THE LAST
WARRIOR
QUEEN

THE LAST WARRIOR QUEEN

Mary Mackey

Seaview/Putnam
New York

Acknowledgments

Special thanks to Sheldon Greene, Jana Harris, Tillie Olsen, Marge Piercy, Carol Murray, and Susan Ryan for reading this novel in manuscript and giving me invaluable suggestions and criticism. I owe a special debt of gratitude to Professor Mignon Gregg, who helped me check the historical accuracy of my account of pre-Sumerian Mesopotamia. Vicki Noble and Karen Vogel shared their extensive library on Goddess religions with me, as did the following institutions: The University of California, Berkeley; the Berkeley Public Library; California State University, Sacramento, and Indiana University.

Many friends and colleagues gave me editorial assistance, ideas, and support, among whom the most tireless were Valerie Miner, Susan Griffin, Charles Dalton, Stephanie Antalocy, Mary Jean Haley, Eve Pell, Craig Blanchard, and Barbara Lowenstein.

Finally I would like to pay special tribute to the great archaeologist Samuel Noah Kramer, whose translations of the poems of the Black Headed People were an inexhaustible source of inspiration.

Library of Congress Cataloging in Publication Data

Mackey, Mary.
  The last warrior queen.

  I. Title.
PS3563.A3165L3 1983   813'.54   82-19270
ISBN 0-399-31016-9

Printed in the United States of America

Contents

The Zagros Mountains and Eastern Mesopotamia 3643 B.C.

An Historical Note:

Many of the names and some of the events in this novel are taken from the great epic poems of the Sumerians, otherwise known to history as the Black Headed People. The Sumerians had over seven hundred gods, among whom An (Heaven) and Inanna (the Queen of Heaven) reigned supreme. In later times Inanna became identified with the Babylonian Ishtar. Traces of Goddess worship persisted well into the Middle Ages in the rituals surrounding the Virgin.

Although the City of the Dove is my own invention, there is good evidence to suggest that the Sumerians may have overrun and absorbed an earlier culture that was matriarchal.

Finally, the reader should realize that the ecology of the area was far different between 4000 and 3500 B.C. when the first Sumerian city-states were appearing, and that what are now barren hills were, in all probability, lush forests.

The Axe

There was once a woman of the tribe of Kur who was unfaithful to her husband. At night when the moon was full, she would sneak out of his tent and run with the wolves. When the time came for her to give birth, the women's children were born with paws and tails. "What can I do?" her husband asked his father. "My wife and her children have torn the throats of my best sheep and devoured my goats." The man's father put a copper axe in his hand. "The name of this axe is Death-to-Bad-Women," the father said. "The name of this axe is No-More-Wolf-Wives."

A story of the Black Headed People

In the time of the Great Drought when the wheat burned in the fields and people were starving, a young woman went walking in the High Olive Grove one day and there she met a snake. "Sleep with me," the snake said, "and I will show you how to make rain." So the woman slept with the snake, and when she got up she gathered the clouds in her cape and carried them down to the City. "Let it rain," she said, throwing the clouds up into the sky as if they were birds. It rained for ten days until the river was full again and the wheat was green. "Thank you," the people said, and they gave the woman a fine house, a necklace of lapis lazuli, and many strong young lovers.

A story of the city people

In the Beginning

Rheti, the High Priestess of the city, stretched out her arms and felt the great shift begin. For thousands of years, for time out of mind, as the glaciers retreated up the mountain slopes and the valleys silted in with loam, the old ways, the ways of the Mothers, had prevailed. Now something new was coming to replace them. Already the battle lines for the next cycle were being drawn in those dark places where things came into being. This morning as Rheti stumbled up the last stretch of the steep trail, she could feel good and evil poised against one another like the baskets of an invisible scale, and it was evil she wanted to win when the shift was over, evil sweet and intoxicating as date wine, for Rheti was the child of evil, and its messenger.

Rheti stopped to catch her breath and cursed the heavy rains that had delayed her for the past three days. Nothing had gone right on this journey, and now there was a good chance that she was going to arrive too late, that the most important part of the shift would happen without her. Curse it! Until a few months ago she'd imagined that the transition would be easy, but then on the twelfth day of the Barley Moon, the Queen had come to her reluctantly, reporting strange signs and commanding Rheti to explain what they meant. A ball of green fire hung over the eastern mountains night after night, the Queen had said, and the sacred snakes hid in the roots of the olive trees, refusing to drink the milk the supplicants left for them. And when Rheti heard all this, she knew at once that a dangerous adversary was about to take on birth, and she set out that very night to find this enemy and kill it before it could upset the balance of things.

Beside her now at her elbow, she could hear the eunuch panting from the long climb. "Where are we?" Rheti demanded suddenly, plucking at his rag of a sleeve. Ah it was the burden of her life that she was blind and had to depend on fools to guide her, especially on this of all days!

"Still on the ridge, muna," the eunuch said between gasps. The air was high and clear here, so thin that it made Rheti light-headed for a moment. She crouched slightly, rooting herself back to the earth, feeling the solidness of the mountain under her feet. Then she closed her pale lids over her

sightless eyes and tilted back her head. "Is there a grove of oak trees to the right and a great rock shaped like the jaw of an ox just above it?" she asked.

"Yes, muna," the eunuch answered. There was no surprise in his voice. For weeks now she, the blind one, had been leading the two of them as if she had eyes, deeper and deeper into the eastern mountains, until their sandals wore out and fell off their feet, and the eunuch had thought he must die from lack of food and sleep.

"Good," Rheti said, "then we're almost there." She grabbed the eunuch's shoulder and pushed him forward in front of her, thinking again that they had to hurry or else they were going to arrive too late. For the child was being born in the nomad camp this minute, make no mistake about it. Just now, when she had closed her eyes, she had sensed the head beginning to press down between the mother's legs, and before that birth was complete she had to bring it to a stop. Not she herself, of course; she and the eunuch would never get past the nomads' dogs, much less into the birthing tent where the young mother lay, but soon . . .

The trail took a sudden turn, and she stumbled and fell to her hands and knees with another curse. Before the eunuch could help her up, she was back on her feet, half running down the slope. Bushes, a stand of high grass, more bushes. She felt the limbs slap against her face, smelled the sharp odor of juniper needles. Suddenly she froze as if listening to something. The eunuch stopped too but heard nothing. Rheti's pale lashes fluttered, and a slow smile spread over her face. "Part the bushes," she commanded. The eunuch obediently pulled back the juniper branches. "Now tell me what you see."

"A meadow, muna, full of goats, and a nomad boy watching over them."

"A tall boy with a scar on one cheek shaped like a snake, who sits by himself looking angry and unhappy?"

"Yes, muna."

The shift was rushing toward them now like a great wave. Rheti felt it pulling the breath out of her body, dragging her up and out of herself until she could hardly stand. Closing her eyes, she fought her way down level after level until she found a quiet place, a place where the energy hadn't yet reached. Slowly she focused her power, reached out for the mind of the boy, and found it open. It was an unformed mind, childish as yet, but already full of fine things. Rheti felt the hatred, jealousy, and pride of the boy wash over her, and she knew that the rest of her task was going to be easy. Quickly she searched through his thoughts until she found what she was looking for: My father's new wife is having a child and I . . .

"Hate her," Rheti supplied.
I hate her . . .
"And the child too . . ."
And the child too . . .
"And I will kill them both . . ."
And I will kill them both . . .
"Because it is right and good, because they deserve . . ."
Because it is right and good, because they deserve to die.
"Wolf-wife and wolf cub . . ."
Wolf-wife and wolf cub, hate her, hate the child too, kill them
both, deserve to die . . . but when?
"Now!" Rhetti thought with all her power. "Now!" but it was too late.
The connection wavered and then broke suddenly, and the boy's mind
snapped away from hers before she could give him the final command. For
an instant Rheti realized that she had failed. The boy would do nothing; the
child would live.

Then the great shift came, and for a long while there was no sound except
time running to an end.

1 THE first thing Inanna remembered was her sister Lilith
chasing her around the smoldering campfires to scrub her
cheeks with snow. She remembered Lilith's laugh, thin and
clear as a goat bell, the warmness of her breasts, the smell of the
apricot oil she used to tame her thick black hair. When Lilith
caught Inanna and hugged her, the little girl knew that this was
love. How I pity anyone who doesn't have a sister, Inanna
thought. When Inanna lay next to her sister at night on a pile of
warm fleece, she listened to Lilith's breathing and knew that the
two of them would be together always, that nothing would ever
change.

Yet secretly she knew that this wasn't really true. In the tribe of
Kur nothing was the same for long. Each evening the women
pitched the tents where the grass was thickest, and each morning
they pulled up the bone pegs, doused the fires, and set out again.
If anyone had asked Inanna what the world was like, she would
have said, "It's a trail that goes nowhere." And sometimes it was a
hard trail, full of dangers. In the spring naked savages with muddy

red hair would come out of the west to lie in wait for any child who strayed from the camp. They would grab a girl by the heels and slap her brains out against a rock, or take a boy away so far that his family would never see him again. Something even worse happened to the older girls whom the savages caught, but Inanna never knew what. She only knew that they too never returned. Then the men of the tribe would have to put on their amulets, sharpen their javelins, and follow her brother Pulal until the heads of savages were stuck on poles all around the camp and the honor of Kur was secured again.

After the battle when Pulal touched Inanna, his skin was as cold as a wet rock, and she would shrink from him into Lilith's arms. He loves to kill, she would think as she looked into her brother's face. On Pulal's right cheek a scar shaped like a snake drew his mouth up into a smile. His teeth were yellow and chipped, and there was something sour about his breath that made Inanna think of cheese. Pulal would pretend to caress her again and Inanna would feel the anger in his hands. How he hates me, she would think. For a moment she would hate him in return. Her green eyes would narrow like the eyes of a wolf cub, but soon she would feel her own powerlessness and break into tears. Back in the tent, Lilith would hold her close and tell her a story to calm her. "I want to know how I came here," Inanna would beg. "I want to know how I was born."

"Your mother Nintu was very beautiful," Lilith would begin. "Her blue-black hair was thick and shiny; her face was the color of doeskin; her nipples were like hackleberries. When our father Cabta first saw her, she was only twelve years old. She was playing with a ball of wool and it rolled to his feet. He was a great warrior, the headman of the tribe, and he fell in love with her like a young boy." Inanna would move closer to Lilith and lay her head on her breast. My mother and father loved each other, she would think, and the thought would make her feel full, as if she had drunk a whole skin of warm milk. "But your mother was from another tribe of the Black Headed People," Lilith would continue. "Her relatives honored the Earth Mother Ki instead of the volcano god Kur; so when she came among us our ways were not her ways, and I think she was lonely. Your father had paid many goats for her. Never in the history of the People had such a bride price been paid, and many of the women were jealous. 'Who does this Nintu think she is?' they would ask each other, and when your mother went out to milk the goats the women wouldn't talk to her, and sometimes they would tip over her basket. But slowly your mother won their hearts, and everyone came to love her except my mother Enshagag, our father's first wife.

"Enshagag hated your mother because she was young and beautiful. Some say it was Enshagag who told Pulal that your mother was a wolf-wife, and because he believed this, Pulal, who was only a boy at the time, did a terrible thing on the day you were born." So this is why Pulal hates me, because he did something bad to my mother and is ashamed of it. Sometimes Inanna would look out of the tent flap and see Pulal, a grown man now, standing with his mother Enshagag in front of the fire, and she would wonder how the two could go on living after doing such evil. Lilith would follow Inanna's gaze and lower her voice until it was no louder than the hiss of the wind in the grass.

"When your mother was in labor with you," Lilith would whisper, "Pulal came into the birthing tent where men are forbidden, and there he put a curse on your mother. I was only a little girl, but I saw him. It was my job to feed thorn branches to the fire while the midwife tried to get your mother to push you into the world. Nintu had narrow hips, and she had already been struggling to give birth for three days when Pulal cursed her. He had stolen a piece of rock from the sacred mountain of Kur, and when the midwife wasn't looking he touched your mother with it on the thigh, and she began to bleed. After you were born, the blood rushed out from between her legs like water, and when the midwife saw there was no hope, she gave you to your mother for a last blessing."

"How did my mother bless me? What did she say?"

"She touched you all over looking for a sign," Lilith would whisper, reaching for the child's hand and uncurling her fingers. In the center of Inanna's palm the lines radiated in a small, perfect star. "When your mother saw this, she said, 'No child has ever been marked this way before.' She kissed you here," touching Inanna's palm, "and here," touching her forehead. "Your mother knew she was dying. She was afraid they would leave you behind on the trail, so she gave you to me." Lilith would run her hands through Inanna's hair and pull her closer. "You were the only gift I ever got," she would say smiling. The words were always the same, each one in its proper order. Each time she heard Lilith repeat them, Inanna felt secure.

"After your mother died, our father almost went mad with grief. People had to sit up with him day and night to see that he didn't take his own life. But that next fall when all the tribes of the Black Headed People assembled at Kur, our father got his way despite his friends. He offered himself up as a sacrifice to the volcano, and Pulal—who was still no more than a boy—became headman."

Outside the tent the sky turned the color of lapis lazuli, and a single star appeared. The earth was the color of goat bone, and threads of smoke rose up from the cooking fires, spreading out like spiderwebs as they hit the cold night air. In the distance a wolf howled twice and fell silent. In the wild pistachio trees the small birds folded their wings. Mountains to the west; plateau to the east; a circle of black tents in the middle ringed by the flocks of Kur. Where do I go when I go to sleep? Inanna thought. Curling up on the warm fleece next to her sister, she shut her eyes.

2 KUR the great god was angry. The dust from His breath covered the yew trees and turned the wool of the sheep gray; it filled Inanna's nostrils and stung her eyes like soapweed; it filtered down from the sky, a black rain, forming a thick dirty film on the milk, clinging to the damp places under her arms, crunching between her teeth like ground almond shells. When Inanna put her hand to the earth, she could feel Kur's anger rumbling, and at night He filled the sky with fire and strange smells. What had they done wrong? Inanna asked herself. She was nearly nine now, old enough to know that when things began to change there was often no way to stop them. For the last two years Enshagag had made her sleep alone by the front flap of the tent so she could get up first and gather wood to start the cooking fire. But there was no wood on the slope of the mountain. This year Kur Himself had burned every tree.

When Inanna looked out over the camp, all she saw were a few white skeleton trunks sticking up like bones, and the tents of the

Black Headed People, who had gathered to beg forgiveness. Five young men and five young women were to be given to Kur that day. Pulal was to pick them out.

Pulal stood quietly while Enshagag slipped the heavy white robe over his head and adjusted the folds. His mother was the only woman he would submit to; for all others he had only contempt. Women were weak, puling things, and the man who gave himself to them became soft, unfit for battle. A man's destiny was to be a warrior. Nothing else mattered.

Pulal knew this for a fact. As a boy, before he felt the heft of a real javelin in his hand, he had been unhappy, unsettled, a stranger to himself. Even the girls had taunted him, pointing at his scar, calling him "hyena face." When his father had taken a younger wife he had been powerless to console his mother. His whole childhood had been unhappy, one long humiliation.

But on the day of his first battle, his whole world had changed. The older men had bet he was a coward. Pulal had heard them whispering the night before that Cabta's son would run at the first sight of a savage. And run he had, but forward, charging the savages until his own people had to pull him back. A joy had filled him, better than wine, better than any woman, and in the middle of the dust, blood, and confusion he had found himself and known that this was what he had been made for.

After that battle the older warriors had looked at him with more respect. Around the campfires they told how he had fought like a man possessed by some god; there was no doubt anymore that when his father died Pulal would become headman. For the first time he was offered wives, but he had no time for women, no interest in them. His mother saw to his needs; why should he encumber himself? Already he was sharpening his javelin, honing his axe, planning for the next battle.

But the next battle had been a long time coming. The savages attacked only once more that year, and after Pulal became headman there were months of almost unbearable peace when the tribe wandered from pasture to pasture unmolested for entire seasons.

Outside the tent Kur was coloring the sky with wreaths of yellow and black smoke. Enshagag offered Pulal a skin of wine, and he drank it without a word. He knew he had no talent for thinking things out; his only power lay in the moment of battle when he came face to face with an enemy. He was headman today not because his people loved him, but because of the way he fought. When his battle strength was on him, he could move the others like the wind moved the ash. He was like Kur; he filled them with fear.

But let there be too much time between battles, and they would forget him. The tribe would grow restless, perhaps even pick a new headman who was better at the day-to-day organizing of their lives. The sacrifices he would select today would keep the fear of him alive for a while, but how long could that last? Peace was an enemy. Sooner or later he would rot under it like a soft pear, be fit only for the flies.

Pulal threw down the wineskin. Someday he would arrange things differently. Instead of waiting to be attacked, he would bring all the warriors of the Black Headed People together to harry the savages out of their hiding places. When the mountains were his, perhaps he would turn to the valleys where the cities were said to lie. Pulal smiled, thinking of the sweet prospect of battles that would never end.

"You look happy, my son," Enshagag observed.

Pulal embraced his mother. Of all women, only she knew his heart. "I am happy," he said. He picked her up and whirled her around until she laughed breathlessly. "Old woman, old woman," he crooned, "you've gotten as fat as a ewe. A man can hardly span you." When he sat her down, she brought him his axe cradled lovingly in her arms.

Pulal came at noon when the sky was the color of an old bruise, and the air was too hot to breathe, moving through the camp wearing his finest robe woven of lambs' wool, embroidered with red flames. When Inanna saw him, she grabbed Lilith's hand so tight that her nails dug into her sister's palm. Her love for Lilith was so great at that moment that she would have gone into the cone of the volcano herself to save her from Pulal. Lilith read the thought in the girl's face, and smiled as if Inanna were still a silly child. "Don't worry," she whispered, "he's our brother. I'm safe." She doesn't know him, Inanna thought. Pulal pointed his copper-bladed axe at the young man standing to Lilith's left, and then at the woman to her right.

"You two," he said. His voice was like honey, and the smile on his face looked almost real. He was playing with Lilith, playing with her death as if it were one of the betting games he played with Enshagag and Aunt Dug at night in the tent. Behind Lilith the mothers of the two victims were already starting up their death wails. The sound undulated like the howl of wolves, making the flesh rise on Inanna's arms. Pulal lifted his axe again, and the copper edges sparkled in the murky light. "You," he said to the woman behind her. Pulal pointed his axe a third time straight at Lilith. Inanna felt the bones knot in her back; her heart was like a cup of blood, spilling over the sides. She saw Pulal lift his axe, laugh, and tell Lilith that she wasn't to be a sacrifice after all. Then she fainted.

"I'm to be married tomorrow to Hursag," Lilith was telling her. They had carried Inanna back to the tent. The black wool rippled in the wind, and the poles arched like the naked trees outside. If the stars went out, Inanna thought dizzily, the sky would be black just like that. Lilith dipped a woolen rag into some cold water and put it on Inanna's forehead.

"I'm to be married to old Hursag," she repeated. "That's what Pulal was telling me. Imagine, Hursag's had three wives already and outlived them all, and his son Zu is older than I am. But the goats! No man in our tribe has more goats than Hursag. What a bride price he must be paying our brother!"

As she chattered on, Inanna saw that none of it touched her— not the desolation of the land, not her own near escape from death, nothing. Lilith shook the film of white ash from her hair and began to rub apricot oil into her plaits. Her cheeks were round and shiny, and her eyes shone like sun on clear water. Her breasts swung heavy and ripe under her robe, and she had a woman's hips. Anyone could see that it was time for her to marry. "If only Hursag wasn't so old," Lilith was saying. "Aunt Dug says Pulal should be ashamed to marry his oldest sister to such a stick of a man, but I say a husband's a husband."

Lilith leaned down and kissed Inanna on the cheek, and the girl smelled the sweet, comforting scent of her sister's breath. Lilith was right; they were safe. It didn't matter that God was angry; it didn't matter that at that very moment the people who had stood around them in the crowd were being hurled into the fire. Their deaths have nothing to do with us, she thought.

They were getting the bride ready, rubbing her body with sesame oil and painting her breasts. Inanna stood at the back of the tent near a brazier of sweet-smelling herbs and watched the four women braiding cowrie shells and strings of brightly colored beads into Lilith's hair. The women's excited voices rose and fell like birdsongs as they tossed things back and forth to one another playfully. Everyone was happy except Inanna. The weight of her own misery pressed her down so she could hardly stand. She looked at Lilith slipping a new robe of light brown wool over her body and felt the energy drain out of her. It was as if her life were water, running down her spine through her feet into the ground where it would be lost forever. Lilith glanced into a polished obsidian mirror and smiled at her own reflection. She didn't even notice Inanna standing in the shadows. One of the women opened a white leather pouch and drew out a strand of goat sinew. From the strand dangled a small, dove-shaped gold pendant. Like sunlight, they kept saying, it's just like sunlight. They hung it around the bride's neck and stood back to admire her. The golden dove was a wedding present from Hursag, who had traded ten of his finest goats and several bags of worked obsidian for it, but that didn't make Inanna like the old man any better.

But Lilith was evidently pleased with the bauble. She turned and posed, letting the firelight catch on the gold at her throat. The other women touched it timidly with their fingers, afraid that—like the sunlight—it might suddenly disappear. When Lilith turned a second time, her fine brown robe floated out around her body like mist. Inanna wanted to go to her sister, embrace her, wish her joy on her wedding day, but she couldn't move. She felt as if there were bone tent pegs in her feet nailing her to the ground.

"Where did it come from?" Lilith asked, pointing to the dove. One of the women said that the gold was brought from a valley to the west where great rivers ran down to a lake of salt. The people who lived along those rivers didn't move on to new pastures each season. It was said that they lived instead in permanent camps, in tents made of mud where they worshiped women and snakes.

The woman's words resonated in Inanna's mind . . . *great riv-*

ers . . . permanent camps. So there were other places besides the land of Kur! places she could run away to with Lilith! Inanna imagined herself traveling west with her sister until they came to the valley, and for a moment she felt full of energy, as if she could fly straight up the smoke hole and be there before sunset. But then the misery closed over her again. Lilith would never agree to such a journey. She was going to marry Hursag.

On the other side of the tent the women were laughing, Lilith the loudest of them all. Inanna felt the bones tighten in her face; a fierce, wolflike anger rose in her. All at once Lilith turned and saw Inanna standing in the shadows, and the laughter dried on her lips. Pushing past the surprised women, Lilith walked quickly across the tent and took her sister in her arms.

"What's wrong?" Lilith's hair cascaded across Inanna's face and the girl breathed the scent of apricots. You're going away, she wanted to say, you're leaving me. Burying her face in Lilith's new robe, she began to cry. Lilith lifted the girl's face to her own and smoothed her hair back from her forehead. Her eyes were brown with violet tints in them, and Inanna suddenly sensed the plainness of her own eyes, the bony unfinished shape of her body.

"Hursag's from our own tribe," Lilith said. "My tent will be next to your tent, and we can see each other all the time."

"But we can't ever sleep on the same rug anymore. You'll have to sleep next to old Hursag who smells like a he-goat." The other women broke into giggles and covered their mouths with the palms of their hands. How she hated them for their laughter! But Lilith wasn't laughing. She put her hands on Inanna's cheeks and looked very serious.

"At night when it's dark," she promised, "I'll crawl away from old Hursag and sneak under the flap of your tent, and we can crack pistachios together until morning." Inanna stared at Lilith, trying to memorize her face. She suddenly had the feeling that nothing would ever be the same again.

Outside the drums were welcoming the dawn and the arrival of the bride. Hursag stood drunkenly on the slope, dressed in a fine black robe, supported on one side by Pulal and on the other by his son, Zu. Inanna noted Zu's curly black beard and straight white teeth and thought that he made Hursag look older than ever. When she married, she'd make Pulal find her a young man, someone who laughed a lot like Zu and had all his teeth.

Hursag leaned forward and presented Lilith with the traditional wild cucumbers and apples. The old man's hand trembled, and as he stepped back one of the apples rolled out of the basket, and Zu bent over quickly to pick it up. When Zu straightened again, he found himself looking into Lilith's face. Zu colored to the roots of his hair and stepped back quickly as his father walked forward to claim the bride. Grabbing Lilith by the hand, the old man pulled her into the bridal tent. Zu gazed after them with a strange expression on his face, like a sleeper who had wakened too suddenly. When the bridal scream came, he started and turned away.

I just saw something happen, Inanna thought, but what was it? She looked at the bridal tent and then back at the slope of the mountain, the stripped trees and ash-covered earth.

After the wedding the feast began. As the smell of roasting goat filled the air, the children darted back and forth between the fires, sucking on pieces of honeycomb and laughing excitedly. Boiled duck eggs stuffed with wild herbs lay next to baskets of dried fruit, piles of moon-shaped cheeses, skins overflowing with wine and fresh milk.

Inanna took a small handful of dried hackleberries and wandered to the edge of the camp where she could be alone. Pulal and Enshagag weren't likely to miss her as long as the wine held out. Outside the last rim of tents, she stopped and took a deep breath but the heavy feeling stayed with her. It was almost too much trouble to move. The trail climbed straight and then doubled back on itself sharply. Inanna trudged along aimlessly, kicking up puffs of white ash and watching them float back down over her bare feet. At one point she sat and looked at the camp. She could never remember having seen so many tents in one place before. Ordinarily it would have excited her to see them stretching out to the horizon, but today she stared at them with indifference. Directly behind her was a row of rocks, higher than her head, all burned by the volcano and pitted like rotten fruit. Inanna got up, walked around the edge of the rocks, and then she saw the men.

There were seven of them, standing in a kind of hollow, hidden so that no one could see them unless they came up, as she had, by accident. The first thing that hit Inanna was the smell of sour wine, and then she saw that two of the men were holding a savage girl by the arms. The girl had a rag stuffed in her mouth so she couldn't cry out, and she was struggling.

Inanna crouched behind a rock and held her breath so the men wouldn't notice her and order her back to the camp. Here was something worth looking at. She'd never seen a savage girl before; how ugly they were. The girl was naked, her strange reddish-colored hair matted with ashes and mud. A necklace of dirty teeth dangled from her throat by a greasy-looking cord, and she had a piece of bone stuck through one cheek. She was short and skinny, as if she'd never had enough to eat in her life, and she couldn't have been much older than Lilith.

Suddenly one of the men knocked the girl's feet out from under her and got on top. The savage girl fought and clawed, but the other men pinned her arms and legs. It seemed unfair, so many against one. The first man made a strange sound, got up, and began to adjust his robe. As he turned toward Inanna, she saw that his sex was covered with blood. Something grabbed her in the pit of the stomach, and she turned and vomited. When she looked back, another man was on top of the girl.

The scene went on forever like a bad dream. Inanna watched, afraid to run away, afraid to move because the men might see her. Each one of the seven took his turn and, after a while, the savage girl stopped fighting and lay still. Later Inanna realized that she must have already been dead before they were through with her.

After the men left, Inanna sat for a long time, too frightened to crawl out from the shelter of the rock. The shadows grew longer, and the air became cold. Inanna shivered in her thin robe. Finally she forced herself to stand up.

In the hollow the savage girl lay sideways with one arm pillowed under her head as if asleep, but her eyes were rolled back in terror and her lower lip stained with blood where she'd bitten through it. Inanna tried to tell herself that it didn't matter because the girl was only a savage, but when she looked into that angry, horrified face it made her sick all over again.

Back at the tent Enshagag was lying in wait for her. "Where have you been?" the old woman demanded crossly. "I've been looking all over for you." Inanna ran up and buried her head in Enshagag's soft belly. "I don't want to grow up," she said. "I'm afraid to be a woman."

"What are you talking about?" Enshagag pushed Inanna back impatiently and handed her a basket full of roasted goat. "Pull all the meat off the bones, and then come in and help me make the cheese. There's work to be done around here and I'm not going to do it alone." The old woman limped back into the tent, and drew down the flap. The leather flap made a slapping sound like a breaking stick. Who will I talk to now that Lilith's gone? Inanna thought. Who will understand me?

The winter Inanna was fifteen was wet and unhealthy. For days it rained without stopping until the grass began to rot and the streams were swollen with uprooted trees and the bodies of dead animals. Everything molded: the fleeces they slept on at night, the pitch-lined milk baskets, even the leather tent ropes. When Inanna got the cheeses she and Enshagag had made the preceding summer, she found half too rotten to eat. Every morning she hurried out of the tent to look at the sky, thinking: maybe it has stopped. But the gray clouds never broke for more than a few seconds at a time, and it soon became almost impossible to find wood dry enough to burn. When the women went out to milk the goats, they discovered that their hooves had rotted and split, and the sheep were so covered with sores that their meat was unfit to eat.

Inanna remembered that winter as a time of constant hunger. At night she dreamed of roasted goat meat, fresh cheeses, milk thick with cream, baskets of succulent berries, and piles of toasted almonds. But in the morning the hunger still gnawed away inside her like a fox. "The girl never stops eating," Enshagag complained to Pulal. Inanna was tall now, the tallest girl in the camp, and when she looked into a stream a pair of smoky green eyes looked back at her. "Foreign eyes," Enshagag said, "wolf-woman eyes gotten from your wolf of a mother." Yes, I'm a wolf, Inanna thought fiercely. She imagined terrible crimes: stealing food from Pulal's bowl, killing a whole lamb for herself. Then she hurried to the back of the tent and searched through the empty baskets for a nut that had been overlooked or a scrap of cheese that was still fit to eat.

One morning when she woke she found Pulal crouching beside her, examining her intently. "You eat too much," he said, "and where does it all go? Look at you." He poked her in the arm with one finger and the smile spread from the scar all the way across his face. "You're a bunch of sticks, a giant. Was there ever such an ugly girl? What kind of bride price do you think I could get for you?" Inanna felt the long bones in her legs, and the hunger in her belly. She was beautiful; he didn't know her. "And those eyes of yours—you should look down like the other girls instead of star-ing at people like you want to eat them." She was a wolf-woman, the daughter of a wolf. Another poke, then another.

"You're going to marry Hursag," Pulal said. "Although why he'd want you in his bed is more than I can understand. I'd have thought our sister would have been enough trouble." She hadn't heard him right; she was still dreaming. Pulal put his hand on her shoulder, and she felt the cold hate in his fingers. "You'll be a good second wife. I can't afford to feed you anymore, and Hursag still has food in his tent." A pat on the shoulder, stiff, like a man pat-ting a dog that might bite. "Hursag's a rich man, so you can't say I haven't done my duty by you."

Hursag! an old man with a hump in his back and legs like sticks! She'd run away and live in the mountains! The idea of Hursag touching her made her feel angry. Then suddenly another thought came quickly like the sparks jumping out of a fire, filled her up as if she'd eaten enough at last. If she married Hursag she could be with Lilith again. She could live with Lilith.

Hursag shuffled around her naked shivering body, clicking his tongue and shaking his head. They were in the bridal tent together, the wild cucumbers and apples scattered on the ground around her bare feet. Dangling from Inanna's neck was the chipped cowrie shell Enshagag had grudgingly donated. A fine bride she made. She felt her skinny arms and protruding ribs and was ashamed.

"Beautiful," Hursag said, "you're a beautiful girl." The words surprised her, and she inspected his face to see if he was joking. "When I was young, I was like a ram, but now . . ." Bending down, the old man took one of her breasts gently in his hand and began to gum the nipple. Inanna started and pulled away. Bodies covered with sweat and mud, the face of the savage girl—all came back to her. Hursag looked at her with amusement. "I couldn't hurt you if I wanted to, child," He patted her reassuringly on the arm, draped a warm blanket around her shoulders, and motioned for her to sit on the bed beside him.

"Now I am a very old man and you are a very young woman," he cleared his throat. "And the two of us must come to an agreement if we are going to share the same tent."

"Yes, my husband." She lowered her eyes meekly, but her wolf heart rose in her throat. She was wicked, not fit to be anyone's wife. Tonight when she was asleep, she'd run away.

"Don't pretend to be so obedient," Hursag said, "because I can tell just from looking at you that you're part she-devil." Inanna found he was grinning at her. Despite herself, she grinned back. "Now we will have some rules. You'll milk my goats, spin my wool, and help your sister cook my meals, and when you walk to the water holes you won't talk to the young men. I, in turn, will feed you and buy you pretty trinkets, and when I die I'll leave you rich enough to marry anyone you fancy." He looked at her slyly. "But don't expect me to die too soon, because I'm a tough old he-goat." Inanna bit her lip to keep from laughing.

"Yes, my husband." The green lights sparkled in her eyes; he had seen the wolf in her and liked it. "Now lie down," Hursag gently pushed her back on the bed, "and I'll show you what an old man can do." Inanna lay back and shut her eyes, wondering briefly if it would be like animals copulating. At least she'd seen enough of that not to be afraid.

Hursag began to touch her softly with his mouth and fingers. Her nipples hardened into little stones, and a warm sensation ran lazily down her spine to the back of her legs. She thought for some reason of swimming in a quiet pool, and when she opened her eyes again she felt tenderness for the old man.

Hursag sat up and sighed. "You should have seen me when I was twenty," he said, "I was such a man . . ." He drew Inanna to him and kissed her on the forehead. "You should scream now, my dear, because your brother and the others are still waiting outside." I won't shame him, Inanna thought, and she screamed so loudly that it made her ears ring. Hursag curled his face in pain and laughed. "Such strong lungs," he said, thumping her on the chest.

That night the rain stopped for the first time in weeks, and the stars came out. The tents were pitched in a deep ravine full of beech trees. Inanna and Lilith lay outside Hursag's tent on a blanket and looked up at the constellations. "Those are the Sheep of Heaven," Lilith whispered, pointing to the stars. Then she told an old story of a woman of the tribe of Ki who died and later sent her soul back to earth again to be reborn.

"And if you died would you come back to me?" Inanna asked. Lilith smiled and squeezed Inanna's hand.

"I'd try to."

Inside the tent Hursag was drowsing over a bowl of warm milk, and the firelight flickered and sank to a bed of coals. An owl circled and dived above them for an instant; a nightbird called three times and fell silent.

3 THE dew was thick and heavy, and the wet flowers and grass clung to her bare legs as she threaded her way around the ashes of the fires to the edge of the camp.

The bright water of my love is in my heart

Inanna sang,

He has kissed me, lain with me
Like a drink of honey wine.

Kissed. Yes, she'd kissed Hursag only a few minutes ago as he lay sleeping, softly on the forehead so as not to waken him. And she'd lain with him too, all night listening to him snore. But it wasn't honey wine. She immediately felt ashamed of herself. A wife for over a year now, and still she hadn't learned her duty. There was still that wildness in her that made her different from other women. Hursag was a good man, and it was wicked of her not to love him.

But I don't, she thought, and then she quickly bit her cheek to punish herself. Her mind ran on this morning like a young goat, leaping the fences she had put up, out of control. It wasn't like the old love songs said it should be. Where were the children she should be having? She put the palm of her hand against her belly and sighed. She couldn't help what she thought, and trying only seemed to make it worse.

Inanna gazed over the rim of the canyon where the creek became a waterfall. In the distance the summits of the western mountains were touched with the first streaks of pink and gold. Forests of cedar, scrub oak, juniper, and wild pistachio, high above the valley a single falcon circled in the still blue air. Down below, in the lower meadow where the stream slowed again and flowed into a natural basin, she could see a flock of wild ducks and further on a herd of ibex.

To fly like a bird! The wind whipped her robe back against her legs. If she could fly she would go west over the mountains to those cities where Lilith's gold dove had been made. She would go where the people worshiped women, and become a goddess. She would sit on a throne and all the young men would bring her their best goats as offerings. But she would shake her head at each of them. "No, none of you are good enough. None of you pleases me." Until the most handsome young man of all would come, and she would take his hands in hers and draw him to her and say, "You. I pick you."

What evil god put such thoughts in her head! She was a married woman! Inanna quickly turned her back on the mountains and stepped into the stream. The shock of the cold water made her gasp, but she forced herself to scoop up a handful and pour it over her face. Forgive me my husband for these wicked thoughts. She would learn to do her duty. The mountains were a wall; they would stand in front of her forever; she would become an old woman and never cross them.

Stepping out of the stream, Inanna dried her feet with a handful of sweet grass. Her body felt heavy, as if stones were tied to her feet. It has been this way as long as she could remember, this feeling that she was forever being defeated by some invisible enemy. Across the stream a dead oak lay crookedly on the bank, its bleached roots spread like fingers. There were holes in the trunk where insects had already bored into the dry bark. Firewood for breakfast. She should gather some. Hursag was always hungry when he woke up, and it was her turn to cook the meal. She would learn to do her duty.

The load of wood on her back, the bark digging into her shoulders—no time to milk the goats now; she'd do that later with Lilith. In the camp the smoke rose from the cooking fires, and the smell of burning cedar needles drifted over the meadow. Inanna balanced the wood more securely and started to hurry back through the tall grass.

To fetch and carry, to walk down the same trail forever carrying the same bundle of sticks: there was no point to it; it made no sense. Suddenly she stopped, threw down the wood angrily, and looked up at the sky. Overhead the falcon was still circling lazily. Behind the bird a single line of pink clouds stretched all the way across the horizon like a streak of ochre. Why had such beauty been created if no one ever had time to enjoy it?

A sound cut through the still morning air like a whistle, shrill, full of infant terror. The bleat of a lamb calling for help. More trouble, she thought, always trouble.

Inanna examined the wall of shale. Where was the lamb? Probably above her somewhere in those rocks. The dry stone flaked off under her fingers and her feet slipped. She could kill herself this way, going up to help that stupid animal. Everyone knew the cliffs were too dangerous to climb. The lamb bleated again, and Inanna jumped for the root of a scrub oak. Pulling herself up to a narrow ledge, she lay still for a moment. Down below the stream rushed into the valley like a tiny thread of white wool. So far to fall. She saw the lamb, its long brown wool snarled with burrs, its right foreleg wedged between two stones. An old ewe stood beside it adding her own bleats. The ewe regarded Inanna with liquid black eyes and butted the lamb gently in the hindquarters.

"That's no way to do it," Inanna told her. Slowly, on her hands and knees, she crawled along the ledge and grabbed one of the rocks that held the lamb's foreleg. Rooted to the earth that rock was, probably the top of a mountain. She pulled again and the rock gave suddenly, slipped out of her hands, and careened down the cliff, taking others with it. With a final bleat of surprise the lamb jerked itself free, turned, and bounded off to suckle the ewe.

Inanna wiped the sweat off her forehead and backed away from the dangerous drop. The wind fell and for a moment everything was quiet, so quiet she could hear her own rough breath, the beating of her own heart. Then, in the middle of that silence, a high-pitched sound rose up on the wind from the camp down below.

A woman was screaming.

Savages! She imagined them burning the tents, stealing the flocks, their mud-streaked faces, the animal bones they used for clubs. But wait: if the savages were attacking, there would be more screams and the noise of the men of Kur giving battle. Pulal would be yelling his war cry. But this was a single voice.

Hand, arm, elbow. Inching her way to the edge of the drop on her belly, Inanna leaned forward carefully and peered over the rim. The tents in the meadow appeared small and unreal like a circle of black stones. In the center of that circle a woman was standing, her red shawl fluttering like a spot of blood against the black wool, a woman screaming, holding a child in either hand. Zu's children; Zu's wife. Inanna's tongue went dry in her mouth, and her heart began to beat wildly. She saw Zu's face again, the way he had looked at Lilith on her wedding day when he handed her the apple Hursag had dropped, the apple Hursag should have given her. Now she knew what she had seen.

Numb, she moved slowly down the face of the cliff, cutting her fingers on the sharp shale. "Lilith!" The word echoed off the rocks and came back to her weakly. In the camp below people rushed out of their tents. Pulal, Enshagag. The sun rose fully at last over the eastern hills. Sunlight flooded the whole valley, turning the mist into a fine gauzy net, changing the drops of water on the shale into beads of crystal. Down below Pulal carried something in his hand as he ran toward the screaming woman. The sun touched this too, turning its copper blade into a mirror. Pulal was bringing his axe.

"Shame, shame, shame!" Zu's wife screamed.

"Lilith!" Inanna reached for a root, missed, and the empty space at the edge of the cliff opened up in front of her. She felt the cold air blowing up from the valley like the breath of death as she fell toward it. Reaching out blindly, she caught herself on a small scrub oak. A push sideways, then another push. Dust in her mouth and eyes. She was safe, falling toward the bottom of the cliff instead of the bottom of the valley. A small tree, a single boulder, then nothing in the way. She came down hard, jarring the bones in her ankles. Breaking into a run, Inanna fought her way through the high grass and briars. It was taking so long to cross the space between the cliff and the edge of the camp; it was taking forever. *He has kissed me, lain with me.* Lilith was Hursag's honey, his wine. Surely he'd forgive her. She'd make him forgive Lilith. And Zu too; Zu was Hursag's son. They'd all forget it, pretend it never happened. Even Pulal would forget. It meant nothing what the two of them had done together.

Zu. Running out of Hursag's tent half-dressed, his bare shoulders shining in the sunlight, coming straight toward her. She'd protect him. Inanna stretched out her arms. Zu come here, come this way. She was at the edge of the camp, inside the first circle of tents, inside the second. Zu lifted his head and looked at her. The sunlight caught in his hair. Handsome Zu; golden Zu. Suddenly a spear struck him in the middle of the back. Dark blood welled up around the spear handle, blood the color of winter honey. Zu opened his mouth, trying to tell her something. Then his body twitched like the body of a spider, and he fell forward, face first into the long wet grass.

She went on running, past Zu, afraid to stop, passing Zu's wife running in the opposite direction, dragging her two daughters after her. The woman's scream had turned into a death wail as if she'd only just realized that she'd made herself a widow. Fool, Inanna thought. Oh, you fool!

As she fought her way through the crowd around Hursag's tent, Pulal came out dragging Lilith by the hair. Hursag followed, half-dressed, looking as if he were still asleep. Pulal pulled Lilith over the cold embers of the firepit, jerked back her head roughly, and ripped open the neck of her robe, exposing her throat. A gutteral moan went up from the crowd, and the women began to intone the wail for the dead. On Pulal's cheek the white S-shaped scar had turned bright red, and he seemed filled with a strange, almost hysterical happiness. Inanna had seen the same look on her brother's face once before, at the volcano when he chose the sacrifices.

"Kill her!" Pulal yelled, handing Hursag the axe. "She's brought shame on us all!" Hursag loked at Lilith and then at the axe. It was a heavy weapon, carved over with twisting vines and strange foreign fruits. "Kill her!" Pulal commanded again. Hursag let the axe fall to the ground and squatted beside it.

"No," he said simply, "I won't do it." He turned away from his wife, avoiding her eyes, and ripped open the sleeves of his robe. Picking up cold ashes from the firepit, he smeared them on his face and arms. "I mourn the death of my son," Hursag mumbled. He wrapped his hands around his knees and began to rock back and forth. "Lost, lost, everything lost." Pulal spat into the dust near the old man and picked up his axe. Still holding Lilith by the braids, he dragged her over to where Enshagag was standing.

"Hold your daughter," Pulal commanded, pulling her into the circle and placing Lilith's hair in her hands. Enshagag took Lilith's braids unsteadily and glanced uneasily at the crowd. The old woman held Lilith so weakly that she could have easily pulled away, but Lilith seemed frozen with terror. The whites of her eyes showed, and she knelt trembling in the dust with her head thrown back like a sheep about to be slaughtered.

"Lilith!" Inanna called out, shoving her way violently through the crowd that separated her from her sister. A flicker of recognition passed over Lilith's face when she heard Inanna's voice, and she seemed to come back to herself for a moment. "Inanna," Lilith said weakly, stretching out her arms as if trying to find something to hold on to. Pulal raised the copper axe over his head, and the edge sparkled in the sunlight, but before he could bring it down on Lilith's neck, Inanna thrust herself through the last ring of spectators and threw herself on her sister.

"Get back!" Pulal barked. Inanna looked up at her brother defiantly and pulled Lilith to her. She had the eyes of a she-wolf protecting her cubs, and even Pulal was intimidated for a moment. Inanna hugged Lilith closer, blocking her sister's body with her own. She could feel the coldness of Lilith's hands; under her robe her sister's heart was beating too quickly—like the heart of a small, terrified bird. Pulal looked at the two women kneeling in front of him and realized that he looked like a fool in front of the entire tribe. The scar on his face went from red to dead white.

"Get back!" he thundered. Inanna took Lilith's head in her hands and kissed her sister on the forehead. "I won't let him hurt you," she promised. Lilith stared at her sister, the terror still in her eyes. She opened her lips to say something, and then closed them and looked at Inanna. Inanna was about to comfort her when, all at once, she was knocked sideways by a blow to her head. Pulal beat her away from Lilith with the flat of the axe, cursing and calling on Kur as he did so. Inanna dug her fingers tightly into her sister's shoulders as another blow smashed across her jaw, shattering the bone.

"She-devil!" Pulal yelled, striking at Inanna a third time. The axe caught her on the upper arm, breaking it in two places: Inanna lost her grip on Lilith and fell back into the dust. She tried to crawl forward again across the few feet that separated her from her sister, but her body wouldn't move. Through a haze of blood and dirt she saw Pulal lift the axe over his head and bring it down with a swishing sound. Lilith screamed a terrible scream that stayed with Inanna for the rest of her life. Then the blade of the axe caught her on the side of the neck. As Lilith slumped forward, Pulal struck a second time, then a third, completely severing her head from her body.

Inanna turned her face away and was sick. She closed her eyes and tried to slip into unconsciousness. She wanted to forget the smile on Pulal's face that looked more like a real smile than it ever had before. For years afterwards it would come back to her in bad dreams, mixed with the smell of apricots and blood, and she would awake trembling and sweating, filled with a hatred for her brother that grew until it became a river that drowned everything else in her.

Smoke. No, not smoke. Birds. Thousands of birds rising in a spiral, circling and circling . . . Inanna felt the cold rush of their wings on her face and opened her eyes. The late afternoon sun was slanting through the long grass in thick folds and Hursag was crouching beside her, waving the flies away with a juniper branch. His face was a comic mask of white ashes, and he was crying. She watched the tears bead in the corners of his eyes and run down his cheeks. A ghost, he was only a ghost. The flowers in the meadow danced before her like colored spots. The world felt so thin that she wondered if she could stick her fingers through it like a spiderweb.

Only the pain was real. It stretched over her in all directions like the blue bowl of the sky. "You'll get well," Hursag said, "and then you'll come back to me." His voice was high and thin like the bleat of the lamb. When he took her hand and lifted it to his lips, she left her body. For an instant she saw herself from a great distance lying far below in the meadow with Hursag beside her. Was she dying? Was she already dead?

She tried to touch something, but there was nothing there. A humming sound like the bees filled her ears. She remembered the honey she and Lilith had gathered last fall, thick golden honey that dripped down the trunk of the tree, stuck to their fingers, matted in their hair—honey enough for the whole camp. They had smoked out the bees, scooped the honey into gourds. Later, when they came to eat it, they found the queen herself, stuck in a piece of the comb, drowned in her own honey.

The buzzing stopped suddenly and it gradually began to grow lighter. She could see now that she was lying in some kind of cave. Black stone walls curved above her, polished like obsidian mirrors. But where was she? She'd never seen this place before. As she lifted her arm to touch the wall nearest her, she realized that the light in the cave was coming from her own hand. The lines in her palm grew, pulsating like a star. She was holding a star. But that was impossible. She tried to rub the light off on the wall, but it stayed in her hand. The warmness of it coursed up her arm, down her spine, to the soles of her feet. Then, without warning, a man's face floated in the air above her. The man appeared to be about thirty, with a hawklike nose, sky-blue eyes, and high foreign cheekbones. Around his neck he wore a small gold dove like the one Hursag had given Lilith on her wedding day, and he looked at Inanna with such an expression of love and pain that she wanted to call out to him, to tell him that everything was all right. She knew she'd never seen him before. She must be dreaming.

She lay back and let the dream unfold. Above her the man's face stretched and rippled like sun on water, and other things filled up the space where it had been. She saw Pulal, only she knew somehow that it wasn't Pulal, but only someone with Pulal's eyes wearing a different body. And she saw herself with long red hair, falling over her naked shoulders, cascading down her back like blood. A dream. None of this was real.

The star in her hand blossomed, filling the cave with light. Inanna shut her eyes, but the light remained, pushing its way into every fiber of her body. It was honey wine, and she was drunk on it. She felt as if Lilith had come back to her somehow, but she knew, even as she dreamed it, that such things were impossible, that the dead never returned.

"Inanna," a voice said. The voice was calling to her. It seemed to come from inside her own body, from the base of her skull, forming and floating to the surface of her mind. "Inanna, a great battle is coming, and you must be ready to fight it." The words echoed inside her, and another face rose up in the darkness. It was the face of a woman, pale as a corpse, her long white hair tangled and matted with filth. "This is your enemy, Inanna," the voice said, "but you will have special powers to fight her, not only in this life but in all your lifetimes to come. You are the chosen one, the champion. No matter what body you are born into, remember your true self." The words were confusing. What enemy, what champion, what lifetimes? She remembered the story Lilith had told of the woman of Ki who came back to earth from the nether world. But what did all that have to do with her?

The face turned into a spiral of white smoke, disappeared, and the darkness closed around her again. She reached out, frightened, trying to find something familiar to hang on to. "Be still," the voice said. Something touched her gently on the eyelids and a bright warm sensation flooded her, draining away the anger and pain. Her confusion broke into pieces and fell away. I'm happy, she thought. She rested for a moment, cradled in an invisible embrace. Everything in this dream was so good now. She never wanted it to end. Her mind began to float away like a leaf on a stream; she felt it going farther and farther, and then she fell asleep.

4 IN the meadow the grass had quietly covered the bare spots left by the tents. Inanna dipped a piece of bark into the toasted acorn meal and ate slowly without tasting the food. The morning air was cold and crisp. Down in the valley a herd of ibex grazed in a dim clump, their curved horns silhouetted against the sky. Everything looked peaceful. Impossible that Lilith could really have died in that green space between the juniper bushes and the stream. A volcano should have sprouted from the ground to mark the spot, and the sky filled with fire and ashes. But there was only a flock of wrens calmly feeding on a patch of oil grass, and a small lizard sunning itself on a stone. Nothing stayed, nothing. The idea had a bleak taste to it, like hunger in the middle of winter. She stood up quickly to throw it off and kicked out the fire. The path twisted away from her in both directions. "Which way should I go," she asked the bird sitting on the branch above her, "east or west?"

Some time later she walked along the path to the east, thinking with each step that she should be dead. The thought had come to her over and over in the past few weeks as her wounds healed, rolling around in her head like a stone in an empty basket, going nowhere. She again wondered if her own people would think she was a ghost. If she tracked the tribe of Kur through these mountains before the snows fell, would the children run from her screaming when they saw her? Would Enshagag and Dug and the other women spit at her and call on Kur for protection? After all, they'd left her for dead, thrown her away like a broken basket. And they'd been right; she should have died. She remembered waking up that first morning to find everyone gone. Her arm had hung by her side, useless; her jaw had been so swollen she could hardly open her mouth. She should have bled to death or been eaten by a wild animal. But something had happened.

The thought kept coming back: she had healed herself. But that was impossible. The weeks of pain must have affected her mind. She dug her walking stick angrily into the ground and tried to concentrate on the trail in front of her. She'd see only this path. She wouldn't think of dreams or visions or plants and broken bones. One step, then another. She'd think of nothing but the walking.

The late flowers of summer bloomed in profusion along the trail and the air was thick with the smell of cedar needles. Inanna felt the strength of her arm as she held the stick, the power of her own fingers as they grasped the wood. That same arm had been the broken one, bones poking up through the flesh, the fat exposed like jelly, the skin torn away. She'd fainted when she first saw it. Healed herself? Healed *that*? Who was it that Aung Dug said made people crazy? Wasn't it the dark gods, the legless ones who lived under the water? Did the craziness start this way, with this feeling that you had powers that other people didn't?

Deliberately she stopped, threw down her walking stick, and held up her left hand. "I'm Inanna, daughter of Cabta, wife of Hursag," she said, looking defiantly at the star lines on her palm, "an ordinary woman." Her voice was so thin and clear in the mountain air that it startled her, and she took a step back. She inspected her palm, the ridges of pink flesh, the curve of her fingers. Why not admit it? For weeks now she had had the feeling that when she touched things they spoke to her: flowers, bones, rocks, filling her ears with chatter, like a flock of birds gone mad.

Was she god-cursed then? No, she'd just been alone too long. Time to stop this nonsense once and for all.

Quickly Inanna bent down and picked one of the plants that grew along the trail. She had spent long hours with Lilith and the other women of Kur gathering berries for dyes, herbs for medicines, bark and moss for love potions, but this little plant was a stranger. She couldn't remember having seen it before. Cradling it in her hand, she felt the pleasure of its silence. There was nothing there, only a root, a few leaves, a small blue flower. Behind her in the bushes the birds sang, and the sun was hot on her back. It was an ordinary day; everything was perfectly ordinary.

The message came suddenly, shaking her to the base of her spine. *Fever. This is used for fever.* Inanna threw the plant away as if it had bitten her, and wiped her hand on her robe. She could not go back to her own people now. She turned and began to retrace her steps, dragging her bare feet over the stones like an old woman. God-cursed. Along the side of the trail the blue flowers bowed in the wind. She'd have to go west after all, away from the tents of Kur.

Jackal, Wild Cat, Great Bear, and Panther lay low on the ridge watching the woman come up the trail toward them. They had seen her campfire at dawn, the thin line of blue smoke that told them there was something to be hunted. All day they had tracked her, as quietly as shadows, without breaking a twig or raising a bird to warn her. Now they were simply waiting. They could lie for hours without moving, so still that even the wary geese would feed next to them, and the small lizards take them for rocks. Great hunters they were, and they had brought their people much meat this summer. But the woman wouldn't be food hunting; she'd be sport.

Jackal sucked the air in through the holes where his front teeth had been knocked out, and made a cautious grunting sound to let the others know he was satisfied with their plan. They would let the woman come to them, and they would harry her like a pack of wolves and have their way of her. How good it would be after she was dead, Jackal thought, to take the strange skins she wore back to his own woman and boast: "Look, your other man brought you only food, but I, Jackal, bring you great things."

Jackal peered carefully over the rim of the rock and calculated how long it would take their quarry to arrive. As he did so, a low moan came from the bushes behind him; the woman on the trail below stopped and lifted her head as if she might have heard it too. Instantly, without disturbing a blade of the tall grass, Panther and Wild Cat slipped away. They should have killed the Captive long ago, Jackal thought as he rubbed the tattooed claw marks on his forehead with the palm of his hand. For weeks they'd been dragging the man with them, hoping to sacrifice him to Oton when they got back to their own people. But he was a sick thing with hands soft as fawnskin, and his leg was rotting. When they had offered him fine raw meat and the blood of their freshest kill, the Captive had refused to eat, and when they had tried to force the food down his throat he had vomited like a young one.

Behind him Jackal heard the familiar sound of a stone coming down on a skull. He grunted with satisfaction at Great Bear, who nodded back lazily. Great Bear's body was so plastered with mud that it was hard to tell him from the ground, and he looked as if he would have been happy to lie there in the sun all day. But Jackal knew that once Great Bear got to his feet he was the fastest of them all. One day when they were hunting in the Big Valley, Great Bear had outrun a baby gazelle just for the fun of it, chasing the startled animal in circles until it dropped from exhaustion.

Quietly as snakes, Panther and Wild Cat slipped back into their positions at the side of the trail. Jackal made a small clicking sound in the back of his throat that meant: "Is the Captive dead?" and Panther nodded, and then leaned over and rubbed noses with Jackal as much as to say: "Only us here now, dear brother." Wild Cat grunted with impatience when he saw this sign of friendship pass between Panther and Jackal, and lifted his head to sniff the air. They could all smell the approaching woman now. "Ready?" Jackal asked them with his eyes. "Yes," Panther, Wild Cat, and Great Bear's eyes said in return, "we're ready."

Except for the occasional call of a wild bird or the quick rustle of a lizard in the grass, the only sound Inanna heard was the crunch of her own footsteps. In front of her the trail narrowed abruptly as it approached the pass; the steep walls of the bank were covered with dwarf juniper bushes, twisted into fanciful shapes by the wind, and clumps of miniature wildflowers growing out of the rocks. Down below it was late summer, but here spring had just begun. The last of the snow was still melting off the high spots, and tiny streams of water dripped from the moss-covered boulders. Inanna stopped, leaned her walking stick against the bank, cupped her hands, and caught a few of the drops. The water was clear and cold as snow, and tasted faintly of juniper needles. Why was she happy here in this place? Inanna turned for a moment to look back the way she had come. Below, the trail wound around the ridge like a piece of brown wool. In the distance the meadow was only a green smear. God-cursed she might be, and still, at this moment, it didn't matter. The air was thin and bracing, and the wind whipped her robe out from her body, making her cheeks glow. Picking up her walking stick, Inanna climbed once again toward the patch of blue sky that marked the head of the pass.

In the Star Country night is day
she sang,
> *The lion doesn't kill there*
> *And the wolf guards the lamb.*

Inanna stared at the trail, lost in thought. When she looked up again a few seconds later, a naked man was standing in front of her.

Muddy red hair plastered into war locks, the bone club in his hand covered with dark bloodstains, the string of fresh hyena teeth around his neck—she saw it all, and the fear came up in her throat so thick that it almost choked her. The naked savage saw the terror in her face, and his smile was slow, taunting, broken in the middle by his missing teeth. Reaching down deliberately between his legs, he took his sex in his hand and began to make it stiffen. For an instant Inanna saw it again: the dead trees, the pitted rocks covered with ashes, the drunken men lying on the savage girl. Then she turned, and ran.

Half way through the narrow part of the pass, she came on the second man standing on the path, blocking her escape, body plastered with mud, urinating in a long, lazy stream. The savage scratched his naked belly, and gestured as if inviting her to come closer. Then, suddenly, he ran toward her with incredible speed, yipping in a high voice like a wild dog. She had to climb! As she grabbed for a foothold on the bank, rocks slipped under her knees and brambles caught her robe, jerking her off balance. She'd lose them both at the top in the brush like a rabbit. Gravel pattered off her head and shoulders; a few small stones rolled down from above. Looking up, Inanna saw two more naked savages sliding down the gully toward her. It was all over; she was trapped.

Dropping back down to the trail, she picked up her walking stick and put her back against the opposite bank. She wouldn't die like the savage girl, beaten to the ground, biting through her lower lip. She'd fight them. And when they'd won there'd be nothing left; she'd feel nothing; she'd be dead. "I have a wolf heart," she sang fiercely as the savages closed in on her. The men of Kur made up their death chants when they were boys, but she had to compose hers now. Still it was a good song, and she could feel the strength of it. "I have a wolf heart, and I'm not afraid." It was true; the fear was leaving, draining out of her with every word. The savages were so close she could smell the rank odor of the bear grease they smeared on their skin. Yelling as loud as she could, she ran straight at them.

The savages stood with their hands at their sides, watching her. Then—so fast that she didn't even see him move—one of the men jumped forward and twisted the stick out of her hand. Inanna felt the pain sear her wrist as she lost her grip; the savage beat her across the shoulders and face, laughing, teasing her like a cornered animal.

"Kur curse you!" she yelled. Nothing mattered but to kill him. A blow struck her, then another. She stumbled back; a piece of the sky turned overhead like a scrap of blue cloth. Ragged edges of pain, dust in her mouth, hands all over her, pulling at her breasts, tearing off her robe. Inanna bit and tasted blood; they hit her again and again, knocking her to the ground. Two of them held her while the other two tried to thrust into her from the front and back.

Instinctively she reached out and touched the shoulder of the naked man who lay on top of her, thinking: if I have power let it save me. But there was no power in her touch. The man only grabbed her tighter as he felt her struggling. The rank odor of his breath made her gag.

Then suddenly it happened, something running through her whole body, warm and light, filling her with power, pouring from the star in the palm of her hand. The savage's body went limp. He tried again to thrust into her and failed. Startled, he let go and jumped back as if he'd been burned. The man yelled something to the others, and they too let go and backed away. Their language was ugly, rasping like the barking of dogs. Inanna rolled to her knees.

When she lifted her head, she saw the four savages looking at her with terror in their eyes. The tall one with the missing teeth untied his necklace and laid it at her feet. "Go away!" she screamed at him. At the sound of her voice the man turned and ran, and the other followed him. The brush closed around them; somewhere in the distance a twig snapped, and then it was quiet again, so quiet she could hear the flutter of her own heart.

Inanna knelt for a moment, catching her breath. After a time, she sat up, pulled her robe back down around her knees, and looked at the string of yellow teeth that lay on the ground beside her. She didn't want to think about it, not yet. But the thought came to her anyway.

She stared at her clenched fist, afraid of her own power. Slowly she spread her fingers and looked at the star mark in the center of her palm. Who are you? she demanded. What do you want? Where are you taking me? A small lizard scurried out on the trail and stared at her with bright black eyes. Overhead great puffs of white clouds floated in a straight line across the sky.

Inanna got to her feet. She had to go on. She couldn't stop here. A single yellow butterfly floated lazily past her and came to rest on a flower. Its tiny shadow trembled on the trail at her feet like a living thing. All this beauty was a trap that made you forget that danger was everywhere. She watched the butterfly circle and pass on to the next flower. Then she threw the necklace into the bushes as far as she could. The teeth made a bright circle in the sunlight as they tumbled out of sight.

Stripping the leaves from a bush, she opened her waterskin and scrubbed her body angrily, roughly. Bear grease, old, stale, like a dead animal: the smell of it was all over her. Grabbing a handful of juniper needles, she crushed them and rubbed the piney scent on her hands and arms. Standing up, she inspected the trail. It was empty, or at least it appeared to be empty. In any case there was nothing to do but go on. Picking up her stick, she walked slowly toward the summit.

The wind at the top was cold and sharp, and she shivered as it blew through her thin robe, picking at her hair, making her eyes water so badly she could hardly see, rushing and dipping in her ears until she was almost deaf. All around her the juniper bushes thrashed wildly like birds caught in a snare, and if there was anything else moving in them it was hidden, drowned in that wild swooping of branches and needles. The savages could be anywhere, waiting for her to think she was safe, waiting for her to grow careless.

A rock covered with salt-colored lichens and grayish moss loomed up, protruding baldly from the brush like a sheep's skull; when she got closer, she realized that she had reached the top of the mountain at last. On the other side a new valley spread out before her, green and vague in the distance, and behind that more mountains topped with glaciers and brown patches of dirty summer snow. Somewhere in that direction was the great valley where people lived in clay tents. Perhaps in that valley there'd be no tyrants like Pulal, no savages, and she could live peacefully. But how long a journey was it? Could she go all that way by herself?

Shaking her head, Inanna turned away from the sight of the next range. There was no use thinking about it. What she should do was get out of the wind for a while and get warm before she started down the trail. Tonight she'd camp at the foot of the mountain, and tomorrow . . . she'd just have to let tomorrow take care of itself.

Inanna stepped behind the rock and felt the wind die down. When she turned, she saw the man.

He was lying on the ground, his face turned away from her, one arm thrown out awkwardly as if he'd been caught by surprise. She started to back away, but when she saw the blood smeared over his back, matted in his hair, she realized there was no need. The man was dead, or nearly dead. This was no naked savage waiting to jump her. His hair wasn't muddy red but black and curly; he was tall, two hands taller than any man of Kur, and there was something taut and spare about him. The muscles in his arms were small but well developed like the muscles of a panther, and that kilt he had wrapped around his waist was unlike anything she'd seen before. It was fringed, made of material thinner than the finest wool, dyed a rich purple like wild grapes.

Inanna took a step forward, forgetting danger in the sheen of that strange unbelievable color. The man moaned, moved restlessly, turning his face in her direction. Hawklike nose, high foreign cheek bones: she knew him! But from where? The planes of his face were slightly uneven and there was a touch of gray in his beard. He was older than she'd thought. Besides the cut on his forehead, he had a deep gash on his left leg. The wound was red and swollen and gave off the sickly sweet odor of rotten flesh.

Inanna approached the wounded man and bent over him cautiously. No danger from this one. Clammy skin, blue lips, a pulse so faint she could hardly feel it. He'd be dead before moonrise.

Well what of it? She should leave. There were signs of the savages everywhere: scraps of rabbit fur, bones, a chipped arrowhead. The sun was already low in the sky and the cold of the long shadows crept toward her. Not a tree to give shelter, nothing but bare rock, low brush, and that constant wind—she'd be a fool to spend the night.

Inanna walked toward the edge of the boulder, out to where the wind blew and the valley spread in front of her. Then she turned abruptly, walked back, and bent over the wounded man again. That face, where *had* she seen it? She was about to leave a second time when the man's eyelids flickered. He might live then, and if he lived she could ask him . . . Ask him what? What was there to ask?

Later, after they became lovers, she often wondered what had kept her from leaving him on the mountain to die. She only knew that from the first she had sensed a bond between them, that it had held her to him like a moth circling a lamp.

Inanna shook her head. She was a fool. Unhooking her waterskin from her belt, she knelt and began to clean the dried blood off the stranger's face.

He nearly died that first night, but she kept him alive somehow, knowing even as she washed out his wounds and piled brush on him to keep him warm, that she was crazy to stay. For years afterwards she remembered the cold—hard, bone-chilling cold that made her fingers ache and her breath sting in her throat. But most of all she remembered her fear that the savages would return. Time after time, she'd pick up her walking stick and start to leave, thinking: this is none of my business; he's going to die anyway. But then she would look at his face again, and it would pull her back. Who was this stranger? What was he to her? Angrily she threw down her stick and went back to him, chafing his hands to warm them, throwing more wood on the fire. She was more than a fool; she was an idiot. Anyone could see he was going to die before morning. She inspected his blue lips, and felt his cold fingers. Finally she gave up and lay next to him, trying to warm his body with her own. In the valley a wolf howled. The stars were cold slivers in the sky. Closing her eyes, Inanna fell into a restless, wary sleep.

Some time after midnight she woke covered with sweat. The stranger was hot now, burning with fever, and his moans were stronger and more frequent. In his delirium he had tried to throw off the cover of brush, and he called out loudly in a language she had never heard. She remembered that the men of Kur almost always died of fever after they'd been badly wounded.

Getting up, she threw more wood on the fire and sat down cross-legged beside the sick man. His lips were cracked and dry, and he was shaking all over. The blood pulsed quickly through his neck and he seemed to be having trouble breathing. What a waste. All this effort and he was going to die before she even got a chance to find out who he was. The man moaned and coughed. Well at least she could make it a bit more comfortable for him.

Uncorking the skin, Inanna poured a little water on his parched lips, and leaned over and unlaced his cloak. Around his neck, a woven cord had twisted, cutting off his breath. Carefully Inanna felt for the knot of the cord, untied it, and lifted the necklace off his throat.

It glittered in the firelight, dangling in front of her, and for a moment she didn't understand. Then she recognized the gold wings, tiny, outspread, the beak, the arched neck and feathers. It was a dove, exactly like the one Hursag had given Lilith on her wedding day. Inanna remembered the way her sister had looked that morning when she stepped out of the bridal tent in her new brown robe. She remembered Lilith's smile, how they had hugged each other, the feeling of peace the two of them shared when they were together.

"Who are you?" she screamed at the sick man, throwing the dove on the ground beside him. "What evil curse of a god sent you to me?" The stranger opened his eyes at the sound of her voice, but there was no recognition in them, only illness and fear. Inanna stood, and stared at him stubbornly. "I'm going to *make* you live whether you want to or not." She picked up the dove and tied it back around his neck. "You're going to explain this to me, understand?"

His skin was burning hot under her hands; he was curled up, shaking like a sick animal, dying before her eyes. How could she break the fever? She looked at the star mark in her palm, almost invisible in the firelight. If she had this power, then why not use it? Nothing else was going to save him.

Slowly, gently, Inanna put the palm of her hand on the sick man's forehead, but nothing happened. She tried again; still nothing. For a long time she worked over him but the harder she tried to push the power through her fingers the emptier she felt. Finally she gave up. Sitting back on her heels, she looked into the stranger's face. "You're going to die after all," she told him grimly. "I'm sorry, but there's nothing I can do."

For hours she sat up watching him grow worse and worse. The fever seemed like a fire in his body; he yelled and thrashed as if trying to stamp it out. More than once Inanna turned away, unwilling to witness this final battle with death. Near midnight the moon appeared, climbing quickly over the peak, thin and cold, so bright she could see her own shadow. When it set, it would take him with it.

Fever. Fever. The word nagged at the back of her mind like a buzzing fly. Inanna threw another armful of dry brush on the fire, and as it flared she remembered where she had heard the word recently. Today on the trail, before she turned back to the west, the blue flower, the one she had picked, hadn't she sensed something about fever from it? Yes, now she remembered! If you fed a tea made from the blue flower to someone who had a fever then he'd get well. That was the thought that had come to her as she held the stem in her hand.

Inanna walked back to the trail. In the moonlight she saw clumps of the blue flowers growing all along the bank, their leaves silvery and wet with dew. If they did cure fever, wouldn't someone else have found out a long time ago? She broke off a handful. The stems were slippery and cold in her hand, and the blooms gave off a faint, sweet smell like crushed almonds. Why was she bothering with these things? She stuffed the flowers into her belt and picked more. They probably wouldn't work.

Hurrying back to the campfire, she poured some water into a

small hollow in the rock, dropped in a few hot coals, and added the flowers. The stranger was panting now, in short jerky gasps like a runner who had come to the end of his strength. Inanna fed him the tea, forcing it through his cracked lips drop by drop. "Quit fighting me!" she yelled, catching at his hands as he tried to push her away. "You can't have your death! Not yet!"

The sunlight drifted under her eyelids, red and warm. Nearby two birds chattered angrily at the other. Inanna sat up and saw the fire had gone out; then she saw the stranger—dead of course. She felt a final, weary sense of defeat; she'd failed after all. She got to her feet, almost angry at the stranger for dying when she'd gone to such trouble to save him. Maybe he was better off that way; maybe everyone was better off dead. After she'd been walking for a few more weeks, she might wish herself in his place. He lay peacefully, his hands folded across his chest as if he'd just fallen asleep.

But wait; did he just move? The stranger moved again, unmistakably. Hurrying over to him, Inanna felt his skin. Cool, damp, a steady pulse: the fever was gone! She sat beside him for a long time, unable to believe that he was really alive, unable to believe that she wouldn't wake a second time and find him dead after all. But it was real enough. A few flies circled in the warm morning air; the birds chattered on in the bushes; the stranger slept quietly. The gold dove that hung around his neck made her remember Lilith again. She couldn't save her, but maybe she could save him. Somehow in her fatigue the two seemed connected. She had lost her sister and found this stranger; she had failed one and she had been given a chance to save the other. The thought was senseless, of course, but she couldn't get it out of her mind.

The sick man turned in his sleep, opened his mouth, and began to snore. Inanna thought of Hursag and smiled. Shading herself with some brush, she lay down on the hard ground beside the stranger and went to sleep.

How peculiar he was, how docile, almost like a child. Sometimes during those first few days he would try to talk to her, and she would listen with pleasure to the strange words. They reminded her of birdsongs or a flute, flowing together with no sense to them, but beautiful like music. When he saw that she didn't understand, he would point to things gently as if saying: "you can bring me that water or not, as you wish. It's all up to you."

Inanna wondered why he didn't order her around, why he didn't get angry. Hursag didn't get angry either, but then Hursag was so old that practically nothing bothered him. He'd eat burned soup and not even notice. But this stranger was no older than Pulal, young enough still to be a warrior with a warrior's temper. Inanna finally decided it was because he'd been so sick. Soon he'd yell or throw a stick of firewood and she'd know he was well for sure.

But the stranger only lay there patiently, eating what she brought him, and when, after a few days, she told him in gestures that they had to move down into the valley to a warmer campsite, he let her help him over the rough trail without protest, even though she could see that it pained him to put any weight on his bad leg. Where was the temper in him? What kind of man was he anyway?

The valley was green, lush with short grass and a stand of nut trees loaded with unripe fruit. As Inanna and the sick man walked down the trail, gazelles bounded away from them and flocks of birds rose with a hum of wings. On a flat stone near the edge of the little lake a huge tortoise sunned itself lazily. Inanna killed it quickly with a rock, and set about cracking open the shell. She wasn't much of a hunter, but at least the two of them wouldn't starve here. Once she got things settled she could weave a few snares for birds.

She glanced up from her work to see the stranger looking back at her with an odd expression on his face, as if he'd just bitten into an oak gall. The man pointed to the dead tortoise and shook his head. "Surely we're not going to eat that thing," he seemed to be saying. Inanna smiled; such a child he was, not knowing anything, not even the things any child would know. "Oh, yes," she gestured. Yes they would eat it, and like it too. Tortoise was good food.

She washed the meat, laid it on the rock, and waded into the water and gathered reeds. The stranger sat on the bank watching her as she tugged at the slippery stems. He seemed exhausted from the long walk, glad of a rest. "I'm going to build a hut over there where the ground's solid," Inanna told him. She mimed plastering the reeds with mud, and the stranger nodded as if he had understood. "It won't be as good as a real tent, but at least it'll keep out the rain. My people build these sometimes when we winter in one place." She saw the confusion in his face and laughed. "I don't know why I go on talking to you when you don't understand a word I'm saying." He smiled and made a tugging motion. "Yes," Inanna said, "I'm going to pull more reeds."

The water was warm around her ankles; tiny silver fish darted through the water lilies. Bend and pull; weave and plaster. Mud covered her hands and dried on her arms, caked in her hair. By midday she had put up the outline of the hut and begun to fill it in. Weave and plaster; back into the water now for more reeds, more mud. The rhythm of the work absorbed her as her body warmed to it. She forgot all about the stranger until he tugged at her sleeve.

"What is it?" She realized he was trying to say something.

"Enkimdu," the stranger repeated, pointing to his face. "Enkimdu."

"Oh, so you're thirsty are you?" Inanna washed off her hands, unhooked the skin from her belt, and filled it full of fresh water. "Here; have a drink."

The stranger shook his head, and pushed her hand to one side. "Enkimdu," he said again firmly. Suddenly it dawned on her that he was trying to tell her his name.

"Enkimdu?" she repeated, pointing to him. The man smiled and nodded slightly, delighted that she had understood him. Inanna pushed her hair out of her eyes and pointed to herself.

"Inanna," she said. The man's smile broadened, and he said a long string of words ending with her name. Reaching out, he picked a wild lily, and offered it to her with formal politeness, gesturing at the shelter.

"*Otla*," he said.

"Does that mean *thank you*? Are you thanking me for building the hut?"

The man grinned at her, happy as a child. "*Otla*," he said again.

"Well *otla* to you, Enkimdu, for the flower." She picked up another armload of wet mud and headed up the slope toward the hut. "*Otla*, Enkimdu."

"In language my people this yellow flower called *dock*; what called in your people language, Inanna?

"This *digging stick*, yes, Inanna? This *fire flint*; this *tortoise meat*. Enkimdu thinking tortoise bad tasting like grass sliding thing. *Snake*, yes, Inanna? Grass sliding thing called *snake*, yes?"

"Yes," she told him, "it's called a *snake*."

"Enkimdu thinking tortoise meat bad tasting like snake. But good tasting tortoise meat is. Inanna good tortoise meat cooking is doing." He talked constantly now, pointing at things as she cooked the food, following her outside the hut to learn the names of the flowers and animals, insisting that she learn his language as well. Even when the wound in his leg reinfected and he could do no more than crawl into a spot of sunshine and sit there all day shivering, he went on with his endless questions. "How are the high hills called different from the low hills?"

"We call them *mountains*," she told him. She asked herself if she minded all his questions and decided finally that she didn't. They made her feel important. That was it: he treated her as if she knew things. She held up the fish she was cleaning and the scales winked back at her. "I am Inanna, Keeper of the Names of Things," she told the unlucky fish. She laughed and threw it on the rock and Enkimdu laughed along with her.

The days began to grow shorter again and the pond dried to half its former size. Frost coated the ground in the morning, and dragonflies laying the last of their eggs hovered over the brown reeds. Inanna harvested baskets of nuts, and at night as they sat around the fire, she and Enkimdu shelled them and ate the sweet meats. His leg was nearly healed now, and when he spoke she found she was beginning to understand most of what he said. But sometimes there were problems.

"My mother," Enkimdu told her one evening, "is a fat woman." Inanna put down the snares she had been weaving and looked over at him curiously.

"A fat woman?"

Enkimdu nodded gravely and pulled his cloak more tightly around his shoulders to keep out the cold. "My mother is a fat

woman from a very long line of fat women." Inanna turned her
face away and pretended to unsnarl one of the snares. She mustn't
laugh at him; he'd be hurt. But the laugh came anyway, and the
harder she tried to stop it, the worse it got. Enkimdu stared at her,
puzzled, a little offended.

"Why the laughing is?" he asked.

"*Fat*," Inanna puffed out her cheeks and made eating motions.
"*Fat*'s the wrong word." He understood his mistake and began to
laugh along with her good-naturedly, his blue eyes sparkling with
amusement. There was color in his cheeks. How healthy he looked
tonight, how handsome. For no particular reason she remembered Zu, how he looked when he ran toward her. Zu had been
handsome too. But why was she thinking these things? She was a
married woman. She pushed the thought to the back of her mind,
but she could feel it prowling there. Wolf part of me, she said
silently, go back to sleep; leave me in peace. Inanna saw that she
had let the snares fall into a tangle. It would take her most of the
night to get the knots undone. She was a fool to let her mind
wander like that.

"I not mean my mother *fat*," Enkimdu was saying. "I mean my
mother is . . ." He waved his arms expansively and looked at her
for help.

"*Great*," Inanna supplied without looking at him.

"Yes, *great* she is. My mother great woman. Powerful, yes.
Headman." Inanna shook her head and begun to unsnarl another
knot.

"A woman can't be a *headman*," she explained. She picked up a
piece of leftover fish and began to eat it without enthusiasm.
"Maybe you mean your mother is the *headwife* to the *headman*."

Enkimdu waved the new word away. "Headman," he repeated
stubbornly. "Yes, headman is my mother. You understanding?"

"But a woman can't *be* a headman," Inanna insisted. Sometimes
he continued to get things wrong no matter how carefully she
explained. But perhaps that was the nature of men, to stick to their
own ideas even if they were mistaken. Oh, the stupid strength of
their stubbornness. How she envied them it, that way they had of
just going on and on.

"Inanna," Enkimdu said, "you understanding?" He was watching her with concern.

"No," she said, a little more sharply than she'd meant to.

Enkimdu patted her hand with his. "Understanding will be coming," he said gently. He picked a half-burned stick out of the fire and sketched two long lines in the ashes. Then he took a small handful of stones and placed them in a row. Was this some kind of game his people played?

"Mountains," Enkimdu said, pointing to the stones. He drew the tip of the stick back along the lines. "Waters. Long waters."

"Waters?" Inanna looked at the lines curiously. She touched them but they were dry. Water? Lines? She felt there was something important behind all this, something she wanted to know, but what was it? If only people all spoke the same language how much easier it would be. "Waters?" she asked again, touching the dry lines.

"Wide waters," Enkimdu said excitedly, putting down his stick and spreading his arms. "To the west. I from." He pointed to a spot near one of the lines.

"You're from the valley of the rivers!" Inanna threw the snares off her lap and leaped up. "You're from the valley on the other side of the mountains?"

Enkimdu nodded eagerly. "From the City of the Dove," he said. "You knowing?"

"No." Inanna threw some more wood on the fire and sat down beside him. "Tell me more about it," she begged. "Tell me everything." She caught the gold dove that hung about his neck. "Where did you get this?" The gold was warm in her hand. "My sister had a dove like this. For a long time I've wanted to ask you where you got yours."

"From my mother," Enkimdu said. Inanna smiled at him, forgetting everything but that she was at last going to find out about the great valley.

"The Black Headed People say you foreigners have no mothers," she told him.

"We say your babies are all fished out of rivers like tortoises," Enkimdu laughed. "And my people say you mountain people wolf-suckled are, got wolf mothers."

Inanna suddenly felt the greenness of her own eyes, the wolf-heart at the center of her. "Your people are right," she said soberly.

Enkimdu leaned forward, looked into her face, and then nodded. "Yes, I am seeing fierceness here, Inanna friend," he said,
"but here I am sweetness seeing too."

The meadow grass grew, unnoticed. One day it was so short
that you had to bend down and scrape off the snow to see it, and
the next time you remembered to look, it was as high as a man's
waist. When did all this happen, and how could she not have
noticed? But the grass must have been growing all the time without her seeing, because here it was, so thick and tall that a child
could get lost in it.

Why did she think of Enkimdu all the time? How did it begin?
She was ashamed of herself; she tried to stop, but it had gone too
far. She was failing her duty as a wife; she was like that crazy
woman from the tribe of Ki who used to wander around saying
"goat, goat," to everyone, only the word in her mind was "Enkimdu," and she heard his name in her head even when she was alone
and silent. At night when they sat by the fire telling stories, she
found she couldn't look in his face. She described the tents of Kur,
and made sure to tell him about Hursag. "I have a husband," she
told him on more than one occasion, but it did no good. She heard
Enkimdu's stories of great brick houses, temples, traders who
came from all over the world bringing pearls and lapis lazuli, and
instead of being excited by these marvels she found herself wondering, "what does he think about me?"

Nothing of course. He thought nothing at all about her. She was
foolish to feel so troubled in his presence. This mood would pass,
she knew it would, if she only kept busy enough. Yet when she
went out to set her snares she sometimes found herself afraid he
wouldn't be there when she returned. Then she dropped everything and ran back to the hut to find him sitting where he always
sat. Of course he couldn't go anywhere. His leg hadn't healed. And
if he did go? What would that matter to her?

She decided that in the future she would listen calmly to his
stories. She would sit by the fire and mend her snares, and when
he talked she would look him straight in the face. She'd feel nothing. It was all foolishness. It was only because she'd been away
from her own people too long. She took her place by the fire, and
found when he came in and sat down beside her that her hands
were shaking so hard that she couldn't separate the knots from the

threads. He offered her a roasted wren breast but she wasn't hungry. "Are you sick?" he asked her. There was concern in his voice, and she let it flood over her for a moment, warming her. No! This was too dangerous! She bit her cheek, trying to force the feeling to go away, and she found that she couldn't look in his face after all. Why? Why should one person be drawn to another in this way? Had he cursed her, put something in her food? She told him that she was tired and wanted to go to sleep soon. Would she like to hear one more story? he asked her. Inanna pretended indifference; she made her voice as flat and empty as she could. "Oh, if you want to tell it," she said. "I don't care." Enkimdu settled down beside her, so close that his sleeve almost touched her own. She wanted to draw her arm away, but she couldn't.

"In my city people worship the Goddess," Enkimdu began. He noticed nothing, and she was half glad, half angry at this. He picked up a small gourd full of hot tea and began to sip it slowly. In her hands the snares snarled into so many knots that it looked as if a weasel had been caught in them.

"The Goddess Ki?" Inanna asked. Her own voice sounded strange to her, far away as if she was speaking from the bottom of a hollow log. Enkimdu took another sip of tea and shook his head.

"No, not Ki," he said amiably. He picked up his stick and drew two pictures in the ashes. One was of a young woman holding a snake to her lips, and the other was of the same woman, older, heavy-breasted, full with child. "The Goddess has two forms, Dark and Light.

"Her name is Lanla the Good; her name is Hut, Mother of the Night." His calm was maddening.

"And how many goats do you sacrifice to these goddesses of yours?" Inanna asked, barely following his words, thinking only of how close his arm was to hers.

"None. To Hut, who used to drink blood, we give nothing." He frowned slightly as if the thought worried him. "To Lanla we give fruits and grains." The name of Lanla made him smile again, and Inanna immediately decided that she liked this goddess better than the other one. "We worship Lanla by singing and dancing and in other ways . . ." He looked at her and a strange expression passed over his face.

"What ways?" Inanna asked. Enkimdu reached over and began

to stroke her hair lightly with the flat of his hand. His palm was rough and steady, and her heart beat wildly, making her dizzy as if she'd run up the mountain.

"When I'm well," he whispered, "I'll show you how my people worship Lanla." His touch moved all through her; she felt it everywhere, in her hands, her feet, in the small of her back. She closed her eyes, letting him stroke her head; like smoothing the feathers on a young bird. Like soothing a child. Then she remembered Lilith.

"You shouldn't touch me," she snapped, jerking away from him. "I belong to another man." Enkimdu looked at her and smiled as if amused.

"In my city women belong only to themselves."

She stood up and backed away from him. This was a trap, and she was no fool. "I'm going outside to check the snares," she said, not looking at him.

"The snares?" Enkimdu said. The snares lay on the ground in front of her. Inanna blushed angrily. "Good hunting," he said. He picked up the mess of knots and tossed it to her. "When you come back I'll probably be asleep."

That night she stood over him for a long time studying his face in the firelight. She should leave now before it was too late. She remembered the fish she had caught that morning, how it had struggled on the end of her spear, eyes bulging, body changing color, and how the birds too fought the snares, beating the feathers off their own wings, twisting themselves hopelessly in the threads. How caught was she? How much of her had this man already taken without her knowing it?

Enkimdu turned in his sleep, hand over his chest, shallow breath. His eyes moved under the lids. Quietly she put her things together: a bag for food, a waterskin, the knife he had made for her out of a piece of bone. She took half the dried lily bulbs out of the basket, a handful of nuts, a flint. She made all her movements tiny, small like a mouse rustling through the stores. Sandals, spear, snares. The fire flared for a moment, and she noticed the scar on Enkimdu's forehead, healed, shrunk to a small red flower. Like a wild rose or a hackleberry stain; he didn't need her anymore. He was healed. She wanted to lean forward and touch him, say goodbye at least. But what could she be thinking! She'd wake him up if she kept standing there.

Outside the hut it was cold and the stars were covered by clouds. Why did she feel so sad? In a week or two she'd probably have forgotten all about him. The wind cut through her robe, making her shiver, and something white drifted down and settled on her sleeve. A snowflake no bigger than the tip of her fingernail, followed by another and another. Inanna threw down her pack, and stared at the sky. A storm was raging above her, burying the trail, sealing off the high passes. She couldn't go, couldn't leave after all. Half a day in the snow without a warm cloak or proper shoes, and she'd be dead. She had to go back to the hut; she had no choice. The two of them were stuck together until spring.

Inanna caught some of the snow in the palm of her hand and put it to her lips. The flakes were cold and gritty. This shouldn't have made her happy, but it did. So happy she was ashamed of herself.

The next morning as Enkimdu was stirring a basket of acorn meal mush, she walked up to him and stood with her arms folded across her chest. "How many wives do you have?" she demanded. Her voice was sharp, sharper even than she had meant it to be, but she looked straight at him, thinking: now I must do it while I still can; things must be settled between us. Enkimdu laughed so hard that he spilled some of the mush into the fire.

"I have no wives. Why do you ask?"

Inanna turned away, angry at him for his laughter. "My husand's name is Hursag."

"So you've told me," Enkimdu interrupted.

"He's very rich," she went on, determined not to let anything stop her. "He has goats, so many that no one can count them." Enkimdu set the basket of mush down on the ground and wiped his hands on his hips.

"He must be a very old man, this Hursag of yours, to have gathered so many animals."

"His age is no concern of yours!"

Enkimdu bit his lower lip as if trying to hold back a smile. "Oh, indeed," he said gravely, "and do you love this old husband of yours who owns you like one of his goats?"

"Don't say such things to me!" she cried, stamping her foot in the ashes.

Enkimdu lifted his hands. "I beg your pardon, *muna*. Let me ask you again: do you love your fine, rich, and undoubtedly handsome husband?"

"Yes," Inanna snapped. "I do."

"Ah," Enkimdu offered her some mush, "how pleasant for you." Inanna turned away from him and stalked angrily toward the door. Curse the snow! Curse the passes! She should have left anyway. He understood nothing, this foreigner. He was an idiot, a fool. Behind her she could hear him chuckling.

"Going out to check the snares again?"

Lilith walked down the hill toward her, balancing a basket of milk on her head. There was something strange about her dress, something strange about the way it floated around her breasts as if it were made of fog instead of wool. The gold dove gleamed at Lilith's neck, and she was smiling. "Inanna," she called out, "come help me with the milk." Inanna began to run up the hill, stumbling over the stones, thinking that it was already late in the day, the wrong time to be milking. Suddenly she looked up and saw that Lilith was beginning to lose her balance. Her sister turned in the path like a dancer, turning and turning, clutching at the milk basket. Her face was white with fear and her hands looked like bird claws. The basket tipped dangerously and a little of the warm milk slopped over the side.

"Lilith, be careful!" Inanna yelled. All at once she knew that if Lilith spilled the milk something terrible would happen.

"Inanna, help me!" Lilith screamed. The basket fell and Lilith's head fell with it. There was blood everywhere, mixed with milk.

Inanna woke screaming, still smelling the blood. In the instant before she was fully awake, she felt as if she were drowning in her own anger, as if the grief had made her heart burst inside her. But an arm was flung around her shoulders, pulling her back from the horror. Enkimdu. He drew her to his chest and stroked her hair. Over his shoulder she stared blindly at the familiar wall of the hut, the fire burning low in the firepit.

"You just had a bad dream." His voice was calm, matter-of-fact. He lifted her face to his and looked at her gravely. "Are you all right?"

"Yes," Inanna said. "I was dreaming about my sister, about Lilith, she . . ." At the sound of Lilith's name she began to cry in fierce, dry sobs. How ugly memory was! Why couldn't it leave her alone! It attacked when she least expected it, sneaking up on her in her sleep.

"Hush," Enkimdu said. He pulled her face closer to his and kissed her lips, took her in his arms and kissed her again, running his hands over her bare shoulders. Her body moved by itself under his touch, like grass blowing in the wind. Suddenly she was giddy, dizzy. Oh, the beauty of it, this dark strange beauty she had never suspected existed. Then she remembered Hursag.

"What's wrong?" Enkimdu asked. He let go of her and she moved to the other side of the pallet.

The words stuck in her throat. Enkimdu poured her a gourd full of cold tea and waited patiently while she drank it. Outside an owl hooted, and the wind rattled in the reeds. How late it must be. She wanted to lie down, close her eyes, never get up again.

"Now tell me everything," Enkimdu said.

She shook her head; she couldn't. She was too tired to go through it all again.

"Please." There was real concern in his face.

Well then, she'd tell him a little. Inanna leaned back against the roof pole and took a deep breath. "I loved my sister more than anyone," she began. The words tumbled out as she spoke of her dream, of Lilith's execution, of Pulal and his axe. She even told him the old story of the wolf-woman who had died for betraying her husband. When she finished she looked up and found him shaking with anger.

"You mean to say your brother beheaded your sister for taking a lover?"

"Yes."

"What a people!" Enkimdu snapped. "In the City of the Dove . . ." He stopped, and continued in a softer voice. "Our women pick their lovers where they wish and there's no shame attached to the act. You understand?" She didn't. "No one will hurt you. I promise that." He drew her close to him again, and she felt the warmth of his body against hers. His hands moved gently over her face and down across her breasts. "This is how we worship the Goddess." He moved his palm across her stomach and then lightly touched her between the legs. "This," he whispered, "is sacred."

As he touched her the bad dreams disappeared and the guilt

began to leave, to drain away. She grew calmer, and the passion rose in her again, irresistible as hunger. Enkimdu ran his hands down her sides, across her chest; her nipples hardened and her breath quickened. He kissed her passionately as if he wanted to devour her, bending her head back, mixing his tongue with hers. Hursag had never given her anything like this. There was some woman part of her that had been cheated until now. Enkimdu wanted her in a way Hursag never had. This must be the kind of wanting that made a husband really a husband and a wife really a wife.

Enkimdu moved down her body, kissing her neck, her breasts, the damp hollow of her belly. Inanna moaned with pleasure, tangled her fingers in his thick black hair, and smelled the fresh clean odor of rainwater and woodsmoke. His body was young and strong. She explored it tentatively as if it were a strange country, feeling the heavy maleness of his bones, the muscles under his skin, the hair on his chest, wiry and soft at the same time. He was like a bear. No, too taut and quick for that. A panther. His manness was wild and unbroken, but gentle somehow too.

As he spread her legs and began to kiss her, moving his tongue in slow circles, she no longer tried to imagine what kind of animal he was like. She was a spring, a stream, a river. He stopped and she floated under him, thinking nothing. Their bodies seemed to melt and float together, light and insubstantial as smoke.

Then he began all over again, probing her with his tongue, drinking her in. She forgot everything except that she wanted him closer. Inanna lifted her hips and grabbed, digging her nails into his shoulders. Her wolf heart rose in her and her back arched. Enkimdu slipped up, sliding along her body on a fine film of sweat. She felt his weight press her breasts against her chest, anchoring her. She pulled at him, throwing her legs around his. He entered her quickly, and together they danced the old dance of hunger, passion, and connection. When she moved, he followed her; when he went away for a moment, she drew him back. Time was nothing; she was no longer in it and neither was he.

The energy built between her legs, carrying her up toward Enkimdu. It vibrated in her womb and at the back of her spine. She was a wolf, biting at his neck, clawing at his back; she gave a sudden, sharp cry and heard him crying with her. His body vibrated inside and outside of her until she couldn't tell the difference anymore. And then there was peace and the sound of his heart beating against her cheek.

"Did I hurt you?" she asked.

Enkimdu laughed. "No, my sweet little wolf," he said. They lay still for a long time after that, wrapped in each other's arms. Finally Enkimdu kissed her softly on the forehead. "This is the way the earth feels after the rain falls on it," he said. Inanna smiled up at him and touched his lips lightly with the tips of her fingers, tracing the outline of his mouth. Enkimdu kissed her again, and then turned over and fell into a deep sleep. She lay beside him quietly for a few minutes, listening to his breath, and the words of the old love song ran through her mind:

He has kissed me, lain with me
Like a drink of honey wine.

5 HE'D always wanted a miracle to happen and now it had. When he was a boy he had lain awake at night begging Lanla to send him a sign to prove that She existed. Later, when he was older, he had joked with his cousins about the Goddesses: their statues were just piles of painted mud; they were both old cows who no longer gave milk; the people who still worshiped them were fools. How smart and bright and witty he and his cousins had been—and how unhappy. He understood now that they had been alone, even when they were with each other. The feasts, the lion hunts, the love affairs and intrigues of the palace were nothing but diversions, ways to avoid the knowledge that there was nothing really worth doing. Even his own adventures—those solitary trips off into the wilderness that he'd been so proud of, that he'd pursued despite his mother's commands and warnings— they too had been nothing.

What good was life without some kind of connection between people? That wasn't the sort of thing he would have admitted thinking even a few months ago before he left the city and a bunch of dirty savages jumped him and carried him off into the wilderness. Even though he'd nearly died, he looked on that as a piece of good luck now because it had brought him to Inanna.

Connection. What did he really mean by that? In the morning, when he sat outside the hut looking at the lake, he would feel a sensation of absolute peace. He would look at the reeds and feel that he himself was swaying in the air; he would look at the birds overhead and suddenly know what it must be like to fly. It was a quiet feeling, so subtle that if he stopped to think about it, it disappeared.

Once when he was a child he had gotten lost in the basement of the palace. For hours he wandered among the great stone jars of lentils and piles of broken furniture, crying, sure that he would never find his way out. All at once he had turned a corner and run into his mother. Her hands and arms were covered with wet clay, and he had seen that she was molding a statue in the center of an empty storeroom. "I've been waiting for you," his mother had said, although there was no way she could have known that he was lost, no way she could have expected him. But he had accepted her waiting for him, and silently gone up to dinner with her. That was what it was like for him now with Inanna, that simple feeling that he was connected to everything and that everything was connected to him.

Just saying her name brought him pleasure. At night he would run his hand over her carefully so she wouldn't awaken, over her high small breasts and the slender curves of her hips. The bones in her wrists were delicate and her skin as soft as those colored scarves the traders sometimes brought from the East, but she was strong as well. There was something half-tamed about her that excited his imagination. She was different from the city women, beautiful and fierce at the same time, elegant and unspoiled. Her long black hair smelled like musk and woodsmoke, and her green eyes were like the eyes of a wild animal. He had lain with many women and never encountered this before, this feeling of touching the core of another human being. Sometimes he thought he had known her all his life.

Other times he would realize Inanna was a mystery, that her mind was as different from his as the mind of a wolf or a gazelle. One afternoon he came back to the hut unexpectedly to find her bending over piles of dried plants and strips of bark. She had a look on her face he'd never seen before, excited, almost greedy, as if these bits of rubbish were something precious.

"What are you doing with those things?" he'd asked her.

"They talk to me."

"Talk to you?"

"Well, not talk to me really, but when I touch them I feel things. Like these." She picked up a handful of juniper berries and held them out to him. "When I touch these I get the feeling that they'd help Bismaya."

"Bismaya?"

"An old woman in my tribe. Her hands and feet are so swollen that she can hardly go out to milk her husband's goats. If I boiled these into a tea and made her drink it, the swelling would go away."

He told her about Rheti, the High Priestess of the city, who claimed to be able to see into the future. "Is it like that? Do you see things?"

"No." She began to put the plants back in her bag, wrapping some of them in little reed packets she must have woven while he was gone. "Is there much sickness in your city?" she asked him at last.

"The river fever breaks when the water gets low," he told her. "Once when my mother was little, there was a great plague, and so many people died that the funeral fires burned for days. I remember everyone saying that it had been a curse from Hut because we had stopped offering her sacrifices."

She had looked up at him with her green eyes, unblinking, like an owl. Then she had opened one of the packets and shaken some small blue flowers into the palm of his hand. "I think this would cure that river fever."

He'd wanted to tell her that nothing cured the fever, but she'd known what he was going to say before he opened his mouth.

"You don't believe it, do you?"

"No," he'd admitted.

"I'm not sure I do either." She had seen the surprise in his face and laughed. "A kiss," she said, "give me a kiss." The blue flowers had fallen on the floor forgotten, but later he had seen her outside, scraping away the snow, looking for more.

He carved a small, elaborate comb out of bone and spent hours combing out her hair, losing himself in the feel of her presence. She seemed to find it amusing that he would want to touch her in this way. Sometimes he reminded her of her sister, she told him. "I think there's a woman hiding inside you, Enkimdu," she said once when the two of them were eating dinner. He wasn't sure how she meant that, for it seemed among her own people only the women were gentle; yet he could sense that she felt there was something wrong with that gentleness, that it was a bit shameful to her. He'd learned her language; she'd learned his, but how little they really knew about each other. He tried to imagine what her childhood must have been like, dragged from place to place, living in a tent that was cold in the winter and hot in summer, never having quite enough to eat. And her husband, who was supposed to keep her in clothes and other necessities: look what he let her wander around in—an old wool robe that looked as if it had been made out of a grain bag. He wondered what she would look like in a linen robe with a good pair of sandals on her feet. Dignity, that's what she'd have, and beauty too. No one could call her a savage, not even his mother, who had always disliked the nomads. Dirty, his mother had said they were, and dangerous. But when his mother saw Inanna . . .

"I want to take you back to the city with me in the spring," he told her one afternoon. They had been sitting together for half the day without saying a word, watching the snow fall on the lake.

"Yes," she said simply, "I'd like that." She put her arms around his neck and drew his face down close to hers. "How I love you," she told him. "I never knew what love was before I met you."

"Neither did I."

But sometimes things went wrong between them. In late winter when the lake was skimmed with ice and the sun had not shone for over a week, a mixture of rain and sleet fell. For three days it poured, dripping through the reed roof of the hut, soaking everything. Inanna sat in front of the fire without complaining. Her lips were blue with the cold, and she had a bad cough, but she never mentioned the rain. Instead she seemed to move into herself like a fox preparing to sleep through the winter. He sensed her leaving him, and though he knew when the sun shone she would be herself again, he felt troubled by her silence. Now that his own leg had healed, he could afford to worry about such things.

"Let me tell you about the city," he began, putting his arm around her. How cold she was under her robe; her hands were like ice. If I lost you, he wanted to tell her, I would want to die. But he knew that it would upset her to hear that, so instead he explained

the customs that surrounded the temple of the Goddess. His voice
was soothing. Picking up his spear, he thrust the wood tip into the
fire to give it an edge.

"The priestesses are all *lants.*" Good. He could see that she was
interested now. "They're holy women," he explained, running his
thumb along the spear tip, "dedicated to the Goddess. Each new
year all the men of the city come to the *lants* and to the other
women of the temple to perform the Sacred Act." She looked at
him for a moment, and then before he knew what had happened
she was on her feet, yelling.

"You lie with these women, these *lants?*" she screamed. "You
copulate with them in the temple?"

What was wrong with her? Of course he did. "To honor the
Goddess Lanla who gives all life," he said, wondering if she was
sick.

She leaped at him, grabbed the spear out of his hand, and
waved it in his face. "If I ever find you sleeping with another
woman," she hissed, "I'll kill you. Do you understand?"

She'd lost her mind from the cold, gone crazy. There was no
doubt about it. "But it's the custom."

She turned from him and threw the spear through the doorway,
then sat down, shaking violently. "And is it the custom for your
father to sleep with other women besides your mother?"

What was she talking about. "My father?"

"Your father, your father. I'm asking you about your father.
Does he sleep with these . . . these *lants?*"

She spit out the word with such venom that he took a step back.
"But I don't even know who my father is." All this was so obvious;
any child could understand it. "My people trace their lineage
through their mothers and grandmothers. I come from an ancient
line of queens and priestesses, but as for my father, who knows? I
suppose he must have been someone my mother met in the temple when she went to honor Lanla, but I never bothered to ask. I
doubt even she knows."

"Your mother had many lovers then?" The anger seemed to
drain out of her, and she walked aimlessly around the hut, touching the wet walls with the palm of her hand.

He wanted to reach out and take her in his arms, but he was
afraid he might upset her again. "Yes," he said simply. He remembered the times he had walked into his mother's rooms and found

her with a new friend. She'd always seemed so happy to him, sitting on a pile of cushions drinking spiced wine and laughing like a young girl. You could hear her laughter all the way down the hall, and the next morning chances were good that he'd find her busy in her workroom. "Love makes me see my art more clearly," she'd told him once when he was mixing up the water and clay for her. But he'd only been a boy then, ten, eleven at the most, and he hadn't understood. Later, when he was older, it had been too late to ask. He thought how impossible it would be to explain that the lovers had been the finest part of his mother's life instead of the worst as Inanna seemed to imagine.

"I don't understand." Her voice interrupted, echoing his thought.

Enkimdu saw that her eyes were full of tears. How hard it must be for her to live here, separated from her own people. The city must seem like a story to her. He remembered how she had cared for him when he was sick, fed him, kept him warm. Why should he expect more of her? Why should he expect her to understand?

"When spring comes," he said, reaching out and taking her by the hand, "I'll take you back to the city with me, and you can see it all for yourself." She sat beside him, put her head on his chest, and he stroked her hair. It was so soft, fine like the shawls the traders brought from the East.

"But you won't sleep with those *lants,* will you?" she persisted, looking up at him earnestly.

"If it means so much to you, we'll only worship the Goddess together, even though it's not the custom." He felt her body relax against his. The softness of her breasts, the smell of her skin made him dizzy. *Lanla, Lanla, how beautiful your gift is.* "We could start our worship now," he whispered.

Inanna put the palms of her hands on his cheeks, and kissed him shyly. "I think I'm going to have a lot to get used to when we reach this city of yours," she said.

"Ah, but you're a quick learner." She laughed at that, and the color came back into her face. Enkimdu put his lips on her neck and kissed the whole arch of it from ear to shoulder, tasting the salty sweet flavor of her skin. He wanted to say something more but words felt clumsy. Reaching up, he untied his necklace and held it out to her. "Here, take this. It's all I've got to give you for now, and the dove is sacred to Lanla." He kissed her and placed the necklace in her hand. "Maybe this will help you get used to Her ways."

Inanna turned pale, and started back with a cry, nearly dropping the necklace.

"What's wrong?"

"There's going to be a terrible battle!"

"What are you talking about?"

"The dove." She looked at the necklace as if she were afraid of it. "When you put it in my hand I felt that I was going to have to fight someone . . . or something; I don't know which. I felt I had an enemy waiting for me in the city, a woman, white and evil, cold like ice. She's blind but she sees everything. I could feel her here," she touched her bare throat, "trying to wrap around my neck, and I could hardly breathe."

A shudder ran up Enkimdu's spine as she spoke. Rheti was blind, and her hair had been white as long as he could remember. But how could Inanna know about the High Priestess? He felt a sense of foreboding, something evil sweeping toward the two of them. Drawing Inanna closer, he tried to conceal his fear. This was ridiculous; it was only a coincidence that she had described Rheti. He was making too much out of it. But still the fear stayed, cold in the pit of his stomach.

"Inanna," he said, forcing his voice to take on a reassuring tone, "how can you have an enemy in a place you've never been?" He smiled and some of his own fear dissolved.

"I don't know. I feel like I've seen her before, but . . ." Her voice trailed off in confusion, and she lay her head on his shoulder. He stroked her hair until she grew quiet and he grew quiet with her.

"If the necklace bothers you so much, you don't have to wear it."

"No, it's all right now." Her eyes cleared, and she smiled. "You're right; I must be imagining things. Here." She handed him the necklace, and sat quietly while he tied it around her neck.

"How do you feel?" he asked.

"Fine. I don't know what got into me." The gold lay against the flesh at the base of her throat like a pool of yellow light. Enkimdu touched it with the tips of his fingers, and then slipped his hand under her robe, feeling her breath quicken, his own quicken with it.

"You mean more to me than my own people," he told her.
"And you more than mine."

Spring came early that year, exploding all around them in a riot
of mountain wildflowers, the spring Inanna always remembered
when anyone mentioned the word. She remembered the damp
smell of the earth, the first pale blades of the new grass, the wrens
that nested in the bushes near the hut; she remembered the lake
swelling from the melting snow, full of frogs that kept her awake
at night, the bear that lumbered down to drink one evening, lean
and hungry from his long sleep. But most of all she remembered
the almond trees, their branches slick and wet from the rain,
loaded with blossoms, petals dropping on the ground and blowing
through the air like a blizzard. She gathered up armfuls of the
blooms and brought them into the hut, hanging them everywhere,
piling them on Enkimdu so when he woke he found himself buried
in flowers.

"Time to travel," she told him. On the summits the snow was
melting, exposing patches of bare rock. The trail wound among
the boulders, clearly visible now from the door of the hut. For a
moment she stood looking at the mountains, thinking of other
springs: the black tents of Kur, people putting away their winter
clothes, the newborn lambs struggling clumsily after the ewes,
children running barefoot through the camp. How could she bear
never to go back, never to see any of them again.

"What's wrong?" Enkimdu asked. She looked at the almond
petals in his hair and began to laugh. What a fool she was to brood
and worry over things she didn't have, when she had so much.
"What are you thinking?"

"I was thinking that when a woman has a husband waiting for
her, it's best that she and her lover travel in the opposite direction." They laughed and he put his arm around her. "Now tell me
again how high the walls of that city of yours are."

"Higher than ten men and wide enough for an army to march
along the top."

"And do people really live there all year round?"

"You'll see."

"Is it true that you worship women, you city people?" He
smiled at her and picked off a sprig of almost blossoms. The petals

clung to the twig like tufts of new wool, and the centers were dusty with golden pollen.

"Yes my little goddess," he said, sticking the flowers in her hair. She slipped her arm around his waist, and they stood quietly looking out over their valley. The poplar trees had just put out their first leaves, and in the lake the water reeds were beginning to bud. "We could leave at the next full moon," he said. She nodded silently. Yes, they should start out soon. There was no reason to wait any longer. She looked at the lake again, the almond trees, the mountains. She would miss this place, and she wondered if he was thinking the same thing.

The next day the weather turned unexpectedly warm and Inanna woke to the sound of the birds singing lustily. Sunlight shone through the reeds of the hut, and the air smelled of new grass, damp earth, wind, and clean water. Stretching her arms over her head, she looked out of the door at the lake. As she started to get up, Enkimdu pulled her back to him and kissed her sleepily.

"Where are you going?" he asked.

"Up the trail to the place we first met. I want to say goodbye to it."

He ran his fingers through her hair and kissed her again. "I miss you every time you leave," he said.

"Even for a little while?"

He took her hand in his and touched the tiny star in the center of her palm. "Even for no more time than you could put here," he said, "I miss you."

"I'll be back soon." More kisses, and by the time she left the sun was already well over the rim of the mountains. The climb was longer than she'd remembered and steeper too, but the morning was so fine that she didn't mind. As Inanna labored up the old trail, tiny rivulets of water from the melting snow rushed across the path in front of her, forming shining pools under the boulders, dropping in threadlike waterfalls over the edge of the ridge. The snowdrifts were pocked and rotten, the sky a clear blue without a cloud. Up past the stunted juniper bushes, up to the great summit: and there it was, just as she'd remembered it, the great boulder, bald as an old man, sitting like a gloomy sentry at the top of the pass. Behind the boulder, out of the wind, she found what she'd come for: some bits of charcoal from their fire; a strap from Enkimdu's sandal; the bones of the dead rabbit, brittle now, green with moss. Yes, it was all still here. She put her hand on the place where she'd first found Enkimdu lying wounded, on a patch of wet rocky soil that looked like all the rest. Sacred ground, part of her life forever now; she couldn't have left without seeing it again.

Later, after she had eaten and rested, she walked back around the boulder and stood in the cold wind looking out over the valley. The hut seemed small and insignificant, as if their whole life together had hardly made an impression on the landscape. The thought made her shiver, and she turned quickly away. A small plant, beaten sideways by the wind, grew out of a crack in the boulder. Red bud, grayish-green stem. "We're both fools to be up here in this cold," she told the plant.

The flower bent and blew, nearly breaking with each gust. Its roots grabbed at the rock, forcing their way into the stone. Amazing how it could hang on like that. "Tell me how you do it," she said, reaching out for it playfully. As her hand touched the stem, a feeling of panic rushed from her arm to her heart, burning her, making her gasp for breath. She had a sense of terrible danger coming closer every minute. She pulled her hand away from the flower and put her fingers in her mouth. Curse it! What a fool she was! She'd grabbed a nettle.

Then she saw the man standing on the slope behind her. He was wearing a flame-colored robe, and his face bore a smile that wasn't a smile—Inanna recognized it the moment she saw it.

"I thought you were dead," Pulal said, walking toward her. Inanna looked at him dumbly, unable to move, unable to think of anything except that she must be dreaming. Pulal strode across the few paces that separated them, reached out, and pinched the skin on her upper arm so hard she flinched. "I see you fed yourself well over the winter, little sister," he said in a honeyed, half-mocking tone. "Your husband will be sad to learn that he's paid another bride price for nothing."

Where did he come from? What was he talking about? How did he find her? Pulal was so close to the edge of the cliff that if he took another step he might see the hut down below by the lake. He mustn't suspect that Enkimdu, that she . . . Inanna's mind began to race wildly. She remembered how Zu had died with a spear in his back for just one night with Lilith. How could Enkimdu escape if the men of the tribe learned he'd been sharing her bed for a whole winter? Pulal would kill them both if he found out.

"Old Hursag married again," Pulal was saying. "The he-goat's taken Aunt Dug for a wife so he'll have a woman to pitch his tent."

Inanna tried to calm herself and listen to what he was saying. She measured his power. Yes, he was stronger than she. She couldn't win if she had to fight him straight on. But if Pulal let his guard down, she might be able to take him. Strength came back to her again, filling her whole body. Pulal was still talking, telling her that the tribe had spent the winter only a few valleys away in a lower meadow below the frost line. "Plenty of grass for the herds," he said, puffing out his chest. "The flocks increase." She tried to smile, but hate gagged her.

"Kur favors you, brother." If he gave her a chance she'd kill him before they got back to the camp.

Pulal looked at her humorlessly. "So at last you've learned to talk like a woman should." He grabbed her more firmly by the arm and led her down the trail on the other side of the pass. Inanna turned her head for a moment and saw the great bald boulder disappearing behind the high bank. The jagged edge of the mountain rose up, blocking out the sky, hiding every trace of the valley, the hut, the lake. Enkimdu, my love, my darling, she thought, at least you're safe. She felt such terrible pain at leaving him that she almost cried out. She wanted to dig her feet and legs into the rock, root herself there like a tree so that nothing could pull her away, not even Pulal. But she went on instead, putting one foot in front of the other. Obedient woman, good wife. Look, Pulal; look at me and suspect nothing.

"Your husband will rejoice to see you even though he's taken another wife to his bed. Aunt Dug complains that his feet are cold at night and that he's no more use to a woman than a stone. How pleasant it will be for him to sport with you again."

Inanna tried to pull away, but Pulal was too fast for her. Snatching her hair, he jerked her head back so she had to stare straight in his eyes. Snake, lizard. What horror had Enshagag copulated with to birth him? Pulal saw the disgust in her face and his grip tightened.

"I'd hate to think what might happen if you don't agree to

return to your husband willingly." His voice was low and threatening. "You'll rejoice to see him, of course, won't you, my sister?"

Inanna thought of Enkimdu and how he would worry when she didn't return before dark. She'd have to wait for a better chance to escape. She pushed her wolf heart down in her breast and looked as meek as she could. "I'll rejoice to see my husband again."

Pulal let go of her hair and the color came back to the scar on his cheek. "Good," he said in an almost friendly tone of voice. "Very good."

The camp dogs licked her hands and the children surrounded her in a laughing crowd. She smelled goat meat roasting on the fires, and watched mutely as the women put down their baskets and ran up to throw their arms around her. "Inanna, wife of Hursag, has come back from the dead!" they called to each other. The women touched her face as if expecting her to disappear, turn into a water ghost, and melt under their fingers. Even the men smiled at her as if she were some marvelous creature. "How did you live through the winter, wife of Hursag?" they inquired politely. Inanna stared at her old friends and neighbors standing around her expectantly; she looked at the familiar black tents, the cooking fires, the dogs, the children. She wanted to say something, tell them how much she had missed them, her own people. She'd be leaving them again soon, going off to the city with Enkimdu. She wanted them to know that she'd keep their memory with her. But the words caught in her throat.

"Are you well?" someone asked. Inanna opened her mouth, but nothing came out.

"She's tired," someone else said. They spread out a blanket and set her down on it as if she were a child.

"Look who's coming to greet you," Pulal said.

An old man was running toward her. His legs and arms were as thin as twigs and he looked so frail that it seemed the least puff of wind might blow him off his feet. "Dear one," the old man cried in a high, shaky voice. There were tears in his eyes. Kneeling down, he enfolded her in a bony embrace. "Great Kur be praised, you've come back to me at last!" Inanna stared dumbfounded, unable to believe how much he had aged over the winter. Pulal caught her wrist and squeezed so hard that the bones ached.

"This time she'll be staying with you for good," he told Hursag.

"I lived on acorns most of the time, wild onions when I could find them, and nuts. There were a lot of nut trees. Alone? Of course I was alone. Afraid? Of course. Is the valley where I spent the winter near here? Oh, no. It's far away. Over there somewhere." A vague gesture. "I'm not sure just what direction. I walked for weeks before my brother found me."

All day she sat in Hursag's tent answering the same questions, taking the small gifts people brought her: a comb, a bit of brightly dyed wool, a piece of yellow quartz. All day as the shadows of the tent poles shrank and then lengthened again, she wove a fine story that left out any mention of Enkimdu.

"How lucky for you that your brother chanced upon you," a young woman named Kisim said, clapping her hands together excitedly. Bowls of goat meat were handed around, and skins of fermented honey.

"Yes," Inanna agreed, "very lucky indeed." Pulal picked up a piece of the meat and held it between his fingers. The gravy dripped slowly back into the bowl. Inside the tent it was so crowded no one could move. People stood outside, listening through the flaps.

"You had no firestick when I found you," Pulal said, "no food. Tell me how it was that you set out to travel without such things?"

Inanna looked him straight in the eye. "I lost my bundle only this morning in a stream. If you hadn't found me, I would have starved."

"Then you owe him your life," someone said.

Inanna looked down. Be humble, grateful. "My brother has always been favored of the gods." There was a mutter of approval from the crowd. Pulal put the goat meat in his mouth and began to chew it contentedly. Good, she had gotten his guard down. He was starting to believe her. She imagined herself tonight rolling under the flap of the tent, escaping. The moon was nearly full so she shouldn't have any trouble following the trail. She would find Enkimdu sitting in the hut waiting for her, worrying that she had been attacked by savages or wild beasts. Perhaps he would even think that she had deserted him. How happy he would be to see her safe and well. She imagined the smile on his face, how he would take her in his arms.

"You look awfully fat for a girl who's been eating acorns all winter," a voice snarled suddenly. Aunt Dug stood in the opening of the tent, looking at Inanna with ill-concealed hostility. The old woman's badly pockmarked face was flushed with spite, and her hands were planted stubbornly on her broad hips. She hates having to share Hursag with a younger wife, Inanna thought, but she won't have to do it for long. "Get out of here all of you," Dug ordered Kisim and the others. "She's got work to do."

After the crowd was gone, Dug thrust a bowl of nuts into Inanna's hands and told her to pick out the meats. "And when you're done with that, there are cheeses to be made. Unless you've become too fine for such work." Inanna felt a sudden twinge of pity for the old woman. Had Dug ever known anything about love? It must make people mean to live their whole lives without ever finding someone to care about.

"Well, what are you waiting for?" Dug snapped. She pushed a greasy strand of hair out of her eyes, and threw sticks on the fire, muttering to herself as she did so. Later, when Hursag came in, she complained to him that Inanna was lazy. "A man with two wives can't expect one of them to do all the work," Dug grumbled. She put her hands in the small of her back and groaned. If I had to live with this all the time, Inanna thought, I'd probably come to hate her. But after all, it's only for today.

But late that afternoon Pulal unexpectedly ordered the tents struck and announced that the tribe was moving on. Deliberately—or so it seemed to Inanna—he led them over a stony ridge, down a rocky canyon where they would leave the least possible trail, pushing them on until the animals were stumbling with fatigue, and it was so dark that they could hardly see to pitch camp. That night, just as the women were cleaning up after the evening meal, Pulal appeared in Hursag's tent with his mother. Enshagag's long gray hair was unbraided, and she carried a pile of sleeping robes.

"I've come to visit, sister," Enshagag told Dug. Dug smiled and offered the two of them some roasted nuts.

"May you have a happy visit, sister-in-law," Hursag said politely, yawning behind his hand. He stretched, and motioned for

Inanna to follow him into the back section of the tent. "I think it's time you and I went to sleep, dear one," he said, looking at her with his old tenderness. The old man had always been good to her, and for a moment Inanna felt ashamed that tonight she would be leaving him again. But then she thought of Enkimdu and her resolution hardened. The way back would be harder now, but she had noted every turn they had taken, and she had no doubt she could still find the trail.

But Pulal had other ideas. Stepping between Inanna and Hursag, he caught her by the arm. "You sleep with her tonight," he said, pointing to Enshagag.

Hursag started to protest, but Pulal cut him off short.

"There'll be time enough for you to take her to your bed later," he said sharply.

"I'll keep your feet warm tonight, husband," Dug said, snatching Hursag by the hand and pulling him into the back section of the tent before he could object. Enshagag spread her sleeping rugs next to Inanna's bed and stretched out without a word. She had become heavier over the last year, and her body effectively filled the space between the rugs and the tent flap. Inanna knew from long experience that her stepmother was a light sleeper.

Pulal kicked the ashes over the fire to bank it. "Don't let her out of your sight," he told Enshagag.

Early in the morning, before the sun was up, Inanna—who had been lying awake all night—tried to slip quietly out of the tent, but Enshagag was awake and grabbing her arm before she could even get up from her bed.

"Where do you think you're going?" Enshagag hissed. She put her fingers to her lips and whistled sharply. Pulal suddenly entered the tent. His hair was slicked back with water, and he had already put on a fresh robe.

"Good morning, mother," Pulal said.

She would find herself in a corral, penned up like a goat, stuffed into a leather bag, trapped under a mudslide. Great boulders lay on her chest, crushing her lungs, pinning her to the ground; she couldn't breathe or move. She was smothering, dying. She had to get out. She would pull at the fence stakes, scrabble at the mud with her bare hands, try to lift the stones, and wake up to find herself in Hursag's tent, lying beside Enshagag. She would smell the sickly, over-sweet odor of her stepmother's body and know that she'd been dreaming of escape again.

Over and over it would happen, the same nightmare, and afterwards in the half-darkness she would lie awake wondering how she was ever going to get back to Enkimdu, knowing that the rocks, the walls, the mud of her dreams were the three of them: Enshagag, Dug, and Pulal.

Everywhere she went, one of them went with her. Milking the goats, gathering firewood, washing out blankets in a stream, she would turn to find Enshagag next to her or Pulal watching from a distance. Looking up from her weaving she would find Dug's eyes following her every move. They knew or at least they suspected that she'd had a lover. But they couldn't be sure.

Sometimes as she lay awake she would imagine Enkimdu had tracked her and was trying to signal to her by imitating the call of a bird or the howl of a wolf. Other times she would convince herself that he must have already given her up for dead and gone back to his own people. No, she wouldn't lose him. Half a day's journey down a canyon toward the rising sun; half a day's journey along a stream with rough water; a tree struck by lightning at the turning. Each night she tried to memorize the way the tribe had traveled, and each night it grew harder. A small meadow with a pile of rocks at one end; a ridge followed to a cleft; the middle fork, the second branch. The trail snarled in her mind like a skein of badly wound wool: three juniper bushes growing in a bare place, the lower path, a stand of nut trees just before the turn. Or was it the upper path? She'd forgotten, but she couldn't forget. If she forgot, she'd never find Enkimdu again.

"Why don't you eat?" Pulal demanded one afternoon.

"I'm not hungry."

"You look like a bag of bones." He put his hand on her arm and she shivered and pulled away from the cold deadness of his fingers. "What are you thinking about all the time?" he asked, dipping himself some fresh milk.

"Quit following me," she hissed. "Leave me alone, all of you; you've won, you understand. You've won." Pulal looked at her coolly, drank his milk, and shook his head.

"I don't know what you're talking about. No one's been following you." But after that, even though they still didn't trust her outside the camp, they at least let her wander among the tents by herself.

"Wife of Hursag, my child is sick and won't take the breast."
"Wife of Hursag, my old mother has pain in her bones."
"Wife of Hursag, do you have anything that could enable a man to . . ." embarrassment, a low whisper, "that could enable a man to continue being a man?"
"My husband has a fever and I'm afraid he'll die. Come to our tent, I beg you, wife of Hursag."
"My throat hurts."
"My arm . . ."
"My baby . . ."

To give in to her grief was to die of it, so on the third day of the new moon Inanna took her bag of herbs and began to wander through the camp looking for sick people. Dried flowers and strips of bark—she remembered the day she had sat in the hut sorting them into piles, telling Enkimdu what diseases each one would cure. The thought of Enkimdu was like a knife twisted in her side, a pain too bad for bearing. Silently begging his forgiveness, she pushed him out of her mind for a few hours. She would think only of the plants: plantain, wild lettuce, ash, comfrey root. These she knew. Like all women of the tribe she had used them before. But others were strangers: a flower shaped like a moth with silver spots on the petals, a root mottled like a snake. Now was as good a time as any to find out if there was any value in them. She had to keep busy. A handful of moss that smelled like wet dirt, half a dozen bitter white berries that no one would eat even if starving, a string of dried seeds that Enshagag insisted were poison. Were they really good for anything, or were they only bits of trash that she'd dragged along with her all this time?

In the first tent she entered an old woman sat by the fire wrapped in a clean wool blanket. Her hands and feet were so swollen that the fingers and toes had almost disappeared and her face was puffed up like a bladder of water. Inanna took a handful of juniper berries out of her bag and showed them to the old woman.

"Grandmother Bismaya," she said, "I think these can help you."

The old woman smiled and shook her head. "Neti of the underworld already has the gate open for me." She lifted her great paw of a hand and looked at it calmly. "Do you remember how fast I could milk the goats when I was younger? I was the fastest milker in the camp." She let her voice trail off and her hand fall back into her lap. "Nothing can help me now."

Inanna wondered if when her own time came to die she would be as resigned and dignified as Bismaya. No. She'd go down scratching and clawing like a wolf—she knew she would—fighting it every step of the way. The old woman gazed at her steadily, her eyes almost hidden by the swelling of her cheeks.

"I can't promise anything, but I'd like to try to help you anyway." She took some hot water, crushed the juniper berries, and dropped them in.

"Will the tea taste bitter?" the old woman asked. "I've had enough of bitter drinks."

"I'll sweeten it with honey."

Bismaya smiled. "It's good of such a young one as you to take an interest in such an old one as me." She drank down the tea, wiped off her mouth, and patted Inanna on the knee with sausage-shaped fingers. "Tell Hursag his wife does him credit."

Inanna took the old woman's hand in hers for a moment. She was going to say something, but she never remembered later what it had been, because the moment she touched Bismaya she lost all sense of being in the tent. Instead she found herself looking at a great lake that was overflowing its bounds, flooding the forest. Dead trees stuck out of the water like bones, and the grass around the rim was black and slick with mold. What was happening? At one end of the lake there was a mud dam with great cracks in it, and even as she watched the cracks began to close of their own accord and the flood waters began to go down. Then, as quickly as it had come, it was all over and she was back in front of the fire holding Bismaya's hand.

"Where did you go just then?" the old woman asked.

"I don't know."

"Did some god give you a vision?"

"I don't know." Inanna tried to stand up but found she was too dizzy. "You're going to get well," she told Bismaya. The words came out of her mouth before she knew she was going to say them. She thought of the lake and the mud dam. "You're going to get well; the water's going to leave your body."

"Are you sure?" Bismaya grabbed Inanna by both hands and scanned her face eagerly.

"I'm not sure of anything." Inanna pulled away, got up, and walked out of the tent in a daze. How could she have said such a thing? How could she have made such a promise? She was a fool, an irresponsible fool. She'd put away her bag of herbs, never touch a sick person again.

But as it turned out, she had no choice. A few days later the water began to leave Bismaya's hands and feet, and from then on Inanna was constantly busy. *The wife of Hursag has powers.* The rumor that she had found new cures ran from tent to tent with the speed of a brush fire, and they began to come—the sick, the injured, the dying—to Hursag's tent, looking for his younger wife, begging her to cure them of things that not even the gods themselves could cure: a missing leg, old age, even death. How could there be so much sickness in one small camp? Why hadn't she ever noticed it before? She sat up until dawn pounding bits of bark into powders and mixing up purges and teas. Later, she would straighten up from the bed of a sick child and realize she hadn't thought of Enkimdu for hours. Was she forgetting him? She would summon up his face again, feel the old loneliness, the pain of his absence, go off by herself leaving the sick to their sickness for a while. But when his memory came back to her unexpectedly it was the hardest to bear.

"The Goddess Ki sent you back as our blessing, wife of Hursag," one of the women said to her after Inanna had cured a bad headache with thyme and boiled thistle leaves.

"It's no blessing my coming back," Inanna had replied with such bitterness that the woman had taken the damp compress off her forehead and stared at her uncomprehendingly.

"But where else could you have gone, wife of Hursag?" she asked.

The seed sprouts in the darkness; the whole tree waits in the nut to be revealed. You crack open a bird's egg and find a tiny bird, feathers and all, where you had thought there was only yolk and shell. Later Inanna wondered why she hadn't noticed the changes in her own body sooner, why she hadn't suspected.

"I feel sick," she told Dug one morning. The two of them were milking Hursag's goats together, their heads resting against the animals' warm bodies. Not as she and Lilith had milked—with songs, stories, and laughter—but with a sullen companionship. The milk flowed into the pitch-lined baskets, and Inanna felt dizzy at the smell of it.

"You're supposed to be working," Dug snapped. "Do you think I can milk these cursed things all alone?" The sky and earth tilted slightly; Inanna turned her head to one side and vomited. "Oh, very well." The disgust in Dug's voice was as thick as scum on water as she thrust a basket of warm milk into Inanna's hands. "Go back to the tent with that and try not to spill any of it this time. If you'd eat less and work more, you'd feel better." Inanna started uneasily down the hill, holding the basket against her chest. "I knew you'd get sick," Dug called after her. "I knew it was just a matter of time. Courting it, that's what you've been doing, playing the healer. Now look at you!"

The next morning Inanna was ill again. "You don't have the stomach sickness, do you?" Dug asked suspiciously, crossing over to the far side of the tent. Hursag put some cold water on her brow and crouched beside her until she felt better.

"It's nothing," she told him.

"Good, dearest one." He never touched her with desire now, and for this she was grateful, but the old tenderness still existed between them. "Rest a while more."

She nodded her head and promised to lie still, but after he was gone Inanna dosed herself with mint and wild cucumber juice, and went to see an old man who needed a splinter taken out of his knee. By evening she'd forgotten all about her sickness, but the next morning the dizziness was there again. What was the matter with her? She went on working, pushing it all to one side of her mind. Later she marveled at her own stupidity, how long she refused to recognize the obvious.

She was lying awake for the fourth morning in a row feeling too ill to get up. Through the open flap of the tent the first gray light of dawn mottled the sky. Awake so early for no reason and sick on top of it. In the background the faint rhythm of Hursag's snoring blended with Dug's. Well, she'd had enough of this! What was the matter with her? Suddenly it came: only as a suspicion at first, but a suspicion that grew stronger and stronger. She was with child, Enkimdu's child.

Joy ran through her. Oh, Enkimdu should be here to share this moment! She remembered how he had held her in his arms the last time they were together. The child must have already been with them, and they'd not even known. Inanna touched her belly and smiled. Enkimdu would be so proud, even if he did claim that his people cared nothing for fatherhood. This would be their first-born.

Great Kur, what was she thinking! What kind of fool was she? This was a disaster. Everyone in the tribe knew Hursag was incapable of fathering a child. Dug knew that since Pulal brought Inanna back from the mountains she hadn't even shared the old man's bed. Her *husband's* bed. How long would Dug wait before she spread the word that Hursag had another wolf-wife in his tent?

Inanna clenched her fists and forced herself to think through to the end. It would mean nothing that she'd healed so many of her people, nothing that she'd brought their babies into the world and saved some of them from certain death. The whole tribe would turn on her with Pulal leading them. It would be Lilith all over again.

Silence. The call of a bird. Inanna sat up carefully and surveyed the dark tent. A few yards away Dug lay on the other side of the firepit, still snoring heavily. The bird called again and then fell still. If she had any sense she'd get rid of this new life before her condition became obvious to everyone. Inanna felt her belly again and tried to imagine how it would look five months from now. How long could she survive before someone discovered her secret? It would be so simple to stop the whole process. There was a bitter plant with purple stems that grew along the trail, a small mint with grayish leaves, a root she'd already used several times to provoke the delivery of an afterbirth. All three made the womb knot and bleed. She could expel this thing overnight, and no one would ever be the wiser.

Getting up quietly, she felt her way to the peg that held her leather bag, lifted it down, untied the mouth, and reached inside. Yes, she had them all. She could smell the sharp fragrance of the mint, the dusty bitter odor of the purple-stemmed herb. The root was smooth and slick under her fingers with bits of damp earth still clinging to the tendrils. She need only get up in the morning and brew herself a bowl of tea, and tell them that her time of bleeding was difficult this month, and that she needed a day's rest. No one—not Dug, not Hursag, not even Pulal—would ever know.

But as Inanna leaned forward to replace the bag on its peg, her left hand accidently brushed against her belly, and the life inside her spoke. She could feel it coiled there under her palm, no bigger than her thumb, its tiny heart already beating, and she knew—as small as it was—it wanted to live as much as she did. This baby would have Enkimdu's high cheekbones and Lilith's eyes, and perhaps she too would have the power to hear the voices of plants.

The next morning Inanna got up early and threw the root, the mint, and the bitter herb into a deep crevice, and when she saw more growing along the side of the trail, she passed quickly by.

Now, knowing that she had the child's life to look after as well as her own, she put her fears aside. She had to escape at once; there was no longer any other choice. Since Enshagag had stopped sleeping with her, Pulal probably believed she had given up any idea of leaving the tribe. Sometime, sooner or later, they were bound to let her go out of the camp by herself, and when that time came she would be able to get away. No matter that she was no longer sure of the exact route back to the hut. She'd find it somehow. She'd hide food for the journey, weave herself a warmer robe, take a sharp knife and a good flint. If anyone tried to stop her, she'd outrun them; if a wild animal attacked her, she'd kill it. And if she got to the hut and Enkimdu wasn't there, she'd keep on going west to the valley. She'd find Enkimdu's city and bring him his daughter. But first she had to get out of the camp.

The opportunity came sooner than she had expected. A few days later she was sitting in the tent mending one of Hursag's sandals, when Dug began to complain that there wasn't enough firewood to cook dinner. "Don't sit there like a lazy slug," Dug grumbled, "go out and get some." Inanna waited for the old woman to offer to go with her, but Dug simply continued to rattle the cooking pots together ill-naturedly. "Well, what are you waiting for? Do you think the goat meat's going to cook itself?"

Picking up her woven carrying sack, Inanna stepped out of the tent and walked rapidly toward the edge of the camp. It was already late and the setting sun had turned the sky behind the mountains a pale yellow shot through with red. Inanna took a deep breath of the clear, cold air, and felt free for the first time in weeks. Looking around to make sure Pulal was nowhere in sight, she threaded her way between the tents and stepped out into the tall grass.

Should she try to escape now? But Dug was back in the tent, waiting for the firewood. If she failed to return in a reasonable amount of time, Dug would no doubt sound the alarm and Pulal would send men out to look for her. Better to wait for a few days until they were used to the idea of her going off by herself, and then she might be able to sneak away unnoticed. Putting the strap of her carrying strap around her forehead, Inanna walked through the flock toward a clump of scrub oaks well off the trail.

By the time she'd picked up enough sticks to make a bundle it was already getting dark, and the light of the cooking fires reflected off the black sides of the tents in the camp down below. Inanna stood for a moment, enjoying the view and the sense of being by herself again. The valley the tribe had stopped in that morning was wider than usual; hundreds of tiny streams poured off the opposite wall of the canyon like threads of white wool. At the base of the sheer slope, sheep and goats were scattered around the tents in dim clumps while directly overhead a star swam in the night sky like a single fish. It was a perfect, calm evening, and she thought—with a slight touch of regret—that soon she would be leaving the mountains, perhaps forever.

Putting the last of the wood into her carrying sack, she hoisted the bundle onto her head, and walked rapidly back toward the camp, trying to calculate how long it would be before the moon was full again. She wanted to be able to travel at night for the first few days, and it would be dangerous to try to follow the narrow trails in the dark. The thought of the moon reminded Inanna of an old song Lilith had once sung to her when she was a child, a song about Nana the baby moon god. She was trying to recall the words when someone grabbed her from behind and clapped a hand over her mouth. Inanna gasped, began to struggle, and the bundle of firewood fell off her head and went rolling down the slope.

Her attacker turned her to him and she suddenly recognized him. "Enkimdu!"

Enkimdu pulled her closer and kissed her hungrily on the eyes and lips. "I've been tracking you for weeks," he whispered, "but you never went out alone before. Great Holy Goddess, how many times I've seen you down there in that camp!" He was thinner than she remembered, his beard longer; he seemed older somehow. "I've come to take you back with me," Enkimdu said simply, "will you come?"

For a moment her feelings were so strong that she couldn't speak. "I was already coming to you," she managed to say at last. Enkimdu smiled and embraced her again. The musky odor of his body greeted her, the clean sharp fragrance of his beard. Her silence broke, and the words came pouring out. She told him in quick, excited sentences how Pulal, her brother, had found her and forced her to return to her husband, how Enshagag had slept with her at night to keep her from running away; she told him of Hursag's feebleness, of Dug's nagging, of the sick people she had healed, and the nights she had lain awake wondering if he had gone back over the western mountains to his city. She started to mention the child, but stopped, realizing that she wanted to save that news for later, after they'd made love again.

"I thought you'd gone on without me," she said instead, grabbing onto his shoulders tightly.

Enkimdu kissed her, and then gently put one finger over her lips to stop the stream of words. "We have to leave right now." He looked at the camp uneasily. Inanna turned to stare at the ring of black tents. There were extra lights moving in and out among the cooking fires, and she thought she could hear the sound of Pulal's voice calling her name.

"If I leave with you now," she whispered urgently, "they'll send out a search party." How worried he looked. She caught up his hands and kissed them. "Wait until they're asleep, and then I'll sneak out of Hursag's tent. By morning we'll be too far away to follow." Enkimdu shifted his weight uneasily and looked up at the sky as if trying to calculate the time. "I've got food hidden." She took his face in her hands. "Please," she begged.

But he still thought it was too dangerous. For a long time they stood in the shadow of the scrub oaks trying to agree, and finally, reluctantly, he gave in to her. "How could I refuse you anything," he said, touching the tiny gold dove that hung under her robe. He picked up his spear. "I'll be there," he pointed to the clump of scrub oaks, "until you come back, but don't be too long." Inanna retrieved her bundle of firewood. As she started to lift it to her head, he grabbed her again and kissed her fiercely. She pushed him away lightly with the palms of her hands, and smiled up at him with more courage than she felt.

"I'll be back before the moon sets."

"May Lanla guard your every step." For a long time he stood on the ridge, following her with his eyes until she reached the circle of tents. Then, shouldering his spear and feeling for the bone knife at his belt, he moved cautiously into the cold shadows of the oak grove.

When she got back to Hursag's tent, Inanna found Pulal waiting for her with a pine torch in his hand. The pitch cracked and popped dangerously, sending out a small shower of sparks. Five other men were with him; as Inanna had suspected, a search party was already in the making. Several of the men looked at her with curiosity, not unmixed with awe. She recognized them as members of families she had visited recently—a case of lung fever, a badly cut hand. Under ordinary circumstances not one of them would have left his dinner to go look for a lost woman, but her healing abilities had given her a special status in the tribe. Even Pulal felt it, and when he spoke his voice sounded more worried than angry.

"Where were you?" Pulal held the burning torch so close Inanna smelled the sap from the wood. His eyes were suspicious. He inspected her carefully as if she were a prize ewe that had been exposed to some unexpected danger.

"I had to go a long way to find this," Inanna threw the sack of dried brush at his feet, "and besides I was gathering medicines." At the mention of medicines the five other men nodded and made approving noises. One of them, a young husband named Ur, strode up to Inanna and cleared his throat nervously.

"My wife," Ur began. His wife had pricked her foot on a thorn and nearly died before Inanna could put wild apple paste over the wound to draw out the infection. Now the woman was weak but recovering.

"I'll come see her in the morning." Inanna brushed past Ur and walked through the flap of Hursag's tent. Halfway over the threshold she remembered that by morning she and Enkimdu would be far away. Reaching into the leather bag at her waist, she pulled out a handful of yellow dock leaves and went back outside.

"Give these to your wife," she said gently to Ur, "and make sure she rests for the next few days." Ur took the leaves in his big, bearlike hand and smiled at her gratefully.

"Thank you, wife of Hursag."

Inside the tent Dug bent over the fire, trying to poke it up with a charred stick. She was coughing from the smoke, and Inanna could tell at once that the evening was going to prove far from pleasant. "Other women found wood close to the camp," Dug said ill-humoredly, pushing a greasy curl off her forehead, "why not you?" She poked at the fire again, sending up a cloud of ashes, threw down her stick, and retreated grumbling outside to get the firewood. On a pile of robes near the entrance to the back section Hursag sat on a fleece, drinking a cup of fresh milk. He looked terribly old, like a dried-up child. Hursag lifted his head when he saw Inanna, stopped coughing, and smiled at her in a gentle way that made her feel a pang. She genuinely loved the old man, and hated to leave him to the mercy of Dug, Enshagag, and Pulal. She wanted to say something to him that he could remember after she was gone, something to let him know it wasn't him she was leaving, but before she could find the words, Pulal came into the tent and sat down on the other side of the fire. Just then Dug came back and Enshagag was with her.

For hours the three of them sat around the fire talking while Hursag dozed on his pile of robes and Inanna pretended to sort herbs. Yellow flowers in this pile, blue in that—and never mind what they cured. She could hardly tell the plants apart tonight. Her mind was on Enkimdu waiting for her out in the oak grove.

Wouldn't Pulal and Enshagag ever leave? Wouldn't they ever stop talking and give Dug and Hursag a chance to go to bed? Just listening to the slow monotonous drawl of their conversation made Inanna so nervous she wanted to scream, throw the leather bag at them, and run out of the tent. She bit her cheeks and continued to sort yellow flowers, red flowers, blue flowers. Curse all of them! Why wouldn't they go to sleep! Had they picked this night of all nights to sit up until dawn? And what were they talking about? Idiocy, nothing.

First Enshagag insisted on relating a long story about a black-and-white goat that gave birth to a three-legged kid. The incident had happened some ten years ago when Inanna was still a child, yet the old woman rehashed every tiny detail as if the birth had taken place that very morning. Pulal, who always seemed to enjoy his mother's rambling, nodded eagerly, encouraging Enshagag to go on even when she seemed to be losing interest in her own story. At the end he grunted with satisfaction, placed a warm robe over her shoulders, and helped her to some of the best bits of food from the communal pot. For a moment Inanna was afraid he might ask Enshagag to tell the story again once she had eaten, but it was Dug's turn instead.

For the next hour—perhaps longer—Dug complained loudly and bitterly that she had been better off as a widow. Hursag had too many goats to tend to; his tent was drafty; Inanna was lazy; the old man himself was as much trouble as three children. As she droned on, Pulal and Enshagag nodded their heads in sympathy, prompting her to offer an even more detailed list of her grievances. Hursag, who was the object of all this, managed to drop off to sleep somewhere in the middle, and Dug, seeing that the most important part of her audience was no longer paying attention, finally stopped talking. For a full minute Inanna could hear only Hursag's snores and the wood cracking in the fire. Surely Pulal and Enshagag would go back to their tent and Dug would go to sleep.

Pulal stretched his arms and yawned as if he were about to announce his departure, but just as Inanna was putting the herbs back in her bag, he pulled a carved wood board and a set of stone markers out of his pouch and sat them down on a flat rock near the edge of the firepit. "Ah!" Dug and Enshagag said. The old women ran their fingers over the polished stones with little exclamations of delight and began to set them on the board.

Great Kur, not this! Inanna looked at the game in despair. From long experience she knew the three of them often gambled together until sunrise, losing and winning until everything finally balanced out. Through the open flap of the tent she saw the moon had already set and she looked around frantically for some way to slip out unnoticed. She touched the side of the tent furtively, trying to see if she could slide under it somewhow, roll forward, duck under the rope. No, too risky. They'd be on her in a minute like a pack of dogs.

She went to the far corner of the tent, lay down on her bed, and tried to still her growing nervousness. Perhaps if she pretended to sleep the others would realize it was time for them to do the same.

Inanna shut her eyes and drew the covers up over her body. She was fully clothed—her knife and herb bag at her belt, her flints in her pouch, a bag of food stuffed under the rug beside her. She even left her sandals on so that as soon as Dug fell asleep she could escape from the tent without another moment wasted.

In front of the fire the gambling game continued quietly, the only sound the click of the stone counters and an occasional murmur from one of the old women when she lost or won more than usual. The fire sank to a dim glow and no one bothered to throw on more wood. It was smoky and hot in the tent, and Inanna's head felt heavy. She had to stay awake. She couldn't let herself go to sleep . . .

Someone was shaking her. Inanna screamed and struck out in the darkness.

"Inanna."

She opened her eyes to find Enkimdu crouched beside her, whispering her name. "Inanna, wake up!" Later, after it was all over, she realized that he must have waited until it was nearly light, and then—afraid perhaps that something had happened to her—slipped into the camp. "Hurry," Enkimdu whispered, trying to pull her to her feet. His hands slipped across her wrists as she struggled to rise out of the tangle of the covers, but it was already too late. Awakened by Inanna's scream, Dug sounded the alarm, calling out that there was a stranger in the tent.

"Help! thieves! savages!"

Inanna heard Hursag in the back section, and the sound of running feet outside. As she fought to stand, she remembered the way Zu had looked when the spear caught him between the shoulder blades. She grabbed Enkimdu by the arms to steady herself and smelled the sharp, clean odor of his beard. If she didn't act at once he would die.

"Run." She pushed him away as hard as she could. Her mouth went dry with panic at the thought of being left alone, but she knew they could not both make it to the edge of the camp. If she stayed behind and delayed Pulal, Enkimdu might not end up like Zu. In the darkness Enkimdu caught her arm and pulled her stumbling over the pile of robes to the side of the tent.

"No. We go together," he whispered. Inanna couldn't see his face, but she knew it bore the same stubborn expression she had seen a hundred times that last winter, the look that meant he wouldn't compromise. He wasn't going to leave her; he wasn't going to save himself.

"Enkimdu . . ." Inanna pleaded. Before she could finish, the tent was full of light. Pulal rushed toward them, yelling the war cry he used in battle just before he moved in on the enemy for the kill. In one hand he held a flaming torch, and in the other his copper-bladed axe. The flames from the torch threw strange shadows on Pulal's face, transforming it into an animal mask, complete with a row of grinning teeth. In one motion, faster than she would have thought possible, Enkimdu put his body in front of hers and drew the knife from his belt.

Pulal glanced at the short bone knife and his smile widened cruelly. Waving back the other men, he came forward alone, stepping carelessly over the firepit. In the other corner of the tent Dug threw her robe over her head and set up a wail. It was an eerie, keening sound that made Inanna feel as if she'd been strung between the two tips of a bow.

"Heh!" Pulal yelled, feigning with the axe. Enkimdu grabbed Inanna by the shoulder and pushed her to one side as the metal blade crashed down inches from her head, sheering off a piece of the tent pole. The tent wavered and the shadows danced crazily on the walls. Pulal circled around the two of them, pushing them back toward the corner, thrusting his torch so close Inanna shrank from the heat. If Enkimdu could only fight alone he might have a chance, since he was the stronger and quicker of the two. But with her to take care of . . .

"Heh!" Pulal lifted the axe and brought it crashing down on a pile of baskets. Nuts and cheeses rolled out on the floor and the smell of sour milk filled the air. Pulal herded them further back, teasing Enkimdu like a dog. It was an insane, deadly dance. As Pulal lifted his axe a third time, Enkimdu sprang in low and quick under his guard, slashing Pulal's upper arm, A cut, then another. Blood spurted and Pulal screamed with pain. His axe swung wildly as he hacked to the right and left; part of the tent pole splintered, collapsing. Baskets split in two and the tent ripped jaggedly as the axe slashed a hole in the side. Enkimdu dodged and struck again, cutting Pulal on the chest.

"Get back!" Inanna yelled at Enkimdu, but this time he wasn't quick enough.

"Heh!" Pulal brought the axe down. As Inanna looked on help-lessly the copper blade caught Enkimdu on the right shoulder, knocking him sideways. The bone knife flew out of his hand onto the dirt floor, and rolled into the firepit. In the moment of silence that followed she heard only the breathing of the two men.

Pulal took a step back and looked at the unarmed man in front of him. Enkimdu's right arm hung uselessly at his side, but he still shielded Inanna's body with his own. Under his robe, his back-bone tensed like the back of a snake. Then, with no warning, he threw himself at Pulal bare-handed. The other men in the tent muttered in admiration, but Inanna heard only her own scream. She reached out for Enkimdu, trying to catch at his robe and pull him back, reached for him and lost him.

"Hyena!" Enkimdu struck Pulal across the face, smashing his smile into an obscene parody of itself. Then the head of the copper axe caught Enkimdu across the chest, throwing him backwards.

Enkimdu's body hit Inanna's, the sudden heaviness knocking her off balance, throwing her into one of the remaining tent poles. She grabbed him under the arms, thinking he was dead.

But Enkimdu wasn't dead. Fighting, pulling away from her, he went for Pulal again. His breath whistled in his throat, and the blood soaked through his robe. Pulal stepped out of the way as the wounded man lunged toward him and looked at Enkimdu for a moment with grudging approval. Then, as if slaughtering a goat, Pulal lifted the axe and brought it down squarely between Enkim-du's eyes.

Inanna caught the body as it fell toward her a second time. She had to stop the blood. She grabbed a blanket from the pile and pressed it over Enkimdu's face, trying not to look at the jagged hole, the white bone of his skull. Blood, warm, gushing out, soaked through to her skin, staining her robe. Enkimdu's lips moved under her fingers as if he were trying to tell her something, and then he went limp and she knew the life had drained out of him.

Dead. The word sputtered in her mind. She felt the edge of a great numbness creeping toward her. So this was the way it was. She sat back on her heels and looked at his body. The one man she had ever loved, the one person she had ever wanted to heal, had bled to death in her arms. Her powers were useless. Inanna noticed that her hands were smeared with something. With

Enkimdu's brains. Then the pain hit her. Bending forward, she sobbed in great, choking gasps.

Someone pulled her roughly to her feet. "So I have another she-wolf for a sister," Pulal yelled. His face was red with excitement. "She-wolf, slut!" He twisted her wrist, forcing her away from Enkimdu's body.

Inanna's grief changed to anger. She struck out at Pulal with her free hand and he slapped her so hard her ears rang. The tent turned sideways, and she caught at a pole to steady herself.

"Slut!" He slapped Inanna again, dragging her toward the open flap of the tent. Inanna lifted her hand, touched herself on the heart, trying to drain off the heat of her own anger. Cold hate, cold hate, she prayed, give me hate like stone. She thought of the child inside her, of how she had to live to revenge Enkimdu's death. Under her fingertips her heart slowed and she took a deep breath. Her head cleared and she could think again.

He sensed the change in her. Twisting her wrist harder, he tried to push her back into the pain. Pretending to yield, she forced her body to go slack like a leaf on the water. Then they were outside the tent and she was breathing the cold morning air. Pulal took a torch from one of the men and held it so everyone could see her shame. Calmly, as if she had infinite amounts of time, Inanna surveyed the situation and saw to her satisfaction that the circle of people hadn't closed around her yet. There were still gaps, places she could slip through. Escape was still possible.

"Slut!" Pulal yelled again, reaching for her braids. As his hand came toward her, Inanna stepped back as if afraid. Then quickly— before Pulal had time to recover his balance—she lunged at him with a loud cry and pushed the burning torch full in his face. Pulal screamed as the flames hit his eyes and the air was filled with the smell of burning hair and flesh. He floundered blindly into the crowd and someone threw him to the ground and began to beat out the flames with a blanket. She broke and ran in the other direction.

Later she realized that if it had been daytime she would have had no more chance of escaping than Zu. But the moon had set long ago; it was pitch dark once she got beyond the ring of torches, and the entire camp was in confusion. Ignoring the sounds of pursuit, she raced between the tents, through spaces too small for a grown man to follow, stumbling around cold firepits, knocking over piles of wool. Would the camp dogs let her pass? She saw recognition in their half-wild, wolflike eyes. The dogs lifted their muzzles curiously and lay back down again without barking. She ran past them to the rim of the camp, and stood for a moment trying to decide which way to go. Outside the ring of tents the sheep and goats appeared as dim white shadows that bleated uneasily as if sensing the disturbance.

Stripping off her robe, Inanna ran to the nearest group of animals and threw herself down on her hands and knees. Now she too was only a dim white shape in the darkness, indistinguishable from all the rest. Slowly, with great caution, she worked her way up the slope away from the camp. The sharp rocks cut her knees and the palms of her hands. Down below, behind her, torches moved out from the ring of tents and the sound of voices grew louder. Well, let them search. They'd have to look behind every rock, examine every animal to find her, and even when morning came she'd be hard to track over the stony ground.

She stopped for a moment to catch her breath. About a hundred paces down the slope a man held a torch and looked out at the hills. It was Ur, the young husband whose wife she had saved only a few days ago. Inanna suddenly felt terribly alone. Her friends, her relatives, everyone was hunting for her—even the children. Crawling behind a rock, she slipped her robe back on before continuing toward that same grove of scrub oaks where Enkimdu had waited.

The branches of the old trees were laced together like the roof of a hut, the shadows cold and damp. Inanna stood for a moment, letting her eyes probe the darkness until she found what she had come for. There, as she had hoped, were Enkimdu's things: a small bag of food, several extra flints, his spear, a blanket made out of rabbit fur. Inanna picked up the blanket and folded it carefully. The sorrow came toward her as she touched his things, but she pushed it away. Sorrow could drown her; time enough tomorrow and in the days to come to grieve for him. Tonight she had to escape. The morning star was already up over the horizon and the eastern sky was getting dangerously light. She felt the tears well up in her eyes, but she fought them back.

Picking up Enkimdu's spear, Inanna turned her face away from the tents of her own people and began the long journey west.

The Dove

Lanla is the barley,
Lanla is the wheat,
Lanla is the dates,
The olives, the sesame,
Milk and honey pour from Her breasts,
Who can praise Her enough?
Lanla gives us children,
Lanla gives us life,
All good things come from Lanla . . .

A birth prayer of the city people

Hut! Let me win this fight!
Hut! Let me kill my enemies!
Hut! I promise you blood!

A war chant of the city people

6 THE path stretched out in front of her forever; it lost itself in creekbeds, wound down ridge after ridge into the purple distance. At night, when the wild animals howled, it was a path bordered with fear, a path that pulled her up into the high mountains where she shivered with cold, a path that dragged her down into the lowlands, burned under her feet at noon like a griddle, until all she wanted to do was lie down in the shade, stop walking, give up. Then she would get to her feet, face the sun, and follow it down to the finish of another day wondering how long she had been traveling, wondering if she would ever come to the end.

Each morning when she woke, she felt the child growing inside her, and her own hunger growing with it. A handful of red berries, a few birds snared one afternoon when she stopped longer than usual, a fish caught on the tip of Enkimdu's spear: she never remembered how she survived those weeks. She only knew that she walked and walked, half crazy with grief.

Every moment of the time she and Enkimdu had spent in the valley came back to her. She remembered the first day of his illness, the hours they had pased by the fire talking together, making love, their fights. Small things tormented her beyond reason. Once—before they were lovers—he had asked her to massage his bad leg and she'd refused, afraid of what such touching might bring. Now that refusal haunted her as she lay on the pallet of dried brush at night, unable to go to sleep. Had he really been in pain that morning? Had she failed him somehow? For days she mulled over how stupid she had been. Why hadn't she foreseen how short their time together would be? Why hadn't she given herself to him at once and enjoyed every minute of their loving? Now he was dead, gone from her forever, and there was no way she could reach out to him and say: "I'm sorry." Enkimdu had died without even knowing of their child. Sometimes as she walked down the trail, Inanna would stop suddenly and put her hand on her belly, thinking: here too I failed him. And then she would go on again, but with no heart.

How long did her journey last? Weeks? Months? She only knew

that one night near the end of summer she woke from a deep sleep to find the full moon had risen, flooding the sky with light. In the distance three dead tamarisk trees stuck out of the ground like bones; beside her, her own shadow lay on the ground, thin arms and full belly etched in silhouette. Her first thought was of the quiet; the world seemed to be holding its breath, solemn and still. All around the moonlight poured in pools on the rocks, covered the leaves of the poplar trees like ice. The air was warm and full of strange smells: jasmine, wild rose, and somewhere—very far away—the scent of fresh water. Inanna felt the moon pulling her to her feet; its energy filled her body.

Restlessly she walked around her campfire for a few minutes, and then abruptly tied up her bundle, and slung it over her shoulder: rabbit skin blanket, spear, herbs, food, flints. She would walk, take advantage of the light while the moon was high in the sky, and rest during the heat of the next day. Kicking out the fire, she turned and trudged slowly up the slope, for once thinking of nothing in particular.

After she had been traveling for some time, Inanna sat on a sandy stump and drank water from a pool. It tasted tepid, musty, almost stale. In the brush a cicada chirruped in a lazy fashion that reminded her of Hursag's snoring. For a moment she was overcome with homesickness, and she allowed herself the dangerous luxury of remembering the black tents, the smell of the cooking fires, the children running through the camp—as if they were all still her own people. But then Enkimdu's face rose before her, and for the hundredth—perhaps two hundredth—time she got up and continued walking.

The slope of the next hill was especially steep and the path narrowed dangerously. Once or twice she nearly slipped over the edge, and she became so absorbed in finding firm footholds that she hardly noticed when she climbed over the crest. So it was the wind that finally grabbed her, rushing on her by surprise, nearly knocking her off her feet—not the tight sharp wind of the mountains, pressed and twisted into narrow canyons, blocked off by walls of sheer granite, but a vast open wind, the kind that blows off an ocean or sweeps across a plain. Inanna caught onto the edge of a rock to steady herself against it, and looked down the opposite slope. For a moment none of it made any sense. It was like looking into the sky, into a vast, flat void. Then suddenly she knew that she had come to the end of her journey at last.

Throwing down her pack, she yelled with joy. It was the river delta! And there, on the bank of the river, just where Enkimdu had said it would be, was a city! Not until the next morning did she realize that the walls had been washed with white clay. Now, in the moonlight, the shining circle seemed like something out of a dream, a great glowing disc, as if someone had caught the moon and tethered it to the earth.

She stood until her body grew numb, filling herself with the beauty of it all. At last, reluctantly, she moved behind a rock where it was warmer.

That night Inanna had a strange dream. In her dream she stood on a ridge, wearing a kind of armor she had never seen before, and heard a voice calling to her out of the darkness, challenging her to battle. The voice was evil and venomous, full of hatred, but when she went forward to fight against this unseen enemy, she found no one: only an empty meadow full of black rocks and large yellow flowers spattered with blood . . .

Two sets of walls, a circle within a circle, and in the center the city itself, domed roofs piled up on top of one another like a termite nest. The next morning Inanna stood for a long time on the bluff taking it all in: date palms, terraces, a spot of green high in the air that must be a roof garden, narrow streets that wound back and forth like the threads in a snare. Two large buildings stood out from the others, decorated in strange designs. Boats shaped like cups floated on the river, and in the fields animals grazed along the irrigation ditches.

In the light of day it was obvious that the great circles of the city walls were far from perfect. Rubble and stones filled the gaps; whole pieces of the inner parts were thrown down or missing altogether. Didn't they care? Weren't they afraid of attack? She looked out across the great plain, at the clusters of mud houses that broke the flatness. Those were villages on a scale she could understand, but the city! What kind of people could afford to neglect their walls in such a fashion? There was something grand about the decay, something majestically careless, as if the people of that city never had to fear savages or hostile armies. As if they were saying to the world: "We have been here forever, and with no effort on our part, we will remain here until the end of time."

Inanna combed her fingers through her hair nervously. How would the city people receive her? Maybe they would kill her simply because she was a stranger among them. Or—worse yet—perhaps they would simply take her in without noticing her. She uncorked the waterskin, took a drink, and splashed some of it on her face and wrists. Even from the bluff she could see that it was already getting hot in the delta. Waves of heat rose in spirals and the ground under the worn soles of her sandals was almost unpleasantly warm. Small figures began to appear on the footpaths that ran through the fields: the people of the city. She stared at them, those dolls no larger than her thumb. There was nothing to do but go to meet them and hope for the best. Picking up her pack, she began the long walk to the river.

As the sun rose higher in the sky, her wool robe clung uncomfortably to her body, and the dust stung her eyes. Her clothes, none of her was made for this land. Under her feet the trail was gradually becoming broader, but, except for a vulture or two circling overhead, there was no sign of life. Where were they all? Why hadn't she met anyone yet? It gave her a strange feeling to be walking down this road by herself as if she were the only person alive.

Dust, heat, more dust. Near mid-morning she came to a large olive grove and sank down gratefully in a patch of shade. Cool shadows, overhanging branches, trunks growing in circles, coiling back on themselves like snakes. They looked old. Above her head, the fat green olives hung in clumps, and doves cooed placidly. Outside the grove the sun shimmered moltenly in the sky, and the glare from the rocks was almost blinding. The real heat of the day was just beginning.

Inanna stretched out her arms and thought of sleep, but it was too dangerous. She could be seen easily from the trail, and there was nothing to hide behind, not even a rock—only dust, olive trees, and shade. She decided to continue on her way, when a noise caught her attention. Above her two doves were quarreling, fighting over something—a nest, food, she couldn't see just what, pecking and calling at each other like children squabbling over a honey cake. They took to the air with a great flap of wings, stirring the leaves, disappearing into the hot sheet of the sky. Inanna peered at the place the birds had abandoned, high up in the crotch of the tree, and noticed that the limbs just below had grown together to form a sort of platform, broad enough to lie on. The perfect solution, and if it hadn't been for the doves she might never have noticed.

Tossing her pack up into the tree, she hoisted herself after it and stretched out on the limbs. They made an airy, pleasant bed, and she would be safe up here out of sight. All around her the silver-green olive leaves fluttered in the breeze, and the limbs themselves moved gently. Putting her hand on her belly, she felt the child rocking with her. Then closing her eyes, she went to sleep.

"I think we should get her out of here."

"But she told us not to touch her, *ordered* us not to, remember? No matter what happened, she said."

"Look how sick she is. We can't just stand here and watch her die."

"If she dies I'll break my spear and shave my head as if she were my own mother, but an order is an order."

"You're right, but when I see her like this all the singing goes out of my heart."

"And mine too."

"Are you praying for her?"

"Yes."

"So am I."

Inanna woke to the low whisper of voices just below her, to musical words that drifted up through the leaves like the murmur of doves. It was the language Enkimdu had taught her, the tongue of the city people. She lay still for a moment, holding her breath, trying to make sense out of the half-familiar sounds.

"Lyra . . ."

"Yes, Seb, what is it?"

"I wish she'd picked anyone but us to come here with her."

"But she loves us the best."

"Since *he* died, she hasn't loved anyone."

Inching her way to the edge of the limb, Inanna cautiously parted the curtain of olive leaves and saw two soldiers standing under the trees: a man of about thirty who must be the one called Seb, and Lyra, a woman. A woman soldier? But it *was* a woman, black as obsidian, dressed in full armor, so close that Inanna could almost reach down and touch the red plume on her helmet. A double-headed axe dangled from the dark-skinned woman's belt, and on her shoulders and arms the pink welts of old wounds stood out clearly in the dim light.

"Ah, you don't know her heart then if you think that," Lyra was saying. She lifted her spear and pointed to someone Inanna couldn't see. "Even now she loves us as if we were her own children." Inanna parted the branches delicately, as though she were taking a small bird out of a snare. Not a noise, not a rustle. She now saw a third person in the grove, an old woman lying on a pallet. Matted gray hair, face covered with sweat, fingers clawing at the hem of the thin blanket that covered her. The woman began to moan and turn restlessly, throwing off the blanket. She was dressed in a course brown shift, and her feet were bare, swollen so badly that they looked like cushions.

Seb walked quickly to the other side of the grove, pulled the blanket over the sick woman, and then came back again. As he passed under the tree, he looked up at Inanna without seeing her, his eyes full of tears. The sight of his face hit her like an avalanche, like a rockslide, nearly knocking her out of the tree. Inanna bit her cheeks to keep from screaming out loud. The man was a stranger, yet his face was as familiar as her own: those high cheekbones, that hawklike nose, the thick black hair, the blue eyes. She had loved that face, awakened with it sleeping next to her, held it in death! It was Enkimdu. She turned her head away, closed her eyes, but when she opened them again and looked down at the soldier, the likeness seemed stronger than ever.

"If there's a curse for touching her," Seb was saying, pointing to the sick woman, "then I'll take it on myself. I can't stand by anymore and watch her suffer this way with no one to comfort her."

"I'll help you then."

"But the orders?"

"To the hell realms with the orders! I can't stand it anymore either." Lyra's arm slid around his shoulder. "Let the curse be on both of us." The two soldiers walked back to the sick woman and sat beside her.

"Ah, don't die, dear one," Seb said softly, taking the old woman's head in his lap and stroking her sweat-streaked hair.

"Come back to us," Lyra pleaded. "Remember the goodness of this world. Don't get lost in Hut's caves. Remember your family and all your friends who love you."

The old woman seemed to hear them; moving again, she lifted her arms as if reaching out for help. On her wrist a red bracelet dangled for a moment before falling to the ground. It was a viper, untwisting, sliding off into the roots of an olive tree. Now Inanna knew what was wrong; the woman was dying of snakebite!

She had to get a better look. Carefully balancing herself between the limbs, she moved forward, but as she did so, her foot caught in her pack, knocking it sideways. She made a desperate grab for it, but missed. With a loud thud the pack fell to the ground. A moment later, a spear slammed into the trunk beside her, inches from her cheek. Looking down, she saw that Lyra had unhooked the double-headed axe from her belt, and Seb was standing over the old woman, his own spear raised.

"Come down and die!" Lyra yelled, shaking her axe in challenge. "Show yourself, coward!"

Inanna put as much of the tree trunk between herself and the two of them as she could manage. "I'm Inanna, daughter of Cabta, wife of Hursag of the tribe of Kur," she shouted back in their own tongue. "And I come in peace!" She looked at the spear still vibrating in the trunk beside her. "I mean no harm," she added.

When the two of them heard her speak their language, they lowered their weapons. The dark-skinned woman strode to the foot of the tree and warily looked up through the leaves. "Holy Goddess, it's a woman with child!" She spread apart the branches and examined Inanna with curiosity. "You up there," she called out, "do you claim sanctuary?"

"What?"

"Sanctuary, do you claim it? Any woman with child can claim the protection of the Goddess. So do you or don't you?"

"What happens if I do?"

Lyra smiled, exposing a row of front teeth with one missing. "We don't kill you."

"Well I claim it then," Inanna said quickly.

The woman threw down her axe and motioned for Seb to do the same. "Come down. My brother and I won't hurt you."

Inanna climbed slowly out of the tree, feeling the spear in her back all the while. Would they wait until she was on the ground to attack her?

"Where are you from?" Lyra looked at Inanna's swollen belly. Her face was kind now, almost friendly.

"I come from the mountains." Inanna met Lyra's gaze firmly, determined not to show any fear.

"Seb," the woman said, putting her axe back in her belt, "did you hear that? She says she's from the mountains."

"Then how . . ." Seb began. But a moan from the sick woman interrupted him. Instantly he was on his knees beside the pallet, taking her hand in his. There was intense grief on his face. But the pain it caused her to see him suffering was ridiculous; she didn't even know him. Inanna forced herself to scan his features, looking for differences. Yes, the mouth wasn't quite the same, the hair was thicker. And his head—this man had a way of holding his head to one side that was nothing like Enkimdu. His bare legs were perfect, no sign of the wound she'd healed. No, she and this man had no past together. It was just a first impression, a trick of her imagination.

Seb rubbed the old woman's palms, pulling the blanket up around her shoulders to keep her warm. On her swollen wrist the marks of the snakebite glittered like two tiny red stones. "Who is she?" Inanna asked.

"I can't say. That is, it's forbidden." Lyra stumbled over the words.

"What's forbidden?"

"To say her name." Lyra's expression was apologetic. "She doesn't have any name here."

Inanna crossed to the pallet, and put her hand on the wrinkled forehead. The skin was cold, clammy; the old woman was dying. Suddenly, before Inanna could remove her hand, energy began to course up her arm. A blinding light blossomed from the back of her skull, filling her eyes, and her palm burned as if she'd grabbed a live coal. Then it was all over, quick as a flash of summer lightning burning itself out in the sky.

"What's wrong with you?" a voice said. In her confusion Inanna thought she saw Enkimdu. But it was only Seb. Turn your face away from me, stranger, she thought, leave me alone! Don't remind me of the dead! Under her hand something moved; her palm was still pressed to the old woman's forehead.

"I can save her." The vision had left a taste in Inanna's mouth like a strange fruit, and she knew she had the power to heal. "Build me a fire." She never knew why they obeyed her; she was a stranger to them too, after all. Maybe because there wasn't any other choice.

A fragrant smell of burning wood filled the grove. In the olive trees doves called placidly to each other, and the leaves rustled together, purling like running water. Taking her knife from her belt, Inanna made four quick slits on either side of the snakebite and began to suck out the venom. Her healing power rose in her, coming to her throat, blocking out the fear, protecting her from the poison. A cut in her mouth, a scratch on her lip, and the death gift of the snake would enter her too. But she knew she was safe. In her hand the star mark pulsed, and the thought of death passed over her like a wave and receded. It was the healing that was important now. Nothing else mattered.

"Let me help you," Seb said.

"Boil me some water," Inanna told him without looking up. The sick woman was still only half-awake. If she closed her eyes, she might never open them again. Inanna saw the lashes flutter and droop. "Wake up!" she slapped the ochre-stained cheeks. Behind her Lyra and Seb exchanged glances, but she saw nothing but the old woman, the swollen face, the tangled gray hair, the eyes opening. A bowl of boiling water was placed beside her; she reached into her bag, and took out the hyssop, dried onion blossoms, and clover. It was like a dance; once you began the proper movements, everything else came along in the right order.

"Are you a healer?" she heard Lyra ask.

"Of sorts." Crumble the leaves and blossoms into the hot water. Smell the sweetness of them. Light, now dark, now the brew is ready. She dipped a piece of clean cloth into the water and washed out the bite. Plantain leaves, chew them into a paste. Spread them on the wound just so. Not in the deepest part, but around the edges. Careful now. Do the other one. Sitting back on her heels, Inanna inspected her work with satisfaction.

"I need more water."

"Let me get it." Out of the corner of her eyes, Inanna saw Lyra walk to the stream, dip her helmet in the water, and carry it carefully back to the fire. "You are a healer." There was respect in her voice, something that almost sounded like awe.

This time when the pot came to a boil Inanna thew in some small bitter-tasting berries. The smell was acrid, unpleasant, and the liquid foamed slightly. Inanna thought of her long journey west, the cold nights, the times she had used these same berries to stay awake and alive. Two or three of them in a cup of water and you could walk for a day without eating or resting. Perhaps the gods themselves fed on such things. But the taste was terrible. She wondered if she'd be able to get the old woman to swallow the stuff.

"Lift her head," she ordered. With obvious affection Seb raised the old woman's head and cradled her in his arms as Inanna placed some of the liquid between her lips. She coughed and tried to turn away, but Inanna caught her chin and forced more of it into her mouth. As she swallowed, two spots of color appeared on her cheekbones, and she began to breathe more quickly. Inanna touched her wrist and felt her pulse beating strongly now, quick as if she'd come to the end of a long race. And it had been a race after all.

The old woman opened her eyes and looked at Seb. "I'm not dead? The Good Goddess Lanla didn't take me, then?"

"No, aunt." Seb pressed her hand, and the sick woman smiled at him gently. There was something surprisingly calm about her face, as if the idea of dying hadn't frightened her at all. Inanna looked over at Seb and then at Lyra. The joy in their faces was unmistakable. Why hadn't they told her the old woman was a relative of theirs? They seemed to love her too much to be ashamed of her just because she was poor.

"I'm going back to get the others now," Lyra said. She took the old woman's hand and pressed it fondly. "We'll soon have you out of here, aunt." As Lyra picked up her shield it caught the light; the figure of a naked woman was painted between the copper bands. The painted woman held a snake to her lips; her feet were birds' talons, her breasts tusks. Now where had Inanna seen that before? Then she remembered; the woman on Lyra's shield was the same as the one Enkimdu had once drawn in the dust for her. It must be Hut, the Dark Goddess.

Seb saw her staring and cleared his throat uneasily. "Lyra's devoted to the Dark One, but I worship the Light."

"That's your mistake," Lyra said. There was no anger in her voice, only a tone that indicated that the disagreement was an old one, hardly worth bothering with.

"Lyra! Seb!" the sick woman snapped. The two of them started guiltily like children caught fighting over a sweet. "I want peace in my family."

"Yes, aunt." Lyra hunched her shoulders as if ashamed.

"Yes, aunt," Seb echoed meekly.

This woman was no beggar living off the scraps of rich relations. But who *was* she?

"Sit me up," the old woman commanded, and when she was sitting with her back against a tree, she motioned for Inanna to come closer. "What's your name, girl?"

Suddenly Inanna felt shy, unable to speak, as if her tongue were tied to the roof of her mouth. Why was the old woman affecting her this way?

"Your name?" the old woman demanded again, smiling as if amused at Inanna's confusion. "I asked you your name."

"Inanna."

"Well, Inanna, you saved my life, for what it's worth. What do you want for that?"

"Want?" The bright black eyes stared straight at her, taking her measure. "I want nothing . . . that is . . ."

The old woman arched one eyebrow and waved her hand in disbelief. "Come now, my own healer would take three weights of silver for that cure. Surely you want something." Three weights of silver! Was the old woman crazy, or was something else going on here? "Come now," the old woman commanded again peremptorily, "name your price. What do you want for bringing me back from the shadow world, girl?"

"Well," Inanna thought of all the things she could ask for and then settled on what she really needed most. "I'd like a place to stay in the city tonight if that's not asking too much."

"So you want a place to stay?" The old woman tilted her head to one side and looked at Inanna sharply. "No payment at all for the healing?"

"My people never take payment for helping someone." Inanna

wanted to explain somehow that the power wasn't hers, that it just came through her, but it was all too complicated. "I was glad to do it," she finally said, "and if you don't have room for me to stay with you, I can . . ."

"Lyra!" A single word, quick like the flight of an arrow, broke through her explanation. The old woman motioned toward Inanna. "Take this girl to your mother's house and see that she's given what she needs."

"Yes, aunt." Lyra tapped the handle of her spear against her forehead in a salute.

"Seb."

"Yes, aunt?"

"You'll stay here with me." The old woman turned back to Lyra and sighed. "Tell the others that the sacred snake who brings us messages from Lanla has gone away, back to her earth caves. Tell them that they can come up to the High Olive Grove now and get me." She suddenly seemed tired.

"Yes, aunt," Lyra said, saluting again. The old woman coughed into her sleeve and then looked back at Inanna.

"No payment for the healing?" she asked.

"No," Inanna said.

"Strange," the old woman said, "very unusual, but good. I think Lanla would approve."

For years afterwards Inanna would find herself dreaming of that day when she and Lyra entered the city. She would see the great broken walls again looming up in front of them, the dirty brown swirl of the river, the fat birds sunning themselves on the battlements, the lizards peering out of the rubble. She would see women, naked to the waist, casting fishnets from the shore; merchants wearing clothes fine enough for a headman; vats of colored dyes, piles of dried dates and melons; traders from faraway lands calling out to each other in strange tongues like flocks of exotic birds; soldiers in their leather armor, priestesses in tall head-dresses, barefoot children carrying trays of sweets, and, over everything, the smell of decay, musky and subtle as perfume. Waking up, she would remember that smell and know that—even before she had first set foot in it—the city had been dying.

She and Lyra had entered through the main gates and walked

down a broad street paved in stone until they came to a large brick building inlaid with red and blue tiles. The building was set on a terrace, and a flight of stairs led up to it, each one as wide as the height of a grown man. "That's the temple," Lyra explained. Inanna had looked around eagerly for the *lants*. Now at last she'd get a chance to see those wicked women who dared to take lovers whenever they wished with no brother or husband to stop them. But all she saw were a few old people sitting on the steps in the sun, and a boy with a cage of white doves. Disappointed, she turned and hurried after Lyra, afraid to lose her in the crowd.

Now the streets became narrow, twisting, with stones worn thin by generations of passing feet, the houses round, piled up on top of one another like beehives. And the women: she had never seen so many in one place before. There were women carving wood, women pounding metal, women soldiers nursing their children, striding down the street with their heads lifted proudly as warriors. The men were there too, of course, doing most of the same things, but it was the women who interested Inanna the most. Even the girls seemed different here. When they ran, they ran like boys, tucking their robes into their belts, and no one called after them to remind them to be modest and quiet.

"There's the palace," Lyra said suddenly, stopping again. Above the walls, crowns of date palms waved slowly in the wind. Half a dozen soldiers snapped to attention in front of the main gate.

"Wait here a moment." Lyra left Inanna standing with her back to a carved pillar, and strode over to the soldiers. After a few moments of hushed conversation, one of them put his hands to his mouth and called something through the gate. Four men appeared at once, carrying an elaborate litter on their shoulders. Could that be for the old woman in the olive grove? If it was, she must at least be a high priestess.

"Why did those soldiers salute you?"

Lyra smiled. "I suppose they like my looks," she said good-naturedly.

Inanna pointed to the palace. "Is the Queen in there?"

Lyra's expression became more sober, and she turned away and looked after the litter bearers, who were half-running down the crowded street, pushing their way through knots of curious people. "Sometimes you ask too many questions," Lyra said, not unkindly.

In the courtyard of Lyra's house a small artificial waterfall tumbled over tiny flecks of colored tiles into a sun-filled stone basin. In front of Inanna stood two men, both good-looking, dark-haired, with bare chests, curly beards, and copper bracelets around their wrists.

"My brothers," Lyra explained. "This one is Ev, and this is Talin." The taller of the two smiled. (Which was he? She hadn't been paying attention.) Lyra sat on the edge of the fountain, took off her leather breastplate, and untied her shinguards. "Do you want a bath?"

Inanna looked at her muddy legs and torn robe and felt ashamed. "Yes, thank you." She wondered how the city people bathed. In the river perhaps? Not knowing made her feel even more uncomfortable. Lyra talked to the two men for a moment, then smiling, picked up her helmet and started out of the courtyard. As she passed through the curtain that hung over one of the doors, Inanna caught a glimpse of a long dim hallway, and at the end a cage of birds with feathers the colors of flowers.

"This way, *muna*." Talin took her hand and led her around the fountain through another doorway. He pointed to a small flight of white stone steps that wound up through the sunlight toward the roof.

The bathing room was inlaid with small blue tiles in the form of fishes and flowers, and the water looked pleasantly cool. How strange to keep your water inside a room instead of out under the sky where it belonged. How strange to live in the middle of a pile of mud instead of in a tent where all you had to do to see the trees was to pull back a flap. Sitting down on a stone bench near the tub, Inanna was homesick for the mountains.

"Here." She looked down and saw Ev kneeling at her feet, pulling at the strap of her sandal. But surely he didn't expect to attend her in her bath! Inanna jerked her foot back, and tried, blushing, to wave the two men out of the room, but they only seemed amused.

"It's the custom," Ev said politely, adding a few drops of sweet-smelling oil to the water. Talin stepped up beside her and pulled her robe over her head before she could stop him. Taking her hand, he helped her toward the sunken tub. I give up, Inanna thought. If they want to stay, then let them. Maybe the customs here *are* different; maybe they think all this is perfectly normal. Well then, I'll just pretend that it's normal for me too. She folded her arms across her breasts, and settled down in the water trying to look as if it were something she did every day.

"It's not too cold, is it?" Ev asked.

"No," Inanna said, unable to meet his gaze. He added a few more drops of scent to the water, and the oil floated toward her in little round drops, coating her breasts and belly. Inanna closed her eyes, and let the tiredness drain from her lower back and legs. Jasmine, musk, and roses. Outside doves cooed on the window ledge. Woodsmoke from a fire somewhere down below and the smell of baking bread. All at once she knew that her journey was truly over. I've come home, she thought, touching the gold dove that hung at her throat. And then she felt Enkimdu's absence so sharply that it was all she could do to keep from breaking into tears.

Talin fished in the water, caught her hand, and pared her softened nails with a small copper knife. Her fingers slid between his, but there was no resistance left in her anymore, only fatigue so deep it was almost frightening. Inanna lay with her head against the tile rim of the tub while Ev washed out her hair, combing through the snarls, rinsing it afterwards with herb-scented water. When Ev was finally finished, the two men helped her out of the tub, and dried her all over with rough towels until her skin glowed.

"You'd like to rest now?" At the end of the room was a narrow platform covered with thin red cushions. Inanna stretched out on the hard pallet and closed her eyes. It was the first bed she'd lain on in months, and as Ev began to massage her shoulders with warm oil she felt herself drifting into sleep. She lost track of time and began to imagine things: a field full of high green grass, a clear cloudless sky. How peaceful it felt; how good.

With a shock she realized that Ev had moved his hands down and was now massaging her breasts, his fingers moving expertly around her nipples. Talin had let his hands drift down her belly, between her legs, circling gently, insistently.

"Stop that!" she said sharply. Sitting up, she pushed them away. Her body tingled with desire. The two men smiled back at her in a friendly, innocent fashion.

"Would you like to worship the Goddess with us now for a while?" Ev reached out and touched her nipple.

As it hardened under his hand, she pulled back quickly, so tempted it made her feel ill. How could she respond to a stranger this way? She was a wicked woman to feel such things. She looked at the two of them in confusion, and saw that Talin had already thrown off his fringed kilt. Taking her gently in his arms, Talin cradled her big belly with his hands. The muscles under his skin were firm, his body warm and reassuring.

Ev touched her belly as if for luck, and knelt down in front of her. "Our women say it pleasures the child as well as the mother." He began to kiss her. "How beautiful you are, like a ripe pear." He ran his fingers through her hair, and then down across her breasts.

"Pleasure's a gift from Lanla Herself," Talin whispered in her ear. For a moment Inanna let herself yield to the sensation of being touched by the two men before the thought of Enkimdu overwhelmed her with shame.

"No!" she said fiercely, pushing Ev away from her breasts and getting up from Talin's lap. She took a few steps forward across the green and blue tiles, and then sat on the edge of the tub and broke into hard, dry sobs.

"Did I hurt you?" Talin asked, upset.

"No." She was hardly able to get the word out. Ev sat beside her and looked at her with a worried expression. "What's wrong?"

"Nothing," Inanna said, "just don't touch me."

"Did your lover die?" Inanna lifted her head and looked at him in amazement. Was he a reader of minds? "Once a lover of mine died of the river fever," Talin continued sadly, "and I couldn't worship Lanla for almost a year afterwards. Every time I touched a woman, the thought of my dead lover made me cry just like you." He put his hand on her shoulder and patted her comfortingly as if she were an unhappy child. "You'll get over it."

"I'll never get over it." Her sobs stopped, as she measured Ev and Talin with cold, distant eyes. "Never." The two men shifted uneasily under her gaze.

Ev left the room and returned with a small cup of hot tea. A circle of red petals floated around the rim. "Drink this. It's a flower remedy for grief."

"It'll make you forget," Talin said reassuringly. Inanna touched the wet flower petals with the tip of her finger, and the red stuck to her skin like blood. She thought of Enkimdu in her arms, wounded and dying.

"I don't want to forget him," she said. "Ever!" She threw the tea into the tub, and put the cup on the floor. Ev and Talin exchanged startled glances.

"Would you like to see your bedroom now, *muna?*" Ev finally asked with wary politeness.

Dinner that night was a haunch of roasted venison, a bowl of stewed field peas, and great wheels of bread stacked in the middle of the table. Leopards danced across the walls, their eyes inlaid with bits of tile that glowed in the lamplight. Inanna ate as much as she could, nodding steadily all the while no matter what was said to her. At the far end of the table, Ev and Talin shared a bowl. Lyra and Seb sat at the opposite side, and near her were three more of Lyra's sisters, an older man, and several children. Sellaki, the mother of the house, sat like a queen in a high-backed chair, eating prodigious amounts of food and washing it down with great gulps of beer as she held forth on the topic that seemed to interest her most.

"I've heard of that tribe of yours." Sellaki wiped off the rim of her goblet with the palm of her hand and took another drink. "Caused us a lot of trouble, you people did, a number of years ago. Came down from the mountains and attacked the city like a bunch of savages. Not that I'm saying you're a savage, mind you." Inanna nodded politely. "I was only a girl then," Sellaki went on. "Ten summers at the most, maybe less. Just before the last great plague it was, and not many left to remember it because of that. If they remembered, they'd keep those cursed walls in repair."

She must have my people confused with some other tribe, Inanna thought, or else I'd have heard the warriors of Kur bragging about it.

"The Black Headed People," Sellaki continued, "and a rough lot you were too, even if all you had were stone weapons. 'Teach those people to make copper blades,' my grandmother said, 'and there'll be no stopping them.' A good fighter my grandmother was. Wielded a mean axe." She pushed up her sleeve exposing a long gash that ran the length of her arm. "You see that scar? One of your Black Headed People gave me that as he tried to climb over the inner wall. Our house was smack up against it, and they'd hidden me on the roof where they'd thought I'd be safe. My grandmother caught him though." She drew her finger across her throat and grinned. "I'll never forget it." The old woman helped herself to more venison and dipped her bread in the gravy. "And we heard they're up to more trouble now," she said thickly between bites. "Well, what about that, girl?" She looked at Inanna sharply. "Is it true?"

How did Sellaki know the name of her people? How did she know what they were doing? The bread dried in Inanna'a throat, and she struggled to swallow. "Is what true?" she managed to say at last.

Sellaki ate another piece of meat, and then plucked several olives out of a small clay jar. "We hear those tribes of yours are getting together under one leader. The traders told us that this year at that volcano of yours . . ." Kur! She knew about Kur, then, too! "The traders told us that at the big camp this year there was a headman who was trying to get the others to join him for a raid on the valley. Seems someone had told him a story of a city full of gold over here . . ."

Inanna started. How could the traders have brought the news so fast when it had taken her months to make the same journey?

"I told the Queen to expect trouble in the spring," Sellaki was saying, "but I doubt she'll listen."

"Well, mother," Lyra said quietly, "if the nomads come, we'll be ready for them."

"I doubt it," Sellaki said, banging her goblet on the table. "The army's not up to full strength, and discipline isn't what it should be. In my day . . ."

"The Black Headed People are coming here?" Inanna asked. She knew at once that it was the wrong thing to say, that she shouldn't have interrupted so bluntly.

Sellaki looked at her and smiled and the tension at the table broke. "If that headman of yours gets his army together they might," she said, toying with her bread. "Ugly man, the traders said he was, big scar on his face."

"Shaped like a snake?" Inanna knew who had gone to the camp at Kur with talk of a city full of gold.

"Why, that's just how the traders described it," Sellaki said. "They said this headman had a big snake-shaped scar on his face, that everyone called him 'the hyena' when his back was turned. You know him?"

Inanna felt her whole body shaking. Pulal was worse than a hyena; he was a vulture, a . . . murdering devil who . . .

But what was she thinking of? She was surrounded by strangers, and if they knew she was Pulal's sister . . . He was her enemy too, but would they believe that? A circle of curious faces stared at her, waiting for her answer. Picking up an olive, Inanna forced herself to eat it with deliberate casualness.

"In a way I know him," she said finally, her voice calm. They would not suspect she was upset, but she had to change the subject. "I don't think I've met your husband," she said, nodding politely in the direction of the older man who sat to Lyra's left.

The man grinned at her, and the whole table broke into laughter. "That isn't my husband," Sellaki roared, almost choking on her food. "That's my brother Zend. Men here like to stay in their mothers' houses." Her broad face turned scarlet, and one of the women pounded her briskly on the back.

"My mother's had her children by traders mostly," Lyra explained. "My father, as she tells it, was a black-skinned man from the west, while Seb's father . . ."

"Was a blue-eyed, blonde-haired devil of a man," Sellaki interrupted, catching her breath again. "Variety is what I like, and the Goddesses have sent me quite a bouquet." The old woman smiled at her children and grandchildren, and they smiled back at her. "Now that's not to say that some women here don't take husbands," she said, growing more serious for a moment, "but it's not the rule. And some live without woman or man, like Seb here who hung his shield up to Lanla when he was thirteen."

Seb lowered his eyes, a serious expression on his face. In the dim light he looked more like Enkimdu than ever.

Sellaki helped herself to the last of the olives. As she stood up, everyone else rose with her. "By the way," she said, turning to

Inanna, "I have a message for you from the palace. The Queen wants to see you first thing in the morning."

Curse that Seb! Why did he always have to take her by surprise? When she opened her eyes the following morning, he was standing over her and in the confusion of first waking her heart nearly stopped with joy and grief when she saw his face. He'd come to take her to the palace, he'd said, and he was sorry to wake her before dawn but the Queen was an early riser. How innocent he'd looked standing at the foot of her bed in his white cloak with only a tiny moon-shaped pin at his throat. Enkimdu had never looked that way. Great Kur, what was wrong with her! She couldn't help the fact that he had someone else's face.

Inanna followed him down the street toward the palace, lost in her own thoughts. The only people out at this hour were old men and women sweeping out the gutters with bundles of straw. She should have been thinking about the Queen, wondering how her presence in the city had come to the attention of the palace, anticipating the questions she'd be asked. Maybe some trader had remembered her face, and revealed that she was the sister of Pulal, headman of Kur, a dangerous enemy to the city. Maybe she would be questioned, tortured, or even executed. These were the things she should be worrying about. But instead she was thinking about Seb, looking at him from behind, being glad that from this angle at least he didn't look quite as much like Enkimdu.

"Do you have any brothers besides Ev and Talin?" she asked him abruptly, just as they came in sight of the palace gates.

"No," he said, smiling back at her, "only sisters." I'm a fool and obsessed, Inanna thought. What kind of god-curse is this? The guards at the gate saluted and let them pass without challenge.

"You see, you're expected," Seb said.

The palace was like an empty beehive, full of narrow hallways that crossed and doubled back on one another, tall ceilings, clay floors burnished smooth as ice. On the walls doves, gazelles, lions, all manner of fabulous beasts had been painted, their eyes set with jewels and brightly colored stones. Cages of birds and great clay lamps hung from hooks by the windows. As they threaded their way along the corridors Inanna caught glimpses of rooms furnished with fine straw mats, sunny courtyards, and fountains splashing in the early morning air. She thought of Hursag's tent—

the largest in the camp—her best embroidered robe, Pulal's carved staff; how crude they seemed next to this. Why there wasn't a single thing in the whole tribe of Kur as fine as the smallest wall painting.

"This way." Seb led her down a flight of stairs into a series of underground rooms. The rooms had small, slitlike windows near the ceiling to let in light, and they were dim and pleasantly cool. Finally Seb stopped in front of a curtain woven out of plain white linen, embroidered with a single small dove. "I'll wait for you out here."

Inanna pushed aside the curtain and found herself in a high-ceilinged room with a stone-lined floor. Directly in front of her an old woman sat on a stool beside a large copper lamp, molding a statue out of a lump of wet clay and a skeleton of wicker. Inanna recognized her at once: she was the old woman from the olive grove.

"I'm supposed to see the Queen," Inanna said. The old woman put down her clay, and wiped her hands on a bit of white cloth. Her dress was made of an exotic silky material dyed bright purple, and gold earrings hung from her ears. On her arms she wore heavy bracelets encrusted with lapis lazuli and unfamiliar jewels.

"I'm the Queen," she said simply. At the look of consternation on Inanna's face she broke into laughter. "Come here, child," she said, "don't be afraid. You couldn't have known."

Inanna felt her face flush with embarrassment. Why hadn't someone told her? Or why hadn't she figured it out by herself? All the signs were there.

"Closer," the Queen ordered. Inanna took a step so near that she could smell the oil burning in the lamp and the earthy scent of the clay. When she was only a pace away from the stool, the Queen leaned forward suddenly and placed the palm of her hand lightly on Inanna's swollen belly.

"How's the baby?"

"Fine." Despite herself, Inanna smiled. The Queen smiled back and gave her another friendly pat. Why, she was human, just like anyone else really. Maybe things would be good between them after all.

"Come sit by me," the Queen motioned to another clay stool near the lamp. She clapped her hands and a servant stepped out of the shadows holding a tray of honey cakes and a goblet of sweet wine. Somewhere an invisible musician began to play on a lyre. The music was a lament, so ancient that it seemed to sing of a grief that came before everything else in the world. The Queen offered Inanna a honey cake and some of the wine.

"Now," she said, sitting back and folding her hands, "there are two reasons why I asked for you to be brought to me today. The first was to thank you again for saving my life in the olive grove. You thought I was a beggar, didn't you?"

Inanna felt herself blushing again. "No, yes, that is . . ." What a fool she was making of herself. Now, on top of everything else, she'd spilled some of the wine. The Queen must think she was a savage.

"Ah, yes you did, but you took care of me anyway. I liked that." A quick, bright, friendly smile. "And you wouldn't take payment for it either. I liked that even more."

Inanna tried to think of something to say, but her tongue caught in her mouth. The Queen motioned to the servant to pour out another cup of wine, and went on as if no reply were expected.

"Second, I had you brought here because I thought you might prove useful to my people." Her face grew sober and she paused for a moment. Inanna tasted the wine and found it strange. Honey was much sweeter on the tongue. When she looked up again, the old woman was studying her.

"Have you seen the temple?"

Inanna thought of the red tiles, the long flight of steps, the boy with the basket of doves. "Only from the outside."

"Ah, only from the outside. Then you haven't seen the healing benches where the sick are laid, or the priestesses who tend them? You haven't heard others weeping over their dead children, or sick men begging the Goddess for a quick death to put them out of their pain. And you don't know what happens when the river gets low, when fish are found in the mud and the rushes start to rot."

"No," Inanna replied. There was a terrible stillness in the room now, and even the music had stopped. The Queen picked up a small lump of clay and began to roll it absentmindedly between her swollen fingers.

"There's a fever that comes at low water. My people call it the Death." The way she spoke the word made a shudder run down Inanna's spine. The Queen paused for a long time; then she took a deep breath and shook her head. "When I was just a girl, an old woman came into the city one day to sell cabbages, and someone saw the signs of the Death on her. They pushed her back out the gate, but before the year was over nearly half the people were dead of it. I can still remember the funeral fires burning along the river, my own mother crying over my three dead sisters. Everybody lost someone. You can't imagine." Her eyes were bright with a passionate intensity. "I never want to see that happen again." She reached out and put her hand on Inanna's arm. "I want you to teach my priestesses the cures you know. Take anything you want in payment, but teach them. Do you understand?"

But I don't really know anything, Inanna thought. Some power moves through me, and I don't even know what it is. I should admit that to her. But when she looked at the Queen, she found she didn't have the heart to tell the truth. There was so much hope in the old woman's eyes; what did it matter where the cures came from as long as they came?

"Will you teach my priestesses?"

"Yes." Inanna heard herself say the word, and knew she had bound herself to the city. For good or for bad she was here to stay.

The Queen's face relaxed. "Good. You'll live in the palace here near me, and when you give birth I'll send my own women to attend you." She clapped her hands together sharply and lifted her voice. "Seb." The white linen curtain parted and Seb stepped into the room and saluted formally. The Queen turned back to Inanna. "I'm assigning my nephew to you as your own personal guard," she said. And then to Seb: "You're never to leave her unprotected for a moment; do you understand?"

"Yes aunt." Another salute. Inanna met Seb's eyes and looked away quickly, cursing herself for her thoughts.

"Why do I need a guard?" she asked the Queen.

"Why, there'll be danger, of course."

"Danger?"

"From Rheti the High Priestess and those who follow her. From all those who whisper that I don't give the Dark Goddess Hut Her due. But you'll be well protected, never fear. Seb will see to that."

"But I don't understand. Why would Rheti want to hurt me? I don't even know her?"

The Queen sighed and shook her head. "I can see that you know nothing about politics and palace intrigues, but understand one thing: from the moment it becomes known that I've made you a teacher of the temple priestesses, your life will be in danger. But find me a cure for the Death, and you can have whatever you want in return. Gold, fine husbands, a great house. Whatever you want."

There's no doubt what I want, Inanna thought. I want Pulal dead. She lifted her head and looked at the Queen. But I can't tell her that; not yet. In the palm of her hand she felt a strange prickling sensation, a warming. The light in the room changed; blackness closed in on either side of her like the walls of a tunnel, and she saw the Queen sitting at the end of it like a light at the bottom of a deep well.

"Come closer," the old woman said. Her voice echoed eerily, and the bracelets on her arms sparkled and clashed together with a sound like silver bells. Inanna stepped forward, trying to fight the trance, trying to push her own power away, half afraid of it. But it propelled her toward the Queen against her will, as if she were a swimmer caught on the crest of a wave. "There's another reason I brought you here," the old woman was saying. Her eyes were falcon eyes, bright and sharp, and the shadows on the wall behind her fluttered like great wings. Something terrible's going to happen, Inanna thought.

There was a moment of complete silence, so deep that she could hear the sound of the fountain outside. Then the Queen leaned forward, reached inside the neck of Inanna's robe, and pulled out the gold dove. The bird lay in the palm of her swollen hand like a fleck of sunlight.

"When my nephews Ev and Talin were giving you your bath, they noticed that you were wearing this." Her voice was thick, harsh. She stared at the tiny lump of gold again, and a spasm of pain crossed her face. "Only members of the royal family are permitted to wear the gold dove of Lanla."

Suddenly the magic of the moment was over, and she was just an old woman, sitting on a clay stool in a dark room. The Queen lifted her head and looked at Inanna almost pleadingly. There was great weariness in her eyes, something very near to defeat. "Where did you get it?"

Inanna's breath caught in her throat. "My lover gave it to me," she managed at last. She met the Queen's eyes defiantly. The dove was hers, a gift from Enkimdu, and no one could take it away.

"And where is he now, this lover of yours?" The Queen's voice was strangely different now, old and dry like the rustle of dead leaves.

"Dead. My brother killed him."

The Queen moaned and put her hands to her face. She looked withered, like a tiny old child. "And what was this lover's name?" she whispered.

"Enkimdu." How hard it was to say the word, as if something precious were being torn out of her, something that belonged to her alone. "His name was Enkimdu. Did you know him?"

The Queen sat back as if she'd been struck. "Yes," she said. "I knew him. Enkimdu was my son."

7

HIGH in the palace, behind carved screens and thick wool curtains, the old Queen sat alone in her chamber thinking of death. It was midwinter and the rain was beating down on the roof, knocking tiles loose, drumming like the festival drums when she was a girl. Outside, under the balcony, the river had swollen until it resembled a living animal, a great humped brown thing that lapped at the walls. The Queen felt the palace tremble with the force of it, and in the lower storerooms the water was as high as a man's waist. If the rain went on like this until spring, her advisors warned, it might undermine the foundations of the palace itself. No one had ever seen such rain.

It's a sign, the Queen thought wearily, studying the half-finished statue in front of her. And she felt a sudden fear for the child who was being born that morning, just far enough away so that the mother's screams wouldn't disturb the royal presence.

My grandchild, the Queen thought, the only fruit to come off this old tree. I've grown fond of Inanna too; she's taught my priestesses well. A natural healer if I ever saw one. The Queen examined the face of the Goddess taking shape under her fingers. Lanla grant Inanna an easy labor.

She sat back, lost in her memories. How quickly her own babies had been born. Hardly any pain at all when they slipped out from between her legs into the arms of the midwife. The pain came later when they all died but one: Enkimdu. And now he was dead too, and she was an old woman because of it. How long ago was it now since they'd quarreled?

She'd told him not to leave the city, but he'd defied her. Proud, stubborn, just like her. He'd been right; she'd tried to protect him too much, but then of the twelve he was the only one she had left. Her only chick, the last bit of her own blood, and they'd parted in anger. "Go hunt your lions then and be damned!" she'd told him. "And may Hut take you for all I care!" And Hut did.

She felt tears coming to her eyes, and she threw her knife on the table with so much force it bounced and fell to the floor. Morbid, foolish thoughts! She must be getting old and soft in the head to wallow in her memories. It had always made her impatient when her own grandmother spent all her time recalling the past. Wasn't there enough trouble today without looking for more? She thought again of the girl Inanna fighting to bring forth the child. "A hard birth," her midwives had told her last night, "she's strong but the womb doesn't open as it should." They had asked if they should cut the child out of the mother's body if the labor went on too long, but the Queen had told them no. She wouldn't be responsible for taking the girl's life, even to get a live grandchild. She was too close to death herself to strike up such a bargain with Lanla; better to let things run their course.

That was something you *did* learn as you got older—that there was really nothing you could do to change things, not even if you were Queen. Whatever happened, happened, and all you could hope for was the strength to accept it. But let the baby be born well and alive, please, she found herself thinking stubbornly, and let the mother live too.

"Your Majesty." One of the midwives poked her head in the door, bringing more bad news no doubt. Well, she'd had enough bad news for one morning, and if the labor was going worse she didn't want to hear about it yet. She looked at the midwife's stringy hair and white face, empty of sleep for three days. The woman looked like a corpse, as if her very breath smelled of bad tidings and death.

"Get out!" the Queen yelled, throwing a ball of clay at the startled woman. The midwife's head disappeared from the doorway so fast that it made the Queen laugh despite herself. Yes, she was a mean, imperious, crotchety old woman. Behind her back they whispered that her ways were wrecking the city, that she didn't repair the walls or keep the army up to strength. But what had walls and armies ever meant? Only war, the most stupid of human occupations.

The Queen picked up another bit of clay and began to mold the face of the statue in front of her. She'd brought them peace and the fools didn't even appreciate it. Over two generations without a war worth mentioning, and no more bloody sacrifices to Hut. And still they grumbled. Her spies said that the people wanted a Warrior Queen to lead them as the queens did in the days of their grandmothers. But what did they remember of those days?

The Queen looked out of the window at the falling rain and thought of the spring the mountain tribes had attacked the city. The Queen's Companions had fought shoulder to shoulder and been slaughtered to the last woman. Children had taken up rocks and spears to beat the black-haired invaders from the walls; her best friend had been killed in front of her, a nomad javelin through the neck. For weeks, until the rains came, the city stank of blood. In the temple the victory sacrifices to Hut had begun. First sheep and oxen, but then, inevitably the children. Babies left at night on the altar, their throats slit; young boys and girls offered up by the priestesses at great public feasts. For almost a year the Dark One had reigned supreme and Lanla was almost forgotten.

"Gentle Mother, protect us from ever seeing such days again," the Queen whispered, running her fingers lightly over the clay face of the Goddess. She knew who was behind this new unrest. It was Rheti, the High Priestess, curse her! She wanted the power of the temple back; she wanted to see Hut rule the city.

"Your Majesty." The midwife was at the door again, blinking like an owl. It was death for sure; she could see it in that puny white face. So her blood had run out after all, and she had no grandchild. But she'd live a while longer yet; she was tougher than they thought. "Your Majesty, the child . . ."

"Is dead, no doubt." The Queen sat back and let her clay-covered hands drop into her lap. All at once she felt terribly tired.

The midwife straightened her orange robe and cleared her

throat importantly. "On the contrary, Your Majesty, the child is very much alive." She smiled and bowed. "A girl has been born."

The Queen felt the blood rush to her cheeks. "And the mother?"

"Tired but well, Your Majesty."

She wanted to laugh and cry; she wanted to dance again like a young girl. So Inanna would live after all, and the child too! She had a granddaughter! She imagined holding the child on her lap, and a tenderness welled up inside her, fierce as the mother-love of an old lioness. Picking up her knife from the floor, the Queen went back to work eagerly, her fingers flying over the wet clay. It was going to be a fine statue of Lanla, she thought happily, the best she'd ever made.

Inanna lay listening to the rain as the baby nuzzled at her breast. She was exhausted but very happy, as if she'd accomplished some great thing. Behind her the midwives whispered sibilantly as they cleaned out the room and pulled the curtains to shut out the light. Their orange robes flickered by her like flames, and one stopped and bent down, a thin woman with gray eyes. The gray-eyed woman carefully pulled back the blanket and looked at the child in Inanna's arms.

"How hard she sucks," the midwife said. "That means she'll grow up strong-tempered like a warrior." She paused and gave Inanna a strange look. "How lucky you were to have a girl, *muna.*"

Later Inanna was to remember those words and the odd, intense look on the midwife's face, but at the time she only felt a great laziness. She was a child again with no responsibilities.

"Tell me a story," she said. She knew vaguely that she was talking nonsense, but they had given her a cup of wine and herbs to help the pain, and now she was floating back in time. "Lilith," she said, looking at the child. "Are you Lilith?"

"My name is Amarga, *muna,*" the gray-eyed midwife answered, thinking the question had been meant for her.

"Lilith said she'd come back to me."

The gray-eyed woman put a cool hand on her forehead. "You should sleep now."

One by one the orange-robed midwives drifted out of the room.

Their sandals clicked on the tiles as they walked down the long hallway, and then she was alone. But no, not alone. Something was moving beside her, rooting at her breast like a tiny lamb. Her child, Enkimdu's child. The love washed over her in one great pulse.

She struggled to a sitting position, and the room seemed to turn with her, dizzy, uneven. She must be careful. She put her hand against the wall to steady herself. She could drop the child, and then what? Cautiously she lifted the baby onto her lap and began to unwrap the swaddling clothes. How small the fingers were. Inanna ran her own finger timidly over the dome of the baby's stomach, feeling the feathery softness of her skin. She was perfect, not a mark or scratch on her. Enkimdu's high cheekbones, Lilith's dark hair—her own daughter. And even if she wasn't Lilith come back, even if that was only her imagination, still what a miracle! Suddenly she understood how the city people had come to worship the Goddess Lanla. Who could see a newborn child and not feel that there was something awesome and mysterious about it?

Inanna lifted the baby and kissed her gently on the forehead.

Welcome new life
she said in the language of the Black Headed People,
I name you Alna.

The baby clenched her fists, opened her mouth, yawned, and stared back at Inanna as if she recognized her. Alna. The name meant traveler. For she's come from a distant place, Inanna thought, and I want her to remember that when she's older. I want to tell her about the mountains, and how the tents of Kur look when the morning sun is still hidden behind the cedar trees. And I want to tell her the old stories Lilith told me, about the wolf-wife, and Utu and his golden boat. But most of all, I want to tell her about her father.

Outside the rain had stopped and on the windowsill a dove in a wicker cage cooed drowsily. The child at her breast. Peace. Sleep.

She woke with the sense that something evil was in the room with her, something cold and menacing. A strange blue light was coming from somewhere, casting eerie shadows on the walls, and she could see her breath as if she were back in the high mountains in the snow. Inanna tried to sit but found she couldn't move. Her arms and legs lay numb, heavy like stones; she was pinned to the bed, frozen like a fish she and Enkimdu had seen once, trapped under the ice of a pond, swimming in the same place for an entire winter. The fear pushed at her, breaking down her resistance, and she had an almost overpowering urge to scream. But if she screamed she'd wake the baby. Against her breasts she could still feel the warm circle of Alna's body. It was only a dream after all. She repeated the words to herself, closing her eyes to shut out the blue light. How long before she woke up from this? But the sense of evil became worse; came closer, surrounding her.

"So this is the child."

Inanna opened her eyes to see a woman standing over her, the whitest woman she'd ever seen. Not only was her robe white, but her hair was white too, long, cascading over her shoulders like a frozen waterfall. Yet her face was the unlined face of a young girl, pale as ice. Memory turned and coiled; the present molted and under it lay the skin of another bad dream, dreamed long ago, a vision in which the same face had appeared, and a voice had whispered *this is your enemy, Inanna.*

White lashes, white eyes. Why she's blind! Inanna thought. Fear rose in her, cold, dark, bottomless. The white, sightless eyes looked back at her, and she was reminded of a snake she had once seen, dancing in front of a small bird, holding it frozen in terror until it was ready to strike.

Suddenly the woman threw back the covers, and began to feel for the baby. Her cold fingers touched Inanna's body, the tips burning into her skin like ice. "Go away!" Inanna screamed, but her voice was only a whisper, caught in the back of her throat. She tried to turn over, to snatch Alna away, but she was helpless. What a horrible dream! In her hand the woman held a small cylindrical stone carved with strange designs. It was made of jade, translucent, like a leaf, delicate, strangely beautiful.

The woman placed the side of the stone against Alna's forehead. "She's mine." When she drew away, there was a mark on the baby's skin, a snake that twisted back on itself, swallowing its own tail.

"Leave her alone! Don't touch her!" Inanna's voice shattered the silence of the room. Her power rose in her, fighting off the evil, pushing it away. "Don't touch my baby!" Her arms suddenly free, she pushed the woman, knocking her back "Get out!"

Inanna's fingers glowed with a brilliant white light; the energy poured from her body, setting up a barrier between the woman and Alna. The woman tried to take another step forward, but stopped as if she had hit an invisible wall. Her pale fingers flailed the air; she was like a great white spider now, blind, helpless, pushed back by the force that was coming from Inanna's hands.

"So you have the power too," the woman hissed. "Well it won't do you any good. When the final battle comes, you'll lose, do you understand?" One pale finger pointed to the bird cage that hung near the window. Inside the dove was sleeping, its head under its wing. "Behold yourself, Inanna of Kur," the woman said. The dove started, and as Inanna watched in horror, it began to peck at itself with high piercing shrieks. Blood spattered the feathers. The dove attacked its wings, tore at its legs, ripped open its own breast, until at last it fell forward in a bloody heap and lay still.

"Honored Companion of the Queen, *muna,* wake up!" Inanna opened her eyes and found the room full of sunlight. It was a warm, lovely day and the rains had stopped at last. "You were crying out in your sleep." The midwives stared at her with worried expressions like a circle of old ewes. In her arms Alna lay sleeping peacefully, her forehead unmarked. So it had been a dream after all! Relief flooded over her. In the cage the dove cooed softly, its gray feathers smooth and unruffled. Alna snuggled closer to Inanna's breast, a small bubble on her lips.

"Would you like some warm broth?" One of the midwives brought a bowl of thick, salty liquid and Inanna ate it gratefully. When she had finished, Inanna placed the bowl back on the table and sat up against the soft cushions.

"Was anyone in the room while I slept?"

"No, *muna.*"

"I dreamed I saw a woman with white hair; she was blind."

The midwives looked at one another uneasily, and the one with the gray eyes cleared her throat.

"Rheti, the High Priestess, is blind," she said reluctantly, "and her hair is as white as flax."

"But I've never met Rheti." Inanna felt the anger come back

again. "They say she has some rooms under the temple and never shows herself. In all the time I taught there, I never once saw the High Priestess."

"Then how could you dream of her?"

Inanna felt her confusion growing. "I don't know. Perhaps she was really here."

But when Seb appeared to look at Alna, he confirmed that he'd been on guard outside her door the whole time. "No one came in," he said gravely, "and if Rheti or anyone else had tried, I would have stopped her." He had Enkimdu's face, Enkimdu's eyes. But she'd grown used to the resemblance, she told herself. "Inanna," Seb said. His face changed, and she saw that he was someone with feelings of his own. Suddenly she knew, as clearly as if he'd spoken the words, that Seb cared for her. She tried to push the idea away, but it came back irresistibly. How much did he care? Did Seb love her? No, he couldn't. But if he did, it would be like having Enkimdu back again.

Wicked, foolish thought! To mix the two men up. What was wrong with her? One minute she was afraid of a dream, and the next she was actually considering a love affair with Seb just because he looked a little like Enkimdu.

"You look well."

"My looks are no concern of yours," Inanna retorted, more sharply than she'd meant to.

Seb looked at her, confused. "I meant no harm." There was pride and hurt in his voice. Inanna was ashamed of herself. They must think she was a savage. What was wrong with her today? It should have been the happiest day of her life, and yet she felt as if everything were going contrary. She remembered the dream, the dove pecking at its own breast.

"I'm sorry. I suppose I'm just tired." She smiled, trying to make up for her sharpness, and Seb smiled back, his whole face lighting up.

"May Lanla give you good rest." Inanna lay back exhausted and watched him leave. His sandals made a clicking sound on the tiles that was strangely soothing. Such soft pillows, she would go back to sleep and not dream this time.

Alna moved restlessly. Soft warm baby body. Inanna reached out to draw the child closer, and her hand brushed against something hidden under the covers—something small and hard like a stone. She felt the anger rise to her mouth, leaving a taste bitter as oak gall.

"Seb!"

He was back beside her in an instant. "Inanna?"

She opened her hand slowly, afraid of what she would see. There on her palm lay a piece of jade, so translucent that you could see through it. On the side a snake had been carved into the stone, twisting back on itself, swallowing its own tail. Inanna looked at the stone cylinder and thought: this is a nightmare, another dream. Green rock, cold as ice against her skin, she could almost smell the evil on it.

"What is it?"

Seb's face darkened. "A signature seal." Cold room, blue light, a blind woman with white hair. Seb picked up the piece of jade and looked at the design. "Curse her!" he spat. "Curse her to the hell realms!"

"Curse who? Whose seal is it?" She wanted to call her question back, not know the answer, but it was too late.

"It's the seal of the High Priestess of Hut, the seal of Rheti herself, curse her!" Seb leaned so close to Inanna that his cheek nearly brushed hers. "I swear to you by Lanla," he promised passionately, "that that woman will never get by me again!"

The Queen was furious. In the center of the Great Hall of the Mothers, among the richly robed and delicately scented courtiers, a badly decomposed body lay on a rough wooden slab dripping muddy river water onto the tiles. He was only a boy, not more than eighteen, and you could see by the muscles in the arms that he had once been an athlete, strong, virile. But now, the Queen thought, his skin is as white as a fish belly, his hair is the color of river weeds, and may the Goddess grant that I never see that expression on another human face.

She looked again at the eyes, rolled back in terror, the open mouth, the missing hands and feet. But most of all she studied the golden cord knotted around the boy's neck, because it was the cord that told the real story of his death. He was the King, and he had been strangled, killed in the old way as kings had been killed each year for time out of mind before she'd put a stop to the custom. Now it was starting all over again.

"Fools," she yelled at the courtiers. "Couldn't you at least have the decency to wait until I was dead!" To her left, along the far wall, fifty-three of the Queen's Companions stared at the floor and tried not to catch her eye. She'd known all of them since they were girls together; in battle those same fifty-three would have fought alongside her and died defending her honor. But now they wouldn't even look her in the face. She was surrounded by fools and cowards. Fluted red robes, gold headbands, soft white hands, sandals fit only for dancing girls: useless like a flock of overfed pheasants, that's what her so-called Companions were. Fit only for the dinner table. And she supposed they'd say it was her fault because she gave them no battles to fight.

The others, were they any better? The Queen gazed down the length of the Great Hall at her white-robed advisors, her uncles and sisters, guards, cup bearers, and courtiers, all on their knees before her, pretending loyalty. Was there ever such a fine-looking assembly, so splendid in its jewels, so richly dressed and delicately scented? But underneath there was only rot and decay, plots and treason. How had she failed them? Was there one she could trust? Was this what peace did to people? Maybe she should have given them a war and let them wallow in blood. It was clear that as soon as she was dead they were going to anyway. But until that time, she was Queen, and she'd make sure none of them forgot it.

"This is treason!" Her voice rang out clear and strong. The Queen stood up, ignoring the pain in her feet, walked to the body, and laid her hand on it. It bothered her that she couldn't remember the boy's name. Not that he'd ever come to her bed. She'd never used the ritual kings, always picked her own lovers even when she was a young lusty girl who'd take almost anyone. But now that this king was dead it didn't feel right not to at least be able to remember who his mother had been. His drowned flesh felt cold, but she let her palm rest on his chest without flinching. Had they cut off his hands and feet before or after they'd strangled him?

"The High Priestess is to be removed from office at once." There was a sound in the hall like the whisper of a great indrawn breath. So they were surprised that she knew who had ordered the killing. Surely they didn't think she spent all her time in her room making statues.

"What's the charge, Your Majesty?" The chief advisor was her sister, Sellaki. For an instant the two women stood confronting each other like old stags about to clash antlers. Sellaki's on the other side, the Queen thought. I've known that for years, and should have done something about it.

"The charge is murder. Rheti killed the King."

Sellaki scratched her shoulder and looked around the hall. Even when she was a girl, she'd never had a royal air to her. Her arms and legs had always seemed twice as long as anyone else's. But she was honest. Of all of them, she was the only one who ever dared tell the truth.

"The High Priestess hasn't been out of the temple in months." Sellaki's missing teeth gave her a comic air, but her words were as sharp as arrowheads. "There's no way she could have killed anyone."

"Remove her from office and bring me her staff."

"It can't be done," Sellaki replied flatly. "The people won't accept another High Priestess. They're afraid Rheti will put another curse on the city. And as for the army . . ." she stopped and rolled her eyes significantly, "there'd be trouble."

"Are you trying to tell me that if I get rid of Rheti I'll have a rebellion on my hands?" the Queen yelled. One look at Sellaki's face told her the answer. The Queen turned and looked down the Hall at the silent, frightened crowd kneeling before her. "Then the Goddess help us all."

8 WHAT are you crying about? Hungry again are you? Here, take my breast. Look at you, getting so fat and big. Who'd ever think you were only five months old? Look at those rosy cheeks, all that lovely dark hair. Oh you beauty, what a fool I am about you! Are all mothers this way over their first ones?

"Seb, I think Alna said *Mama*."

"No, Inanna, she's too young."

"Why are you standing in the doorway? You don't have to guard me all the time. Come sit on the bench next to me. Now, just look how it's raining again. They tell me the river's never been so high. Isn't it ever going to stop? I haven't been dry since I can remember."

"I've got a message for you from Lyra."

"What does she want?"

"She wants you to come to the barracks to see a captive the soldiers brought in from the foothills last night."

"Why me?"

"She didn't say."

"But Alna isn't finished with her dinner yet."

"Bring her along."

The barracks proved to be two long rows of ordinary round houses surrounded by walls low enough for a child to climb over. In the center there was a large flat space that must have served as an exercise yard in dry weather, though at present it looked more like a lake. Inanna was disappointed, having imagined it to be more grand, more like the palace. Ever since she arrived in the city, she'd been meaning to come here and ask Lyra to teach her the arts of war so she'd be ready to fight Pulal when the time came. Why had she waited so long? She thought of Lilith and Enkimdu, and the old hate rose in her, fierce and bitter as ever. Alna's birth had overshadowed her desire for revenge, but not stilled it. In one corner of the exercise yard half a dozen women were drilling in full armor, so covered with mud that they looked more like turtles than human beings. Their red plumes were wet and bedraggled, but their faces glowed with energy. Soon she would join them.

"Over here," Seb said, leading the way through the ankle-deep clay. He stopped in front of the first doorway and pulled aside the piece of sacking nailed over the opening to keep out the rain. The flicker of lamps; a smell of wet leather, oil, and woodsmoke. A military smell. The idea amused her.

"Come on in before you drown," a friendly voice called. Lyra was sitting on a rough wooden bench with the captive tied to a post beside her. One look at the man, and Inanna knew why she'd been summoned.

"He's one of your people?" Inanna nodded, not trusting herself to speak. The man was dirty, sullen, his hair tangled, his face covered with dried blood. She'd never seen him before; he meant nothing to her. Yet the sight of him made her homesick. She took in his sandals, the familiar blue designs on his robe that identified him as one of the tribe of Enlil. Hadn't some of the men of Enlil feasted at Lilith's wedding? Perhaps she'd served him goat meat and honey wine when she was a child.

"We caught him prowling around outside the walls," Lyra said. "We think he's a spy." She picked up one of the lamps and held it close to the captive's face. The man glared back defiantly. In the light Inanna could see that a long gash ran down the side of his head; his lower lip was split and bloody. Had Lyra's soldiers done that? But what did it matter if they had?

"Ask him who he is," Lyra said.

"Who are you?" The words were heavy, unfamiliar on her tongue, and the captive started when he heard them. He studied her suspiciously, taking in her finely woven linen robe, her tooled sandals, the baby at her breast.

"How do you come to know the tongue of the Black Headed People?" His voice was almost a whisper, but there was no mistaking the tone: hatred, fear, suspicion.

"My name is Inanna, wife of Hursag of the tribe of Kur," Inanna said proudly, "Healer to the Queen of this city." But there was no word for *queen*, so half the meaning was lost before she began. "Tell me where you came from. Are there others with you?"

The captive looked at her with more hatred than she'd ever seen before. "Slut, she-devil, how much did they buy you for?" His words stung; she felt some truth in them, but then she thought of Pulal and her resolution hardened. What did it matter what names this man called her? She'd been bought by no one.

"If you talk I might be able to convince them to spare your life," she told the captive flatly. She let his hatred wash through her and pass away. "I ask you again: who are you?"

"Tell your masters, slut, that my name is Sippar, son of the headman Nergal of the tribe of Enlil, and that my life isn't for sale."

"What's he saying?" Lyra asked. Inanna told her the man's name and his tribe. "And were there others with him, more spies? A scouting party?"

"He won't say."

Lyra shook her head wearily and got up from the bench. "Leave him with us a while. By this evening I think he'll be ready to talk." She put a hand on Inanna's shoulder. "I don't like doing this any more than you do, but there's no other way. The whole city is in danger if these nomad tribes move on us. They probably outnumber us a hundred to one." Inanna thought of the camp of Kur, of the black tents stretching as far as the eye could see. "The army's a mess," Lyra said. "We don't have more than a *magur* of soldiers who could actually fight if it came down to it." She glanced at the captive, and her expression darkened. "Leave him with us; it's the only way."

When Inanna came back, she hardly recognized Sippar. He lay on the bench, his arms and legs strangely twisted, his whole body limp, like a sack that had been emptied of grain. One of his eyes was an empty socket, and bloody rags were wrapped around his feet. There was no pride in him now, only pain and fear. Inanna's anger at the savagery was so great she could hardly control it. She hated Lyra, Seb, and everyone in the whole city. Cruel, stupid people! What did she care what became of them? She would save Sippar, make it up to him for this thing she had let them do. But when she thought of Pulal, her confusion deepened. She was being pulled in half. Who was she betraying? Her own people? Lilith and Enkimdu?

"Ninazu?" the captive mumbled. It was a woman's name, maybe one of his wives. His head lolled to one side, and he seemed to have trouble forming the word.

"He's been drugged," Lyra said grimly. "I think he'll talk." Inanna walked past her without a word and knelt beside the man.

"Sippar?"

"Ninazu?"

"No, it's Inanna of Kur. I've come back to help you. Sippar, listen . . ."

"You're from Kur you say?" His voice was dreamy, his one good eye distant, glazed. "From Kur; then you must know the mighty Pulal." Mighty Pulal? Inanna drew back. What had happened in the tribes since she left? She remembered Sellaki at the dinner table telling her about the man with the snake-shaped scar who was uniting all the Black Headed People. The *mighty* Pulal?

"A great leader, Pulal." His words were coming faster now, stumbling over each other. She could feel the desperation in his voice; he was reaching out to her like a drowning man. "My name is Sippar, son of Nergal, of the tribe of Enlil."

"Yes, Sippar. You told me that before. Tell me more about this Pulal." Her heart went cold as she spoke her brother's name.

"This year the mighty Pulal drove most of the western savages off their lands, so now our flocks graze in peace, and our women sleep safe." So the little red-headed men had been taken care of at last. So much the better. Inanna remembered the pass where they had attacked her, the rank smell of their flesh, the wound in Enkimdu's leg, remembered so much she could hardly attend to the captive's words. He was rambling, speaking of a hunt, making little sense. "Soon Pulal says we'll take the whole valley."

Inanna started. Had he just said what she thought he'd said? "Take the whole valley?"

Some kind of awareness seemed to return to Sippar's face, and he lowered his voice. "From what I've seen they've got no warriors to speak of, only a few women and a handful of green boys to defend this city of theirs. Is that true?"

Yes, it was true, but she could hardly admit it to him. "No," she lied, "they have a great army, over sixty *magurs* with sixty soldiers in each." She spread her fingers and held them in front of his face so he could see that the army was too great to be counted. "Many warriors, javelins, arrows."

Sippar was disappointed. "Are all my goats in the corral?" He had again lapsed into a dream world of his own. He rambled on about his goats and sheep until Inanna nearly lost patience. Then suddenly his expression grew sharper again, and a look of greed crossed his face. "Is it true that the city's full of gold?"

"No." Inanna could feel the weight of the dove at her throat, Seb and Lyra's eyes fixed on her back. "There's no gold here."

"Ah, well," Sippar's eyes glazed dreamily again, "at least we'll have the women. Pulal himself promised us that. 'Women to the warriors for our sport and pleasure.' " He smiled an ugly smile, lecherous. "But only the virgins, of course. The rest . . ." He brought up one hand and made a weak slashing motion across his throat.

"What's he saying?" Lyra's voice interrupted the rest of Sippar's story. Inanna was grateful; she hadn't wanted to hear it. What would he and his like do if Pulal ever got into the city? She found herself thinking of Sellaki and her daughters, of the midwives who had saved her life when she was giving birth to Alna, of the temple priestesses, of the Queen, of Lyra who was still waiting for an answer. From her childhood she remembered a woman being held down, raped by half a dozen drunken men, the blood on her afterwards, the terror on her face. There was no further doubt in her mind which side she was on.

"What was the captive telling you?"

"He says the Black Headed People have an army that can take the city," she said flatly.

Lyra sucked her breath in through her broken front teeth. "Is he lying?"

"I don't think so."

"Is he a spy?" Ianna looked at Sippar. His life was on her. She had only to shake her head *no*, and maybe the soldiers would take him back where they caught him and let him go with a message for Pulal to stay away from the city. But if they knew he was a spy, they'd never let him live. She thought of the smile on Sippar's face when he passed his finger across his throat. *Sport and pleasure.*

"He's a spy." She left the room without looking back. Behind her Lyra and Seb talked excitedly. Near the gate she stopped for a moment. The rain was coming down more lightly than it had in the afternoon, scratching the evening sky in long pale streaks. The water feathered her eyelashes, wetting her cheeks, but there was no freshness in it. She had betrayed one of her own people. But she had to betray someone, didn't she?

In the middle of the forty-fifth summer of the old Queen's reign, on the first day of the Barley Moon, the skies finally cleared and the river returned sluggishly to its bed leaving behind fields of mud and rotting wheat. The heat was intense, and Inanna, along with the rest of the court, moved underground into the great cool chambers beneath the palace where melons were served on small metal trays, and flowers lay in bunches on the floor to cover the smell of mildew and rot. A strange lassitude seemed to overtake everyone, a sense of endlessly marking time, and whole afternoons were spent gossiping and drinking chilled fruit juices.

They buzzed at each other like flies around the melon rinds, Inanna thought, as if waiting for something to happen. But what was it? She looked at the Queen's Companions, their red robes stained with sweat, their jewels sparkling in the dim shadows of the hall. Why didn't they tell her? She felt the loneliness of being a foreigner in the city, and drew Alna closer for comfort.

Only the Queen seemed fully awake. Night and day, she worked on her statues of Lanla, throwing her tools aside as if she no longer had time to put them away with care. Her rooms at the top of the palace were like an oven, so hot Inanna nearly fainted every time she entered, but the Queen didn't seem to notice the heat, or the end of the rain, or the smell of the river, or even her own servants. A cheekbone pushed into the damp clay, a hand turned just so, the feet set apart supported by a wicker frame that would later be covered: these were her obsessions.

At noon, when the streets scorched the sandals of the water carriers, the Queen would wrap herself in a thick wool blanket, order another charcoal brazier lighted, and push aside her meal without tasting it. She must be sick, Inanna thought, and she spent days worrying how to break the news she had learned from the captive, Sippar. What if it was too much for the Queen? She was an old woman; what if it made her worse?

"You have to tell her soon," Lyra warned.

"She loves you; she'll listen to you," Seb insisted.

Finally one morning when it was still cool, Inanna put on her best robe and dressed Alna in a new red smock. She went up the long stairs to the royal chamber and threw herself on her knees among the baskets of wet clay and piles of reeds. "An army of the Black Headed People plans to invade the city," she said.

The Queen didn't even look up from her work. "That signifies nothing."

"The destruction of the whole city means nothing?"

The Queen selected a small, sharp tool, and began to work on the head of her latest statue, forming each curl rapidly, as if she were racing against time. "I've heard those stories of invasions before." She turned to Inanna, her mouth set stubbornly, but when she saw Alna in the red smock her expression softened, and she stretched out her arms. "Give me the child." Inanna rose and handed her the baby, and the Queen bounced the child in her arms until Alna laughed and clapped her hands with delight.

"What cures do you have for old age?" the Queen asked suddenly.

"What?"

"My own mother died in this very room. Did you know that? An arrow scraped her arm and the cut became infected. It was one of her own arrows, an accident. Does that strike you as funny?"

"No, Your Majesty."

"Well, it should."

What could she say to make the Queen listen? Inanna decided to try again. "The Black Headed People have joined into a great . . ." she began, but the Queen silenced her with a gesture.

"It's only a false rumor, a plot to get me to build up the army here."

"But I talked to the captive myself. He said . . ."

"A plot." Her jaw locked; her black eyes were as hard as pebbles. "This city will have peace as long as I'm alive and afterwards too, I hope, if Lanla permits."

"You're a stubborn fool," Inanna blurted out before she could stop herself. The servants gasped behind her, but she was too angry to care.

The Queen laughed. "That's what I like about you; you've got no manners at all. Say just what's on your mind, don't you?"

"Yes, I do." The Queen handed Alna back to her and picked up the carving tools again. "You could at least send out scouts. I'd take them myself. I know those mountains."

"You'd take scouts against your own people?"

"I have a blood score to settle."

"Against whom?"

"Against my brother, Pulal. He's the one who's leading on the tribes with stories of gold and women in the city. He killed my sister and your son."

At the mention of Enkimdu the Queen's face hardened. "A Queen must be above personal revenge."

"But it isn't just personal revenge! If you don't stop those nomads now, they'll overrun this whole valley. They outnumber your people ten to one. Can't you understand that sometimes you have to start a war to prevent one?"

"An interesting concept. Every year or two one of my advisors comes up with it again."

"Please." Inanna knelt at the Queen's feet. "I beg you in the name of your Goddess Lanla to build up the army and attack the nomads."

"You mean you beg me in the name of your hate for your brother."

"I don't mean that at all!"

The Queen laughed. "You make a poor petitioner; humility isn't one of your talents." She made a gesture of dismissal. "Now go, and come back when you've cooled off."

She could at least send out scouts, Inanna thought as she strode angrily out of the room, but she doesn't want to know the truth. She can't face the fact that she's failed. Peace she says she wants, but she's letting everything fall apart. Why did she give up? What's wrong with her?

Later, when she was Queen, Inanna realized that if it hadn't been for that conversation she would never have agreed to the meeting with Rheti. But she had been angry.

How differently things might have turned out if the Queen had listened to her warning, Inanna would think as she sat on the throne stool looking out over her own court. She would wonder if it had been pure chance that the message from the temple had been waiting for her when she returned from the royal chambers. Was some god directing her life, or had Rheti's spies been better than she thought?

"The High Priestess wishes to see you, *muna*," the eunuch had said. His lips were painted discreetly, and he had smelled faintly of musk and incense. Officially he was considered a woman with all a woman's privileges, but Inanna had never been able to see it quite that way. Smooth faces, old men with boy's voices pure as bells, she had taught them along with the temple priestesses, but never got used to them. How had such a custom started? They made her uneasy, these men who had chosen to dedicate themselves to the Goddess, and she couldn't help wondering if any of them had secret regrets.

But this eunuch was an old man, so thin his robe hung on his body like a sack, the kind of messenger who would frighten no one. He was hunched in an obsequious half-bow as if she were royalty, and he cleared his throat cautiously as if taking great pains not to offend her with the sound. "The High Priestess . . ." he began again.

"When?" Inanna interrupted.

"Now, *muna*," the eunuch said smoothly, as if he'd been expecting the question, "in the temple." Inanna studied him for an instant, measuring the risk, and then decided. Or rather her anger decided for her. If the Queen couldn't run the city, maybe Rheti could. Perhaps the High Priestess wasn't as bad as everyone made her out to be. In the back of her mind the memory of her dream pushed itself forward: white hair, blue light, something evil. But she had been overwrought from giving birth to Alna. It was time she saw for herself.

In the temple the votive lamps burned dimly and the air was dank with stale flowers and incense. Shadows crawled up the walls, and Inanna began to wish she hadn't been so hasty. Was it her imagination, or was it cooler than it should have been? She pulled her robe around her and looked up at Lanla for encouragement. The statue of the Goddess was old, blackened with smoke; her purple robes hung limply, the gold fringe tarnished and broken in places. The sacred animals on either side of her—the deer, rabbits, and doves—looked neglected: a chipped ear, bits of paint flaking off the horns. On the stone healing bench an old priestess snored fitfully, her head pillowed uncomfortably on her arm. One of the famous *lants* she had argued with Enkimdu about. Inanna wondered briefly if the old woman had had an attack of indigestion and come to the Goddess for relief, or if she had simply found her own quarters too hot.

"This way please." The eunuch led her across the main cella past the statue of Hut. On this altar someone had placed a small dish of water and a wreath of fresh flowers. It was easy to see where the sympathies of the city lay. Inanna walked faster, her footsteps echoing on the tiles.

There was something wrong here, but she couldn't quite place it. She shivered and folded her arms across her chest. She was cold, yet it was so hot outside that the stones in the street were still warm. She was reminded of the Queen, sitting in her wool blanket, shivering as if she had been caught in an invisible snowstorm. There seemed to be a connection, but what was it?

"Here," the eunuch said, interrupting her thoughts. He had pulled aside a tapestry, exposing a doorway so small that they both had to stoop to enter. She walked down a narrow hallway plastered with black clay, noticing the vultures drawn on the walls in red ochre. The cold increased, and she shivered in a distinct draft.

"Wait a moment, *muna*, and I'll see if the High Priestess is ready." The eunuch bowed as deeply as the narrow hallway would permit and smiled, exposing a row of startling white teeth. Turning quickly, he disappeared down a flight of stone steps. Inanna held her breath, listening to the sound of his footsteps until they faded away. In the odd silence, she felt smothered, buried alive. Ridiculous. She was frightening herself by thinking such things. She closed her eyes and thought of all the times she'd faced dangers and overcome them, but the sense of approaching evil grew worse. Wolf eyes, wolf heart. But the words didn't work this time. The plaster behind her was so cold that she shivered when she touched it. In the darkness something moved. A rat?

"There you are; that's better." The eunuch stood before her, holding a smoky bundle of reeds. Strange that she hadn't heard him return. The light from the torch was dim, but Inanna imagined she could feel the warmth of the fire. The eunuch cleared his throat uneasily. Even under the paint his face was unnaturally pale.

"Be careful," he warned, leading the way down the stairs, "it's slippery." Evil growing with every step, expanding, cold and slippery as a lizard's back. Inanna concentrated on the stairs. They were ordinary, nothing odd about them except that they felt colder than they should have. The masonry on either side was crude but sturdy, and, except for a few niches in the wall where lamps might once have stood, the plain gray stonework was unbroken. Evil, cold and icy, it grew stronger, pulling her down like a seductive whisper. If she wanted to, she could turn and go back. The sound of running water, then a smell from down below as if a sewer emptied somewhere just out of sight.

"This way," the eunuch whispered. His breath came in white puffs like steam. They had reached the bottom of the stairs at last. To the right the hallway branched out into five narrow passages; to the left there was only a single tunnel, twice as tall as a man, vaulted with old stonework. The walls opened into shallow caves full of white things. It took Inanna a moment to realize that the things were bones.

"Where are we?"

"In the burial vault under the temple." He leaned so close that she could smell the stale incense on his robes, the sour milk odor of his skin. "They say the bones of the first Mothers are down here somewhere, but no one knows for sure."

"I thought you were taking me to the High Priestess."

"And so I am, my dear." The politeness was gone. The old man smiled at her as if she were a spoiled child who asked too many questions. "And so I am." The stench was overpowering, worse than anything Inanna had ever smelled. Behind her water trickled into an invisible pool. How deep were they? below the river itself?

"Here." They had come to the last cave, and the eunuch was pointing to a filthy bundle covered with excrement. Something moved, and Inanna caught sight of white among the rags. "She's been down here ever since the boy-king was strangled," the eunuch whispered, holding the light over his head so it shone into the cave.

A naked woman with long white hair crouched on the floor, staring blindly as the torchlight crawled across her face, filling the hollows of her cheekbones, glinting off the hard white centers of her eyes. Inanna strode forward, pushing past the eunuch. She knew that face; she had seen it in visions and bad dreams.

"High Priestess, I've brought you the woman Inanna." Rheti wheeled at the sound of the eunuch's voice, got up, and glided forward, touching the sides of the cave to guide herself. Stick arms, skin white as a fish belly, long white hair matted with filth: evil radiated from her. Something entered Inanna's mind, something cold, indifferent. It was a horrible feeling, like being stripped naked. She lifted her hand to push Rheti back, and as she did so it seemed to her she saw light streaming from her own palm, yellow and clear as a sunbeam.

"I'm not afraid of you." The other presence in her mind dissolved and Rheti stopped. Inanna looked and saw nothing there in her hand, only the shadows from the torchlight.

"You have the star mark," Rheti said in the thin, cool voice of a young child. "Come, bring me my basket." A basket of peeled reeds lay in one corner of the cave.

"Take it to her," the eunuch said. Inanna stared at the basket and then back at Rheti. If they thought she was still frightened, they were wrong. She carried the basket to the Priestess and dropped it in front of her.

"Here." The top of the basket rolled off, revealing a mass of black ropes. The ropes moved, slid over one another. One lifted its head and gazed at Inanna with cold inhuman eyes.

"I have a message for you, Inanna of Kur."

Inanna kept an eye on the snake and held her ground. "Give it to me then," she said.

"You won't like it."

"I'll be the judge of that."

A look of satisfaction crossed Rheti's face. "Remember, you're the one who asked." Her hand was in the basket, among the snakes. There was a sudden thrashing, a movement so quick Inanna could hardly follow it, and Rheti drew out her hand and held it up to the light. Blood ran down her wrist, and she stiffened, her eyes rolling back in her head, a choking sound in her throat.

"In a little while," the eunuch said calmly, "the Priestess will speak to us."

"But she's killed herself. No one could be bitten that many times and live!"

The old man licked his painted lips nervously and shook his head. "Wait and see."

They waited until the torch burned down to a smoky stub, listening to Rheti's labored breathing. Then, with her eyes still closed, she began to speak. Or perhaps she was only making sounds; Inanna couldn't tell which. The noises were animal-like, meaningless.

"The High Priestess speaks the old tongue," the eunuch said proudly. "The tongue of the first Mothers."

"What's she saying?"

The eunuch laid one skinny finger over his lips and motioned for Inanna to be silent. "She's praying to Hut."

For a long time the sounds went on, monotonous, guttural, until finally Rheti's eyes opened and she pointed to Inanna. *"Lave na pollu tah koh ved ah mok . . ."*

"The Priestess says that you want to be Queen and kill your brother," the eunuch translated. He caught her by the sleeve and held her back. "Wait *muna*, please; there's more."

"She's insane!" Shadows slid ominously up the walls, festooning the ceiling. The torch in the eunuch's hand wavered. "I never wanted to be Queen!" But even as she denied it, she knew it was true. She did want to be Queen; she wanted to take the army, march into the mountains, and kill Pulal. Rheti had tempted her with the one thing she couldn't refuse.

The eunuch coughed and waved away the torch smoke. "The Priestess says you must do two things to get your desire."

"What things?"

He seemed reluctant.

"Tell me."

"The Priestess says that to be Queen you must . . . do nothing."

"Nothing?" It made no sense. "And the second thing?" Down on the floor of the cave Rheti rocked, repeating the same phrase over and over again. The eunuch shifted his eyes, and cleared his throat nervously.

"The Priestess says that if you want to kill your brother . . ." He stopped, as if afraid to finish.

"What do I have to do?"

"Give your daughter to Hut."

For a moment Inanna didn't understand, and then she realized what Rheti was asking for: Alna's life.

"No!"

The word echoed off the stone walls and down the long hallway. Inanna clenched her fists so hard her nails dug into her palms. Angry beyond words, she would have killed Rheti on the spot if she'd had a spear. But something held her back. "Tell her . . ." the words stuck in her throat. She pointed to Rheti, who was curled on the floor, muttering incoherently. "Tell this High Priestess of yours that if she tries to harm my daughter I'll kill her myself. Tell her that."

The old eunuch shook his head sadly. "The Priestess says that your fate isn't your own. She says that she's seen into the basket of the future, and that you'll order your own soldiers to bring the child to Hut after you're Queen. The Priestess says . . ."

"May your Priestess rot in the hell realms!" Inanna cried.

"Where is she? Where's Alna?" Inanna ignored the nurses's startled white faces. "Where's my baby?"

"Here, *muna*. Asleep in her bed."

Inanna hugged her child, pressed the warm firmness of her small body, kissed her fiercely. Alna awoke and began to cry, rubbing her eyes with her fists. "My dear one, my darling, I didn't mean to frighten you. Don't be afraid. No one will ever hurt you as long as your Mama's alive. I swear it!"

"What happened?" Seb stood in the doorway, his face clouded with concern. "Where did you go?"

Inanna sat down on a three-legged stool, put Alna to her breast, and gazed around the room. She saw the familiar surroundings as if for the first time: cream-colored walls decorated with geometric designs and birds; copper and clay lamps set on low tables; the floor covered with thick grass mats, her bed draped with blankets so thin that they rippled as the evening breeze blew across them. Peace, harmony, security. She thought of the cave, the basket of snakes, and another wave of anger passed over her.

"The High Priestess is god-crazed."

"You went to the temple?"

"Yes."

She could see the worry in his face, the hurt that she had gone without him. "You could have been killed." He reached out as if to touch her, and then drew back his hand. "Rheti's dangerous."

"Why doesn't the Queen get rid of her then? Or at least order her into exile?"

"Rheti has too much power."

"Power? She's half dead; she hasn't got any guards. I could have killed her myself tonight. I should have."

Seb shook his head. "You underestimate her. People here believe she can curse the crops, bring on a plague, make the river rise and flood the city."

"And can she?"

"Who knows?" Seb sat down and put his hands on his knees. "But it doesn't matter if she can put a curse on the city or not. What matters is that people believe she can. If the Queen moved on Rheti, there'd be a rebellion."

"The Queen's a coward! If I were her, I'd go down to that cave under the temple and . . ." She stopped suddenly, realizing what she had just said. They sat in an uncomfortable silence.

"You look pale; maybe you should eat something." Seb lifted the cloth off of a dish of stewed partridges, steamed wheat with grapes, pears preserved in honey, and a jug of beer.

"I'm not hungry." Inanna leaned back in the chair and held Alna closer, letting the baby's nursing soothe her anger. Seb helped himself to the cold stew, washing it down with beer. He ate in silence, stolidly, lost in thought. When he was finished, he wiped off the blade of his knife, and stuck it back in his belt.

"You don't know how things were in the city before Rheti became High Priestess," he said at last, "so how could you understand? I should have told you the whole story a long time ago."

"What are you talking about?"

"Rheti's changed everything around here."

"What do you mean?"

"Before she became High Priestess the worship of Hut was different."

"Different how?"

He stopped as if hunting for the right word. "Happier. We honored both sides of the Goddess equally in those days." He held out both hands, palms up. "There was balance." He got up and took a few quick steps across the room. "Hut was decay, but She was life too! She was the half cycle of the winter seasons that made the year whole; She was the rotten stalks we plowed back into the land to feed the wheat. Then Rheti changed all that."

Inanna had never suspected that Seb had so many words in him. "Why? What happened?"

Seb shrugged. "I'm not sure. All I know is that Rheti disappeared for more than a year. I was a child at the time. I only overheard what my mother and her friends said: that the High Priestess had gone east or north, and met some strange people with golden hair who rode on the backs of great animals with feet of stone."

"Great animals with feet of stone?"

"In a land where the river is as big as the sky and made all of grass."

"Sounds like a dream."

"Dream or not, Rheti believed it. When she returned she claimed that the gold people had given her special powers. She claimed to have flown through the air and talked to the spirits of the dead. She said that the gold people had told her a great change was coming."

"What kind of change?"

"Rheti refused to say."

"And the Queen did nothing?"

"No," Seb's face grew grim, "she did something all right, but it didn't work."

"What did she do?" Why couldn't Seb just tell the whole story at once? It was maddening to hear it a piece at a time like this.

"She arranged to have Rheti killed. The night before the deed was supposed to take place, there was a banquet in the Queen's chambers. By morning all the guests—including the six assassins—were dead. Only the Queen survived, and she's never really been well since. The High Priestess claimed it was a curse from Hut."

"More likely poison."

"More likely, but people were frightened. The next day Rheti turned up in the market yelling that the gold people had told her Hut and Lanla were at war, and that she'd chosen to side with Hut. There was a riot and some of the shops were sacked and a few of them burned. Lyra wanted to muster the army against the mob, but the Queen stopped her. Finally the rioters wore themselves out and went home."

"And then?"

"The Queen confined Rheti to the temple and forbade her to make any more public appearances, but that didn't work either. This new, evil worship of Hut continued to grow. There were secret sacrifices; children disappeared. Finally the Queen proclaimed that if Hut and Lanla were at war, then only Lanla would be worshiped in the city as long as she reigned."

"So in a way Rheti won after all; your Goddess was cut in half."

"Yes." Seb slumped down in the chair, picked up the empty beer jar, and toyed with it thoughtfully.

"And what do you think will happen next?"

His blue eyes were clean and unafraid. "More trouble."

After the dinner dishes were cleared away, Inanna's women worked quickly, unobtrusively, washing her feet in lightly scented rose water, combing out her hair, and helping her into her linen night robe. Inanna gave herself over to them as if she were a child, glad to feel cared for, to think of nothing for a time. The linen gown smelled faintly of jasmine and the feel of it against her skin was comforting. The jasmine reminded her of Ev and his scented oils, the first day she'd come to the city. How long ago was that? How much time had she wasted? Her whole body ached as if she'd crossed the mountains all over again. All she wanted to do was sleep, forget the things Seb had told her until morning.

"Here." Seb put Alna in her arms. The baby had been swaddled in fresh linen; her eyes were already closed. "I'll be right outside your door." She nodded at Seb gratefully, too tired to talk. "Sleep well." He blew out the lamp and left the room.

But Inanna didn't sleep well. She lay awake for a long time, staring at the ceiling, hugging Alna's body close to her own. How could she have been so blind to the danger? She should have asked more questions. She should have been training herself in the arts of war all along; she should have argued more with the Queen, made her realize that the only way to get rid of Rheti was to strengthen the army. If the army was strong and loyal, there wouldn't be a rebellion.

Inanna turned restlessly. The Queen was a fool, not facing reality. Why hadn't she tried harder to make the old woman see the need for war? Rheti could be deposed, the nomad tribes quashed once and for all, Pulal killed along with them.

Weeks, months wasted! Motherhood had made her a coward. What had happened to her vow to revenge Lilith and Enkimdu? Had the birth of this child tamed the wolf in her? Curse it, she should have been doing something instead of just sitting around the palace like a fat dove in a cage! This very minute Pulal was living, enjoying himself. What was she planning to do? Let him die comfortably of old age?

The moonlight streamed in through the clay lattices, casting bright lozenges on the white plaster; a nightbird called and fell silent. Inanna sat up, uneasy. Was she safe, even here in her own chambers? The walls were sheer, no handholds, the windows barred. She measured the thickness of the lattices in her mind and found that she was still afraid. But how many nights had she slept alone in the mountains with wild animals howling around her? Finally, completely exhausted, she curled closer to Alna, closed her eyes, and slept.

Sleep was thick on her, matting her eyes. Inanna struggled up from the dark quiet bottom of it and found the moon had already set. It was pitch-black in the room, so dark it was like another sleep. Alna breathed softly next to her. The only other sound was the fountain out in the courtyard. Or was it? Inanna sat up and listened. A rustle, like dry leaves blowing across stones, very soft, almost a hiss. She heard the sound again, close at hand. Reaching out in the darkness, she ran her fingers over the top of the cover and felt something slick and cool slide under her palm and over her bare arm.

She could never remember screaming. She only remembered Seb standing over her, a torch in his hand, and the cobra spread out on the blanket, its hood flared, its head inched from Alna's face. The baby lay quietly, her cheeks flushed with sleep. But if she began to cry or made the slightest movement, the snake would strike. Inanna froze and Seb froze too. For a moment the silence in the room was complete.

Then it came, hissing, lunging, a flash of white fangs. Seb lifted the torch and struck out, catching it in midair, shoving the flaming tip against the flared hood. The cobra flew off the bed, turned convulsively, and struck out again, just missing Seb's arm. Inanna grabbed for Alna, pulling her out of the way. With one quick motion, Seb unhooked his axe from his belt and threw it, catching the snake just behind the head. The cobra slumped forward on the grass mat, its hood collapsed. Stepping forward, Seb put his foot on the snake's body and cut off its head.

"A greeting from Rheti," he said grimly. Blood splattered the straw; the body of the snake still twitched. The smell of the cave came back to Inanna; she tried to speak and discovered she couldn't. Alna blinked at Inanna sleepily. She yawned and put her fingers in the pink circle of her mouth.

"Are you all right?" Inanna nodded mutely. Seb sat beside her. "You and the child . . ." He stopped, pulled her close, and kissed her. "You fool! You almost got yourself killed!"

Later she tried to tell herself that she'd been confused, frightened, not really aware of what was happening. But she knew that was a lie. She'd wanted comfort; she'd wanted to close her eyes and lose herself, forget Rheti and the snake, the room, the moonlight, the city itself. So she had given in, let Seb's passion wash over her, let him lay her down on the bed and take off her linen robe. He had tangled his fingers in her hair and kissed her neck, her breasts, her hands, the soles of her feet. She had let him call her his darling and his love, and still she hadn't turned from him. She had let Seb make love to her, but when she cried out with passion it was Enkimdu she cried to.

It was Enkimdu who pulled her body to his, the thrust of Enkimdu's loins, his lips on hers. And for a short time after, she was happy again the way she'd been back in the valley before Pulal found her and the nightmare began. And when she slept, she dreamed—not of Rheti and her horrors—but of a small reed hut, a range of snow-capped mountains, and a pond full of blue-tipped water lilies.

But the next morning when she woke and found Seb still lying beside her, she knew she'd done an unforgivable thing to him, and she felt wicked and ashamed. Putting on her robe, she slipped out of the room and began to walk aimlessly through the palace, losing herself in the maze of hallways. At last she came to a small courtyard where the sun was beginning to turn the stones pink. A blue fountain was sending up a delicate spray of water, and someone had planted white flowers in a broken jar. Inanna sat for a long time, staring into the blue basin. The fish were dark shadows; the water was so clear she could see the cracked tiles on the bottom.

"If you can't forgive yourself, who can forgive you then?" Inanna turned quickly, wondering who had spoken to her, but the courtyard was empty.

Seb's mother, Sellaki, had always said that he was like the river: smooth on the surface, but full of swift, dangerous currents. When he was just getting his first beard—and proud of it as lion's whiskers—she had called him to her in the barracks where she was drilling the army. It had been a big army in those days, four *magurs,* maybe more, and when he arrived the air was so thick with dust that he could hardly see across the practice yard. Seb had found his mother at last, sitting near the well in full armor, her shield propped beside her, her long brown hair tied back with a scrap of red cloth. How strong she'd looked to him at that moment, as if she'd never grow old. Her skin had been as smooth as an eggshell, and her teeth were so hard that she could crack nuts with them. Sometimes now it was hard for Seb to believe the old Sellaki he ate with every night was the same woman who once threw a javelin the length of ten men as easily as if it were a pebble.

"What do you want to do with yourself, son?" She'd asked him, drawing a jug of water from the well and sluicing it over her head to take off the dust. She had shaken out her hair like a big healthy dog and looked at him with a motherly frown. "You're almost a man, and it's time you did something of use."

Seb had looked back at her, and then at her shield. He remembered it had an unusual design painted on the leather: a white crane flying above a willow tree. Which Goddess had that shield favored: Hut or Lanla? Sellaki had never said.

"Well?"

"I want to be a soldier, mother," he'd told her, meaning: I want to be like you. She'd looked him over for a moment grimly, and he knew she was thinking that he'd had the crippling sickness as a child. Until he was six seasons old, he hadn't been able to walk without someone to help him, and even now his left leg was shorter than his right. But he wanted to tell her he'd changed all that. He'd run every path in the delta until he was ready to drop; he already knew how to use an axe and a javelin, and there wasn't a boy in the city who could beat him in swimming. Once—although she didn't know it—he had even crossed the river out where the currents were worst, with a stone tied to his bad leg, just to prove he could. But he hadn't said any of that. As always, he'd held his tongue and endured her glance. Sellaki had seen the worry in his face and laughed suddenly, clapping him on the shoulder as if he were already a comrade in arms.

"I guess you'll do," she'd said. His relief had been so great that he'd wanted to cry, laugh, and yell at the same time. "Report here tomorrow at sunrise, and your sister Lyra will fit you out with some gear."

"Thank you, mother," he'd said, feeling, as he always did, how he never had the right words to tell her what he meant. After that they'd walked back together through the city, and she'd told him what he already knew: that his aunt, the Queen, didn't favor the army and that things were beginning to fall apart.

"Then you'll have all the more need for me," he'd said proudly, feeling like a soldier already. He remembered that his mother had put her arm around him after he'd said that, drawn him to her like a baby, and he'd felt angry with her for not seeing that he was a man.

"You like lost causes, don't you, Seb?" she'd said. And it wasn't until years later, when he met Inanna and began to love her, that he knew his mother had been right.

Inanna. When he thought of her, Seb wanted to put his fist through something—through a shield or a wall—because he had no words to tell her what he was feeling. Why had he been born unable to speak his mind like other people? When he tried to talk of love to her, he heard himself stumbling, lumbering about like a great ox until he was too humiliated to go on, always afraid she might start laughing. To her credit, she never had. I love you, he'd wanted to say. The first time I saw you, big with your child, facing down me and Lyra as bravely as any warrior, I thought: there's a woman worth having! I love your beauty, your courage, your quickness. Your eyes are green like the river in spring, your hair is as dark as a crow's wing, and when I hear your voice I feel at peace with myself.

But he'd never said any of those things to her, not even when she'd finally let him come into her bed. He knew all along that she didn't return his love, of course; he knew so many more things than she suspected. He even knew about Enkimdu. The two cousins had often been mistaken for twins when they were growing up, and there were even whispers in the palace that they'd had the same father, although no one knew for sure. Once an old temple *lant* had told him that the Queen and his mother had both entertained the blue-eyed trader at the same time—a strange-looking giant of a man who'd come from the far north bringing magic stones that could be burned. The stones had smelled like cedar trees, the *lant* said, and all the women of the palace wanted one because the trader told them that they brought an easy labor.

"Sons-of-the-foreigner-with-the-sky-blue-eyes, people called you both when you were born, not a day apart," the *lant* had said, "and as alike you were as two beans."

But she'd been wrong. Enkimdu had always been the quick one, born with a honeyed tongue, *able to talk the river fish into his net,* people said of him. While everyone had thought Seb was strong but slow, a good man but passionless. Only Sellaki, his mother, had seen the truth, the whirlpools and currents, the dark, fierce places in him.

So how could he blame Inanna for not understanding. He knew he'd found the only woman he'd ever really wanted, and if she pretended to herself that he was someone else, what did it matter in the long run? Seb was a practical man. Enkimdu was dead, and he was alive. Perhaps someday Inanna would see his love for her, even though he couldn't tell her about it in words; perhaps someday she'd call him to her bed again and take him for himself.

Then again, maybe not. He was willing to wait and see.

"Throw, curse you!" Lyra yelled. One of the four soldiers—a short girl of perhaps fourteen or fifteen, lifted her arm and sent the shaft of her javelin straight through the center of the bale. "Good work, Tarna." The girl beamed with pleasure and ran to retrieve her weapon. With a little practice she'd make a passable recruit, better than most they sent these days. Chips of plaster rained off the wall and fell onto the hard baked clay of the practice yard. Great Goddess, was it possible that every one of the other three had missed the target? Were they blind?

"Put your backs into it! Look what you're aiming for, you useless pack of water snails!" No pride, that was the problem. Unless she was out here watching them all the time, they wouldn't even practice. No wonder they couldn't hit anything. When her mother had been in command, things had been different. The army'd had the pick of the city. But now . . . Lyra looked at the two beardless boys and the two skinny girls and thought what a sorry lot they were. Days like this made her wonder if it were any use trying to keep things together.

Tarna continued to batter away at the target. "Take a break, I said." No use letting the girl overdo it and hurt her throwing arm. Tarna stopped reluctantly and ran to catch up with the others. Lyra watched the four of them disappear into the guard house, then went over to the well, drew herself a jug of water, and took a long, cool drink. She noticed that the lip of the jug was broken, cracked straight across where someone had carelessly let it strike against the side of the well. Endless, petty problems. She'd have to remember to get a new jug.

Sitting with her back to the wall, she took off her armor and began to polish the metal parts with wet sand. The copper started to take on a dull sheen, and Lyra examined it with satisfaction. She liked to put things in good working order. After a while, she gazed up from her polishing and saw Inanna coming across the practice yard with Alna on her hip. Now what were they doing here at this time of the morning?

Alna was laughing, tugging at Inanna's braids, squirming and kicking like a swimmer. A pretty child, getting big too. Lyra smiled at the baby. She loved all children, but Alna more than most. Then she caught sight of Inanna's face and her smile faded.

"I have to talk to you," Inanna said as soon as she was in ear-shot. Pale face, dark circles under her eyes—was she sick? Lyra saw her glance warily at the soldiers who stood near the guard-house. It was obvious she didn't want to say anything in front of them.

"Come to my quarters. We can talk there." The relief on Inan-na's face was as sharp as the cutting edge of a good spear. Lyra put her hand on her shoulder, and the two of them walked silently toward the barracks. I know something's wrong, Lyra thought, I can see it in her eyes.

Small room, roughly plastered walls, packed dirt floor, narrow bed hard as the ground, two clay stools without backs. Lyra inspected her extra shield hanging on the wall, her javelins and arrows standing in the corner in a neat bundle. On one of the stools was the awl she used for repairing her sandals, her whet-stone, and half a round of coarse bread. She liked the barrenness of it all, the cleanliness and order. Her room was simple—the way life should be and almost never was.

Picking up the awl, the whetstone, and the bread, she placed them carefully on the windowsill, sat down on the stool, put her hands on her knees, and confronted Inanna. "Now tell me what's the matter."

Inanna sat on the other stool, and shifted Alna from hip to lap. "I want to train here along with the soldiers."

"Why?"

"I need to learn to defend myself."

"Against whom?" But Lyra already knew the answer.

"Against Rheti. Last night she tried to kill me with a snake; it nearly bit Alna." Lyra looked at the baby and felt herself growing very angry. Plots, intrigues—when the army was weak everything else fell apart with it. No one was safe, not even the children. Curse Rheti and curse the Queen too!

Standing up, Lyra crossed the room in two steps, grabbed one of her javelins from the pile, and held it out to Inanna. "Here, give me the baby and take this outside. There's a bale of hay against the wall near the well. When you can throw this javelin through the center of it three times in a row, come back and we'll talk some more." Did she have what it took to be a soldier? Her arms looked strong, but it was the will that counted most. Did she have the will? "Learning to fight isn't easy."

Inanna took the javelin and measured it grimly. "I didn't expect it to be." Green eyes, stubborn, something wild in the depths of them. Where have I seen that look before? Lyra thought. In a wolf cub she and her sisters had trapped when they were girls, a tiny thing no bigger than a rabbit: that cub had had the same look, and when they'd tried to take it out of the net, it had clawed through all five of them and escaped.

Out in the practice yard, soldiers were sparring with blunted spears, and the air was already thick with dust. Lyra watched from the doorway as Inanna hurled the javelin at the target, missing every time but one, and then called her back.

"I forgot to tell you something."

"What's that?" The sun was coming up now, and the eastern sky had turned the color of pomegranate juice. Lyra looked at Inanna standing there, the javelin in her hand, her white robe tinted red by the light. Blood color, she thought, and later she was to wonder if it had been an omen.

"Don't let the Queen know you're coming here. Try to go out the side gate by the kitchen, and give the guard something so he'll look the other way. If she found out you'd taken up soldiering, she might decide not to adopt you after all."

"Adopt me!"

"Holy Goddess, you mean you didn't know? Why it's all over the city. She's going to recognize Alna as her granddaughter, and make you the *Joyta*."

"The what?"

"The *Joyta*, the heir to the throne." Lyra put her hands gently on Inanna's shoulders. "That means after she dies, you'll be the next Queen."

"But I don't want to be Queen!" The javelin dropped from her hand and rolled in the dust. Alna screamed at the top of her lungs at the sound of her mother's voice. "I can't be Queen!"

Yes, she could, and a good one too. Besides, if the old Queen made her the *Joyta*, she wouldn't have any choice. The trouble with Inanna, Lyra decided, was that she thought about things too much. People weren't made for so much thinking.

Lyra picked up the javelin. "Get back out there in the practice yard and start throwing." But instead Inanna went back into the room, grabbed Alna, and held her to her breast for a long time. She looks as if she's worried about the baby, Lyra thought, but what does that have to do with being Queen? Somewhere a great disorder was blossoming. She could almost feel the confusion growing up around her like mushrooms on a rotten log. But those were foolish thoughts, and not worthy of a soldier.

A few weeks later, on a smolderingly hot day in the month of the High Wheat, the Queen officially adopted Inanna as her heir.

The Power

My long spear I shall hurl upon Kur,
My throw stick I shall direct against it,
In its forests I shall strike up fires,
At the neck of its headman I shall set my bronze axe,
I shall remove its dread like a mountain,
Like a city cursed it will not be restored,
I am Inanna the Warrior,
I am Inanna the Slayer of Dragons,
I am Inanna Heaven's Queen . . .

A Sumerian poem
Taken from a tablet now in the Hilprecht
Collection of the Freidrich-Schiller
University (Jena)
Date unknown

The gods foresee everything but their own destruction.

Motto on a Babylonian cylinder seal
Second millennium

9 WHAT is time? Who can see it pass? Is time like the wind—a great, invisible force that changes everything—or is it only part of some collective dream? The river rose, fell, and rose again; the wheat was planted and rotted in the fields a second season. Alna took her first step, and the Queen retreated to her rooms permanently, refusing to see anyone but a few servants. No one knew if she was sick, bewitched, dying. Panic was in the air; flowers in the royal gardens wilted because no one had given orders for them to be watered; piles of broken crockery were tossed carelessly in odd corners. All around her Inanna could feel the court falling apart like a broken water wheel. Then one morning, just before the first rains, she came back from the barracks to find six of the Queen's Companions waiting for her. They were dressed in their finest red robes, holding their sandals in their hands to symbolize their humility.

"You must run the city, *Joyta*," they begged. They bowed down and refused to rise. "You must sit on the throne stool in the Queen's place until she comes to her senses again."

"But I can't. I know nothing."

"*Joyta*, the city is on the edge of ruin. There's silt in the irrigation ditches; the walls are falling down; people in the outer villages are on the verge of famine. Please."

"Let the Queen tell you what to do."

"But she refused. She stays in her rooms."

"Well I refuse too. I don't know how to rule a city. You'd be better off doing it yourselves."

But the next day they came back, and the day after, and the day after that, until finally she agreed to come to the Great Hall and hear the petitions.

Three cows from the village of Molli loose in the communal wheat fields again; a man who claimed that his sister stole a bag of salt from him; an architect who insisted she receive new gutters to put in the market or the streets would wash out in the next rains. Inanna felt helpless, inadequate. What did she know about salt, cows, and gutters? There was so much to learn.

"You'll learn in time," Seb kept telling her. "Being a Queen's like everything else. It just takes practice." He'd become such a good friend. How lucky she was to have him near her. Often when she sat on the throne stool, she would ask Seb to stand beside her so he could whisper advice. Did he remember that night they'd spent together? She liked to imagine he'd forgotten. "Take what you want from me," his eyes seemed to say, so she took the safe parts only, the support and kindness, and as for the passion, she left that, pretending it was gone, that it had never existed.

But sometimes she would glance up unexpectedly from the petitioners in front of her and catch Seb unawares. Then for a moment she would see the passion in his eyes before he had time to hide it. On those days she would weaken, let that love wash over her, and then, angry with herself for taking where she couldn't give, she would push it aside.

She would look again at Seb's face, and see the ghost of Enkimdu. That face would drop to the bottom of her like a stone down a dark well, and she would get up suddenly, walk out of the hall without a word, and go back to her rooms. Taking off her gold diadem and fine robes, she would spend the rest of the day throwing her javelin with such fury that it often went straight through the target, shaft and all. Twenty times, thirty, forty. The heft of a good axe in her hand, a bow that bent at her touch as if it were part of her own arm: these were the important things in her life, the things she could measure.

"You're a soldier now," Lyra told her one morning. The days were short and cold again, the sky full of clouds the color of dirty ice. Inanna shivered under her armor, and slapped her hands together to warm them.

"How good a soldier?"

"Not so strong as some of the men, but stubborn and aggressive."

"That's not good enough." Fifty times through the target, sixty. Her muscles grew harder under her robe, and in the throne room the petitions suddenly began to make sense.

The seasons changed again. Outside the walls of the city flowers bloomed among the patches of barley and wheat; new onions came up, thin and green as a goddess's eyelashes; in the market fish lay in wet reed baskets gasping for air, and new gutters ran toward the river carrying fruit rinds and the last of the spring rains.

Time passed and she hardly noticed it. In midsummer, on the first day of the Barley Moon, Lyra took her aside after practice and offered her a seat in the shade. The sky was a copper bowl and the dust already three fingers thick in the yard. "You're becoming a warrior and a queen both," Lyra said, "but you're pushing yourself too hard."

I'm still not good enough at either one yet, Inanna thought. She looked at Lyra, the row of barracks, the well, the soldiers sparring in the dust. There was still something missing, something she couldn't identify. And she had the sense of a great battle coming toward her like a thundercloud.

Late summer, the river a low green ditch, lizards crawling over the walls, heat thick enough to cut: during the afternoon the whole city slept, and only at night was it cool enough to practice. Inanna sat in a great stone tub playing with Alna. The baby laughed and splashed the water, her naked body slipping out of reach, cool and slick as a fish. When Alna was older she'd take her down to the river and teach her to swim. Alna threw her arms around her mother's neck and kissed her on the cheek. Then she turned back to the toy boat that was floating away toward the other side of the tub, a round boat shaped like a cup.

"The Queen wishes to see the *Joyta* in the royal chambers."

"What?"

The servant stood in the doorway bowing uneasily. "I'm sorry to disturb you in your bath, but the Queen said you were to come at once."

Alna laughed and grabbed at the boat, sinking it. "What does the Queen want?"

"She didn't say, *muna*."

Inanna kissed Alna, took her out of the tub, and handed her to the two nurses. Then she dressed herself, slipped into a pair of fresh sandals, and hurried toward the Queen's chambers. As she climbed the stairs it grew hotter and hotter; the air was stale here, stagnant, like a pool that had been left behind when the river went elsewhere. Why had the Queen sent for her? Had she found out about the time she'd been spending in the barracks? Was she angry at her for sitting on the throne stool? And if that was it, why had she waited so long to do something?

Inanna felt the questions tossing through her head like puffs of wind, scrambling her thoughts as if they were dry leaves. How many months had it been since the Queen had wanted to see anyone? She tried to count and gave up; it was too hot to think.

At the entrance to the royal chambers, the guards stood in full armor, their shoulders covered with sweat. The stones felt hot under her sandals, and there was a strange smell in the air, thick, sweet as pomegranate juice. She found the Queen sitting on a cushioned bench, wrapped in heavy wool blankets, her swollen feet propped up on a small clay box full of hot coals. Stifling heat, servants stripped down to their linen undergowns, dripping and red-faced: over the windows heavy drapes blocked out all light and air. How could she stand it? The Queen's face was sickly pale, her legs swollen like bladders, her eyes two bruised plums, no life or fire in them.

"Well, what do you see?" the Queen demanded.

"Nothing," Inanna lied.

"Nonsense. Any fool can see that I'm dying." Her voice was still stubborn and strong, and when she smiled she had the look of her old self for a moment. "Well, sit down, sit down. Don't stand there staring at me like that."

Inanna sat down on a bench. The baskets of clay and the carving tools were nowhere in sight. Along the walls, the niches that had once held the Queen's sculptures were bare. "Where are the statues?"

The Queen wiped her mouth with a square of cloth, and took a drink of hot water to clear her throat. Her hair was plastered to her forehead; her hand shook as she reached for the cup. "Some I gave to the temple; some I had broken up. I couldn't stand having them around to remind me that I couldn't work any longer." She took another drink of the hot water. "I can't touch the clay any more. It's too cold; gets into my bones." She lifted her head and measured Inanna with bright, clear eyes. "Help me up."

As she struggled to her feet, the table fell to the floor with a crash, and the cup shattered on the tiles. Inanna caught the Queen under the arm. "There's something I want to show you while I can still walk."

The servants scurried around picking up the table and the bits of broken pottery. One of them tried to take the Queen's other arm, but the old woman waved her away. "No, only the *Joyta*. The rest of you stay here." She whispered in Inanna's ear: "You see, I'm still as mean and hard to get along with as ever." She chuckled. "I'm taking you up to the Queen's Aerie. Cursed lot of steps it is too, all the way to the top of the palace." She began to hobble toward the door, clutching at Inanna's arm, swearing at every step. "Curse my feet, and old age, and whoever wove this wretched spell! May Hut take her to the hell realms!"

"A spell?"

"Of course, what did you think?"

"I thought you were just sick."

As they started up the first steps, the Queen gasped for breath, moved slowly like a swimmer kicking to the surface of a pond. "Rheti's put the cold curse on me."

The coldness of the underground caves, her own breath coming in puffs like steam. Inanna shuddered, thinking: please let her be wrong; please don't let there be a curse. What could a javelin do against such evil?

The stairs led to another flight of steps, narrow, twisting. "This way." The walls were whitewashed, and bars of light alternated with bars of shadow. They were now high above the rest of the palace. Through one of the lattices Inanna saw the city below, the white circle of the walls, the fields of grain and dusty foothills. Behind the hills, just visible through the haze, the mountains rose up, the highest peaks barely dusted with the first snows. A chill passed through her body. The cold curse. Ahead the Queen still climbed and swore. Inanna put her hand in the sunlight and felt its reassuring warmth. The Queen was an old woman, sick, imagining things.

They came to the top of the stairs at last, and a dusty red curtain blocked their way. Inanna wasn't sure what she expected to find on the other side of it: a storeroom perhaps, or some kind of lookout post. With one hand the Queen pushed the curtain aside. "Welcome to the Queen's Aerie. Well, don't just stand there. Go on in."

Inanna found herself in a garden, small, open to the sky, lush with flowers of every kind and color: long-stemmed lilies, cornflowers, sweet-smelling vines, jasmine. There were great orange flowers that smelled of spice, and small purple irises no bigger than her thumb. In one corner a miniature waterfall trickled into a small pool, and beside it in a niche stood a statue half hidden by wild roses. Full body, heavy-lidded eyes, a smile as serene as if the stone itself were dreaming.

"It's beautiful," Inanna said, "all of it."

"It's yours," the Queen said, "only you must tend it yourself. That's the Queen's gift to the Goddess: to keep one perfect garden with her own hands." She folded her swollen fingers under the edge of the blanket. There was pride and sadness in her eyes. "Today I give it to you. The steps have become too steep for me. I won't be coming here again." A pause. "I remember the day my own mother brought me here and told me what I'm going to tell you. That was the last time we were together before she died." The Queen stood for a moment, looking at the flowers without appearing to see them. Then she shook her head. "Stupid to stand here thinking about the past. A disease of old age. Come." She reached for Inanna's arm. "I've got more things to show you." They walked over to the statue, and Inanna touched the stone face tentatively with the tips of her fingers, feeling the worn quality of the rock. It was soft as kidskin.

"I've never seen anything like it. Who is she?"

"The First Mother."

"She must be very old."

"Older than the city itself. She was the one who set me to carving statues. I used to come up here, look at her face, and go back to my rooms and try to capture that smile of hers in the clay. I think the sculptor who made her must have been something more than human." They walked to the other side of the garden where a small apple tree had been trained onto a trellis against the wall. The apples were tiny and hard.

"But they're sweet," the Queen said, offering Inanna one. Bending down, the old woman began to tug at a large stone. "Uf," she said, "curse these things!"

"What are you doing?"

The Queen laughed. "Giving you your inheritance, but if I were you, I'd refuse it. Want to run back to those mountains of yours? Well, now's the time to do it. Wait around a little longer and it's going to be too late."

Inanna helped the Queen lift the slippery, moss-covered stone. Underneath was something wrapped in a white cloth embroidered with small gold doves. It looked moldy, as if it had lain there for years.

"Lift that thing out and unwrap it," the Queen said. Inside the bundle was a small stone no bigger than a good-sized radish. The stone was pocked and honeycombed, blackened as if it had been in a fire. Inanna was disappointed. But what had she expected the Queen to give her? A magic axe that would cut through anything? Still this was only a cinder. She wondered why anyone had bothered to hide it so carefully.

"What is it?"

"A changing stone."

"A what?"

The Queen lowered herself onto a small carved bench and sat for a moment looking at the lily pads on the pond. "Come sit beside me," she said at last, "because I've got a story to tell you. It's the same story my mother told me, and her mother told her, and you can believe it or not as you like." In the garden the only sound was the trickle of the waterfall and the monotonous scraping of a single cicada. Inanna rested on a patch of moss and put the stone in her lap.

"A long time ago—before the second ring of walls was built around the city—a star fell from the sky. And when people went out in the fields to look at the great hole it had made, they found that stone you're holding." Inanna felt new respect for the rock. A piece of a star. She wondered idly why the stars were white, but this bit of one was black. Maybe they were like campfires that burned down to charcoal . . .

". . . people were afraid of the stone and they wanted to leave it where it was, but a very old woman picked it up and carried it to the Queen. She told the Queen that some day a new Queen would come out of the east, and that she would be a great warrior with magic powers. But the odd thing would be that this Warrior Queen wouldn't know how to use her own powers. So the old woman—who people later said was Lanla in disguise—left a message for the future Warrior Queen. Not much of a message, I grant you, but a message nevertheless: '*Let her hold the changing stone,*' the old woman said as she pushed the star rock into the Queen's hand. '*Let her do nothing, think nothing, wait for her power.*'"

The Queen snorted and pulled her blanket more tightly around her shoulders. "Well that's it. That's the story my grandmother told my mother, my mother told me, and I'm supposed to tell you. Every *Joyta* as far back as anyone can remember has been forced to listen to it. But if you ask me, it's all nonsense. As far as I know, that changing stone has never changed anyone. But a whole line of Queens have gotten dirt under their fingernails and bad backs hiding it. You see, there was a curse that went along with it: that if the changing stone were lost, the city would be lost too."

But Inanna wasn't listening; she was seeing the eunuch, the underground cave, the basket of snakes. *Do nothing and you will be Queen.* Rheti must have known about the old prophecy. The part about Alna dying must have been added on to frighten her. It hadn't been a vision of the future after all, just an ordinary threat.

Still, that didn't mean the old prophecy itself wasn't true. Maybe she was the Warrior Queen the old woman had foreseen so long ago! Her excitement rose, ebbed, and turned into confusion. Surely if she had been destined for greatness she would have known it. And the changing stone, could it really give her control over her own power? Or was the Queen right: was it just a rock?

"What's wrong with you?" Inanna found the Queen staring at her. The old woman shook her head and sat back on the bench with a sigh. "Here I give you a whole kingdom and a garden to go with it, and you sit there looking as if you'd swallowed a hive of bees." A breeze blew and the iris bent and dipped in the wind; rose petals fell into the pool and floated on the water. Dust, shade, the odor of jasmine. A low white wall and beyond it the mountains.

"Take the stone; use it if you can, and if you can't, bring it back here and bury it again." The Queen looked at the flowers wearily, as if memorizing every petal. "Lead me back down the stairs. I think I've had enough of gardens."

Do nothing. Think nothing. Wait. It sounded easy enough, but it didn't work. Inanna found herself thinking of everything: of the petitions she had heard that morning, of Alna's newest tooth, of what she had for breakfast, of the fact she was supposed to be thinking of nothing. She'd come to the garden every day for a month, and even there her mind never stopped for a minute. It unwound like a ball of wool, leading her to all sorts of things, but never to silence.

Maybe a bird can have an empty mind, or a hyena, or a lion—but not a human being. Her legs ached from sitting, and she imagined that ants crawled up her spine. In the palm of her hand the changing stone grew sweaty.

Inanna began to feel like the victim of a bad joke, generations old. Or maybe she wasn't the one who was supposed to be the Warrior Queen. But it had to be her. She was from the east, and had special powers: plants told her their secrets; savages backed away at her touch; even Rheti herself shrank from the light that came from her hand.

Inanna imagined the statue of the First Mother was laughing at her. Maybe she imagined everything. The sky above the garden grew plum-colored, and the doves put their heads under their wings. Down below the whole city began to settle into sleep.

Blank. A gray cloud. Long time. Silence.

This must be a dream because nothing is the right color: the sky spreads in a sheet of thin gold above a city of pearl; flowers bloom in obsidian and bone. In copper trees flocks of strange birds flash like jewels. Inanna sits and waits; the dream goes on, and in the dream she sleeps.

She wakes to something burning below her navel. It comes over her quickly, flows through her before she can stop it, liquid like molten gold, river of fire, and oh the joy of it. Navel, to heart, to throat, to face. Spine, fingers, arms. The fire blinds her; she spins into darkness and her body becomes a sack.

All at once the mouth of the sack opens and she leaves it behind in one great leap. Long hair grows on her face and chest. She senses the soft splay of her pads on the stone, the arc of her tail, the sharpness of her teeth, the muscles under her skin taut as a bowstring, the courage of her heart. Green eyes, wolf-woman. She springs to the top of the wall. Looking back, she sees her old body sitting there in the garden.

I am a wolf, she thinks. *This is the true body I got from my wolf-mother, the body Pulal and the rest tried to take from me. But I've won it back.* For a moment she's lost in the sense of her own power. Then she feels the presence of the Other. The Other is cold, evil, angry that she's discovered it. The Other knows that she is as strong as it is, and Inanna feels its fear.

Green eyes, her claws on the wall. Inanna throws back her head and howls a challenge. All around her the sky breaks up like a basket of tiles tossed off a balcony.

Nothing. Blank. A gray cloud.

A long time later—it seems forever—she opens her eyes to find herself sitting in the middle of the garden. It is night and the stars twinkle above her in the dusty sky. Did she dream all that? She looks at the changing stone, dark and heavy in the palm of her hand, and begins to feel foolish again. Surely it must have been a dream. And yet . . . She has the feeling that she has won a battle, but that another, greater one is still to come.

Deep in her breast she imagines she can still feel her wolf heart beating.

10 *"JOYTA*, they say that the Queen is better." The servant combed out Inanna's hair, rubbed in a bit of scented oil, and began to braid it quickly, chatting all the while. It was the first day of the Dry River Moon, and outside the window the sun had already rolled over the peaks of the eastern mountains, clear and round as a gold ball. "They say the Queen's put out the fires in her braziers, and called for all the wool drapes to be pulled off her windows. They say she's moving down to the cool rooms soon. I heard the Queen might even go back to the Great Hall again, which would be a blessing on the city as I see it . . ." The woman's voice stumbled suddenly and her fingers slipped. "Not that you haven't been a blessing too, *Joyta*. I only meant . . ."

Inanna smiled at her. "The Queen can't come back too soon for me."

"Ah yes, *Joyta*. In the month of the Dry River Moon a Queen is especially needed, yes?"

Outside, round purple clouds floated across the sky, and then dissolved out of sight. Inanna stopped listening. Soon the rains would come, and a good thing too. The river was so low that the rushes were beginning to rot along the shore, and a few days ago the fish had started to die. Yesterday she had gone outside the walls with Seb and seen them stranded above the water line, flapping in the mud. Odd how the fish changed colors. At first their scales were like rainbows, their gills pink and clean. But at the end they were brown, black-finned, hard to tell from the mud itself. And the smell! Those fish smelled so bad that you couldn't even eat them.

When the rushes start to rot and fish are found dead in the mud . . . Who'd said those words? A bat wing of fear, the sense of something disappearing around a corner before she could see what it was. Then calm again, the familiar contents of her room, the open window, a perfectly ordinary morning.

"What's wrong, *Joyta?*"

"Nothing." The sky was an unmarred blue, and sunlight fell through the lattice and spread itself out across her robe like a gold chain. She worried too much, worked too hard. She needed more time for herself. Maybe she wouldn't go to the hall or the barracks. Maybe she'd spend the whole day with Alna instead.

That was it. She would take Alna outside the city walls to gather wild berries. They were at their peak this time of year, big, sweet, juicy. Not that Alna ever got many berries into the basket. Seb would come along too, of course, and when it got too hot for berry picking they would eat their midday meal under one of the big willow trees. They'd have honey cakes and dates, and sleep all afternoon until the evening mosquitoes drove them back to the city.

"Ask the toymaker to come here," she told one of the guards.

The man smiled at the command and saluted. "Right away, *muna.*"

She would take Alna something special. Inanna remembered how Lilith had made her dolls out of wool with acorns for eyes. What other toys had she had as a child? She seemed to remember a miniature spindle and carding comb that fit into the palm of her hand. And then there was the little stone hatchet she had been given to break up firewood. Enshagag hadn't believed children should waste time playing.

"Good morning, *Joyta*." The toymaker was an old man, so bent at the waist he could hardly lift his head to look Inanna in the face. As he spread his wares out on the table, he made constant clucking sounds as if each toy were a surprise to him too.

Tiny oxen, boats the size of cups, pigs and birds made of baked clay, colored marbles, a whistle, a hoop, a drum inlaid with cowrie shells and brightly polished stones. Inanna looked through the toys for a long time and finally settled on a clay bird with wings made out of real feathers, even though Alna would pull them off in a minute.

"A good choice, *muna*," the old man said happily.

Inanna stamped her signature seal into the wet clay tablet he held out to her, and sent him off to the palace storerooms to get his quarter measure of grain in payment.

It was still cool when she hurried along the halls, and up the stairs that led to Alna's rooms. Flowers in clay pots in the balconies, servants singing as they washed out clothes in the back courtyards: a fine day. Maybe the heat had broken at last. She found herself looking forward to the winter rains. And then she saw the nurse standing outside Alna's door, her usually florid face white as a bone.

"We were just about to send for you, *muna*." Behind the nurse everything was in confusion. Servants were running in and out with bowls of broth and cold water.

"Send for me?"

The nurse studied her hands, avoiding Inanna's eyes. Her voice was slow, full of fear. "The child isn't feeling well, that is . . ."

Alna was sick. The fools, why hadn't they sent for her sooner? Inanna pushed past the nurse. The child was lying curled up on her cot, her cheeks flushed with fever. Hot dry skin, sores around her mouth, and her breath heavy, laboring like a bellows. Inanna heard that breath, and something caught at the base of her own throat.

"How long has she been sick?" Anger in her voice, fear.

The nurse folded and unfolded her thick fingers, and stared at Inanna with undisguised terror. "Only a little while, *muna*. Only a little while. I'd just come in to get her up for her morning bath when I heard her choking and by the time I got to her bed she was all . . . stiff and blue. But now . . ." The nurse pointed to Alna as if trying to convince Inanna there was no cause for alarm. "She's not blue anymore, as you can see."

In a jar by the cot black specks floated on the surface of the water. "Did you give her this to drink?"

"Yes."

"Where's it from?"

"I don't know. From the river, I suppose."

"Who brought it?"

"An old man, *muna*. A stranger. He said our regular water bearer was sick."

Inanna knocked over the jar and it broke, spattering water on the hem of her robe. The water was muddy and had a foul smell. "How could you feed that dirt to my child!"

"But it looked clean, *muna*."

Alna stirred and began to cry irritably. The river fever, the *Death*, the Queen had called it. *Everybody lost somebody. You can't imagine . . . Mothers crying over their dead children . . . the funeral fires burned for weeks.*

Inanna grabbed Alna's hand and held it to her own cheek. It was so hot! She felt the panic rising, threatening to drown her.

"Get out!" she yelled at the nurse. The woman fled from the room. Inanna picked up Alna and cradled her in her arms. "Hush, baby, don't cry." The child's sobbing stopped, and she grew calmer. I can't let myself panic, Inanna thought. I have to think. Maybe she doesn't have the river fever at all. It could be a spell, some kind of curse like Rheti put on the Queen. She reached into her pocket and felt the changing stone. How much power do I have? Enough to save my own daughter?

Laying Alna back on the cot, she put the palm of her hand on the child's forehead. "Let me know what's wrong with my child," she prayed—although to which god she couldn't have said. And then she closed her eyes and thought of nothing . . .

When Inanna opened her eyes, she knew that Alna had the river fever and was going to die.

She couldn't accept it. She thought of Enkimdu, how sick he had been from the wounds the savages had given him. Enkimdu had been on the edge of death too, but she'd brought him back, kept him alive. How had she done it?

She remembered the blue flowers.

In the outer room the nurse was sitting on a bench looking dolefully at the floor. When she saw Inanna, she jumped to her feet.

"Keep the child covered," Inanna commanded, "and if she asks for water, give her *clean* water. Do you hear me?" She was almost out of the door, already thinking of the halls and stairs that separated her from her own rooms. How long would it take to get there and back?

"Yes, *muna*." The nurse, Inanna realized, was well-meaning but stupid.

"If you forget," she warned, "I swear I'll have you thrown in the river."

The nurse turned pale and bowed. "I love that child as my own."

Inanna felt ashamed for threatening her. "Take care of Alna, please," she said in a softer voice.

The old nurse shook her head. "May Lanla give her health again, poor thing," she said gravely. But her face said that she doubted it was possible.

Leather bag, rawhide knots shrunken by years of wet winters. Inanna cursed and tried to use her teeth on the drawstrings. Everything inside could be rotten. Picking up a copper knife from the table, she slashed impatiently at the rawhide. The bag spilled open and packets of herbs tumbled onto the floor. Rosemary, juniper berries, dried roots, strings of lily fruits. Inanna noticed that some of them were moldy, and she breathed a prayer that not everything in the bag had spoiled. Where were those flowers?

Near the bottom, under a bunch of mallow stems, she found what she had been looking for: a small straw pack filled with dry petals. The petals had faded but she could still see the blue in them. Great Goddess, there was so little of the stuff! She shook the petals out of the packet and they barely covered the palm of her hand. Why hadn't she picked more, filled up her whole bag when she had the chance? She'd never be able to find the place where those flowers grew, even if the Queen gave her an armed escort to get her past the nomads. They were rare; in all the time she'd spent gathering plants, she'd never seen others like them. Too late now for regrets. There had to be enough here to break Alna's fever. And if she herself got sick . . .

Inanna pushed the thought aside, poured the petals back into the straw packet, and hurried out of the door. She found the nurse fanning the sick child with a palm branch.

"How is she?"

"She woke and cried for you a little while ago."

"Bring me a brazier and a bowl." Tea, pale and thin, the color of new grass. What a weak thing it was to set against fever. Inanna dipped the hem of her robe in it and began to feed it to Alna drop by drop. The little girl's lips were blistered, and she turned her head aside, refusing to swallow.

"Hurts, Mama," she said.

Inanna stroked Alna's hair and tried to force herself to speak calmly. "Drink just a little of it, please."

"No," Alna said firmly, and Inanna recognized her own stubbornness in the child's voice. She remembered the toy she had brought that morning, still in her pocket.

"Look here, Alna." The little girl's face lit up with pleasure as she saw the bird, and she tried to reach for it.

"Drink a little of the tea and I'll give it to you." And I'll give you anything else you want too, Inanna thought, only please help me keep you alive.

"Give me."

"After you drink your tea." Alna opened her mouth, sucked up some of the liquid, and swallowed. "Just a little more." The tea was nearly gone now. Inanna placed the clay bird in Alna's hand and the child examined it closely.

"I like real birds better, Mama, but this is pretty." She smiled at Inanna, her eyes bright with fever. "Can I have a real bird someday?"

"Yes, as soon as you're well."

"Good. I'd like that. Real birds' wings don't come off, do they?"

"No," Inanna said, "they don't."

Each day Inanna watched helplessly as the fever took the child farther and farther away. Alna was like someone going out on a boat; her features seemed to change, blur as if a great distance separated her from the rest of the world, and when she spoke it was in incoherent fragments, to people whom no one else could see. When Inanna looked at that thin, yellow old-woman's face, she felt a strange tearing sensation in her breast. How could one small body stand so much pain? She began to think of things she had never considered before: that death might be a sort of kindness, that life itself was mysterious, painful, terribly short.

In the outer rooms presents from the Queen piled up against the wall untouched: baskets of grapes, lemons, melons, jugs of spiced applejuice, branches of fresh dates, rugs, pillows, a whole set of dishes with tiny birds painted on the rims. Each morning and evening, the old woman sent a messenger to ask one question: "How is my granddaughter?"

"Dying," the nurse said flatly on the worst day of all, the day Alna began to choke on her own tongue.

Inanna turned on the nurse in a rage. "Don't ever say that!" She dipped a piece of clean linen into the tea bowl and forced some of the liquid between the child's lips. So few of the blue flowers were left. "Tell the Queen that her granddaughter is getting better, that she'll soon be well."

"As you wish, *muna,*" the messenger said.

Inanna felt the exhaustion dragging her down like stone sandals. For five days she hadn't had any sleep, and still Alna did nothing but slip deeper and deeper into the fever. "No, don't tell the Queen she's getting well," she said. "Just tell her we're doing all we can."

Night came and the lamps burned smoky and low. The air in the sickroom was musty, and Alna's breath began to rasp in her throat. She turned restlessly, throwing off the light cover, and then fell into a heavy, unhealthy sleep, one arm dangling over the side of the cot. This night would probably decide things one way or another; there was nothing more anyone could do.

"You should get some sleep yourself," the nurse said, "or you'll be sick too."

"I can't leave her."

"Then let me make you a bed on the floor." The nurse piled up the rugs, and Inanna stretched out on them gratefully.

"For years I slept on rugs on the ground," she said, "in a tent."

"You did?"

Inanna closed her eyes and lay back. "Have you ever slept under the stars?" she asked after a while. But the nurse had already left the room and there was no answer.

Sleep. Quiet, cool, dreamless.

"Mama!" The voice cut through her sleep, and she was on her feet before she was fully awake. "Mama!"

"Alna?"

The child was sitting up with frightened eyes. "I dreamed you were gone."

"No, sweetheart, I'm right here." She touched the little girl's forehead, and it was cool and damp. Had the fever broken at last? Inanna looked in Alna's eyes and they were clear.

"Mama, make more light," Alna said sensibly. "I don't like it so dark."

Inanna pulled up the wicks on all the lamps and lit them. Then she took Alna in her arms and held her tightly. "You're going to be all right."

Alna put her thumb in her mouth, closed her eyes, and curled closer to her mother. "Do I get a real bird then?" she asked sleepily.

Inanna saw that no time had passed for the child; the five days of fever hadn't even existed. "Yes, you can have a real bird."

By the end of the Dry River Moon, Alna was well enough to run across the palace courtyards with the other children. Inanna would watch them playing, and for a little while she would feel perfectly happy. But at night, when she slept and the children were no longer there, she sometimes had strange dreams. She would find herself poling a boat down a low river, picking up dead fish and putting them in sacks. The fish stank terribly, and the more she picked up, the more there were. I have to hurry, she would think in her dream. And then her boat would begin to sink under the weight of the sacks, and she would know that she had failed—although in the morning she could never remember how she had failed or why.

11 ALNA'S grandmother was dying. Everyone had thought she was getting well again, and now she was dying. Well, Alna thought, that must be the way it was with people who were so terribly old: they just broke like toys and stopped. She had had a top once and the string had come off.

Maybe it was like that for her grandmother. Only it sounded almost funny when you said it that way, and Alna knew that this was no time to think funny things, not when all the grown-ups were going around with long faces, walking so quietly that they came up behind you before you even heard them.

Besides, she would really miss her grandmother, who had always held her on her lap and given her sweetened pomegranate juice. Her nurse, Lagsha, never gave her pomegranates because she said that they stained too much, but grandmother was different. She had told Alna all sorts of stories too, about when she was a little girl—good stories about a frog that hopped across the river (which couldn't really be true, of course) and a magic stone that changed everything that touched it.

"What would you be if you could be any animal you wanted?" her grandmother had asked once, and Alna had said that she would like to be a bird with big wings. "I'd fly up high where no one could catch me, and then I'd go back to the mountains where Mama says we really belong." Then seeing the sadness on her grandmother's face and not understanding it, she had added: "but sometimes I'd come back to visit you." Her grandmother had laughed then, hugged her, and they had both drunk pomegranate juice together until their tongues turned pink. But now grandmother was breaking like a toy, and Lagsha had said Alna might never get to see her again.

Mama had acted so strange this morning when the messenger came with the news. She'd turned all funny-looking, and grabbed Alna, and then let her go, and then grabbed her again, until Alna was so frightened that she'd started to cry. Then Mama had run out of the room, knocking over the best lamp on the way, and the lamp had crashed to the floor, and oil had spilled everywhere. Alna had expected Lagsha to get angry at that, but she hadn't. Lagsha'd mopped up the oil in the oddest way, as if she were listening for something all the time, and when she was done there were still big slick spots on the tiles, which wasn't at all like Lagsha, who usually got mad if you even had a grass stain on your robe.

So what were they afraid of? She loved her mama better than anyone in the world, but she didn't know why she did the things she did. Yes, grandmother was dying, but why break the lamp?

It was quiet this morning, so quiet that something seemed to be wrong. On the floor the oil stains made little rainbows in the sunlight, but Alna tried not to look at them. Every time she did, she wondered if maybe old people weren't the only ones who broke. Maybe other people did too. If Lagsha died, who would clean up the rest of the oil? Who would bring her breakfast tomorrow?

Could Mama die? Could everyone?

What would happen to her then? If she were the only one left? If she were all alone?

The Queen lay on her bed, curled on her side like an old baby, her swollen hands clasped around her knees. Her face seemed to have collapsed, fallen away like the side of a cliff. The room smelled musty, sweet, the way Alna's room had smelled. Fever and death, Inanna thought. I can't go through this again. Not so soon.

"She is very sick, *Joyta*, yes?" The two priestesses stood on either side of the Queen's bed, their bare arms round and soft as fish bladders. Green light filtering in through the linen shades, an underwater scene. Inanna remembered her bad dreams, the low river and the sacks of dead fish. The priestesses were looking at her as if they expected her to perform a miracle. Inanna put her hand on the Queen's wrist. The old woman stirred slightly and moaned. There were white blisters on her lips and tongue, the size of millet grains.

"How long has she been lost to the waking world?" she asked one of the priestesses. The woman patted down the edge of the embroidered sheet nervously.

"She's only asleep, *Joyta*."

"No," Inanna said, lifting the Queen's eyelid and examining the yellowness, "she's not asleep. You understand?"

The priestess peered over Inanna's shoulder at the Queen, and then stepped back quickly as if trying to take up as little space as possible. Inanna slid her hand to the sick woman's throat and felt for her pulse. Fast, sharp, a small animal clawing its way out of a trap, a chick pecking through the shell of her skin. Inanna felt pity and then fear. The Queen was dying, there was no doubt about it; she was old, weak, and Alna's pulse had never been that fast, not even when she was at her worst. But the Queen had been nowhere near the child, so if she had the river fever, then that meant soon everyone else would be getting it too. *The funeral fires burned for weeks. . . . You can't imagine . . .*

"*Joyta.*" The pair of priestesses still looked at her hopefully. The older of the two cleared her throat and folded her heavy arms across her breasts. Her skin was splattered with pale freckles and a mole on her upper lip bobbed up and down distractingly as she talked. "We were told," the priestess said hesitantly, "that you know of a cure for the fever. Some kind of tea—that when your daughter was sick you made her well again with something you brought from over there." A fat white arm waving in the direction of the mountains. "So now that the Queen has fallen ill, perhaps . . . ?" She stopped and let the last half of her question hang on the air unspoken. Inanna saw that the priestess too was afraid.

The Queen moaned and turned restlessly. Yellow face, breath coming in gasps like a bellows. She's been kind to me, Inanna thought, and I've grown to love her even though she's got a tongue sharp as a spearhead. She's Enkimdu's mother, Alna's grandmother. But how many of the blue flowers are left? Half a packet? Less? Suppose Alna gets sick again, or I do. She touched the old woman's skin, feeling the heat of it, looked at her swollen hands and feet. Already dying even before the fever, even if by some miracle I cure her, how long will she live? Why take her out of one death into another?

In the brazier the charcoal flared, casting shadows on the walls. The heavy drapes hung motionless at the windows, and the only sound was the rasp of the sick woman's breathing.

Inanna found the two priestesses still waiting for her answer. "I can't do anything." Blue flowers, less than a handful left, and Alna might get sick. She forced herself to continue. "The remedy comes from the far side of the mountains, and it's all been used up." She felt horrible as she said the words, as if she'd just condemned the Queen to death. She took the old woman's limp hand in hers. I'm sorry, she thought. Please forgive me. You understand, it's for the child.

"Nothing left?" the older priestess persisted.

"Nothing." Inanna turned away and let the Queen's hand fall back on her breast. She examined the old woman's face for a moment. There was no calm there, no peace, no forgiveness either.

The older priestess pulled the sheet around the Queen's shoulders and shook her head sadly. "Then the old Queen must die."

The younger priestess picked up a palm leaf fan and stood with it in her hand as if she didn't know what to do. Outside a dog barked, then stopped as if someone had silenced it. Inanna noticed how quiet the palace was. As if they were all waiting. She imagined that if death had a face it would be like the arms of these priestesses—without eyes or a nose, soft and round as bread dough.

"Alna, we're going on a trip."

"Yes, Mama."

"Put on your warm robe and your sandals. We're going to live outside for a while. Would you like that?"

"In a black tent like you told me about? With goats?"

"No tent or goats. Just you and me. We'll sleep under the stars and keep each other warm at night."

"Can I take my bird?"

"No, but we'll get you another one as soon as we can."

"Mama, why are you running? I can't keep up."

"Here, let me carry you." Empty silent halls, and suddenly a wailing like the howl of a wild animal. Inanna heard footsteps before she saw the woman, robe torn, hair and cheeks smeared with ochre, eyes already wild with the fever.

"The Queen is dead! Have you heard? The Queen is dead!" The woman threw her arms over her head and began to wail in a high-pitched voice. She stumbled forward, blocking the passage.

"Get out of my way!" Inanna commanded. The sick woman leaned against the wall and stared at them dully, her wail dying in her throat. On her lips were tiny white blisters, and her skin was the color of melon rind.

"I don't feel well," she whispered. She reached out to steady herself, and stumbled forward into Inanna. "Please," she begged, plucking at Inanna's sleeve, "please help me." Hot fingers, hands full of sickness.

"Get back!" Inanna gave a push and the woman slumped and fell to the floor in a sitting position. She looked around as if she didn't know where she was.

"I want to go swimming," she said almost sweetly. "It's so hot in here. Take me down to the river." She vomited and some of it splattered on the hem of Inanna's robe. Inanna picked up the child and ran.

A courtyard, a hall, another courtyard, and then the main gate:

Inanna put Alna down and stopped to catch her breath. Outside the walls of the palace voices took up the cry that the Queen was dead. The courtyard itself was deserted. A dog lay in a patch of shade near one of the date palms, and the tiles were littered with broken crockery and mud. A bright red pillow sat incongruously on a heap of straw; a spear lay on the ground as if someone had just thrown it down. Where were the servants? the guards?

The heavy wooden bar that spanned the gates was thick as a man's body, two arms wide. She could never move the thing! They'd have to try to get to the small gate, the one she used when she went to the barracks. It was on the other side of the palace, near the kitchen, but the cross-bar was light, and if she had to, she could lift it alone

A woman in a yellow robe stepped out onto one of the upper terraces and began to throw things aimlessly into the courtyard below: bedding, clothes, a stool, pots of face paint. She looked like one of the Queen's Companions, but from this distance it was hard to tell.

In the hallway the sick woman lay sideways, still blocking the way. Her eyes were closed, and Inanna couldn't tell if she was breathing or not. Flies had gathered on her face and on the pool of vomit. Inanna felt sick. She should move her out of the way, but she couldn't bring herself to touch the body. One fly began to crawl lazily up the woman's right nostril. Picking up Alna, Inanna ran choking and gagging down the stairs that led to the basement storerooms. Putting her forehead against one of the great jars of wheat, she tried to steady herself.

"Are you all right, Mama?" Alna was tugging at her robe.

"Yes, I'm fine. I'll be fine." She waited until the nausea passed. The storeroom was cool and smelled of spices and dried onions. Wineskins hung from hooks and jars full of nuts and lentils were stacked along one wall. She tried to force herself to smile for the child's sake.

"Don't be frightened."

"I'll try, but it's all dark."

"Take my hand." Light came in through narrow slits high up near the ceiling. Shadows and dust, strange smells. The store-rooms led into one another like cells in a honeycomb. Piles of spears, scythes, winnowing screens—how easy it would be to get lost. Broken furniture, jars with cracked spouts, a few of the

Queen's statues covered with dust sitting abandoned in the corners. And finally cooking pots, sacks of charcoal.

"We're almost there." Inanna squeezed Alna's hand reassuringly at the sight of the charcoal. They must be under the kitchen by now. Soon they'd be coming to the stairs that led up to the side gate. Over the entrance to the next storeroom hung a curtain. Strange: it seemed to be made of new material, and it was fastened to the wall with wooden pins. What was so important that someone would take that much trouble to close one room off from the rest?

Inanna tugged at the curtain, and it fell in a heap at her feet. For a moment she stood in the doorway, not understanding. Then she screamed, grabbed Alna, and covered the child's eyes.

"Don't look!"

Arms, legs. Bodies piled up like firewood, some of them half-decayed. Sightless eyes stared back at her, and somewhere in the dark there was the soft scuttling sound of rats. Yellow skin, tiny white blisters on their lips the size of millet grains: no doubt how they'd all died. How long had the plague been in the palace? How long had the old Queen tried to keep it a secret?

On the other side of the storeroom a flight of narrow steps led up to the gate. A thin beam of sunlight fell on the wall from a patch of blue sky no bigger than her thumbnail. Inanna took off her cloak, threw it quickly over the little girl's head, picked her up, and carried her past the dead and up the stairs. In front of them only a few steps away the gate was hidden by wild roses and trumpet vines. Inanna snatched the cloak off Alna and kissed her fiercely. There were so many things she never wanted the child to know or see.

"Are we there, Mama?"

"Yes, we're there." The bar on the gate moved easily, and the doors swung open revealing an empty street. Soon they'd be out of the city. There were olive trees outside, berry bushes along the ditches. Food would be no problem; they . . .

"Good morning, *muna*," a voice said, "I've been waiting for you." Rheti's eunuch stood against the wall beside the gate holding a small tasseled umbrella over his head. He was eating a slice of melon, spitting the seeds neatly into the palm of his hand. "I have a message to give you from the High Priestess." He bowed and smiled. "Why, what a pretty child. Is she yours?"

Inanna pulled Alna behind her. "Get out of here." She took a step forward, and the eunuch put his umbrella between them as if it were a shield. She struck out at the thing, feeling ridiculous.

"The High Priestess says thus . . ."

"I don't want to hear what she has to say."

"Tell the former Joyta, *Inanna of Kur, that I congratulate her on becoming Queen by doing nothing just as I predicted, and tell her that now . . ."*

"Let me by!"

Bony fingers caught at her sleeve. "There's more, *muna*."

"I won't hear it, I tell you!" She tried to shake him off, but he clung to her, weaving his bony arms through hers.

"The High Priestess says . . ." She pushed at him, breaking his grip, but he caught her again. *"Muna.* Listen, *muna*." For a long time afterwards she remembered that painted face inches from her own, those hands reaching out to touch Alna. The child shrank back and began to cry.

"What's going on here?" Seb strode down the street in full armor, his head lowered like an angry bull. Grabbing the eunuch by the neck of his robe, he pulled him away from Inanna. "What were you doing, curse you!" The eunuch opened his mouth, but no sound came out.

"He was bringing me a message from Rheti." Inanna knelt, took Alna in her arms, and tried to hush her crying. Seb's face darkened at the sound of Rheti's name.

"I was going to find you," he said to Inanna, "because I thought you might be in trouble, and it looks as if I was right. Are you hurt?" The look in Seb's eyes said he'd like nothing better than to throw the eunuch in the nearest cistern if he'd done any harm.

Inanna shook her head. "Not really."

Seb dropped the eunuch in a heap. The old man got up, retrieved his umbrella, and hurried away muttering to himself. Seb straightened his helmet and picked up his spear. "I don't think he'll be bothering you anymore."

"No, I suppose not." The melon rind lying in the dust had already attracted a few flies. The sight of them made Inanna shudder. Picking up Alna, she started down the street. There was no time to lose.

"Where are you going?"

"I'm taking Alna out of here." Another street, smaller, leading toward the main gate. Inanna tried to remember how long it took to get out of the city when you went by the back ways.

"But you can't leave." There was genuine surprise in Seb's voice. "You're the Queen."

"I don't care; let someone else be Queen." She and Alna would live in the fields, even go back to the mountains if they had to. High meadows, stands of cypress trees, no river fever there. The thought crossed her mind that Seb was going to die along with the others.

"Seb." She reached out and touched him gently on the arm. "Come with us, please. You can't stay here."

"No!" He grabbed her by the shoulders, forcing her to stop. "You can't leave. Do you hear me?"

"Let go of me."

"Don't you understand?" He stumbled over the words, producing them painfully one by one as if they were being cut out of him. "Rheti . . . you leave and she'll be . . . Queen. How many children like Alna do you think it will take to satisfy that . . . that Hut of hers? Twenty? A hundred?"

"Seb, stop it!" But he only held her tighter, compelling her to listen.

"If you go, who'll keep order? And who'll give out the food . . . and see that the seed grain doesn't get eaten? You're the Queen! You can't leave."

"I thought you cared about me and Alna. What kind of friend are you?"

"I do care about you, I . . . ." There was pain in his face, confusion. His grip slackened a little.

"No you don't. You want us to stay here and die."

"No, I don't. I mean yes, you have to stay. Please." She saw that he still loved her, that he was pleading with her, but she was too angry to care.

"You can't tell me what to do!"

Seb looked at her with a kind of hopeless passion that made her feel almost ashamed. Releasing her suddenly, he turned away. "You're right." His voice was full of defeat. "Do what you want. Go if you want to. I won't try to stop you." He leaned against the wall and stared at her wearily.

Inanna thought of the eunuch's painted face, the room under the temple, Rheti wrapping her evil around the city. But what about Alna? What about her? Had Seb seen the fever yet—what it did to people? A room full of the dead, blisters on their lips.

Rheti the Queen. Twenty children. A hundred. Alna's dirt-streaked face. How do you make a choice when death has you boxed in like a goat in a corral? Inanna put her hand in her pocket, clasped the changing stone, and closed her eyes. She was beginning to feel foolish when suddenly something shoved her and she fell to the ground, and when she rose to her feet, she was no longer in the city; she was back in the camp of Kur and Lilith was in her arms.

Pulal stood over them swinging his axe. The copper blade glinted in the sunlight. In a moment he would bring it down and the nightmare would start all over again. Lilith trembled; Inanna could smell the apricot oil in her hair. "Get back!" Pulal yelled, lifting his axe. The scar on his face was dead white, twisting over his cheekbone. Inanna glared at him with her wolf eyes. "I won't let him hurt you," she promised Lilith. "This time I'll fight him to the end."

And as she said the words, Lilith's body dissolved in her arms and became the city, and she found herself embracing it: walls, streets, people, down to the last drop of blood, the last stone. The vision shifted and the city changed into Alna, and Inanna saw that the child and Lilith and the city were the same, that everything was connected, that there was only one battle to be fought.

"Mama?" The real Alna was tugging at her sleeve anxiously. "Are you asleep, Mama?"

"No, I'm not alseep." She ran her hand over the child's hair. How calm she felt, empty and clean as a new jar. There was courage in her of a kind she'd never felt before. She picked up Alna and held her out to Seb. "Get her out of the city, and when the fever's over, if I'm still alive, bring her back to me."

"You mean you're staying?"

"Yes."

The blood rushed to Seb's face and he seemed about to say something more, but instead he took Alna without a word. The child put her arms around his neck and snuggled comfortably against his chest. Seb walked away down the street.

"Seb!" He stopped and took a few steps back in her direction. The red plume of his helmet danced in the breeze. How strong he was, how fine. Alna would be safe.

"What is it?" Seb asked.

"Find a pet bird for her if you can." She touched Alna's hair and kissed her on the forehead.

"Don't worry about her. I've got a cousin in one of the villages up the river. No one ever comes there." Seb drew her to him and kissed her quickly. "I'll be back," he promised.

Through the gate, up the stairs, past the kitchen where a fire burned untended and joints of meat lay on the tables where the fleeing cooks had left them. In the passageway to the Great Hall Inanna at last came across someone else: a palace guard, curled up, already shaking with the fever. She recognized the man as someone she had sparred with in the practice yard at the beginning of the Dry River Moon before Alna got sick. His name was Rel.

"*Muna*," Rel said. His skin was already yellow, and white blisters covered his lips like the eunuch's paint. There was fear and pain in his eyes, and his big hands trembled like the hands of an old man. "Water please." Anyone could see he was already past saving. But what did that matter? Kneeling down, Inanna uncorked her wineskin, lifted the sick man's head, and gave him a drink. Rel lapped at the water greedily, and when he was finished he lay back and closed his eyes.

Inanna stood over him a while, wondering how much longer he would last. She thought of the days to come, the funeral fires that would soon be burning along the river. Maybe she would envy him.

Her sandals clicked against the tiles of the deserted Great Hall as she walked toward the throne stool. So now she was the Queen. She sat down and looked out over the empty room.

What was there left to be Queen of?

12 THE Moon of the First Rains, only no rains came. The river was a rotten green thread; snowflakes of salt as big as a man's hand lay in the fields, killing everything they touched; the water tasted foul; there were no fish left to die.

How do you describe a great plague? Do you say that it's like a journey in which many people start out on the trail with you and only a few arrive? Do you say it's like a nightmare in which waking is the worst part? Houses were deserted; roofs fell in and no one bothered to repair them. Along the riverbanks the funeral fires burned day and night, and the walls of the city were soon coated with a film of gray ash.

Later she would look back on it as an oddly peaceful time. The merchants had closed their stalls, and the country people no longer came in through the gates. Most of the traders had moved on to the north, and even thieves and robbers seemed to be too ill to commit their usual crimes. A strange silence settled over everything, broken only by an occasional death wail. In the marketplace grass began to grow in the street, and flowers appeared in unexpected places.

But what she remembered most about those days was the smell of death, heavy, sickly sweet like rotten cabbage. As the bodies piled up, those who could still walk hurried through the streets with scraps of scented cloth tied over their noses and mouths. The smell was everywhere. Even scrubbing the Great Hall with pitch and pennyroyal, and scattering fresh flowers on the floor failed to mask it. When Inanna went up to the Queen's Aerie, the smell followed her, and when she sat down to eat she imagined she could taste the stench in her food.

Blue sky, sun so bright it made her eyes water. Each morning she stood at her balcony and watched the crops parching in the fields. The heads of the wheat shrank and withered; the kernels crumbled into dust between her fingers. Plague and now—soon—famine too. Inanna gazed at the burned wheat, and a great sense of helplessness came over her. Was there really a time when she had sat down to dinner knowing that she'd be alive to see the next day? Had there really been afternoons when she and Alna had gone berry picking along the canals, and then come home and taken a bath together in the big tiled tub without thinking about anything but their sunburns and mosquito bites?

Alna. Sometimes the thought of her seemed worse than the plague itself. Inanna didn't dare send messengers for fear they'd take the sickness with them, so she had no way of knowing if Alna was still well. Had she caught the fever? Inanna worried about the child constantly. She tried to tell herself that there was nothing to be afraid of, that the plague hadn't reached the remote villages, that Seb could be relied on. But often she woke in the middle of the night sure she had heard Alna calling. Then she lay for hours imagining the most unlikely disasters: a bad fall, a scythe left out where a small child could step on the blade, and always the fever itself, the yellow skin, the white blisters on Alna's lips. Sometimes she fell asleep again and dreamed of a great field of blue flowers, and Alna running toward her with a bouquet of them in her hands.

The morning after such a dream, Inanna rose with the feeling things would work out after all. She would wonder why she worried so much about Alna, and if all mothers were as foolish. The day would seem fresh and clear, and she would get up full of energy, eat breakfast, dress herself in the Queen's robes, and go down to the Great Hall to conduct the business of the city, thinking: perhaps today things will be different.

But things never were. Often she sat on the throne stool for an entire morning without receiving a single petition. The sun beat in through the lattices, drying the flowers on the floor, filling the air with dust, while outside the funeral fires burned and the death wails went on. Why am I here? Inanna would ask herself. And then she would see the frightened faces of the people and know: she was there to give them hope. She was their Queen. The word would take on a new meaning for her, and she would feel tied as if a great pack had been strapped onto her back.

At the foot of the throne stool, the old Queen's Companions stood in a half circle, fanning themselves with palm branches, their faces covered with sweat. How old they all looked, how fragile. Their gray hair was like dust, and Inanna imagined their red robes as flames, dying out one by one. Soon there would be none of the old order left.

The idea made her feel unaccountably bad, and for the first time she realized how much she missed the old Queen. Could she have saved her? She would put the thought out of her mind, tell herself that she'd had no choice. But always the love, pain, and guilt would be there, mixed up together.

"You need to pick new Companions," Lyra suggested one morning, "ones your own age."

"No," Inanna told her, "not yet."

But the next day Lyra brought a hundred and twenty of the strongest women in the city to the Great Hall and presented them to her. The women all wore short tunics and their hair had been oiled and tied back so Inanna could see the freshness and health in their faces. They were like something out of another, happier time. The muscles in their arms were taut, their legs strong, their breasts firm. Their eyes were sober and calm, and they looked back levelly, unafraid. Lyra had chosen well. For a moment Inanna forgot about the plague and the burden of being Queen, imagining instead the army she might build someday. These women could be the core of it. She imagined them in full armor, fighting beside her against Pulal.

"Pick out the sixty you want," Lyra said, nodding toward the women.

"I'll take all of them." Inanna put her hand on Lyra's shoulder. "Teach them to fight."

"That's what I like to hear," Lyra smiled.

By the end of the Moon of the First Rains, the original hundred and twenty was down to ninety-seven, but all in all—given the times—the new Companions lasted well.

Things grew worse.
"Who are you?"
"The Queen."

The sick woman laughed and then began to cry. Fever made people do strange things. She was a blacksmith; you could see it in her arms, knotted muscles, wrists like tree limbs. The small room was littered with the tools of her trade: a straw fan, a special jar to catch the melting copper, a stone grate for the charcoal. The round walls were black with smoke, and a few flies buzzed lazily along the dome of the ceiling. A poor room. In the tribe of Kur there hadn't been such great differences between people. Some had had more goats, others a few more baskets of nuts, but everyone had had something. Here there were those who had almost nothing at all. How long it had taken her to find that out.

The sick woman reached up with one hand and touched the folds of Inanna's robe, feeling the weight and luxury of it. Her fingers were thick and calloused, and the skin under the nails was already yellow. "What would the Queen be doing here?" she asked. Inanna considered telling her the truth: that she was finally tired of watching everyone die, that sitting in an empty hall hadn't suited her. But she knew that the woman wouldn't understand. No one had, not even Lyra. When she'd announced that she was going to start visiting the sick, Lyra had thought she'd gone mad.

"I was a healer before, back in my own tribe," Inanna had insisted.

"But you'll catch the fever."

"I'll probably catch it anyway."

"But you're the Queen," Lyra had said stubbornly. "If you die, who'll rule the city?"

"Does it matter? If someone doesn't do something soon, there won't be any city left to rule. Hand me that leather bag."

"What's in it?"

"Herbs, medicines, all sorts of things."

"You should be praying to the Goddesses, asking them to help us. That's what the Queen does."

"Not this Queen."

In the small hot room, the sick woman began to talk loudly, accusing Inanna of being her mother in disguise. But Inanna knew the real mother had died only yesterday, along with an uncle and a brother. It had taken three of the Queen's Companions to carry the bodies to the funeral fires. The mother had been a big woman with broad shoulders and a gruff voice.

"Mother . . ." the sick woman coughed and tried to sit up.

"Be still." Inanna took some osier bark out of her bag, chewed it into a paste, and put it on the blistered lips, knowing that at the very best it would only buy the woman a little time.

"You can't make me eat that stuff." It was a childish voice, the voice of a little girl. The sick often traveled backward in time near the end; she had seen it happen again and again. The sick woman spat and began to claw at her face, breaking the blisters.

Inanna grabbed her hands and held them still. The sickness coiled inside the woman like a hank of wet rope. Each time the fever felt different: sometimes she sensed it as a bitter taste in the back of her own mouth, sometimes as a pain in her arms and chest. Sometimes when she touched the hands of the dying, she saw vast panoramas, things she could hardly understand: whole mountain ranges exploding, great forest fires raging out of control, whirlwinds sweeping up entire cities.

Is the land of the dead a place of constant disaster too? Could it be so much like life?

Along the river the funeral fires crackled and blazed. At night as Inanna lay in the old Queen's bed, she dreamed of them: of flesh falling from the bones, blackened and shriveled, of the sightless eyes of her people looking at her accusingly. Why couldn't you save us? Why did you let us die? Then she would dream she lay down beside them on the fires and gave up. The flames would lick at her spine and the back of her neck; her body would turn into a fine white ash. *Snow,* she would think, and she would wake up shivering, covered with cold sweat.

But there were the good times too, the times when she touched a forehead or a hand and knew that the person could be saved. For a moment she would feel her healing power come back to her, and later, when she returned to that house, the fever would be gone from it. And because one or two recovered after she touched them, strange rumors grew up about her: that the Queen could cure anyone, that she could even bring the dead back to life. But Inanna knew the truth: the dead stayed dead.

"People are saying you've got divine powers," Lyra had told her only yesterday. "They're saying you're Lanla come back to them."

"Well, they're wrong."

"They say you heal the sick by your touch."

"Only a few, and those probably would have lived anyway."

"Are you a Goddess?"

"What do you think?"

"I think that if you keep going out of the palace at all hours you're going to get sick. Do you know what kind of mess things are going to be in around here when you die?" She had put her hand on Inanna's shoulder and looked at her with love and concern. "Slow down at least; get some sleep. You've lost weight. I'm worried about you."

"But there are so many sick . . ."

"Is killing yourself going to make them well?" Lyra had handed Inanna a clay tablet covered with lines, in rows like tent stakes. "Do you know how many bodies the Companions carried to the riverbank yesterday?" One scratch for each of the dead.

"So many?"

"And more to come. You can't stop the plague by yourself. No one could."

"When do you think it will end?"

"Maybe when the rains come."

The clouds drifted over the city and disappeared. In the Queen's Aerie the waterfall stopped flowing and the flowers began to die because there was no water to spare for them. Now when Inanna reached for the changing stone, she felt herself come up against a wall with nothing on the other side of it. Did that mean she was going to die before the plague was over, or was something resisting her, holding her back? Was she fighting a real enemy, or only herself?

In the tiny room the sick blacksmith curled on her side and closed her eyes. By morning she would be another body on the funeral fires. Her son, no doubt, would follow her in a day or so. On the ceiling the flies buzzed and circled endlessly, and outside the sky was hard and blue. The woman, her son: they were all leaving one by one. Like Alna, Inanna wondered what would happen if she were the only one left.

Two months later, at the end of the High River Moon, Inanna finally made peace with Rheti. But it wasn't the plague that drove her to it. It was her brother, Pulal.

"*Muna,* come look!" The servant ran into the room, cheeks pink with excitement, eyes sparkling. Inanna hadn't seen so much happiness on a human face in a long time.

"What is it?"

"A rain cloud."

Out on the balcony the stones were so hot they burned through the soles of her sandals. Blue sky, fields rutted with empty ditches, baked hard. "No, not that way, *muna,* over there!" Inanna turned to the east and saw the cloud, black and heavy with the promise of rain, big enough to fill up the river again. And then something moved inside her, a tiny thread of fear, a warning. Strange how that cloud seemed to be hugging the ground, moving across the delta instead of rising. A crawling cloud—there was something ominous about that, something unnatural. Suddenly she realized what it was: it wasn't the rain blackening the sky: it was the last of the harvest.

"It's smoke."

"What?"

"I said it's smoke. The fields are on fire." She went back inside and sat for a moment staring at the wall, unable to move. At least

Alna was safe. The village Seb had taken her to was on the other side of the delta, up the river. Outside the sky was taking on a peculiar reddish color, and the light that filtered in through the lattices was tinged with pink. Like wine or blood. Like bad luck that never came to an end. She sat for a while longer; finally she put on her robes, and went down to the Great Hall to wait for the first runner to arrive.

He came a little before dusk, a young boy with a bad shoulder wound, half-dead, out of breath, his face smeared with soot. When the boy was shown into the Great Hall, he fell down in front of the throne stool and lay there quaking, from exhaustion or perhaps fear. Inanna felt pity for the boy, for herself, for the whole city. She had a good idea what kind of news she was about to hear.

"Where are you from?"

"From the village of Shubur." The boy got to his knees, wiped his arm across his forehead, and stared uncertainly at the Queen's Companions in their armor.

"Don't be afraid. No one will hurt you. Now tell me what message you bring."

The boy met her glance gravely, opened his mouth, and broke into tears. "The savages burned everything." He wiped the tears away with his fists almost fiercely. He was so young, ten or eleven at the most, only a child really. "They fell on my mother and grandmother like dogs, copulated with them, and killed them. They killed all my uncles too and my baby sister. I saw them throw her against a wall and knock her brains out. My uncles and I tried to fight, but there were too many." The boy stopped crying. "The savages set our house and fields on fire and went away. I hid in a ditch until they were all gone, and afterwards I went back to the place where our house had been. My mother was still alive, but her skin was all burned off so you could see the bones and . . ." The boy stopped, and then finished quickly. "She told me to come here and tell the Queen what happened to our family."

"Your mother did well."

"She told me that I shouldn't forget to say that the savages had their women with them, children too. She said, 'tell the Queen that it wasn't just an ordinary raiding party.' "

"And what did these savages look like?"

"Short, ugly."

"Black hair?"

"No, red. They wore animal skins, and some of them had strings of teeth around their necks."

All night and the next day more runners arrived, each telling the same story: a family killed, houses and fields burned. The savages seemed to be coming out of the foothills in small groups, and most of the time the villages were able to fight them off. But the most interesting report came from an old man who arrived in a litter from a remote village called Kardam.

"I used to worship the Goddess with a savage woman for a while," the old man told Inanna. His face was pale with fatigue, and there was an owl-like look to his eyes, as if they'd seen too much.

"Why do you bother the Queen with this?" one of the Companions demanded. She looked at the old man with disgust.

The old man sighed patiently. "Because I learned a bit of their language, that's why," he said. "When we saw them heading for our village, my niece hid me in the loft under the straw, and later I heard some of the savages talking."

"And what did you hear?" Inanna asked.

"They were complaining that they'd been driven from their own lands by some other, bigger tribe who'd been killing them off like rabbits all summer, pushing them further and further west. They kept calling that other tribe the Black-Haired-Ones."

"The Black Headed People?"

The old man stared at Inanna with surprise. "Why, yes, it might be said that way too. The Black Headed People. And these savages said that their enemies were being led by a hyena with a scar on his jaw who smiled as he killed. They were worried about stopping in the delta because this hyena and his warriors were right behind them, and would probably be here by spring as far as they could figure."

After the old man left, Inanna went up to the Queen's Aerie and sat for a long time. White scar, hyena face, so by spring he'd be here. She closed her eyes and saw Pulal's smile as he brought his axe down on Lilith's neck, on Enkimdu's forehead.

Along the riverbank the funeral fires flickered in an endless procession. To the east the stars were blotted out by the smoke and the new moon rose blood-red in the sky, no bigger than a sliver. Plague, hunger, and now this. The city must be cursed. Inanna reached in her pocket for the changing stone, but nothing happened. It lay in her hand, heavy and cool—a rock and nothing more. What should she do? Where could she go for help? She'd need an army to fight Pulal.

All night she sat in the garden, until the stars disappeared and the sky began to turn a dirty gray. At dawn she went back down the stairs to her rooms, woke her servants, and told them to lay out her finest robes.

"Go to the temple and tell the High Priestess that I'm coming to see her." She saw the surprise in the guard's face as he saluted. "Tell Rheti I want to make peace."

13 IN the temple the incense rose up in front of the altars in long twisting spirals, and the lamps blinked dimly through the smoky air. A *lant* was waiting for Inanna beside the statue of Hut, a tall thin woman with kohl-rimmed eyes. "Welcome from the High Priestess, my Queen," the lant said, bowing with exaggerated politeness, and crossing her long pale hands over her breasts. There was something spidery about the woman that made Inanna uneasy, a hungry cunning glint in her eyes. The *lant* straightened up and began to move quickly across the sanctuary, past the healing bench and the offerings to Lanla. "We go this way, *muna*," she said.

"Not to the caves under the temple?"

"No, *muna*." The *lant* walked so rapidly that Inanna almost had to run to keep up with her. They hurried down a short corridor, across a deserted courtyard, and then—to her surprise—out onto the street.

"Where are we going?"

"To the High Priestess," the *lant* called back over her shoulder without breaking her stride. She disappeared around a corner and Inanna ran after her, feeling angry and foolish. The streets were so dark that she tripped over a loose stone and nearly fell. Curse Rheti for dragging her around in the middle of the night like this! What was the point? Inanna stopped for a moment to catch her breath, and realized that she was being separated from her guards. Was this some kind of trap? An ambush?

"*Muna!*" The *lant* was calling to her up ahead. Inanna put her hand on her knife and moved cautiously around the corner. The attack could come from anywhere. She wondered briefly how many Rheti would send against her and if she could hold them off long enough for help to arrive.

But there was no one around the corner but the *lant.* The street itself came to a dead end, butting up against the inner wall of the city. Crumbling bricks, a single jasmine vine dead from the drought, a gutter full of garbage—nothing more. The *lant* smiled and bowed. "The High Priestess said you should see this."

Inanna felt more confused than ever. "What are you talking about?"

"The gate."

"What gate?"

"The one in the wall, *muna.* The High Priestess said you'd need to use it yourself soon."

"I don't see any gate."

The *lant* touched a large stone and a whole section of the wall swung back without a sound. Inanna found herself looking at the riverbank outside the city. The *lant* smiled and brushed her hands together with a soft, slapping sound. "It's a secret gate, *muna.* You can only open it from the inside."

The river was low and murky, and the mosquitoes bit fiercely. As Inanna slapped at them, she wondered how many other things there were about the city that she didn't know. To the right, the main sewer emptied into the river; the stench was almost unbearable. Inanna stepped out on the bank, and tried to keep from gagging.

"Take me to the High Priestess and get on with it," she said sharply. The *lant* began to half run, half stumble through the mud, and Inanna followed her, tripping over dead branches, trying not to lose her footing in the ankle-deep muck. On the bank ahead the funeral fires glowed in the darkness, sending up showers of sparks. As they got close to the first one, Inanna saw a woman in a white robe crouched beside a burning body, throwing small sticks on the coals. Face and hair smeared with ashes, blind colorless eyes. Rheti.

The High Priestess lifted her head at the sound of their footsteps, and pointed in the direction of the burning corpse. "Look at what we'll all come to someday, my Queen," she called. Inanna looked and saw the body of a young girl on the fire, twisting in the heat in a macabre parody of a dance. As she watched in horror, the flesh on the corpse began to blacken and fall away from the bones. The girl's delicate eyelids shriveled and the eyes themselves exploded with a pop. Blood boiled up from the open mouth, and the smell of burned meat filled the air. Inanna turned away, sick at the sight. She never should have come to make peace with this madwoman.

"No, look," Rheti crooned, grabbing for her arm. "Really look and see what you've brought on your people." A cold white hand clutched at her sleeve, and Inanna shook it off. She felt repulsion, as if she'd touched something vile, then a terrible rage. Wolf heart and claws, it was all she could do to keep from falling on Rheti and slitting her throat. Inanna forced herself to take her hand away from her knife and speak calmly.

"You're the one who cursed the city." Inanna heard the bitterness in her voice, and turned away, not trusting herself to go on. On the opposite side of the river a stand of willows loomed up in the distance, and the thin crescent of the new moon floated over the mountains.

"No, not me, Queen." Rheti got to her feet and grabbed for the *lant*'s shoulder to steady herself. "The curse is from Hut, the Dark One. I've spoken with Her and She tells me She's very angry." Rheti lifted her hands and the sleeves of her robe slipped back exposing red wounds all over her forearms. Inanna shuddered at the snakebites. She knew she should turn and leave at once, but something held her there. Only afterwards, when it was too late, did she realize that that something had been Rheti herself. "Would you like to know *why* the Dark One is angry?" the High Priestess was saying.

"No!"

"Yes, yes you would." Her voice was strangely penetrating. She lunged and grabbed Inanna by the wrists. Inanna tried to pull away, but Rheti hung on. Her fingers were icy; her touch went to the bone. Inanna imagined she could feel those cold hands moving through her whole body, wrapping themselves around her heart. "For many years now," Rheti hissed, "there have been no sacrifices to Hut. The Dark One is hungry, you understand, so She's sent us hunger. She must be fed soon, before it's too late."

Inanna thought of Alna and the prophecy. "No!" She jerked

away, breaking Rheti's grip. "No sacrifices. If I hear of a single one, I'll order the army into the temple. Do you understand?"

"Good," Rheti said, smiling in a mad way. She passed her hand over her face, smearing the ashes.

"What did you say?"

"I said good. Then Hut will have the whole city." She stumbled in a blind circle, waving her arms as if she were dancing, and then sat down on the ground in front of the funeral fire. "Why not let Hut Herself decide?" she said, poking at the ashes.

"What?"

"The sacrifice without the sacrifice. The Death-Not-Death." Rheti lifted her blind eyes toward Inanna, and tilted her head to one side.

I've had enough of this, Inanna thought. Either she's god-crazed as she pretends to be, or she's making a fool out of me. She looked at the funeral fire, the *lant,* and finally back at Rheti herself. Pulling her knife from her belt, Inanna walked over and held the blade to the High Priestess's throat. Behind her she heard the *lant* gasp, but she paid no attention. "Stop talking in riddles," she said quietly. "Tell me how to lift the curse on the city without sacrificing any-one or I swear I'll kill you on the spot."

"Let Hut decide," Rheti said quickly. Her voice sounded per-fectly sane, and she sat still, not moving a muscle. "For three days give Her any strangers who come through the gates of the city." Inanna made an angry motion, and Rheti shrank back as if afraid. "No, wait, listen. You don't understand. If Hut wants sacrifices then She'll call many strangers to the city, but if no one comes that too will have been Hut's will. The sacrifice will have been properly offered; the curse will be lifted. It's an old custom. It's been done for generations, for time out of mind."

Inanna thought of the refugees who had started to trickle into the city since the savages' attacks. They were only strangers, and yet at the idea of ordering the death of even one of them her stomach tied itself in knots. Besides, she suspected a trick. Why should she trust Rheti? No, she couldn't do it. It was out of the question.

She stood up and put her knife back in her belt, feeling the confusion roil in her mind. On the other hand, suppose Rheti was right. Suppose a sacrifice was the only way to stop the plague.

Where was Pulal by now? Halfway across the mountains? More? By spring he'd be outside the walls; unless the fever was over and she'd trained a new army, there'd be no one left to fight him. What were a few lives—no matter how innocent—measured against Pulal and the whole city? Curse it! It was the old Queen dying all over again, an impossible choice. The more Inanna tried to think it through, the more confused she got.

On the funeral fire the body had burned down to a heap of glowing coals. Inanna stared at the ashes and wondered what one human life was worth. She only knew she didn't have the answer.

"Lyra."

"Yes?"

"I want you to tell the guards at the main gate that for the next three days they're to take any strangers who come into the city directly to the temple."

"What am I supposed to make of an order like that? I thought you didn't want anything to do with the temple. What do you want strangers taken there for?"

"To worship the Goddess," Inanna said quickly. Later she knew why she'd lied: she'd been ashamed. Four days ago she'd secretly sent a runner to the village, a healthy boy with no signs of the fever on him. He'd returned with the news that Alna was well, that Seb had no intention of bringing her back to the city until the plague was over.

She was doing something terribly wrong. No. She was doing the only thing she could.

"Are you all right?" Lyra gazed at her with concern. "You look terrible. I told you you should be getting more rest."

"I'm fine." She forced herself to smile. After all, there was still a good chance that no strangers would come, that there'd never have to be a sacrifice. Why should she admit to Lyra that she'd given in to Rheti when no one might have to know. Later she saw that Rheti had counted on her silence, on her shame too.

Inanna cleared her throat. "I thought that if strangers went to lie with the *lants* they might bring us luck," she said. Lyra smiled, exposing her missing front tooth. It was an honest, friendly smile, and for a moment Inanna envied her her innocence.

"Good idea," Lyra said, "and it can't do any harm, can it?"

"No." Inanna looked away, not meeting her eyes. Who was this woman who lied so easily? She felt like a stranger in her own body.

"I'll tell the guards right away." Lyra walked out of the room with the healthy directness of a woman who knew just where she was going—or thought she did at least. Does she ever worry? Inanna wondered. And if she were in my place, what would *she* do? She sat for a long time, lost in her own thoughts. Finally she roused herself, called for a brazier and charcoal, and brewed a cup of tea from hops and skullcap. The tea was bitter and hot, and she drank it in two gulps. Sleep without dreams.

"I don't want to be disturbed."

"No, *muna.*"

Inanna lay down on her bed and closed her eyes. Hours went by during which she knew nothing. When she finally woke again, she heard the sound of rain.

Water everywhere, running over the edges of the balconies, filling the pots of dead flowers, soaking the linen curtains, drumming on the roof. Fresh cool air without the smell of death. In the eastern fields the last of the fires smoldered and went out.

Inanna stood under the open sky and let the rain fall on her, soaking through her robe, matting her hair. She felt as if it were washing her clean again, as if she were already more like Lyra. The city walls were whiter, and the river was rising between its banks. Surely the worst was over; the plague would stop.

She threw back her head, opened her mouth, and drank in the rain, reveling in the sweet taste of it. She was being silly, like a child. She thought of Alna and laughed with joy at the idea of seeing her again. Seb too. She'd missed him more than she'd thought possible. Soon they'd all be together.

Going back inside, Inanna put on a soft blue robe, and had her servants dry and braid her hair. Then she went down to the Great Hall and sent one of the Companions to fetch Lyra. When Lyra arrived, her sandals were covered with mud, and there were tiny drops of water caught in her curly hair. She shook her head, spraying the drops in every direction, ran forward, and gave Inanna a big hug.

"It's raining!"

"I know." Inanna laughed and hugged Lyra, armor and all. "What a way to treat your Queen."

"For a moment I forgot." Lyra backed off smiling. "I've got the army drilling in the mud again, and you should see them. They're positively happy about it. The plague took some, but as I figure it we've got about two complete *magurs* left, and maybe half another." She grinned at Inanna. "Now what was it you wanted?"

"You can tell the guards that there's no need to take any strangers to the temple now. They can forget about it."

"Fine." Lyra ran her fingers through her wet hair. "By the way, they took a few last night, you know. You were right. They must have brought us luck." All the joy suddenly went out of the day. Inanna looked at Lyra, too shocked to reply. So there'd been a price for the rain after all.

"How many?" she managed to say at last.

"How many what?" Lyra looked confused.

"How many strangers did the guards take to the temple last night?"

"Oh I don't know. Half a dozen, maybe more. I didn't ask."

"Who were they? Where were they from?"

"I don't know where they were from. I think I remember the guards telling me they were refugees when they came to ask if they should take the children along to the temple too. I said yes because I figured that as long as the parents were spending the night, the children might as well . . ."

"There were children?" Inanna suddenly felt sick.

"Only two. A brother and sister, I think."

It wasn't until Inanna was halfway back to her own rooms that she realized she must have got up and walked out of the hall.

"Good morning, *muna*," her servant said. "You're back early." Two bundles lay in a pile near the door, wrapped in wet linen, tied up with strips of bright orange cloth. Inanna didn't have to look twice to know who they were from. "One of the High Priestess's eunuchs brought these a little while ago, *muna*."

Inanna wondered grimly what new horrors were inside. But when she had untied the knots and folded back the linen, all she found were some crude cooking pots, a pile of blankets, a bird in a broken wicker cage, several bags of meal, and an empty waterskin. She examined the things, puzzled why Rheti had sent them to her. Then, all at once, she understood: these were the possessions of the refugees who now had no further use for them. The message was clear.

"Hello," the bird said, cocking its head sideways and looking at Inanna with small, beady eyes. The bird's tongue was split, and its black feathers covered with dust. It was probably thirsty, hungry too for that matter. Reaching into one of the bags, Inanna took out a handful of meal and scattered it on the bottom of the cage. The bird pecked at it greedily.

"Give this bird some water, and take it into my room and hang it over my bed."

"Why?" the servant objected. "It's dirty, *muna;* it'll get all over everything."

"I paid a price for something," Inanna told her, "and I want to remember what it was."

By mid-afternoon the rain had slowed to a drizzle, and the weather had turned cool. Inanna went out on the balcony and stood in it again for a while, but it brought her no pleasure. A long line of funeral fires still smoldered along the riverbank. If the plague didn't stop what would Rheti—in the name of Hut—demand next? *How many children would it take* . . .

"Someone to see you, my Queen." Inanna turned and found the servant beckoning to her from the doorway.

"Who is it?"

"I don't know. He wouldn't say." Now what was that about? More trouble no doubt. Hurrying back inside, she began to dry her hair with an embroidered cloth.

"Hello," the bird over the bed said. Someone had scattered more fresh meal in his cage, and his feathers already looked sleeker and less rumpled. *Half a dozen, maybe more . . . refugees* . . . Quickly turning her back on the cage, Inanna opened a chest and took out a light yellow robe. She wasn't ready to think about the bird yet and what it meant to have it hanging over her bed. She drew her cloak around her shoulders and thrust her feet into dry sandals. She'd think about it later, tonight.

In the main chamber a man was waiting for her, dressed in muddy armor. The plume on his helmet was wet and frayed, and his sandals were worn. He was standing with his back to her, looking out at the rain when she entered, but Inanna knew him at once.

"Seb!"

Seb turned, smiled, and then hurried toward her with his arms outstretched. Before she knew what he was about, he had picked her up off the floor and was spinning her around.

"You look wonderful," he said. He planted her back on her feet and gave her a kiss. "No sign of the fever in your face." Inanna always remembered that moment because it was the last time she was ever really happy. She remembered feeling love for Seb, joy at his touch, and sometimes later—when she was alone—she wondered what might have happened between the two of them that night if things had been different.

Seb sat down beside her on the cushioned bench. "Now tell me about Alna," she said. "How is she?" She smiled. "From the look on your face, you can't be bringing me bad news."

"Alna?" Seb said.

"How is she? The messenger said she was well, but that tells me nothing really. Does she miss me, or has she forgotten she has a mother? Tell me everything at once. I can't wait."

"But you should know better than I do how Alna is."

"But how should I know? Except for that one message, I haven't heard a word about her in weeks. I knew the village was off the main paths, of course, and I didn't want to risk sending runners, but now that you're here, I expect that . . ."

"But isn't Alna here with you?"

"With me?" Suddenly she was afraid. "What are you talking about?"

Seb stood and walked quickly to the other side of the room. "Three days ago, right after your messenger left, savages attacked the village." He stumbled over the words. "We had some advance warning, so I sent my cousin and Alna back to the city along with three or four men to guard them. I thought that even with the plague they'd be—that is Alna would be—safer inside the walls. My cousin's an old woman, and the child had to be carried, but they should have been here yesterday or last night at the latest."

"Last night!" She was on her feet, and something in her face made him run to her and throw his arms around her.

"Inanna, what's wrong?"

She stared at him mutely, unable to speak.

"Hello," the bird in the next room said. Seb's face relaxed, and he smiled. "Alna *must* be here," he said. "I can hear her pet bird. Talks well, doesn't it? It should; I trained it myself."

The High Priestess says that she's seen into the basket of the future, and that you'll order your own soldiers to bring the child to Hut after you're Queen . . .

Inanna stumbled and Seb caught her. "Great Holy Goddess," he said, looking at her face, "tell me what's wrong."

In the temple the lamps had burned down to a smoky dimness, and the main cella was deserted. Seb put his arm around Inanna's waist, and they walked slowly toward the statue of Hut. A dozen bodies covered with white cloths lay in a semicircle around the altar. Strangers, sacrifices. She wouldn't know any of them, Inanna told herself. She felt numb, as if her body had frozen. Ice everywhere, heart, backbone, legs; the old Queen, the cold curse. She forced herself to put one foot in front of the other. Wreaths of white roses were scattered on the corpses; the air was heavy with the smell of incense and fresh blood. Strangers all of them; they had to be.

"Wait here." Seb stood next to her for a moment, looking at the altar. Then, abruptly, he strode up to the smallest of the bundles, grabbed the corner of the sheet, and pulled it back. A boy, curled on his side, three years old—maybe less. His baby hair had been combed neatly back from his face, and, except for the thin red line across his throat, he could have been asleep. Inanna looked at the child and knew that, no matter what happened, she had done something unforgivable.

"I never saw him before," Seb said grimly. Inanna took a deep breath.

"Are you sure?"

"Yes."

More corpses. Seb jerked at the sheets and they floated up in the air like great white birds and settled back to the stone floor: a man in a tattered brown robe, a woman with a mole on her cheek. "Strangers," Seb said, "all strangers." He walked around the altar to the fourth corpse and pulled off the cover. The wreath of roses rolled down the steps to Inanna's feet. She picked it up, and crossed slowly to where Seb was standing.

The dead man wore a rough breastplate of untanned leather, and there were gashes all over his arms and shoulders. The mark on his throat was jagged and uneven. He must have fought his executioners to the last. Seb bent down and gently closed the man's eyes. "I knew him," he said in a voice so faint Inanna could hardly hear it. "His name was Hansea. He was a carpenter from the village."

Under the next sheet lay an old woman dressed in a robe of fine brown linen cut in the country style. Her hair was so thin that the pink outline of her skull shone through her braids, and her cheeks were sunken and hollow. No need for Seb to tell her who this was. The dead woman was an older version of Sellaki.

"My cousin," Seb said. Grimly he stepped over the remaining bodies to the only other small bundle left. Without a word he leaned forward and pulled back the sheet.

A scarlet robe embroidered with gold doves, a small pair of pale muddy feet: Alna lay peacefully on her stomach, her face partly covered by her hair. Numbly Inanna walked over, sat down, and began to run her fingers through the soft, baby-fine curls.

I did this, she thought.

Then she picked up Alna, hugged the small, cold body to her own, and began to cry.

14

"RHETI! Rheti, where are you?"

"She's gone, *muna*." The *lant* crouched in fear against the wall of the cave, shrinking from Inanna and the six armed guards.

"Where did she go?"

"I don't know." The cave was empty except for a broken basket and a pile of dirty rugs. Inanna grabbed the *lant* by the neck of her robe and put the point of her spear to her throat.

"Tell me, curse you!"

"The High Priestess went away the same night the sacrifices were made." The *lant*'s eyes were wide with terror, and she stuttered over the words. "She didn't even take her waterskin with her; she said she was going out in the desert to talk with Hut."

"Where in the desert?"

"I don't know. I swear I don't."

"Did she go alone?"

"No, her eunuch went with her." Inanna examined the *lant* with disgust and pushed her away.

"Kill her," she commanded the guards, "and seal up the temple."

For a week Inanna lay in her rooms at the top of the palace, mourning Alna, refusing to see anyone, tormented by the same nightmare. In her dream she would come to a great white wall, higher than a hundred men, made out of stones fitted together so cleverly that there was no way to get a handhold on them. Inanna would put her forehead against the wall, feeling the solidity of it, its impassability, and then—very faintly—she would hear Alna calling to her from the other side. The sound of the child's voice would drive her to desperation, and she would try to climb the sheer stone, throwing herself against it until her hands were torn. When that failed, she would run along beside the wall, looking for an opening. She would run for a whole night and day until she fell to the ground exhausted, and then she would get up and run again.

Finally, near the end of the week, she came to realize that there was no end to the wall, that she would never get to the other side. On the seventh day she gave up. Turning her back, she walked away until she could no longer hear Alna's voice.

In the dream Inanna looked down at her hands and saw that she was holding a wreath of white roses stained with blood. This is my grief for Alna, she thought, and I'll always have it with me, but it won't destroy me. For the first time since the old Queen's death, she felt her wolf heart beating in her again, and she knew that there was still another battle to fight.

Two hundred and forty leather shields rising in unison, locked together in a single wall; a rain of arrows, the creaking of armor and the tread of sandals as the troops advanced. Rabbits running for cover in the hedgerows, flocks of startled sparrows taking to the air.

Three days later Inanna began to drill the *magurs* of the new army. In the early mornings before it was light, she would get up, eat a quick breakfast of dried dates, and go outside the city walls to the practice field where she would spend the rest of the day, returning only when it was too dark to see the targets. Fifty times through the center, a hundred. She would take her grief for her daughter and make it into a weapon against Rheti and Pulal.

More and more often now as the days passed, Inanna had the feeling that the two of them were connected. She would look at the eastern mountains and think that Pulal was a tool for Rheti's evil, that she didn't have two enemies to fight, but only one—dark and ugly, hidden at the center of things like a worm in an apple. Although she knew that if she examined these thoughts closely they made no sense, still they had a feel of truth to them that she couldn't shake off.

Two hundred times into the target, three. The weight of the javelin in her hand, the feel of the mud under her feet, the lifting and throwing: her arms grew hard and the pallor left her skin. At night she slept soundly. Her pain was a spear and she threw it thus! Blade and tip. If this bale of straw were Rheti's body there would be blood on the ground, and so she threw again and again.

As the weeks passed she felt her power growing strong as a shaft of sunlight. At night now, when she took the changing stone in her hand, Inanna could sense Pulal waiting for her just on the other side of the mountains. He was so close that sometimes it seemed she could reach out and touch him. She sensed Rheti's evil under his smile, hard and sharp as an axe blade, and she knew more clearly that the greatest battle of all was still to come.

In midwinter Inanna called in the farmers from the villages to form ten new *magurs*. The army had to be bigger; there was so little time left. In the storerooms below the palace, empty clay jars that had once contained lentils lay stacked in the corners. Some of the seed grain was baked into loaves to feed the new soldiers, and the last of the millet was scraped from the sides of the bins. Dams that should have been repaired during the dry season broke; the rich river loam washed away; streaks of white sand and salt lay in the furrows. There was no time to worry about such things. By spring Pulal would be outside the gates. Already Inanna could feel him gathering the tribes, and in her new dreams she saw black tents spread out over the delta from horizon to horizon.

Wicker shields braced with pitch and hide; a thousand spears with handles so green they still oozed sap. How could she find enough metal for the axe blades? Points for the spears? Inanna ordered every copper vessel and bracelet in the city melted down for weapons, and still half the spears had to be tipped with stone. During the day smoke rose up from the blacksmiths' braziers, and the sound of hammering could be heard even outside the gates. Along the river, the willow twigs turned yellow, and sparrows built nests in the bare branches. The first wildflowers appeared in the fields; the olive trees broke into bud. So little time left! Almost none at all. At night Inanna saw Pulal moving forward, dragging the black tents with him like a dark glacier.

"We should be training the army to fight *inside* the walls," Lyra said one afternoon as she and Inanna sat under a date palm watching Seb drill another group of recruits. Lyra took a drink of water, wiped her mouth on the back of her hand, and clicked her tongue disapprovingly. "The way you've been training the *magurs* lately, they couldn't hold off the nomads for a week."

Inanna shaded her eyes and inspected the practice field. "We aren't going to wait for the nomads to come to us. We're going out and get them." Picking up a stick, she sketched a rough map of the foothills and the mountains beyond. "I know the trails, and where they're likely to camp." A long crooked mark for a canyon, then a rough circle: "If they come with their animals, they'll need pasture." She stuck the tip of the stick into the dirt at the center of the circle. "We'll fight them here, where the foothills begin. That way if they try to turn and run, they'll have the mountains at their backs."

"And if *we* want to run?"

"What do you want me to do? Patch the walls? Reinforce the gates?"

"Yes."

Inanna shook her head. "I've been trying to tell you: there isn't enough time to do that *and* train the army." In the practice field the soldiers knelt, put their arrows to their bows, and shot together at Seb's command. There was a humming sound and sunlight glinted off the shafts. Overhead small white clouds moved briskly toward the west, and the breeze from the river brought the smell of fresh water and new grass.

Lyra looked at the map and shook her head. "We've always defended the city from inside," she said. "My mother, Sellaki, tells stories of years when the nomads outnumbered us ten to one but the walls always held. And now look at them."

Inanna examined the walls, the cracks and broken places, half-rotten gate timbers, gaps filled with rubble. It would take weeks to shore them up to full strength. Out on the field the soldiers marched forward, their red plumes snapping in the wind. She thought of how the Black Headed People fought—a confused mob of men, each one deciding for himself where to strike. Why, these *magurs* would walk straight through them.

Or would they? Inanna recalled how many things had gone wrong unexpectedly in her life. She thought of Lilith, Enkimdu, Alna, of the old Queen, of Rheti. How many mistakes she'd made. When she was younger, she used to believe she knew what she was doing, but now she wasn't so sure. Out on the practice field the soldiers released another flight of arrows. The fronds of the date palms blew in the wind, casting long spear-shaped shadows on the ground. What if she was making another mistake? What if Lyra was right? Then what?

"Pick out the soldiers that miss the targets and set them to working on the walls," she told Lyra at last, "but not more than half a *magur* at the most."

"That's not enough, but at least it's a start," Lyra said.

Late that spring, when the leaves on the willow trees were the size of small fish, the message they had been waiting for came. It was a hot day; Inanna was out on the practice field, stripped down to her tunic, throwing her javelin at a bale of straw, when she noticed Lyra motioning to her from the willow grove.

"Come here," Lyra shouted. Beside her was a man covered with dust. Even from a distance Inanna recognized him as one of the scouts she had posted in the foothills. Tossing down her javelin, she broke into a run.

"What news do you bring?"

"The nomads are here, my Queen!" There was a bad wound on his forehead, but his eyes were bright with excitement. "They fell on us while we were asleep, and I was the only one who got away. I guess all the sentries had their throats slit, because we didn't get any warning."

"How do you know they were the nomads?" It was all she could do to keep the excitement out of her own voice. "Savages slit throats too, you know."

"I hid in the brush, and in the morning I got a look at their tents."

"What color?"

"Black." He smiled proudly. "There were black tents pitched on the hillside above the Sacred Olive Grove, as many as I have fingers on my hands." Inanna remembered the great camp at Kur where the tents had outnumbered the stars. So the main force hadn't arrived yet; there was a little more time.

She took a silver ring off her finger and tossed it to the scout, who caught it and bowed gratefully. What a pity silver couldn't be used for spear tips. But it bent; it never held an edge.

The next morning Inanna led a *magur* of the Queen's Companions up the road to the Sacred Olive Grove. Sixty pairs of legs walked in perfect rhythm, armor well oiled, spear tips glittering in the sunlight, copper studs on their shields so brightly polished it was almost blinding to stare at them. In the hedgerows birds' eggs lay in nests no larger than a man's fist, and the fawns grazed alongside the does in the fields. Everywhere nature seemed to have exploded with particular abundance. Wild cyclamen grew along the irrigation ditches in a pink carpet; mustard sprouted waist-high; the apricot trees were covered with petals, and blood-red poppies lined the path. Could anyone fight or die on such a day? For a brief moment the whole world seemed like the Queen's Aerie, Lanla's perfect garden. Then Inanna saw the black tents—pitched in plain sight just above the Sacred Olive Grove.

She stopped, motioning the column to a halt. Something was wrong. She examined the tents, trying to figure out what made her so uneasy. The camp was too exposed. What scouting party would come so openly? And where were their sentries, their dogs? It could only be a trap.

Inanna looked again, and her mouth went dry at the familiarity of it all. Everything was just as she remembered: the small herd of goats grazing on the new grass, the cooking fires, the piles of dry wood stacked under the tent flaps. Those robes drying on the bushes could have been Hursag's. Her own blood; her own people. No, not her people anymore: her enemies.

"Make sure there aren't any more of them around," she commanded the scouts grimly. In a little while the scouts came back with the news that the surrounding countryside was empty of everything but deer and rabbits. So it wasn't a trap. Inanna gave the signal for the Companions to move forward again. Maybe the nomads had been beating the savages so easily that they'd become overconfident. But there was still something about it all that made her uneasy. She recalled how carefully Pulal had always planned his battles. Why should he have changed?

Walking toward the camp was like a dream. For a long time nothing happened. Except for the tread of the Companions' sandals on the trail, and the call of an occasional bird, the silence was complete. So this was her first real battle. Inanna discovered she was afraid, and she wondered if the others were feeling the same. Was all that practice worth anything if you'd never really gone up against an enemy before? The Companions' arms were strong, their faces eager. Would they turn and run, or would they stand and fight?

They fought. When the nomads finally realized soldiers from the city were coming up the trail, they ran out of their tents and stood on the ridge, yelling insults and singing their battle songs.

"Cowards, come taste my spear!"

"Let me teach you how to fight!"

"Cowards, are you ready to die today?"

The sound of her own language sent a shiver up Inanna's spine. She remembered Pulal and the other men hurling the same insults at savages who had attacked the camp when she was a child. It had been a moonless night, and Enshagag had hidden her under a bundle of dirty blankets to keep her from being carried off. Lilith had hidden with her, holding her in her arms, and the two of them had cried with fright, stuffing the ends of the blankets into their mouths to keep from making any sound. Tents had been burned; the next morning three children and one of the women were missing. The bodies of the dead savages had been stripped, their heads stuck on poles as a warning to the others. For weeks the warriors of Kur had tried to find the rest of the raiding party, only giving up when the winter snows set in.

Reluctantly Inanna pulled herself away from the memory, and inspected the nomads on the ridge, trying to see if there was anyone she recognized. Black hair like her own, but no familiar faces. She wondered what would have happened if these first warriors had been the men of Kur. Could she have ordered the *magur* to kill them? She wasn't entirely sure.

"Sluts!" one of the nomads yelled suddenly. So they'd finally realized the Companions were women.

"She-devils!"

"Come copulate with my axe!" Laughter. "Come let me show you what a man can do!" The insults made Inanna think of Pulal and her sympathy disappeared.

"Shields up!" she commanded sharply. The front row of the *magur* lifted their shields, locking them together in perfect order. Kneeling behind the protective wall, the archers made ready to shoot. The nomads hesitated for a moment, watching the maneuvers with obvious astonishment. The tallest man turned back and seemed to confer with the others.

"Are you dancing for us, sluts?" he yelled.

"Arrows to bows," Inanna ordered. Suddenly the tall man lifted his axe over his head and began to run down the hill, moving as lightly as a deer over the uneven ground. There was something about the way he kept his balance that was almost beautiful, and Inanna felt respect for him despite herself. There was a warrior! For a moment—before she remembered again that her own people were no longer her own—she was proud. The rest of the nomads followed, charging as Inanna had known they would, all at once in a single, screaming mass. No order, no training. Just raw courage. She understood why the savages had always been afraid of the warriors of Kur.

"Shoot!" The archers released their bowstrings at Inanna's command, and the arrows hummed through the air. Five nomads fell, one pierced through the neck. One wounded man began to scream, and then stopped with a wet, choking sound. The others ran past him without even looking; a stone-tipped spear slammed into one of the olive trees, followed by another and still another. Inanna ducked so she too was protected by the shields. The nomad warriors were so close that she saw the battle amulets around their necks.

"Arrows to bows!" she yelled over the din. She put her own arrow in place and took careful aim at the tall man. "Shoot!" Pulling back her bow she sent an arrow straight into his chest. The man stopped with a look of surprise on his face, and slumped to the ground, clawing at the shaft. She'd hit him! Blood poured out of the man's mouth, and his body twitched and lay still. She'd killed him! But she had no time to think. The other warriors were still running toward them, so near that in a moment they'd break through the shield wall.

"Arrows to bows! Shoot!" Suddenly there was no sound in the olive grove except the scrape of the branches rubbing together. On the ground, scattered like dead wood, lay some twenty nomads, all dead. There was a moment of stunned silence as the Companions contemplated what they had done. Then one of the women broke into a cheer, and the others joined in.

"Victory to the Queen!"

"We beat them!"

Pushing her way through the first row of shields, Inanna walked up to the man she had killed and motioned for two of the Companions to turn over the body. She felt exalted, as if she had just drunk a whole jar of strong wine. Bending down, she pulled the arrow out of the body and held it up for everyone to see.

"Hail to the Chosen of the Goddess!" the Companions cheered. "Hail to our Warrior Queen!"

Maybe they were right. She was dizzy, lifted out of herself on the wave of excitement. Maybe she was the chosen one after all. Hadn't the old prophecy said that a great Warrior Queen would come out of the east? Inanna inspected the dead man with a peculiar sense of a job well done. She felt no pity, only a sense of power that grew, sweeping her up with it. A single arrow, life and death in her hand. It was almost like being a god! No wonder Pulal fought the way he did. At that moment she understood her brother better than she ever had.

"This is the first of our many victories!" she shouted over the cheering of the Companions. Behind her on the ridge the flaps of the black tents blew lazily in the wind; the sky had clouded over. The air was thick, as if a storm were gathering, and the olive leaves had begun to sweat. Inanna thought of Enkimdu, Lilith, and Alna; and then of Pulal. She didn't have any more doubts. She looked at the dead man's face, and knew which side she was really on. Turning, she lifted the bloodstained arrow and pointed up the ridge toward the tents. "If there's anything alive up there," she ordered the Companions, "kill it."

But on the way back down the road, she changed her mind— not out of any lingering love for the nomads, but because there was something that still bothered her about the whole morning, something she couldn't quite put her finger on. Every step the feeling got stronger, as if something were trying to warn her that she'd proclaimed her victory too soon.

"Wait." The soldiers who were climbing the ridge stopped and turned toward her expectantly. Why had she stopped them? She wasn't sure. Inanna walked through the olive trees, pausing in front of the largest. The bark was silver-gray, and the old roots had forced their way out of the ground, curling over each other like snakes. She turned away and examined the canopy of branches that arched above her. On the twigs the first olives were already there, hard green globes no bigger than the tip of her little finger, buds really. Inanna picked one of them, and put it in her mouth. They had to be cured to taste right, of course, and the flavor was bitter as she'd expected. Tiny green olives. In the long summer ahead these same fruits would swell and ripen until they were fit to harvest. The nomads would have that whole summer to move against the city. She spit the bitter bits of olive onto the ground. By the time these olives were ripe there might be no one left to pick them unless she stopped the invasion.

Inanna put her hand against the trunk of the old tree, testing its steady solidness. Lyra had said that their only strength lay in fighting from behind the walls, but then Lyra didn't know Pulal. If he got the idea the city was full of gold, women, or anything else he wanted, he's stay outside it until they all starved. She looked down the hill at the delta. There was probably enough pasture between the foothills and the river alone to keep the sheep and goats of the Black Headed People fed for years. It wouldn't be an ordinary seige; it would be a permanent camp.

Inanna turned back to the five Companions who were still waiting halfway up the ridge. One of the women had taken off her helmet; her thick brownish hair cascaded down her back. Inanna recognized her as Tarna, one of the best javelin throwers.

"Put that helmet back on! Where do you think you are? In your mother's house?" The girl grinned sheepishly and quickly buckled on her helmet. It was hot, but that was no excuse. There could be another twenty warriors in those tents. Inanna pointed again to the nomad camp. "Bring me anyone you find in there alive," she commanded.

"Yes, my Queen," Tarna said, touching her spear to her forehead. The five started back up the ridge, holding their shields ready, all caution now. Inanna went back to the olive grove and sat down in the shade near the stream with her back to the tents. It was cool here, almost cold. Over there was the place the old

Queen had lain, the spot where Lyra and Seb had stood. Even the platform of branches was still there, high above her head. How many years ago had she climbed up to take a nap? Four, five? She'd been a raw mountain girl then, younger than Tarna. She'd been pregnant with Alna.

At the thought of Alna, Inanna felt such pain that she pressed the arrowhead into her palm until her own blood was mixed with the blood on the tip.

A little while later the Companions returned with five women they had found hiding in the tents. Inanna could tell that four of the captives were from the tribe of Enlil. Only the women of Enlil rubbed blue dye into their wool and dressed their hair in a single braid. The fifth wore a muddy red robe and looked older than the others, a senior wife perhaps or a widow. The white beads that fringed her forehead gave her a fierce look, and she glared at Inanna sullenly with drooping cheeks, like a dog ready to attack if it saw the chance. What tribe wore that shade of red? Ki? Utu? Inanna couldn't remember. How terrified the younger ones seemed. She felt almost sorry for them. Second wives, no doubt, women of no status who had been taken along with the scouting party to cook the food and pitch the tents. If Hursag had been younger and a warrior, she herself might have gone on such a journey. Yes, second wives. But then if that were true, why the older one? None of it made any sense.

"How far away is the main camp?" she asked abruptly. The four younger women stared at her in amazement as they heard their own language, and the older one folded her arms across her breasts, and clamped her teeth together as if no power on earth could pry them open. If she didn't do something to make them less afraid, it was going to take all afternoon to get them to talk. Inanna remembered that the Black Headed People never ate with their enemies. Once you shared food with someone, you were bound by custom to treat them as a guest. Maybe food was the answer.

"Bring some fruit and some wineskins from the provision cart, and rugs."

When the rugs were spread, Inanna sat down on the nearest one and motioned for the women to do likewise. The younger wives touched the wool timidly, exclaiming at its softness. But the older woman took her place as if she'd seen such rugs all her life. Inanna unstopped the wineskin and held it out to them with a polite gesture. "Don't be afraid. No one's going to hurt you." Their relief was so intense that she almost felt sorry for them again. "Now," she said more gently, "tell me your names and your tribes." The four younger women identified themselves haltingly, and, as Inanna had guessed, all were from Enlil. "And you?"

The woman in red took the wineskin and her expression seemed to soften slightly. "From Utu," she said curtly. She drank and made a disapproving face. "What's this?"

"Wine."

"It doesn't taste like wine. The honey's gone sour."

"It isn't made of honey. Would you like something sweeter?" The older woman appeared surprised at the courtesy.

"Yes."

Inanna ordered a sweeter drink brought, one made from fermented dates. All five women consumed it greedily, wiping their mouths on the sleeves of their robes until their lips were stained with dye. As they drank, the faces of the women took on a slight flush, and relaxed. The older woman smiled slightly, and crossed her legs comfortably.

"How long a trail did you walk to get here?" Inanna asked casually. From what the women said, she quickly calculated the main force of the nomads must be somewhere in the last range of mountains, not more than two or three days' march away. She remembered the spot Pulal must have chosen—a narrow canyon with a good stream and plenty of firewood. Hard to approach except single file. She tried to keep her voice casual. "Who's milking the goats while you're gone?" She helped herself to some of the fruit.

"My mother," the youngest of the women said, pulling absently at the hem of her robe. She had a pale, round face, like a mirror, and she still looked more nervous than she should have. Was that her nature, or was she lying? Three of the other women said their husbands' eldest wives were doing the milking, and the older woman said nothing at all. She took another drink of date wine and pressed her lips together as if to say: "You'll get nothing out of me." Inanna put the stopper back in the skin, and stretched out her arms as if she were growing bored. "I hear the women of Enlil are the best milkers," she said, "not like the Kur women."

"Kur women don't know how to talk to the goats," the older woman said, and then shut her mouth quickly as if she'd surprised herself by the outburst. Inanna nodded at her and smiled reassuringly.

"Are there many Kur women in the main camp?"

"I didn't notice," the older woman said stubbornly. Somehow her reluctance made her more believable.

"But some from Kur," Inanna persisted.

"Yes," the woman said, "some."

"Women from other tribes too, I suppose?"

"Only from Utu and Enlil. The rest stayed behind with their husbands on the plateau." She glared at Inanna. "Many weeks' walk away." She looked as if she were delivering the worst possible news.

Three tribes! Inanna thought excitedly. That fool Pulal's come with only three tribes! It couldn't possibly be true. If it were that meant that he couldn't have more than five hundred men with him at the most. Five hundred undisciplined nomads against her forty trained *magurs*. It wouldn't even be a fight if the women were telling the truth. But suppose they weren't; suppose it was an ambush. She thought of the great camp at Kur, the way it had looked the day Lilith was married: tents pitched on the slopes of the volcano and out onto the plateau as far as she could see in either direction. Lyra was right. If all the Black Headed People joined together, there'd be no way to fight them off except from behind the walls. But according to these women, the main force was still weeks away on the other side of the mountains. If she moved quickly, she could get to Pulal before they arrived. But were the women lying or weren't they?

"Why did the other tribes stay behind?" she asked sharply. The older woman pressed her lips together as if she had bit into something sour. It was obvious that she didn't like talking, but maybe that too was only an act.

"They said the snow was still too deep on the passes, that they'd lose too many goats in the crossing." Suddenly a small snake that had been sunning itself on one of the branches of the olive tree slipped down the trunk into a hollow near the roots. Inanna felt her flesh crawl at the sight of it as if Rheti herself had been watching.

"A good sign, my Queen," one of the Companions said, smiling. "The Goddess sends us her messenger for luck." The other soldiers also seemed pleased to have seen the snake, and the girl Tarna bent down and poured a little wine on the ground as an offering. When Inanna looked back at the captives, the color had drained from their faces.

"Is it true that the women here take serpents to their beds instead of their husbands?" the youngest woman asked in a frightened voice. Inanna looked at the girl, then back at Tarna, who was still kneeling beside the tree.

"Who told you that?"

"Unan of the tribe of Ki," the girl said. She put her hand over her mouth, and looked at Inanna with terror. The other women gasped, and the older one got to her feet. Inanna crossed the rug in two steps, and grabbed the girl by the chin, tilting her head back so she could look into her eyes.

"I thought you told me that only the tribes of Kur and Utu had come with the people of Enlil across the high mountains; now you say a woman of the tribe of Ki was with you as well." They were lying, all of them. "How many tribes are here? Tell me the truth, girl, or I swear I'll have you killed!" The girl's lips trembled so hard that she was unable to speak, and her eyes blanked with fright. The older woman put her arm around the younger's shoulder.

"Unan of Ki married a man of the tribe of Utu," she said quickly, regarding Inanna with ill-concealed hostility. "Only the tribes of Utu, Kur, and Enlil crossed the high mountains."

"Why should I believe you?"

The older woman folded her arms and faced Inanna stolidly. "Because it's the truth," she said.

That night the full moon appeared, thin as a wafer of sweet dough. Inanna climbed the long, twisting steps to the Queen's Aerie and sat for a long time on the bench, looking out over the delta at the mountains. In the dim light the distant peaks floated like a bank of low, dark clouds. Somewhere, over there, not more than two or three days' march away, Pulal was waiting. But who was with him? If only she could be sure those captives had been telling the truth. She put her hand on her chin and stared into the pool, and a dim reflection of her own face stared back at her.

She could send out more scouts, but there wasn't time enough for that. And besides, if the whole of the Black Headed People had come with Pulal wouldn't she have seen some sign of them by now: smoke from their fires, more savages running from them, stray animals? You couldn't hide a group that size. Or could you? She felt nothing but frustration. Obviously the safest thing to do would be to let the nomads come to the city and fight them from behind the walls. But then she'd lose the element of surprise; Pulal might escape altogether, or the other tribes might have time to reinforce him. If the captives hadn't been lying, she had to act quickly. But on the other hand . . . curse it! It was an impossible decision, yet everything hung on it. What was she supposed to do?

Inanna walked over to the wall and back to the bench again. She broke a sprig of jasmine and began to strip off the flowers and scatter them over the surface of the pond. The petals floated on the water, and her mind went in a circle and came back again to the place it had started. She sat down on the bench and stared absentmindedly at the jasmine twig in her hand, wishing the old Queen were still alive. What would she have done? There was no one she could ask for advice, not even Seb. She had to think this through by herself.

She took a deep breath and started all over again. Had Pulal come with three tribes or fifty? It was still winter in the mountains and the Black Headed People always kept as far away from the snow as they could. The chance that he could have persuaded more than a few clans to follow him over the high passes this time of year was slim. But then why had he come at all? Why hadn't he waited until midsummer? Maybe he thought the city was weak from the plague, that the army still wasn't up to full strength. Perhaps he anticipated getting through the walls without much of a fight. But there was no way to tell for certain.

Curse it all! She really didn't have any choice, when you got down to it. She'd have to wait, send out more scouts, take the chance that Pulal would march on the city in the meantime. She couldn't risk the whole army on a guess. She'd have to stay here doing nothing until she got better reports, and even then there'd always be the chance that the *magurs* would be marching into an ambush.

Inanna sat on the bench until the sky turned light and the birds began to sing. She had a foreboding of great forces shifting around her. This was more than just a battle against Pulal. For some reason she didn't fully understand, it was important in a larger way. And yet in the end she was the one who had to decide what would happen. She walked over to the garden wall and looked to the east. Mist was rising off the fields, shrouding the foothills. What was Pulal doing this morning? What was he thinking? Had he slept during the night, or had he stayed awake too making plans?

Inanna knew her own time for wondering what to do was over. Hurrying to the Great Hall, she called her best scouts to her. "Look for signs of a great army," she told each of them. "Look for tents, flocks, and smoke, for dust rising in the air, and secret camps." And each day for a week the scouts came back with the same message: there was no great army; the mountains were empty, waiting for her.

15

FORTY *magurs*, each with its own banner, over two thousand trained soldiers in full armor; men and women marching side by side, their spears a forest, their shields an invincible wall: in the third week of the Willow Moon, eight days after the Battle of the Olive Grove, Inanna led the army through the main gates of the city. For the first time since the plague crowds of cheering people came together to stand on the walls and throw flower petals down on the soldiers. It was a bright, sunny day, and the river was high and full. Mothers lifted their babies to their shoulders to see the sight of the army crossing the delta so that they would remember it for all time. "See that woman in the red tunic," they told their older children, pointing to Inanna at the head of the column, "that's our Warrior Queen, the one the Goddess chose to bring back our fame and honor. That's the one who will destroy our enemies and lead us to victory." In the *magurs* the soldiers themselves joked and sang as if they were going off to a feast.

By late afternoon they reached the Sacred Olive Grove and the road turned into a narrow, twisting path that wound up into the foothills. The soldiers scrambled forward in single file using the handles of their spears as walking sticks. Thorn bushes, rocks, dust: the festival mood went out of the day. Pull, climb, turn and give a hand to the one behind you. The leather armor was hot and heavy; the waterskins soon went dry. By the time they got to the top of the bluff from which Inanna had first seen the city, the army was tired, thirsty, exhausted, the moon already high in the sky. They began to set up camp by its light.

What are tents and cooking fires to city people? Inanna watched in amusement as the soldiers struggled to set up the flimsy linen canopies that wouldn't stand anything stronger than a mild rain. No matter: with any luck they weren't going to be there long. Her own tent was simple and bare as Lyra's room: a pile of rugs for a bed, a small clay brazier, a cooking pot. Everything superfluous had been cleared out of her life. A sharp axe, two javelins, a sheaf of arrows with white-tipped feathers on the shafts: everything was ready.

That night before she went to sleep, she stood again on the bluff and surveyed the valley. The white circle of the city was familiar now; by day she might even have been able to pick out the palace and the temple. Inanna stayed there for a long time, drinking in the beauty of the sight, the bend of the river, the great curves of the fields. She'd made the right choice; all her life she'd felt she was going to have to fight a great battle someday, and now that time had come. Calmness and order settled over her. She felt in her pocket for the changing stone, weighing it in the palm of her hand. Her power was steady, secure; her own past a circle inside a circle like the walls of the city. Everything was in its place, even perhaps the future. The moon drifted across the sky, and the cicadas droned in the thorn bushes. After a while, she went inside her tent and slept.

Two days later the column marched into the first range of mountains; for Inanna it was like coming home. She breathed the brisk, cool air and realized how smothered she'd felt in the city. Squirrels sat on the rocks watching them pass, and once when she looked up at a tall cedar she saw an eagle sitting on a branch like a sentry. Hazel, oak, hornbeam, pistachio, maple, plum, ash: the familiar trees were like old friends. She tasted the melted snow in the water and smelled the sharp odor of the forest. This was where she was born; this was where she belonged.

At midday the advance scouts returned with the news they had found the main nomad camp less than a day's march away. The three scouts, two men and a woman, moved so quietly that they were in front of Inanna before she knew they were there, small people with the quick, sharp eyes of wild animals. The woman scout bowed like a dancer, straightened up, and adjusted the bowstring between her breasts. The bow was nearly as big as she was; she carried her arrows slung over one shoulder with a careless, self-assured grace.

"How many tribes of nomads are there?"

"Only three, my Queen," the woman scout said, "camped in three separate groups in a long closed canyon." The scout took a stick and drew a line in the cedar needles. "Here, here, and here," she said, making three quick jabs, "each a little separate from the others."

"Many tents?"

"Not too many."

"And the sentries?"

"Posted here and here at the entrance to the canyon. We came this way over the top slope. There's a narrow trail that runs along the ridge. We got in close enough to smell their cooking fires."

Inanna bent over the crude map and studied it. "Where were the sentries along this part of the camp, the part next to the back wall?"

"There weren't any." The scout looked uneasy. "At least we didn't see any." The others nodded in agreement.

"No sentries," one of the men observed. "It seemed strange."

"The trail slopes, but maybe they think it's too steep to attack from that direction," the other men suggested.

Inanna studied the map and felt suspicious again. What kind of chance was there that Pulal didn't know by this time that an army was marching in his way? He had to have scouts of his own. There should have been sentries all around the camp. When she was a girl the men had always kept watch for weeks when savage raiding parties had been sighted. She traced the line of the canyon with her finger. It had to be a trap, but what kind of trap could you set when you were outnumbered five to one? It just didn't make sense.

Then she thought of another possibility: maybe Pulal wasn't planning to fight after all. Maybe by now he'd been told how badly he was outnumbered, and he was planning to break camp and make a run for it back into the mountains. That must be it! She imagined finding the camp with nothing left but a few dead fires and bare spots where the tents had been. The Black Headed People could disappear overnight, and once the tribes were scattered there'd be no way to get them into a battle even if she could flush them out. Curse it! Why hadn't she thought of all this before? Why hadn't it occurred to her that Pulal might run? There was no time to lose. It would be a miracle if they weren't gone already.

"Seb." Seb got up from his meal and hurried over to her. His face was streaked with dust, but his eyes flashed with excitement when he saw the scouts.

"What is it?"

Inanna pointed to the woman and two men. "They've found the nomad camp in a canyon about half a day's march away. Three tribes, maybe four hundred warriors, five hundred at the most."

"Good," Seb said. "We outnumber them five to one; we should attack at once."

"We can't."

"Why not?"

She explained that as soon as Pulal's scouts reported the army was closing in, the nomads would probably decamp.

"So you think they're going to run?"

"Yes." Inanna turned and walked to the cedar tree and then back again. She was angry with herself for being such a fool. "The *magurs* move like water snails through these mountains. We'll never catch up with Pulal. You've got no idea how fast the Black Headed People can travel. When I was a child my sister used to pick me up and run with me so I wouldn't get left behind. And that was just an ordinary move. We did it nearly every day. Once their advance scouts let them know we're getting close, they can break up the whole camp and disappear in less time than it takes to boil a bowl of water. I thought Pulal would stand and fight, that his pride would keep him from running from a bunch of women and city people. But they haven't got enough sentries around that camp, and that can only mean one thing: they're leaving, curse it!"

Seb looked at the soldiers spread out along the side of the narrow path. Some were sitting on the boulders drinking from their waterskins, while others stretched out on the few patches of level ground and put their cloaks over their eyes to shield them from the sun.

"Have you ever heard the story my mother tells of the time when the nomads attacked the city, and the people propped dead bodies on top of the walls so it looked as though there were more alive inside to fight than there were?"

"What does that have to do with anything?" Inanna asked irritably.

"Everything." Seb's words were quick and precise, and Inanna looked at him in amazement as he spoke, marveling that Seb could have thought of such a clever plan. "Listen," he said, "march the army on for a while, and then stop and make camp for the night. The nomad scouts are sure to see that and carry word back that there's no immediate danger. After the moon goes down we'll take a small group—a hundred, maybe more—and sneak up on the nomads. We'll go by the back way where you say they don't have any sentries."

"And what do we do when we get there?"

"Trick them, make them think there are more of us than there are, that the whole army's fallen on them. Like those bodies on top of the walls. They can't run; they'll have to fight us because they'll think there's no way to escape so many. Meanwhile, Lyra marches the main army up to meet us. It'll be light by then and they can travel fast. We'll only have to hold the nomads down for a little while."

Inanna studied the map and thought with amazement that it just might work.

Near sunset the column began to move again, so quietly that the loudest sound was the hum of the cicadas in the long grass beside the trail. No use giving the nomads scouts any more warning than necessary. The soldiers moved like ghosts: weapons muffled in their cloaks, sandals wrapped in rags. The only noise as they marched over the stony ground was the impact of their feet, like the soft, irregular beating of a great heart. Sometimes when Inanna shut her eyes for a moment, she could almost believe she was alone again in the wilderness. Then she would open them, look back down the trail, and see the great column winding up the steep slope behind her.

They made fair progress and by the time the moon was near the rim of the western horizon they had reached a wide meadow bordered with oaks. Inanna called a halt. Without speaking, she motioned to Seb, half of the Queen's Companions, and two other *magurs* to follow her. In complete silence they glided out of the camp and disappeared into the darkness.

The sky was overcast and there was a rainy chill to the air. Walking under the cedars was like being blind. The only way Inanna could tell that the soldiers were following her was when an occasional rock slid over the edge of the trail and went clicking down the slope. Soon it became clear that they were going to have to hang on to one another to keep from getting separated. Their progress became slow, clumsy. Twice the scouts realized they had made a wrong turn, and led them back the way they'd come. Tall grass, tangled underbrush, a stream that seemed to come out of nowhere, blocking the path. The water was icy cold, and they had to wade across, holding their unlit torches and spears over their heads. Inanna watched the gray streaks in the eastern sky and tried to calculate how long it would be before the sun rose and caught them still on the trail. A long climb up a steep ridge, an awkward scramble down the other side—suddenly the woman scout stopped short, motioning for the others to do the same.

"We're here," she whispered to Inanna.

The walls of the canyon sloped gradually into a long, narrow meadow. As Inanna measured the fall of the slope, she realized it had been fortunate that they had been so long on the trail. A little earlier, when it was dark, they might have stumbled over the black tents before they knew where they were. Now in the dim blue light of early morning she could make out the blurred shapes of the sheep, the thin threads of smoke rising from the banked cooking fires. The familiar sight made her homesick. There below, pitched in a circle on the ridge closest to the trail, were the tents of Kur. The tribes of Utu and Enlil had taken the lower end of the meadow, just as the scouts had reported, but it was to Kur she turned the longest. One by one Inanna named the occupants of the tents in her mind. That big brownish-black one was the tent of Kisim's family; the smaller one next to it belonged to Ur and his wife: the tents of Nirrda and Amurru, old Bismaya's tent, the tent of Saptu who lived by himself and always chased the children away when they played too near his fire.

At the fringe of the camp Hursag's tent was pitched under a large oak. Inanna felt a strange mixture of nostalgia and guilt. The air was so still that not even the front flap stirred, and the banked embers glowed dimly in the firepit. How many times she'd slept in that same tent. Hursag had been good to her. Was he still alive? Did Dug still burn his food and grumble at him when he coughed? She found herself hoping that somehow Hursag would escape when they attacked. But then she turned to the other half of the camp, and her sympathy disappeared.

It was a big tent, one she'd never seen before, pitched on a knoll so that it dominated the others. A fine canopy of flame-colored wool stretched over the entrance, and beside the firepit a staff of white ash stuck into the ground like a standard. Inanna's hands grew cold with excitement. There was no doubt in her mind that Pulal was sleeping inside that tent. She studied the flame-colored canopy and remembered the robe he'd worn when he'd chosen the sacrifices for the volcano: flames on the hem dyed with hackleberry juice—so many years ago when she was a helpless child who could only watch and do nothing. Inanna touched the changing stone in her pocket and wished victory for herself and death for Pulal. The wolf in her leaped up, ready for the fight. Good morning, brother, she thought. Dream quickly, because you don't have much time left. Carefully, without making a sound, she crawled back to where the soldiers were waiting.

Now? Seb asked with his eyes.

Yes, Inanna nodded back, *now.*

Muddy ground, torches quickly stuck in a line along the ridge, a small fire kindled behind a rock. It took no time at all, and they were ready. The plan was simple, but Inanna ran over it again in her mind just to make sure she had it straight. She would take a raiding party of about twenty soldiers into the heart of the Kur encampment. They'd set fire to as many tents as they could, and those flames would signal the troops on the ridge to light the torches and begin beating the drums. Other raiding parties would hit the remaining camps, fall back, and strike again somewhere else. The idea was to harry the nomads, confuse them, make them think they were surrounded until Lyra came up with the main army. Seb had tried to convince her he should lead the raiding party while she waited behind, but she'd insisted on being among the first. She inspected the camp, memorizing the exact location of Pulal's tent. No matter what else happened this morning, one score was going to be settled.

Inanna took a deep breath, tightened the straps on her armor, picked up her unlighted torch, and began to crawl down the slope, motioning for the rest of the raiding party to follow her. The tall grass was wet with dew; the sheep moved uneasily as the strangers crept through the flock. One old ewe put her head back to bleat a warning, then turned and ran instead, her hoofs clicking over the stones. A clump of oak trees, level ground: no use hiding now. The soldiers stood up and began to run; for a split second there was nothing but the sound of their sandals hitting the wet ground. In front of her Inanna saw the black tents getting closer and closer. The camp dogs were barking, raising the alarm, but it didn't matter anymore: they were inside.

Inanna shoved the head of her torch into a firepit and put it against the side of the first tent she came to. For a moment nothing happened, and then the wool burst into flames, shrinking and twisting. Black smoke billowed up in the air; inside a woman began to scream. A half-dressed man ran out with an axe in his hand. Inanna caught him through the neck with her javelin, knocking him to the ground. Smoke, confusion, a great dog that ran up out of nowhere to lick her hand as if welcoming her home. Behind her, up on the ridge, she heard the beating of the drums.

"This way!" she yelled to the Companions. She ran toward the center of the camp, up the knoll, half a dozen of the others following her. The flame-colored canopy billowed in the morning breeze, warriors in a semi-circle surrounding it, spears in hand. Pulal's guards. Yes, he would have guards now. Five, heavily armed, and only one familiar face. Strangers from other tribes sent to protect the headman of Kur, the mighty Pulal, leader of all the Black Headed People. Who was in that tent. Who was going to die.

Yelling a war cry, Inanna threw herself at the nearest guard, swinging her axe around her head. The man fought back, catching her on the breastplate, throwing her to the ground. Inanna felt the wind burn in her lungs, and pain wrenched in the pit of her stomach. When she looked up, the warrior was coming at her, his axe descending, and she knew she was seeing her own death too late to roll out of the way. Suddenly the warrior turned awkwardly to one side and fell on his face, a spear between his shoulder blades. The axe head buried itself in the soft earth a few inches away from Inanna's cheek, so near she could see the sweaty marks of the man's fingers on the handle. The Companion who had saved Inanna's life was already fighting with someone else. Axe, javelin, no time to think. Inanna got to her feet, picked up the torch, and ran straight toward Pulal's tent. Lifting the burning bundle of reeds over her head, she threw it onto the canopy. Fire licked the sides of the poles; the whole top burst into orange flames.

All at once Pulal exploded through the burning entrance with his copper axe in his hand. For one brief moment, before they started to fight, Inanna saw her brother's face in the firelight, the whole grinning skull of it. Pulal ran straight toward her, but there was no recognition in his eyes.

"Brother!" she shouted, and she knew he knew her. His face turned red and seemed to swell. Behind him the whole tent was burning, filling the air with ashes and smoke. Yelling his battle cry, Pulal charged. Inanna stepped aside quickly, and his axe crashed down on one of the stones in the firepit, nicking the blade. With a bellow of anger Pulal swung at her again; again she moved easily out of the way.

Why, he was clumsy! she thought in amazement, clumsy and untrained! The hours she had spent on the practice field came back to her; she began to study him coldly, looking for an opening. Pulal turned and came charging back at her. Once again he flailed out with his axe, but this time as he attacked, Inanna dodged in under his guard and brought her own blade crashing down on his shoulder. Pulal yelled and struck out wildly, hitting her on the side of the head with the flat of his axe. The blow knocked her back, and she stumbled, catching herself on one of the burning tent poles.

Blood was spurting from Pulal's left arm; white ropes of fat protruded where her axe had split his skin. Quickly, before he could recover his balance, she struck him again. This time she felt her axe blade bite into the bone, nearly severing the arm from the body. The sound made her feel sick.

With a scream of pain, Pulal stumbled back, dropping his axe. He stared at his left arm in horror. It was hanging by a few strings of flesh. Frantically he fumbled for his belt and tied it around the stump, pulling at the thongs with his teeth as if he'd forgotten she was there. Inanna watched him, unable to strike again. The blow on her head had left her dizzy, the physical sensation of having nearly chopped through his arm, nauseous. She should kill him. She should finish this ugly business. She was no good as a soldier. But her hatred had disappeared. She looked at Pulal again and realized that if she didn't kill him now she'd never have the heart to do it later. Wearily, with no pleasure, Inanna lifted her axe.

Pulal looked up and whimpered like a wounded animal. His eyes were full of fear; he stumbled across the firepit, his good hand outstretched, catching at her robe, pulling at her. Suddenly he was on her like a wild dog, trying to wrench the axe from her hand. Inanna pushed him back with all her strength, lifted her axe, and struck at him as hard as she could, catching him straight across the neck, cutting off his head. The body stood, spewing blood, splattering her, and then fell forward into a heap on the ground.

Inanna looked at Pulal lying dead in front of her, and triumph rushed through her, so strong that it almost made her drunk. Behind her the Companions yelled their battle cries, and weapons clashed. There was no time now to savor the moment. She turned from the body and ran toward the meadow where the battle was still going on. The tents of Kur were burning like bonfires, filling the air with foul black smoke. She took two strides toward it all, still filled with her own power, feeling invincible, when suddenly something cold and evil swelled up around her, and she knew that Rheti was there—watching, invisible, but growing stronger every minute. There was a wild, gloating happiness to Rheti's presence, as if she were glad Inanna had killed Pulal, as if she were feeding on it. "Rheti," Inanna yelled, "where are you?" Her voice echoed off the cliffs, and then the answer came, hard and quick, hitting her in the middle of the back.

The pain was so intense that it blinded her. She let her axe drop from her hand, reached back, and clawed at the thing, and not until she felt the shaft did she realize she'd been hit from behind with a spear. Inanna turned in agony to see who had struck her. Rheti, she thought, Rheti has done this. But it wasn't Rheti at all, only an old woman standing in front of the flaming tent, another spear already balanced in her hand.

"Enshagag," Inanna whispered in amazement, stumbling toward her stepmother. Enshagag's hair was singed, her face black with soot. With a scream of anger, she threw the second spear, grazing Inanna on the arm. The burning canopy fell, covering her with flames. Enshagag beat wildly at the fire, a human torch. Smoke, the smell of cooked flesh. She was running down the knoll, her robe falling off her body. The last thing Inanna remembered before she fainted was Enshagag, her mouth open in a scream, her face surrounded by a halo of flaming hair.

Inanna opened her eyes as Seb was pulling the spear out of her back. Bad pain, like ice, cold heat that poured into her without stopping. Please stop the pain, Seb, she wanted to say, but she had no voice to say it. He had carried her part of the way up the slope, out of the camp, but behind him she could still see the tents burning. She forced herself to watch Seb as he tore off a piece of his cloak and wrapped it around her to stop the bleeding. He kissed her and she felt the warmness of his lips, but the pain was behind it all the time, like the sky, she thought dizzily; pain is like the sky the birds fly through, so wide maybe I can fly through it too.

"Inanna," Seb was saying. His voice was so far away; she wanted to call out to him to speak louder. She saw that he'd been crying.

"Seb," she said, but something caught in her chest and she started to cough. The coughing ripped through her, each breath like a knife edge. Seb lifted her in his arms and stumbled through the high grass toward the ridge where the torches still burned in long uneven rows.

"Be quiet," Seb commanded harshly, "be still."

Inanna felt her chest relax and her coughing stop. She managed a weak smile. "I'm all right," she said, and fainted again.

The next time she opened her eyes, the worst of the pain was gone, and a clean bandage had been wrapped around her chest. Seb was sitting next to her; they seemed to be under bushes of some kind. Yes, juniper bushes. Inanna recognized the familiar blue berries, the acrid scent of the needles. The sunlight drifting through the branches was full of the late afternoon, gold as summer butter.

"Why are we hiding?"

Seb put his fingers to his lips and motioned for her to be quiet. He took his waterskin and placed a few drops on her lips. The water was stale, tepid, but she drank it eagerly. When she struggled to sit up, the pain cut through her again, taking away her breath. Seb caught her under the arms and held her. Now she could see that there were only a handful of soldiers with them. They seemed frightened, and one was holding a drum with a broken head.

"Where are the others?" she whispered.

Seb put his mouth to her ear. "They never made it out of the camp," he said grimly.

That didn't make any sense. She'd seen the soldiers fighting the nomads and winning. She remembered the burning tents, the black smoke, Pulal lying dead at her feet. What was Seb talking about? They had to have won the battle. "But the main army?" Her breath rasped in her chest and each word caught in her throat like a fishhook. "Lyra . . ."

"They never showed up."

"But why?"

"We don't know." He lowered her to the pile of leaves and put his hand over her eyes to shade them from the sun. "Try to sleep now," he said.

Next morning the one remaining scout returned with the news that the nomads had disappeared entirely during the night, leaving nothing behind but burned tents and the bodies of the dead.

"And our own people," Inanna managed to say, "did you find any trace of them?"

"Yes, my Queen," the scout said soberly. He held out a small woven bag. Inside were locks of hair taken from the heads of the soldiers of the city who had died in battle. Some were singed, others splattered with blood. Inanna counted, growing more angry with each lock.

"Why didn't Lyra come?" she demanded sharply. She wanted to say more, but coughing wracked her. Seb took the bag from her hands, lifted her head, and fed her a little wine sweetened with honey. After a while she fell asleep.

When she woke the third time, she was lying in a poplar grove. Inanna searched for the woven bag, opened it, and again counted the locks of hair the scout had taken from the dead soldiers. Over two *magurs* worth. In the corner of the grove two men and a woman were cutting down young poplar trees, filling the air with the clean scent of green sap.

A clump of mallow plants grew nearby. Slowly Inanna stretched out her hand and touched one of the cupped pink blossoms. She had been a healer once; maybe she could have healed herself, but now she didn't know if she could. She felt in her pocket for the changing stone and found it empty. Panic came over her.

"Seb!" Seb appeared above her, his face swimming against the sky like a flat, white moon. "I had a rock."

"A rock?"

"A stone. It's gone." She wanted to tell him how important it was to find the changing stone again, how the city might be lost without it, but the pain confused her, and she lost track of the thought. Something like a black cinder, something that had come from a star. She'd had it and now it wasn't there.

"Inanna, lie still. You have a fever." His hand was cool on her forehead. The mallow plant seemed to swell until it was as large as a tree. She remembered vaguely that mallow was good for the lungs. Hadn't she given Hursag mallow stems for his cough? At the thought of Hursag she started to cry in short gasps like a sick child. She was angry at herself for being so weak, but she couldn't seem to stop.

"What's wrong?" Seb's voice came from a great distance. "Is the pain worse?"

"No."

"Then what is it?"

"I don't know. I can't remember." She wanted to tell him more, about how something important had been lost, something more important than either one of them. A balance had shifted in the wrong direction. She could feel the result of that shift everywhere now, rising up around her like an evil white fog. But at least she'd killed Pulal; at least she'd put a stop to some of it. Something good had been saved after all. The thought comforted her. That good would be the seed of something better. She envisioned it growing,

blooming like a great blue flower, pushing aside the fog of igno-
rance and evil. "Seb." She wanted to tell him that they'd won a
little bit at least, but when she tried to speak the cough caught her
instead, lifting her shoulders up off the ground. Grabbing for the
mallow plant, Inanna picked a stem and held it up to him as if that
would explain everything. Seb took the leaves from her hand and
gently lowered her back to the blanket.

"Hurry up with that litter," he called to the soldiers. "The
Queen's getting worse."

By mid-morning the litter was finished, two long poplar poles
laced together with cedar branches and strips of cloth. Inanna let
Seb lift her onto it without a word. The branches swayed under
her as the four soldiers carried her down the steep trail. Once she
had taken a nap in an olive tree, high up among the branches, and
the wind had rocked her like this. Her mind wandered to the past,
and came back again to find Seb still walking beside her, spear in
hand. He had Enkimdu's face, but she hadn't thought about that
for a long time. So she had come to love Seb for himself after all,
though she never thought she could. She wanted to tell Seb how
she felt about him, but he seemed too far away.

Sky, branches, branches, more sky. Strange to look at things
from this angle. Once the edge of the litter struck against something, and she had to bite her lower lip to keep from crying out,
but for the most part the pain was gone. Twice Seb ordered the
soldiers to stop so she could rest, but no matter how many cool
rags he put on her forehead, she kept getting hotter and hotter.

"In a little while we'll see the main camp," he promised. "It's
just over the next rise."

"Put me in the stream," Inanna pleaded. "Make me cool."

"No." Seb turned away from her with a strange look on his face.
A little later he stopped the litter bearers and lifted Inanna in his
arms. A thick black spiral rose over the top of the hills. "Look, you
can see the smoke of the camp already." He kissed her, wiped off
her forehead with a damp cloth, and motioned to the soldiers to
pick up the litter again. "You'll feel better soon," he said, trying to
smile, but his eyes were so grave they spoiled the effect.

"That . . . smoke," Inanna said with great difficulty. She
pointed to the black spiral.

"What is it?" Seb leaned forward to catch her words. Inanna

coughed and tried to sit up. It wasn't smoke; it was something else, something evil. She had the feeling that she had seen it all in a dream once a long time ago. What was it? What was wrong? Suddenly she remembered the dream, the rush of wings against her cheek, cold as snow.

"What is it?"

"Birds." The word was like a stone, and after Inanna said it she lay back numb with defeat. Seb shaded his eyes, examined the black spiral again, and all the color drained from his face.

"Great Goddess, you're right," he said. "Those are vultures up there."

16 THE litter jerked sideways as the soldiers broke into a run; Inanna clung to the sides to keep from being thrown off. Blue sky, a cedar bough, a thin plum branch covered with delicate green leaves. She could hear the birds now over the sound of the men's labored breathing, an ugly high-pitched squawking, the rush of wings beating the air. Then everything stopped, and she saw the first vulture.

It flew slowly above her in long, lazy circles, its great wings spread, its head a fleck of white against its black body. It veered, froze for a moment, and dived straight down, out of her line of sight. One of the soldiers turned away and was sick. The others stared at something on the trail.

Sprawled sideways in front of the litter lay the body of Tarna, the javelin thrower. Tarna's spear was broken, and her throat had been slit straight across. The birds were all over her body in a black heap, pulling and tugging. Under their beaks Tarna's arms and legs jerked as if she were dancing. Blood, shreds of flesh, a rope of intestine dangling obscenely from her waist like a belt.

"Get off her, curse you!" Seb ran at the vultures, beating them with his spear, smashing their skulls. But the rest of the birds seemed in no hurry to escape. They flew off awkwardly, dragging their heavy feet just above the ground, coming to rest just out of reach. Inanna looked at Tarna's face—or rather what was left of it.

"Cover her up." Seb was shouting. "Put something over her

body to keep those things off of her." The vultures perched in a semicircle, regarding the little group of living people with greedy black eyes. Their bald heads trembled like the heads of old men, and the obscene red wattles under their necks swung back and forth. One of the soldiers threw his cloak over Tarna's body and weighed it down with stones. "Pick up the litter," Seb commanded grimly. Inanna lay back and let them carry her forward again. Above her head more vultures wheeled across the sky.

The sun was hot and her throat parched. Each time the litter moved the pain in her back grew worse until it became a dull ache that filled her whole body. Vulture beak eating at me like Tarna, invisible beak, she thought. But that was only her imagination. She closed her eyes and saw a trembling bald head, a red wattle. "Go away!" she screamed.

"What did you say?" Seb asked.

"Nothing."

A grove of cedar trees, another hill, the open sky thick with birds. In the distance the sound of a pack of hyenas fighting over something. The soldiers stopped abruptly, and one of them gasped.

"Why don't we go on?" Inanna's tongue was thick, so swollen in her mouth she could hardly form the words. She struggled to sit up, but she didn't have the strength. No one answered her question. They were all looking to the east, down the slope at something she couldn't see. Grabbing one of the men's arms, Inanna pulled herself upright and looked too.

They had come to the hill above the meadow where the main part of the army had camped. She recognized the spot at once: the stream, the grove of oaks, the gray face of the cliff. Only there were rocks on the ground where she hadn't remembered rocks before—black rocks, strewn all over, half hidden by the tall grass and yellow flowers. She realized she was looking at dead bodies covered with birds.

"There's nothing alive down there," Seb said. "It looks as if the nomads killed the whole army."

Burned tents, entire *magurs* lying side by side, their shields still in their hands; blood and everywhere birds and the stench of death. The bodies of the nomads were there too, more than two for every one of their own. Near midday they found Lyra lying beside a stream, an arrow through her neck, surrounded by the bodies of four dead nomads. Her shield had been shattered by an axe blow, but she still clutched the leather strap, and there was a look of serenity on her face as if she offered them a job well done.

"She must have fought hard," Seb said. He sat down, cradled Lyra's head in his lap, closed her eyes, and began to brush the dust off her face gently as if she could still feel it. "I should have been with her."

Behind Seb, near one of the gutted tents, two soldiers walked among the dead, hunting for the bodies of friends and relatives. They wandered in circles as if drunk; each time they took a step a cloud of vultures rose squawking and protesting into the air, landing just behind them. Seb took off his cloak, covered Lyra's body, and began to pile stones on top of her.

Inanna examined the dead nomads, the designs on their robes, their battle amulets caked with blood. Ki, Enten, An, Enki: each from a different tribe. The captive women had lied. Pulal hadn't come across the mountains with only a few warriors; he'd had the whole of the Black Headed People with him. It had been an ambush. While her scouts had been looking for the nomads in the mountains, they must have been hiding in the valley all along, in the dry lands where there were no villages to raise the alarm.

She understood it now. Pulal camped where he did to lure the army out of the city, never imagining that she would take him by surprise before the other tribes could close the jaws of his trap. The nomads must have swooped down and massacred the army. It had been ten to one; the *magurs* had never had a chance. And it was all my fault, she thought. I underestimated Pulal as a strategist. I expected him to do anything but out-think me.

Lifting up the frayed edge of Seb's cloak, she looked at Lyra's face one last time. "You were right, Lyra," she whispered, "we never should have left the city."

The rest of the journey was a trail through a dream, a path on which day and night blended together. The sky above the litter moved, but Inanna no longer had a sense of going anywhere. She imagined that the dead came back to her instead: Enkimdu, Lilith, the old Queen, Lyra, Alna, even her real mother Nintu with her green wolf-eyes and hackleberry-colored nipples, bending over her now and then to put a cool hand on her forehead.

Sometimes Inanna dreamed she was a child again, cutting firewood with her small stone axe, feeling the wet grass under her bare feet, hearing the bleat of the goats in the distance. The mountains would be cool and blue, and she would pretend that her life was like them, solid and unchanging. Other times she found herself buckling on leather armor, sending her javelin through a bale of straw, enjoying the power in her arms. She would see a willow in front of her, and as she watched the tree would run through all the seasons—from bud to leaf to bare branch to bud—and she would understand that her life was like a circle that changed constantly, always returning to the same point.

But then she would wake again back on the litter. The hot sun would beat down on her face; the pain would dig into her, and she would call out for water and fall back into bad dreams like the ones she had had so long ago after Lilith died.

Near sunset on a day that had no connection to any other, she opened her eyes to find it had grown cooler.

"You're awake," Seb said.

"Yes."

He lifted a skin full of sweetened wine to her lips, and she drank hungrily. In the sky the first stars appeared; the cicadas droned monotonously in the tall grass. Inanna felt the peace of the evening settle over her like a blanket. Closing her eyes, she fell into a dreamless sleep.

All night the soldiers stumbled forward through the dark carrying the litter over the rough trail. At dawn they stopped and Inanna woke again. She felt clear-headed, and the pain was less.

"Seb."

"Yes?" His face was pale with fatigue.

"Where are we?"

"At the edge of the foothills."

"Help me sit up. I want to see the valley." She looked down at the plum-colored river, the blue-white walls of the city. In the early morning light the tents of the nomads were black shadows, each no bigger than a pebble, but pitched everywhere, along the irrigation ditches, under the date palms, on the riverbank, around the walls. Smoke rose from the cooking fires, staining the morning sky. It was like the great camp at Kur, more tents than the stars.

"So many." Seb's voice was full of awe. At that moment the sun climbed over the last peak, and morning light struck the city walls. Circles within circles. The city was more beautiful than ever.

"Seb," Inanna begged, "take me home."

"No." His voice was almost angry. "Look for yourself. Those tents are pitched so close together not even a dog could slip through unnoticed."

"I'm dying, Seb."

"Be quiet!"

She remembered the gate in the wall, the one the *lant* had shown her. "You can take me in by the river. Please." He turned away and stared at the nomad tents grimly. Then he motioned for the soliders to pick up the litter.

The boat was a big cup woven of reeds, covered with hides and lined with pitch. Inanna lay in the bottom, listening to the sounds on the shore, the nomad children calling to one another, the noise of cooking pots being placed on the firepits, the restless bleating of the sheep. The smell of boiled mutton drifted out over the water, and someone in one of the tents began to play a pipe. She recognized the tune. She had danced to it once, a long time ago on Lilith's wedding day. She coughed and Seb gave her some rags to stuff in her mouth.

"Hush," he whispered, taking her by the hand. The shadows of the black tents drifted by them; sentries patrolled the riverbank. A noiseless current, full and quick: don't let them see us. The cup boat turned in the water until she felt dizzy; then all at once the outer wall of the city was rising up, white and clean as the edge of a glacier. She was home.

Gently Seb took her in his arms and carried her up the bank to a clump of willows. The long boughs hung over the water, a screen of leaves, and beyond them the nomad campfires, the black tents. Not a sound, not a whisper, she thought, or they'll hear us. A man appeared at one of the tent flaps, urinated, and went back inside. A baby cried. The cicadas droned in the burned stubble of the field on the other shore; the water slapped against the wall.

"Now!" Seb whispered. Silently one of the soldiers stripped off her armor and dived under that part of the wall where the main sewer emptied into the river. Inanna imagined the woman holding her breath, swimming through the cold darkness until her lungs were about to burst. In the nomad camp the fires burned down to a dull glow, and the voices grew still. A dog barked and fell silent.

Suddenly a thin wedge of light spilled out on the riverbank. The gate in the wall had opened at last. A woman was standing on the other side, motioning to them frantically. "Now!" the woman hissed. It was Seb's mother, Sellaki. "Bring her this way. Hurry, curse you!" The soldiers carried Inanna quickly through the gate, and Sellaki slammed it behind them. "Pack of water snails!" she yelled. "What were you waiting for? Permission from the nomads!" She coughed and then bent over Inanna. "Welcome home, my Queen," she said, bowing formally.

Inanna felt new hands pick her up and lay her on the royal litter. The cushions were soft. A servant covered her with a light blanket, and someone else put a cool cloth on her brow. The cloth was scented with rosewater, and the smell of it made her feel light-headed.

"Is she going to live?" she heard Sellaki say. Somehow, despite the lateness of the hour, a crowd had started to gather. Inanna had a vague impression of a sea of faces staring at her curiously.

"When's the rest of the army coming?" a man's voice asked. "We've only got two *magurs* in here."

"There isn't an army anymore," Seb said.

"What?"

"They're all dead, massacred by the nomads." A moan went up from the crowd and someone began to wail. Behind her, Inanna heard voices spreading the incredible news. Suddenly Sellaki's face loomed over her again.

"What have you done to Lyra, Queen? What have you done to our people?"

"Leave her alone, mother," Seb commanded.

"We've got no food thanks to her," Sellaki was saying.

"We've been fighting off the nomads with paving stones!" someone else called out. An old woman began to scream hysterically that the whole army had been destroyed. The crowd surged forward, jostling the litter.

"Curse the foreign Queen!"

Hands reached out, pulled at Inanna's robe, tearing it. A stone hit her on the cheek. Suddenly Seb was beside the litter, his axe in his hand.

"Let the Queen through," he thundered. The crowd backed away, and the bearers carried Inanna down the street, half running. She lay back on the cushions and looked at the high, white wall, so close she could have reached out and touched it. She felt empty, exhausted, hurt. They'd all turned against her. If Seb hadn't stopped them, they'd have killed her. Were they right? Had it really been her fault that the whole army was lost, or would it have happened anyway? She didn't know. She only knew that she'd done her best, and it hadn't been good enough. Still she did kill Pulal; she did save something for them. If he were still leading the Black Headed People, they'd already be inside the city.

She pushed the thought away without finishing it. The litter rocked and her mind began to wander. She imagined for a moment that she could see into the future, to a time when the Black Headed People and the people of the city had become one tribe. They were building a new city together on the ruins of the old: great temples, towers terraced with gardens, a chain of canals that changed the course of the river itself. There would be much evil in this new city, but good too, she thought dreamily, and life would be . . . what? not perfect, but perhaps endurable. The thought was a comfort to her. Did I win the battle or lose it in the end? she wondered. And then she realized that she no longer knew what she was asking.

The palace was nearly deserted; the hallways had a hot, stale smell. Inanna could feel the walls twelve hands thick, rooms piled on top of rooms, mud and clay cutting her off from the air. She didn't want to be inside. For some reason she remembered a night when she and Lilith had lain together on a blanket outside Hursag's tent looking up at the constellations. *Those are the sheep of Heaven*, Lilith had said.

"Seb."

"Yes, Inanna?"

"Take me up to the Queen's Aerie, please. I want to see the stars."

In the garden the flowers hung limply from their stems; water trickled over the rocks and into the pool, and there was a faint scent of jasmine in the air. Overhead the stars spread out in all their majesty, bright and endless. Inanna lay back and let herself merge with them. She felt them drawing her up like old friends.

"Bring more blankets and a brazier," she heard Seb say. "She's shaking." He knelt down beside her and took her hand in his. "Inanna," he began. She put her fingers over his lips to silence him, but he pulled them away. "I love you," he told her.

She was feeling love too, but not only for him; for something greater, something to do with the stars. Seb was included in it; everything was. She wanted to tell him that, but all at once he started to float away, getting smaller and smaller, like someone in a boat going to the far side of the river. An invisible current pulled at her; she was drifting on the starlit surface of a vast, dark ocean, her body heavy and at peace. Above her the stars were strung out in glittering rings across the sky, like the campfires of the Black Headed People. Inanna closed her eyes, lay back, and began to sink slowly, leaving the pain behind.

"The Queen is dead," the servant said. The old woman wiped her eyes on the sleeve of her robe and coughed to hide her grief. Giving Seb a mournful look, she began to pull the soft wool blanket over Inanna's face.

Seb caught the servant's wrist and pushed her to one side. Throwing off the blanket, he took Inanna in his arms and felt for her heart. Something fluttered under his palm. Joy and terror filled him: joy that she was still alive, terror at the weakness of her heartbeat. Seb brushed Inanna's hair out of the way and put his mouth to her ear.

"Dear one, don't die," he whispered softly. "Come back to us. Remember the goodness of the world. Don't get lost in Hut's caves. Remember all your friends who love you."

For hours Seb sat whispering to Inanna, trying to call her back, knowing that at any minute she might leave him.

17 SOMEWHERE *far west of the city in the great desert, a woman sat with her back against a rock, waiting for the night to end. The woman's hair had once been white, but now it was so* matted with dirt and twigs that if there had been anyone to see it, they would have had trouble saying what color it was. For weeks now the woman had walked toward the setting sun until the last traces of the rivers had vanished and the whole world had become sand and sky. But the woman hadn't seen the change, because she was blind. She had only felt things falling away around her, until now she seemed to herself to be lost in a great, empty void, like a stone plummeting down a bottomless well.

Something moved in the darkness. Rheti reached out quickly and snatched at the sound. Her hand closed around a hard-shelled insect—a beetle or locust grub—and she put it into her mouth and began to chew greedily. For over a week, ever since the eunuch died, she'd had nothing to eat but a lizard that had made the mistake of coming too close. But the fasting had only made her senses sharper. Even now she could feel the soul of the Being that had called itself Inanna passing from the world.

Rheti moved to a more comfortable position and waited for the death to be over. The soul had been powerful, but young and ignorant, easy to outwit. Except for its one small victory, it had been defeated at every turn, but she knew the next time would be harder. The soul would be reborn, guarding itself against her and the evil she offered—that evil that was the true destiny of all living things if they'd only recognize it.

What would happen next? Rheti closed her sightless eyes and sat for a long time without moving, probing into the dark spaces where things came into being. Out on the desert the night wind blew the sand into strange shapes, and after a time the eastern sky began to turn gray. Finally she opened her eyes and lay back content: she'd seen into the basket of the future, and she knew now that the mistakes the Being had made in this life would follow it into the next. The killing of the brother had been the worst mistake of all, and Rheti thought with satisfaction how many rebirths it would take for the Being to cleanse itself, how much her own power had increased as a result.

"She who killed her own blood will be killed by her own blood," Rheti chanted. "She who betrayed her lover will be betrayed by him." Her voice was dry, more like the croaking of a frog than anything human, but she went on, repeating the same words over and over. Finally she stopped and there was a long pause, broken only by the sound of the wind blowing fitfully over the stones.

Some time later, Rheti noticed with annoyance the death was not yet complete. The Being was putting up more resistance than she had anticipated. Something was giving Inanna strength, holding her back from the final moment. Rheti cursed the delay. The wind had already lessened and the desert was growing warmer by the minute. Soon the sun would be up, and the walls of sand around her would turn into an oven. Last night when she had picked this exposed spot to rest in, it had made no difference. She had planned to die along with the Being long before morning, to track Inanna into death, be reborn with her like a thorn stuck into Inanna's very soul. But Rheti hadn't counted on this new turn of events. If the sun caught her too soon, she might die first; her power over Inanna would fade, the connection would be broken—perhaps forever.

Lowering herself on her stomach, Rheti crawled forward, scrabbling at the sand. In her haste she tore off a thumbnail, but the pain was nothing. Her fingers closed around a rock, and the edge of it dug into her palm. It was a piece of flint, sharp as a knife. Good. Her luck was still with her.

Rheti coiled on her side, feeling the first waves of heat starting to rise off the sand. The sun must already be on the rim of the horizon. She was too weak to sit up again, but that wouldn't be necessary.

Slashing at her arm, she drew a thin stream of blood. She was old and bled slowly, but even a small amount would do. With the blood she could see what was going on back in the city. Rheti smeared it quickly on her eyes and lips. Her thirst was terrible, but she didn't drink a drop. She saved it all for Inanna.

"Show me what it is that keeps her from death," she whispered. A red cloud boiled up in her mind, as if the sun itself were finally piercing her blindness. When the cloud cleared, Rheti saw Seb holding Inanna in his arms. The power of his love surrounded Inanna like a wall.

Rheti gave a cry of rage and frustration. What right did Seb have to come between her and her prize! She had been cheated! Well, the battle wasn't over yet. She would wait, find some shade, watch until Seb grew weary and slept. Then she would finish things the way they should have been finished hours ago.

The sun rose higher, flooding the desert with light. As the dunes turned from pale violet to brown, the flint in the rocks sparkled. Heat rose in liquid waves, and the horizon trembled. Rheti could not see the sun, but she felt her skin tighten under its rays. Her breath came in gasps; she was being cooked bit by bit. Past and present melted together in her mind; she saw the funeral pyres along the river, the bodies dancing in the flames. Her own body too was dancing, twitching in the heat. But soon she would find some shade.

The sun climbed in the sky, drawing the last bit of moisture out of the sand. Rheti crawled on and on, into the heart of the inferno.

SOMEONE was lifting Inanna into the air. She opened her eyes and saw Seb.

"I'm alive?"

"Yes, dear one." The endearment was awkward on Seb's tongue, but his eyes were so full of joy that it didn't matter. Sunlight streamed into the Queen's Aerie, embossing the undersides of the leaves, making rainbows in the spray from the waterfall. The sky was a sheet of blue without a single cloud. Inanna felt weak but strangely cleansed, as if something evil had been purged from her.

"You're going to get well," Seb told her. He carried her as if she were weightless, his body warm, his grip firm and secure. She saw now that she loved everything about him: his high cheekbones, the smell of his hair, his hands, his eyes, even his quietness. It was different from the love she had had for Enkimdu but just as strong. She marveled that it had taken her so long to realize all this. What a fool she had been! Human beings had so little time; every moment of life was a reprieve.

Seb carried her quickly down the steps. In the sunlight the narrow walls of the stairwell looked like banks of snow. Through the window she saw a building burst into flame. Orange tongues of fire climbed over the roof; a date palm exploded, a torch scattering a leafy crown of sparks.

"What's happening? Where are we going?" Inanna asked. Sounds came from the street below, loud voices, the clash of arms.

"We're going to the storerooms under the palace," Seb said.

"Why?"

Seb kissed her. "I'm going to hide you there. The nomads are attacking the city."

The walls held until midday. At the main gate the last of the Queen's Companions fought on, the dying passing their javelins to the living before they fell. The white walls of the city were stained with blood and smoke, for the fire spread quickly, running through the narrow streets, leaping from roof to roof, turning the water in the gutters to steam, drying up the fountains, charring murals, statues, and human flesh. A black column rose hundreds of feet into the air, and in remote villages farmers looking up from their work were startled to see black soot sifting down from a cloudless sky.

Inanna saw none of this. Despite her protests, Seb carried her into the depths of the palace, to the great cistern under the kitchen. She was in no condition to fight, he argued; her death would accomplish nothing. She would actually be in the way of her own Companions, who would feel obliged to protect her. The only thing she could do, Seb told her, was to live so that after the battle the city would still have a Queen. She had only one duty now: survival.

Reluctantly, Inanna agreed. All during that terrible day as the nomads poured over the walls, looted the city, and then finished burning it to the ground, she lay in the dark at the bottom of the cistern, on a narrow ledge just above the water. Seb sat beside her, ready to fight if their hiding place were discovered. But there was no need to fight, for soon the palace itself was on fire and nothing human could have gotten to them through those flames.

Even at the bottom of the cistern the heat was almost unbearable. As the fire raged above them, smoke filled the air and Seb had to moisten his own robes and Inanna's to keep them from bursting into flames. If it hadn't been for the underground tunnels that let in air from below, they probably would have suffocated.

They lost all sense of day or night. Sometimes sparks fell hissing into the water beside them, and they heard great crashing sounds as the beams and walls of the palace fell above their heads. They spoke little during those hours, but the ordeal welded them to each other as nothing else ever had. When Seb finally carried Inanna back to the surface, they both knew that, if she lived, they would live together.

Afterword

The city that Seb and Inanna came back to was little more than a pile of smoking rubble. The intense heat had destroyed even the bones of the dead so Seb never knew what became of Sellaki and the rest of his family, and Inanna never heard of the Companions' last, gallant stand. It was as if history had stopped and begun all over again.

The nomads had taken everything: not only gold, but tools, small statues, even the tiles from the murals. What they could not carry, they had destroyed. Priceless porcelains lay smashed in the fields near the main gate; fine rugs hung in tatters; bolts of cloth and baskets of seed grain had been dumped in the river; oxen rotted where the invaders had slaughtered them. But the miracle was that the nomads themselves had disappeared.

By the time Seb and Inanna came up to the surface, not a trace of the black tents remained. Later Inanna liked to think that this mysterious disappearance was in part due to her, that without Pulal to lead them the tribes of the Black Headed People had broken down into small, quarreling groups and gone back to the mountains. But the truth was that no one really knew why the nomads had left—only that they were gone.

For months the few survivors lived in fear that they would again see the invaders pouring down into the delta. They had no way of knowing that it would take three more generations for the Black Headed People to complete their conquest of the city, that it would be their granddaughters and grandsons and not they themselves who would fight the final battle.

As time passed and there was no sign of the nomads, life began to return to normal. It was obvious that the city would never be as great as before, but that it would continue to exist no one ever doubted. Although there was no gold to put in the new temple, the people took the fact that their Queen had survived as a sign from the Goddess that She still had faith in them.

Inanna healed slowly but steadily. That first winter she, Seb, and the others lived in reed huts like the one she had built for Enkimdu so many years ago. They might easily have died of starvation, but nature was kind. The weather was mild; rain fell at the right time, and even though only a few fields had escaped the nomads' fires there was enough to last until spring.

By the time the wheat started to sprout a second time, the city walls had been repaired. The next year, in the first week of the Willow Moon, Inanna raised Seb up beside her on the throne stool and made him King, proclaiming that from now on the two of them would rule as one. That same day she planted a row of jasmine on the roof of the new palace, which was smaller and less grand than the old one, but already full of happier memories.

Every day after, she and Seb came to work together on the garden until the Queen's Aerie was once again a place of beauty and peace. And there, among the fragrant white stars of jasmine, a little more than three years after the great fire, Seb watched over Inanna as she gave birth to their first child: a boy with sky-colored eyes whom they called Enkimdu.